Priest Hole

Wings Press, Inc.

Priest Hole

Lorna woke abruptly to find Jude staring at the wall in terror.

"Jude! What is it? Were you dreaming?" Lorna rubbed the sleep out of her eyes and sat up, trying to subdue an inward groan at being disturbed.

"I dunno," Jude replied. "I heard summat. Don't know what it was. Someone crying—wailing, more like."

Lorna frowned. "Where? Was it outside or inside?"

"I dunno. Seemed like it came from that wall," Jude said, pointing at the chimney breast.

"That's just a chimney, Jude. I suppose it may be open in the room below, but the fireplace is all blocked up on this floor."

She pushed back her quilt and went over to the window, pulling back the curtains to reveal a starry, quiet night. No sign of any wind, certainly nothing like a gale that might set up wind noises in or around the chimney.

"Someone was crying, I tell you. I heard 'em. Crying fit to break their heart."

The Tresayne Family Tree

Gordon Tresayne 1865–1901
m.
Maria Lloyd-Winston 1867–1917

Lionel	Edwin	Frederick	Maud
1890–1914	1893–1916	1896–1916	1898–1979

m. Gerald Booker

1895–1965

Edith   John Tresayne

1919–1922   1928–2001

m. Georgina Carey

1934–2015

Helen Reynolds (1) m. Theobald Landry m. (2) Jeannette

b. 1952   (div.1992)   b.1945   b.1960

Deborah   Marcus   Olivia

b.1981   b.1983   b.1987

Priest Hole

Jane Anstey

A Wings ePress, Inc.

Mystery/Romance Novel

Wings ePress, Inc.

Edited by: Jeanne Smith
Copy Edited by: Christie Kraemer
Executive Editor: Jeanne Smith
Cover Artist: Trisha FitzGerald-Jung
Images: Pixabay

Wings ePress Books
www.wingsepress.com

Copyright © 2024 by: Jane Anstey
ISBN 979-8-89197-997-0

Published In the United States Of America

Wings ePress, Inc.
3000 N. Rock Road
Newton, KS 67114

Dedication

To my friend Caroline Latham

Author's Notes and Acknowledgements

Tresayne House is entirely fictitious, and I have placed it on the upper reaches of the River Lynher, somewhere between Trebartha Estate and Plusha, where no comparable house exists. The church and cemetery where the Tresayne family are buried is, likewise, fictitious. Ridge, however, is a real piece of moorland, and there are real farms with grazing land on the moor there, but Jude's family's farm is completely fictitious and unconnected with any of them.

All the characters in the story are also imaginary and bear no resemblance to any of my acquaintances and friends in the area, but the setting—east Cornwall during the spring 2020 lockdown—is how I remember it from living there at the time. Any misremembering of it or misrepresentation of it is my responsibility, and I present my apologies for any mistakes in advance. As is true for other places, it was a strange time, and one that seemed appropriate as a background to a tale of a mysterious old house and what happened there.

The Great War story interwoven into this tale of lockdown is also completely fictitious, but I based some of the background to it on my researches into the life of Robert Southey, a teenage officer in the 1st DCLI (Duke of Cornwall's Light Infantry) during the early part of the Great War, who died on the Somme in July 1916. His letters home to his mother in Westward Ho! give a very vivid picture of life at the Front in the battalion during the period. I have read these letters, with the permission of their owner, Robert Southey's great-niece, my friend Caroline Latham, whose family now own Trebartha Estate and Gardens in North Hill, Cornwall. Thanks also to the DCLI museum in Bodmin, for giving me access to the DCLI war diaries for 1915–1916.

One

"I've had a letter from Marcus," said Theo.

His wife looked up from her magazine in surprise. "Your son Marcus?" *The one you never talk about?*

"The very same."

"What on earth does he want?" *Help of some kind? Money, perhaps.*

"To come and see us."

This time Jeannette was speechless.

"When the lockdown restrictions ease, he says, so we have a few weeks to think about it." There was a pause. "I'd like to see him, Jeannette. You wouldn't mind, would you?"

She swallowed, ashamed of her instinctive cynicism. "Of course not, Theo. I think it would be wonderful to meet him."

Her husband handed her the letter. "Read it. I think the pandemic has made him re-evaluate his relationships a bit."

"He certainly wouldn't be alone in that." Jeannette unfolded the piece of notepaper, which fluttered slightly in a breath of air that moved across the lawn where they were sitting.

"Dear Dad," she read. *"I'm sorry I haven't been in touch with you for such a long time. I hope you and Jeannette are well and not finding lockdown too onerous. I am on my own at the moment, and have found it more difficult than I expected. During these long hours, I have found myself thinking about you, wondering how you are and hoping you have not been afflicted by this terrible virus. I would like so much, when the restrictions are lifted and we are allowed to travel, to come down to Cornwall and see you both. Maybe we can get to know each other again. Your loving son, Marcus."*

Loneliness, then. Not help. Not even money. "How extraordinary," she said aloud. "When did you last hear from him?"

"I saw him at Danielle's wedding, but nothing since."

Jeannette handed the letter back, frowning. The wedding of Theo's daughter Danielle had taken place all of ten years ago, and as far as she knew, neither of the children had made contact with their father either before or after that event, which made Marcus's overture even more unexpected—and perhaps significant.

"Of course you must invite him," she said again, smiling at him warmly. Suddenly, Marcus seemed much less of a threat. A young man made lonely by lockdown. Her fear receded and at once her natural generosity revived. "As soon as it's allowed."

Theo folded the letter and tucked it into the breast pocket of his jacket. "Thanks, Jeannette. I'll email him. The government are talking about opening some things up in June—but that's more than a fortnight away, and I'll believe it when I see it. I doubt we'll be able to have guests, even then, for a bit."

"Well, let him come as soon as he can."

Jeannette pushed herself up from the cushioned bench and stretched, her practical self once more. "I must get some more weeding done before I make supper." She pushed her hands through her short curly hair, which was always on the edge of untidiness, pulled her gardening gloves on to her broad, capable hands, and picked up the trug of hand tools from the ground beside her. "Will you take the tea tray inside when you go?"

He nodded, but absently, and she saw that he was reading the letter again. She watched him affectionately for a moment before taking her tools down to the herbaceous beds that flanked the driveway on the other side of the house to give him some privacy. They had been together for nearly twenty-five years, but he was still, in some ways, an enigma to her, and his personal reserve was often impenetrable. Perhaps he felt the same about her.

She put her tools down beside the flower border nearest the gate where, in spite of the dry weather of the past few weeks, a number of weeds were pushing up their heads. Theo's young cat was sitting under the big hydrangea bush, watching intently for any unwary bird that might come within range. He stalked away angrily when she arrived. Just as well, she thought, watching him vanish under some rhododendrons on the other side of the driveway. A very bold robin sometimes liked to prospect for worms in the turned soil when she was weeding, and she would prefer him not to join the ranks of Cato's victims. She welcomed the cat's abilities as a mouse-killer, but birds were another matter.

It was pleasantly cool in the dappled shade of the big beech tree by the gate, which was just coming into full leaf. For country-dwellers like themselves, the good weather had been such a boon during the long weeks of lockdown that she refused to complain about the unseasonable heat. At least they had been able to get outside and enjoy the sunshine without flouting the regulations that compelled them to stay within their own boundaries.

These thoughts were interrupted by voices in the narrow lane that ran past the gate. It was a no-through road, becoming a grassy footpath further down, which meant that any car that braved its potholes and sharp bends must be heading for Tresayne, but pedestrians passed the house fairly often, especially in the tourist season, because it was a pretty walking route to the river and the clapper bridge that carried the footpath across to the other side. Under lockdown restrictions, however, only the few who lived locally had been around to walk it, and there had, therefore, been little in the way of pedestrian traffic.

She recognised the two men as they came into sight, however, for they passed by regularly on their daily dog walk. She recognised the dogs, as well, spaniels belonging to a retired professor whose cottage lay along an adjoining lane a few hundred yards away. From time to time, he spent a month or two in Oxford using the resources of the Bodleian Library, and he usually left his dogs in a nearby boarding kennel. She guessed that in these unusual circumstances, with the kennels closed, he had arranged to have a dog-sitter instead—though she thought it was unlikely the Bodleian would be open. Perhaps lockdown had caught him unawares, as it had so many.

The two men appeared to be of different generations—one a tall, lean, middle-aged individual with greying dark hair, whose shirt had a clerical collar, while the younger, perhaps in his late teens, was of similar height but broader in the shoulder and fairer in colouring, and carried a camera bag on his shoulder. Father and son, perhaps?

The boy, clearly uninhibited by any notions of privacy or reticence, looked over the gate and, seeing her, waved a cheerful hand. His father seemed to be in a reverie and oblivious to his surroundings, but when on impulse Jeannette pushed herself up off her knees and went over to greet them, the older man stopped and smiled. The smile struck her as a weary one, a habitual expression of kindliness rather than a cheerful invitation to casual communication, and she wondered uncomfortably whether he had lost someone to the virus.

"Hi," the teenager greeted her. "How are you? I expect we're not supposed to stop and chat to you, officially, but it's very boring to pass people in the street and not say anything, don't you think? Especially as you're inside your garden gate!"

"I rather agree with you. Are you dog-sitting for Cedric? I recognise the dogs."

"Spot on. He and Dad know each other in Oxford—that's where we live in normal times. I'm Mike Swanson, and this is my father, Jeremy—Remy, everyone calls him. We can't shake hands, but it's nice to meet you."

"Jeannette Landry," she responded, amused. "You quite often walk this way, don't you?"

He nodded. "It's a lovely path. The river's a bit low at the moment, but I like to take photographs down at the bridge sometimes." He indicated the bag over his shoulder, grinning. "I got the camera for my eighteenth."

This cheerful openness was endearing. "As soon as we're allowed to meet and talk properly—whenever that is," Jeannette found herself saying, "you must come and have tea in my garden."

"We'd like that, wouldn't we, Dad?" was Mike's instant and enthusiastic response. "Thanks, Mrs Landry."

His father laid a hand on his arm. "We must be getting on, Mike. Your sister won't thank us for leaving her in charge of the twins for too long. And I expect Mrs Landry must want to get back to her weeding."

He smiled at her again, in mute apology for cutting short their conversation, and she wondered why he had wanted to.

Jeremy seemed to realise his response had been inadequate, even rude. "It's a kind invitation," he amended. "Thank you for it. If we are able to take it up in due course, then we would very much like to." He whistled to the two spaniels, who came racing back from their activities in the undergrowth further down the lane, and moved on with Mike in his wake.

Jeannette returned to her weeding thoughtfully. She found herself speculating where the mother of the family might be, if

Mike's sister was being left to babysit. Perhaps she was working from home, like so many at the moment? But it was after five o'clock and surely she would be able to stop by now? Or perhaps she was a key worker and had been left behind in Oxford. Jeannette hoped fervently that nothing too terrible had happened to her. The coronavirus—Covid-19 as they were learning to call it— affected older folk disproportionately, so it was unlikely that so comparatively young a woman would have become seriously ill— but nothing was certain in these dreadful days. It only took an unknown weakness in the immune system, a history of asthma, or other respiratory problems, and even the young could join the crowds inhabiting the makeshift Covid wards at the local hospital, many of whom never made the return journey home.

In normal times, she reflected, she would never have spoken spontaneously to passing walkers for fear of encouraging unwanted intimacy, or of being obliged to hand out invitations of the sort she had just found herself giving. In Cornwall, holiday-makers—known as 'Emmets', which meant 'ants' in local parlance—were all too ubiquitous, especially in summer, and apt to discover even quite obscure or non-existent footpaths and make a nuisance of themselves. How different everything was now. After weeks of isolation in which so few people passed the gate, human contact, even with strangers, seemed a precious privilege. She pitied anyone stuck in a city flat. It obviously hadn't been a pleasant experience for Marcus. *Thank goodness Olivia was at home in March, so she could stay here instead of being in London on her own all these weeks.*

But she found herself, uncomfortably, by no means certain her daughter had seen it in the same way. While Cornwall had seemed to Jeannette the perfect place to spend the national lockdown, pottering in the lovely weather in her own garden, she wasn't sure whether Olivia had thought so. Perhaps she had missed her social life in London, though she never mentioned her friends.

Not for the first time, she wished she were on better terms with her daughter, and that Olivia's thoughts and feelings weren't such a closed book to her. But the slightest attempt on her part to gain her daughter's confidence invariably led to the hostile reaction that had bedevilled their relationship since her teenage years. *It must be something I'm doing wrong. Or something in my character that makes me put her back up. If only I knew what it was, perhaps I could put it right.* But any attempt she made to change the way she dealt with Olivia only seemed to make things worse.

She sighed. Why were family relationships so problematic? She wondered again why Marcus had decided to make contact with his father. Theo's children were her stepchildren in name only. She had never met either of them, and she knew very little about them. Theo's divorce had been rather acrimonious, and his first wife had refused to allow him more than the minimum of access to his children, thus making sure he had never spent enough time with them to create much of a relationship. She suspected their mother had poisoned their minds against him as well, though Theo had never said so. In any case, they had made no effort, as they grew up, to keep in contact with him independently. But that seemed to be the way with young people, these days. They grew up and went their own way, and parents were left behind.

She wondered suddenly how Olivia would react to the news that Theo's son was coming to stay. Tresayne House had been Olivia's childhood home, even if, working in London for years, she had spent little time there as an adult. But Olivia and Theo had always been good friends, ever since he married Jeannette when her daughter was ten. Indeed, it sometimes seemed Olivia felt closer to her stepfather than to her mother. Would she feel threatened by Marcus, and his attempts to reanimate his own relationship with Theo?

Osborne House, Monday September 30th 1915

It's a year to the day since Lionel was killed. Mother has drawn the blinds, and put the whole household into mourning for the day. He was the eldest, the heir, the one she and my father had pinned their hopes on. Now that role is mine, but it sits badly on my shoulders. And I know she secretly wishes it were I who had gone to fight and die for my country, not Lionel. She could have spared me more easily, lost me with less regret. As for Freddie, I dread to think what will happen if harm comes to him.

I can't resent her favouritism, even though I envy him. Freddie is the best of us—he always was, the golden boy. From his letters, it sounds as though he's having a great time at the moment, enjoying parties and racing horses against his fellow-officers during the battalion's nine days' rest away from the Front. He was cock-a-hoop that he'd won the scurry by a short head, as well as his individual race, though the horses sound like a pretty rum lot. You'd think the war was a game! But so far, he doesn't seem to have seen much action, apart from the general run-of-the-mill daily shelling, which randomly kills or maims a few men here and there. And of course, the nightly bombing raids under cover of darkness. He seems to enjoy those grenade expeditions—I think he relishes the challenge of getting across No Man's Land and back without being spotted and tormenting the enemy soldiers into the bargain.

That is Freddie all over. But I know he feels the responsibility of looking after his men very much, and eighteen is too young to be fighting such a war, let alone leading others. Freddie's company are going back up to the Front today, and that isn't helping Mother to cope with Lionel's anniversary. What a miserable thing war is, whether you're at the Front or not!

Yet we are an Army family, I know I must remember that. It is I who am the anomaly, the changeling, the renegade. The one who would have refused to fight even if my useless foot hadn't made it impossible. If I were not a clergyman, people would show me the white feather. Perhaps we did have to defend Belgian neutrality when the Huns invaded, but can it ever be right to kill other men, even in war? I suppose now I'm ordained I could go to the Front as an Army chaplain. Mother wouldn't see me as a coward then, and she would still be able to hope it's I who would be lost, rather than Freddie, her darling, her baby. But is that what I want for myself?

Besides, I fear I would not have the courage to face the suffering I would have to witness, or the possibility of becoming a casualty myself. I know I am a coward. But chaplains must encourage the troops, must believe in the rightness of the cause. And I do not. It would be false, and they would know it. Better for me to tend to the needs of those left behind. With casualties as they are, there is much to do in comforting the bereaved and fearful.

Two

After they'd said goodbye to Jeannette, Jeremy and Mike crossed the river and took their normal route along the footpath and out on to the minor road that led up past Stonaford Manor towards Twelve Men's Moor. The moor itself was a bit far for the hour's exercise they were allowed under current regulations, so instead they turned left towards the Trebartha crossroads, and followed the lane home to the professor's cottage. The verges were full of wild flowers, celandine and campion, cow parsley and dandelion clocks jostling each other for space in the Cornish banks beside them, but neither of them noticed. Mike kept up a cheerful flow of chatter, but Jeremy walked silently, deep in his own thoughts, and eventually his son gave up attempting to engage him in trivial conversation.

"What's up, Dad?" he asked, confronting that relentless silence head on.

Jeremy sighed. "Nothing, really. Or at least, nothing you can do anything about. But thanks for asking, Mike."

There was a pause. "That won't do," the boy pursued. "I can tell there's something wrong. So can Lorna. We aren't blind, you know. And we aren't kids anymore."

Jeremy smiled a little at this but didn't argue. At eighteen and sixteen respectively, Mike and Lorna, like most young people, were sure they were grown up and knew everything. He had probably been the same at their age, but everyone learned as they went through life that there was always plenty more you didn't know.

"Yes, I understand that," he said. "But I can't explain it to you. It's too complicated. I expect I'll be better when we get home to Oxford. If we ever do."

"Don't be so defeatist. Of course we're going back—sometime in the summer if not before. Lockdown can't last forever." He paused, but there was no response. "Well, if you won't talk, you won't. But don't forget I'm here if you change your mind. I know I'm only your son, but...."

"There's no 'only' about it, Mike," his father interrupted. "I really appreciate the offer, and I'll tell you if I feel it would help to talk. But at the moment I don't. It's just something I have to think out for myself."

"Okay, Dad." His mother would be Dad's first choice of confidant, Mike knew, and not for the first time he wished she had been able to come with them. But work had kept her in Oxford, and Dad couldn't be finding it easy.

The cottage driveway appeared only a few yards ahead of them, and Mike began to run, the spaniels gambolling beside him on the end of their double-leash, full of new energy and excitement as they responded to his sudden turn of speed.

He let the dogs off the leash as he went into the house and hoped his father had remembered to shut the gates as he came in. Dad seemed to spend most of his day in the study. Mike supposed Cedric's theological library might be a draw to someone of Dad's intellectual interests, but if so, his reading didn't seem to be doing him much good. Mike didn't remember him ever being so morose, although occasionally, when he was a parish priest, he used to suffer a downer because of some local problem or other. But in the last three years, with his parish responsibilities behind him and a part-time college chaplaincy as replacement, along with looking after the family while his wife worked full time, he had been as sunny as Mike had ever known him. What had gone wrong?

Maybe he should have a chat with Mum. Not that there was much she could do, stuck in Oxford while they were down in Cornwall keeping safe from the Coronavirus—something that was quite easy to do, it seemed to him, this far from the centres of population where the virus seemed to be most active. He didn't want to worry Mum unnecessarily, but she wouldn't want to be kept in the dark if something were really wrong with Dad.

Unless... could it be that there was something wrong *between* her and Dad? Surely not. They were always so united, so comfortable with each other, and had been so all his life. But Dad hadn't taken much persuading to come down here and look after Cedric's house for him, leaving Mum behind in Oxford. And now that all the colleges were closed as well as the schools, and the exams had been cancelled, surely Mum could have come down to Cornwall and joined them if she had wanted to? Or wasn't she allowed to travel, now that everything was locked down? He had a vague feeling that might be the case. Still... *Could* there be a problem? He hoped not. It didn't bear thinking about. He wondered whether Lorna had noticed anything.

He took a quick look through the window. The drive gates were safely closed. He propped the kitchen door open again to let some air flow through the house, and the dogs, having slaked their thirst at the big bowl of water standing in the corner of the kitchen, flopped down on the cool slate flags where they could feel the breeze in their fur.

"Is it down to us to cook dinner?" his sister asked, coming in at just that moment. "I see Dad's in his study again, so I guess we'd better get on with it. It's nearly six." Her voice held no trace of anxiety or resentment, only a simple acceptance of her father's apparent desire for solitude. Perhaps that was all it was—if Dad was struggling with something, he had to work it out for himself, as he'd said. Lorna never worried unnecessarily, which made her a comforting person to be around if you were feeling anxious.

"There's plenty of salad ingredients in the fridge, aren't there?" he asked instead. "No cooking required. And I'm sure Dad bought quiches at the supermarket, so there'll be vegetarian stuff there for you."

She smiled at him. "You get things out and lay the table, and I'll make a green salad. Will Bethan and Chris eat that, do you think? Should we fry some chips? I don't want to use up the last of the pasta in case we can't get any more. It still seems to be in short supply at the supermarket, according to Dad. Along with toilet rolls—can you believe it? A run on toilet rolls?"

Mike grinned. "No chips," he decided. "They can eat salad and like it. Little devils. Dad lets them get away with murder. Mum would have a fit."

"I guess it's easier than having a stand-up fight with them over a meal. They don't want to be told what to do anymore, do they? Not by us, anyway."

"They'll be awful when we get home." He sighed. "I do wish Mum were here."

Lorna patted him on the shoulder. "Mum will come when she can. Or maybe you and me and the twins will be able to go home, even if Dad stays on here to look after the house and the dogs."

Mike grimaced. "I certainly wouldn't want to leave Dad on his own."

Lorna glanced up at him. "I know what you mean," she said. "But there's nothing much we can do to help him, is there?"

"I asked him straight out just now what was wrong. But he just said he couldn't explain. He had to work it out for himself."

"Well, then, it's no use pestering him, is it? All we can do is look after the twins and keep them out of his hair as best we can."

"Lorna…" In spite of himself, Mike found he wanted to confide his fears and take the sting out of them. "You don't think there's anything—anything wrong between Mum and Dad, do you?"

Lorna gaped. "Of course not, stupid! Mum and Dad—when have they ever been at odds with each other?"

"They've never been apart this long either," Mike pointed out glumly.

Lorna shook her head. "Whatever's wrong with Dad, it's not that."

~ * ~

After Mike had disappeared ahead of him with the dogs, Jeremy had trudged on steadily, trying to ignore his exhaustion, trying not to be alarmed by it. Three miles they had walked. Before lockdown, he had often walked double that distance along the river towpaths in Oxford or in the meadows beyond and thought nothing of it. But then, he had been happy and fulfilled and had slept soundly every night. Now he was depressed, and his sleep was disturbed by nightmares or by long periods of wakeful anxiety—and for that state of affairs the pandemic was largely responsible.

"I'll be in the study if you want me," he called to Mike, closing the kitchen door behind him as he went in, and missing entirely his son's concerned glance at him as he went past. He knew he was too firmly locked into a private mental hell, which was more daunting even than the physical restrictions they all had to cope with, but he had shut his children out of it for their own sake. They seemed, with the optimism of youth, to be able to slough off the daily predictions of disaster, the dire statistics as the pandemic raged out of control across Europe, the terrible descriptions—and sometimes images—of Covid sufferers on ventilators, of doctors and nurses clothed head to foot in plastic protective gear, of mortuaries piled high with bodies waiting for burial as funeral directors and crematoria struggled to cope with the excess. But he couldn't ignore it, and the horror of it bore heavily on him, disturbing his peace, threatening his faith.

Most of all, it had upset him deeply that the churches were closed—not since the whole country was excommunicated by the pope in the Middle Ages had church buildings been closed for worship. What were the bishops thinking of, to go along with this prohibition? Some of the more technologically adept clergy had taken services online, with individuals contributing from home—which was better than nothing, but it gave no feeling of corporate worship. Recently the BBC and the Church of Wales had done some really good work with broadcast compilations containing a sermon accompanied by video clips from past Songs of Praise programmes recorded in Welsh churches. That had lifted his spirits a little, but in between they drooped again. He was ashamed of himself and the doubts he found creeping in. Always before, he had found easy answers to the questions people asked about how God could allow terrible things to happen. You could blame human sin or weakness for war, and the fine tuning of the geophysical world for natural disasters, to an extent. But a pandemic... He wondered how Christians who had lived through the Black Death in Europe had coped. Somehow, he must wrestle his way through it, to a new spiritual place of prayer and trust, but as yet he had failed to do so.

Liz made her usual phone call later that evening, and Jeremy, expecting it, made sure he got to the landline receiver first. She used the landline so she could speak to everyone in turn, rather than phoning all their mobile phones—which made sense, but sometimes he wished she would contact his mobile so they could have a more private conversation.

"Everything okay at your end?" came her brisk, competent voice, her tone assuming it was.

In view of his earlier reflections, he found it quite difficult to answer her question honestly, particularly with the children listening.

He carried the receiver into his study before replying. "The kids are being really good," he told her, finding the positives as best he could. "Mike and I went out with the dogs as usual this afternoon, and we had a chat with a local woman as we passed her gate." He wracked his brain for more to say. "Lorna stayed home with Chris and Bethan. And she made supper, as well, I think—though perhaps Mike helped. I was in Cedric's study and lost track of the time."

"Lorna is really shaping up now, isn't she?" Liz responded warmly.

There was a pause. "She hasn't started worrying about her GCSE results or anything, has she?"

"Doesn't seem to have. If the grades are going to be decided by predictions, then she'll be all right. Her teachers seemed to think she'd do okay."

"I'm not sure how they *will* be decided, though," Liz said. "Some algorithm or other, but it's all a bit vague at the moment. Lorna only has to do well enough to go on into Year 12, but what about Mike? His A-level predictions are high, but there's some doubt about whether universities will accept them. There are so many imponderables, even in subjects where there's enough coursework to make some kind of judgement. And with this fear of the virus sticking to surfaces, I wonder whether schools will let them send stuff in on paper. Most of my students are working online anyway a fair bit, but the science practicals are a problem. They won't be able to hold those."

"Mike doesn't seem to care, but that may be just Mike being Mike."

"With his uni place deferred for a gap year, he can always re-take, I suppose. But I don't think there'll be much doubt about his getting the grades for Cardiff. It might have been different if he'd gone for Oxbridge."

There was a silence while they contemplated their disappointment about Mike's decision not to aim so high. One of the brightest and most able students in his year at the independent school in Oxford that had awarded him a scholarship when he started there three years ago, he had been expected to apply to Oxford for his university education—or Cambridge, if he didn't want to stay too close to home. But Mike had decided on Cardiff, and when asked, had said he didn't want the pressure that an Oxbridge place would involve. He liked Cardiff city, and he liked the university, and it would do quite well for him. He didn't want to be an academic, after all.

When asked what he *did* want to do with his life, he'd murmured something about photography, or detective work. The photographic ambition had led to his eighteenth-birthday present, but neither of his parents could visualise him as a policeman of any kind. It was true he shared his father's love of solving mysteries, which had got him into danger on one never-to-be-forgotten occasion, but Liz had no wish to encourage him into anything further along those lines.

"What about you, Remy?" Liz asked. "How are you bearing up?"

The question sounded casual, but that didn't mean Liz hadn't already had a report from Mike by text or email or had just made an educated guess.

He hesitated. It was never easy to lie to Liz, but he found it no more possible to explain his problems to her than he had to his son. "I'm okay."

She snorted. "Now I *know* there's something wrong. You never use that word unless you're trying to pull the wool over my eyes. What aren't you telling me?" Her voice was as robust as usual, but he sensed the anxiety behind it. She probably found it just as hard as he did to have the family separated. He thought, in fact, it must be particularly difficult for her, being alone in the midst of all the daily turmoil, especially in a city. But as she was head of her department at the further education college, she hadn't felt able to swan off to Cornwall with the rest of them in March when they were given the opportunity. Having made that decision, the sudden onset of lockdown had meant she was stuck with it, even though most of her students were at home like everyone else, and not in their classrooms waiting to be taught.

"It's nothing special, Liz. Nothing more than everyone else is dealing with. It's just that I find it overwhelming sometimes—the news, and all the deaths, and the queues of ambulances, and the fear ..." His voice trailed away.

"Everyone else's fear," she pointed out quickly. "Not yours, I hope."

"Not for myself, no. We're safe enough here, I think anyway, and I'm sure you're keeping to the rules. But even with all these restrictions, people are still going down with it like ninepins. Where will it all end?"

He knew, but didn't want to burden Liz by complaining about it, that part of his problem was that here in Cornwall he had no work to do. In Oxford, he had his official Permission to Officiate and acted as assistant chaplain at one of the colleges. If he'd been down here in Cornwall in normal times, he would have offered some help at one of the local churches and, since clergy were in short supply everywhere, he was sure that would have been welcomed. Indeed, when they first arrived after the children's schools had closed early for Easter, just before lockdown began, that is what he had intended to do, and he had "met" the local incumbent early on, on a socially distanced walk. But he knew Liz wouldn't see church closures as such a catastrophe as he did, with years of parish ministry behind him; she would probably think the bishops were right to go along with whatever the government said, and it was difficult to explain his unease with it.

"The number of new cases is levelling off now," Liz reminded him. "There is some light at the end of the tunnel. There's even talk of letting us travel a bit further for exercise, as long as it's fairly local. Take the kids to the beach or something, Remy, as soon as you can. Get a change of scene."

"The beach might be a bit far," he objected. "The nearest beach is Trebarwith Strand and that's nearly ten miles away. Even in Cornwall, I'm not sure that counts as local."

Liz was dismissive of this argument. "I can't believe anyone is going to be lurking at Trebarwith to catch you."

He was silent. He didn't have the energy to argue with her, but his instincts were cowardly, to stay close to home and not take any risks. He smiled grimly to himself. He had not always been so fearful of breaking rules, or of danger in any form. What on earth had this pandemic done to him?

"Are the kids around?" he heard Liz ask.

He got up from his chair and went out into the cottage hallway. "Mike? Mum on the line."

Mike appeared, took the receiver from him and went back into the kitchen, shutting the door behind him.

Jeremy sighed and returned to the study. It was strange, not having his books around him. Was it better to be in your own familiar surroundings in times of crisis, he wondered, or to be somewhere different and unconnected with normal life? At the beginning, it had felt like a holiday. Now it seemed more like exile.

He sat at the desk and tried to keep a mental hold on his own privileged state and be thankful for it. Cornwall was as yet comparatively untouched by the scourge, Liz was working from home, and his family was safe enough. None of them was taking the risks run daily by key workers. Yet he had felt, over the past few weeks, as though his spirit had walked hospital corridors beside exhausted doctors and nurses, and watched rows of patients on ventilators, hovering between life and death. He had sat with the lonely struggling for breath, untended in their homes, or desperate for human companionship, and wept with the bereaved denied their final farewell to those they loved. At some deep level, he had felt their pain as his own. And the questions had besieged him: why was this happening? And where was God in it all?

Osborne House, Friday October 15th 1915

I'm still trying to work out what I should do next about my ministry. I don't particularly fancy being a curate in the back of beyond, at someone else's beck and call, but I know several of my fellow ordinands have volunteered to go to the Front as chaplains, so that must mean there'll be vacancies here at home. Perhaps, I should make more effort to find one, instead of waiting for Mother to hear of something via her friends. Spineless, she sometimes calls me, and I think she may be right. I didn't enjoy school because I had no friends, and the other boys called me names because of my club foot. University was a little better, and I'm grateful to Mother for finding the money for me to go—it can't have been easy, now that she is a widow. The estate brings in less than it used to, and Lionel can't have contributed much from his pay as a subaltern, even before the War began. At least Maudie hasn't had to be presented at court. That must have saved the family a fair amount. But I know I should stop hanging on Mother's sleeve and start to make a career of my own.

In one way, I want to. The Church is what I have chosen, and at least it makes it easier for me to follow my heart as a pacifist. But I am apprehensive. Will I be able to do the job properly? I feel desperately inadequate when it comes to dealing with ordinary people. Will I be able to cope with pastoral visiting and giving the sort of advice that might actually help them? Anyone can say the words of the Office and lead the prayers, but some men seem to bring something mystical to the celebration of the Eucharist, and I'm sure I won't manage that. As for preaching, I know that will be a disaster. I lack the fire and zeal you need to get the congregation's attention, and no one wants to hear the kind of intellectual ramblings I tend to come up with, although they are a useful way of working out my own ideas about religion and the service of God.

But I won't get any better by avoiding the issue. Perhaps practice will make perfect. Perhaps I will learn how to be less awkward with people if I see them every week as their vicar. I know I must try.

Three

Olivia signed out of her Findom Twitter account and closed her laptop. Another few hundred pounds had been paid into her bank account, and the prospect of having to live off her mother and her stepfather receded again.

She smiled. The 'pigs' paid and, in return, she delivered the right blend of domination and mental cruelty to satisfy their fetishes. Poor sods. They had to be pretty lonely—or pretty twisted—to put up with it, and the ones who actually enjoyed it must be emotionally damaged. But that wasn't her problem. She provided an online service and earned some kind of a living from it. There was nothing illegal about her activities—though no doubt some would disapprove, and others would be shocked, if they knew what she was doing—and she even got a kind of perverse satisfaction from the exercise. In the virtual world of Findom, by definition the women were in charge, and that appealed to her. The interactions were quite addictive, in their way, much like the more dangerous liaisons she had engaged in before lockdown in the real world.

Once—how strange it now seemed—she had been satisfied with a career as a personal assistant, a grand name for what was often not much more than a glorified secretary, to an executive male in a position of power. She had despised the feminists who wanted power for themselves, or worse, wanted to drag the whole female sex with them through the glass ceiling. She had gloried in her ability to run the show from behind the scenes. Now, she wasn't so sure it wasn't an illusion, and worse still, one that perpetuated the outward dominance of men. Being a dominatrix, even a virtual and financial one, seemed to give a greater power, though she certainly didn't want to see it as a career. Once lockdown was over and restrictions eased—which was being promised for June, with further moves in July—she would think again. She was conscious, for a moment, of an unease with the whole set-up. There were times when it seemed to drag her even further into a dark and angry mindset that was threatening to get out of control.

She pushed the feeling away quickly, plugged the laptop into the socket by her bed to charge and went over to her wardrobe. Inside was her collection of designer dresses and shoes—some acquired for her work as a personal assistant to that succession of middle-and high-ranking executives, but the more recent paid for by the 'paypigs' who used her services as a Findomme. It was a pity she'd had, as yet, no opportunity to wear any of the clothes, apart from posing for selfies to share with whichever paypig had bought them, but the day would come for that, when the pandemic was over, and she could get back to London and start afresh. Some of the clothes she would probably never wear, particularly the shoes and boots with their absurd platforms and long stiletto heels, and the leather lingerie, but those she could sell. There would be plenty of buyers.

Her mother had looked askance at the number of deliveries that had arrived for her during lockdown, but as yet had not gone so far as to question her on the subject. She rather shrank from

Jeannette's probable reaction to any explanations she tried to give. What would she say? God knew what they would make of the explanation: 'Some men are weird and like to be dominated by women and told to give them money.' Again, that creeping, insidious sense of unease chilled her. It didn't matter that much to her what her mother thought—they hadn't been on very good terms for a long time, not since her father died. But Theo... That was another matter. She didn't want Theo to know about her Findomme activities—he would be disappointed in her, and she couldn't bear that.

In the distance, she heard the sound of the handbell that was still rung to let the inhabitants of the house know the evening meal was on the table. She opened her bedroom door, nearly falling over the cat, who liked to sit like a big black smudge in the early evening sunshine that poured through the window at the end of the corridor. He got up with dignity and batted her sandalled feet with a large paw, fortunately with the claws retracted, before setting off ahead of her along the corridor.

The three bedrooms on this landing had been created on what had been the gallery floor of the original seventeenth-century house. Two of these—one had been turned into a study sitting-room for her when she lived there as a teenager—had been her headquarters while she studied for her A-levels and during university vacations, and she had been glad to be offered them again when she had come home, jobless, just before lockdown restrictions began.

Their only defect, as far as she was concerned, was their proximity to the other bedroom in the old wing, which she had to pass as she went along the landing to the stairs. It was smaller and felt colder, a square room facing northwards on to the courtyard at the back of the house where once carriages had been poled up and horses saddled. The bedroom was seldom used, because there were more pleasant guestrooms elsewhere in the house, and Olivia never entered it if she could avoid doing so. In her teens, she had sometimes imagined she could hear sounds coming from it, unhappy sounds she usually managed to attribute to the wind that moaned around the eaves as it rushed past on its way down the river valley. She had never mentioned these to her mother and thought she had said goodbye to such fantasies when she left home. But during the past few weeks, more than ten years on from her university days, she had felt at times an irrational sense that there was someone living there, unbeknown to the rest of the household.

She shook off these fantastic thoughts with annoyance and walked quickly past the cold little bedroom and whatever dark and imaginary secrets it contained. The stairs led down into the spacious, but gloomy, seventeenth-century hall. This had once no doubt been the heart of the house but was now sparsely furnished with a round Georgian table on a three-pronged carved leg, which bore a big bowl of flowers in the centre of it, and a venerable and faded Persian rug on the flagged stone floor. In front of her, as she turned the corner of the staircase, was the original front entrance to the house with its heavy oak door on enormous black metal hinges, flanked on each side by a long narrow window in a deep embrasure. Opposite it was a massive seventeenth-century fireplace that must, she thought, in spite of its size, have struggled to heat the large space. It would certainly have consumed a great deal of fuel, no doubt further depleting the local forest resources. Much of Cornwall was treeless, whether open moor or farmland fields, as a result of the use of wood for pit props in the mines, and makeshift houses for the miners, even without the depredations of fuel for fires.

The kitchen, reached through a deep archway leading out of the old hall, was the oldest room in the house. It was a spacious sunny room, by contrast, with a big window facing east and a scrubbed oak table with a cloth over it in the centre. In one corner of the northern wall, another archway led into the nineteenth-century scullery that was used in modern times as a utility room;

here lived the dishwasher, washing machine and freezer, along with cupboards containing cleaning equipment. In the main kitchen, the sink and the run of cupboards and worktops either side of it stood under the window, looking out at the clematis-covered brick wall of the kitchen garden, while the oil-fired cooking range, already turned off for the summer, inhabited the chimney alcove opposite, backing on to the hall. This was a modern Aga, and the Victorian copper pots and pans on their hooks and the bread oven let into the wall were now ornamental rather than functional, but Olivia often thought of the hive of activity there must have been in earlier days as servants worked to prepare the family meals.

This evening, Olivia saw, cold meat and salads had been set out on the table, as so often on those unseasonably warm spring days; the mixed green salad and sliced tomatoes put together by her mother just beforehand, the cold beef and prepared salads in plastic containers bought at Tesco by her stepfather on his weekly supermarket outing in Launceston. The evening meal was habitually eaten together, just as it had always been during her childhood. One part of her resisted this family togetherness, but she admitted, if only to herself, that, in the present circumstances, if they were to abandon the practice, she would miss it.

"Help yourself," Jeannette invited her daughter, breaking in on these reflections. She handed Olivia a plate. "Nothing very exciting, I'm afraid, but what can you expect from Tesco?"

Olivia seated herself at the table. "There isn't much choice in Launceston, anyway, is there?" she agreed, serving herself a slice of cold chicken and some green salad. "Though you could always go to the Marks and Spencer foodhall and do some of the shopping yourself."

Jeannette sighed. "But M&S wouldn't stock everything we need, Olivia. Don't forget we're only allowed to go shopping once a week—one person at a time. Besides, Theo likes Tesco, and it's the only time he gets out, at the moment. He's no walker, so it's a good thing, really. Otherwise, he'd sit in that music room of his all day every day."

"And why not?" asked her husband, arriving at that moment. "It's what I have a music room for, after all." He smiled at both of them before taking his place at the table. "Old habits die hard, Jeannette."

Olivia took this as a reference to his working life as a musicologist, which, it seemed to her, had been very little affected by lockdown. True, there were no reviews of live concerts to be written for the newspapers, no TV presenting to be done, and CD recording sessions had been severely curtailed—which meant no reviews of the latest recordings to write for specialist journals either. But his current book project on Benjamin Britten was continuing, based on internet research and the resources of his own library, in the absence of access to London facilities, and he had started compiling a history of Tresayne House in his spare moments, mining the archive of Jeannette's family papers that no one else had bothered to look at for years. Theo was long past the age when he could have retired, but she thought he probably never would, unless physical or mental frailty forced him into it, and neither seemed at all imminent at the moment. At seventy-five, his tall spare figure was still upright, his grey hair thick, his distinguished air and good looks unchanged.

"Do you miss London, Theo?" she asked him, suddenly curious.

He considered. "No, not really. Especially not when there are no concerts to go to, and all the libraries are closed. I mean, what would one do? I'm better here, quietly getting on with my work." He looked at her intently from under bushy grey eyebrows. "What about you?"

It was a serious question, and the blue-grey eyes held genuine concern for her welfare. In the twenty-three years since he had married her mother, Olivia thought gratefully, she had never experienced anything but kindness from Theo Landry—along with a generosity that had culminated in his adopting her when her own father died.

"I do miss it, but as you say, London as it was, not London as it would be now, empty and quiet. It's the buzz I enjoy." It seemed invidious to admit to loneliness, with her family around her.

"Have you made any plans for when the restrictions ease?" Jeannette asked her. "Surely soon people will be getting back to work, and you'll be able to find another job."

Olivia sighed inwardly. Her mother would be glad to see the back of her. It was a long time since Olivia had spent more than a few days in Cornwall, and they both preferred it that way. But at the moment she didn't have much choice. There was nowhere else to go, and no immediate prospect of restrictions easing so she could surf the job market again. Her experience was all administrative and in large organisations, and no one was going to be taking on in-house staff in such uncertain times.

"I think most people are going to be working from home for ages, probably, which wouldn't be much good in the type of job I'm used to. Anyway, I don't know what I want to do next. I'm fed up with being PA to a series of self-satisfied men, and what else am I qualified for?"

As soon as she had spoken, and heard the bitterness in her own voice, she wished the comment unsaid. Jeannette would neither understand Olivia's dilemma nor sympathise with her uncertainties. Instead, she saw everything in uncompromising black and white. She would offer whatever seemed to her the most obvious solution to the problem, and be put out when Olivia rejected her suggestion, as she always did. This was a well-worn groove in the record of their relationship and Olivia had no wish to revisit it just then.

She saw Theo shake his head slightly, warning her mother not to press the question. "Another lovely day today," he commented gently. "You must be well ahead in the garden, my dear?"

"I don't remember a spring like this, in all the years I've lived here. Now that Ben is working again, he and I have got nearly all the beds tidied and the greenhouse is full of seedlings. Thank goodness the government decided gardeners were allowed to go to work as usual, or I should have been in dire straits by now."

Ben was a jobbing gardener for other local people as well, but Tresayne House was his priority, and his bread-and-butter, and she paid him well. The three acres of intensively cultivated garden had first been developed by her grandparents during the nineteen-twenties and nineteen-thirties, and they required of her many hours' work, for gardening was an endeavour in which the rest of the family took no part. Although Theo enjoyed sitting on the bench under the copper beech tree with a cup of coffee or tea on warm days, and appreciated the beauty of his surroundings when he was in them, he had no appetite for any of the hard work necessary for their maintenance, while her daughter had early on reacted against her mother's enthusiasm for the garden by deliberately choosing other leisure pursuits, just as she had turned her back on the Cornish countryside after she graduated from university, and become a dedicated urbanite.

Olivia, eating steadily, tuned out her mother's boring description of progress on her latest garden projects, just as in earlier years she had tuned out tedious stories of her great-grandparents creating the garden after the First World War. Until she heard Jeannette comment, "I met a couple of interesting people today when I was weeding the driveway flower beds."

Olivia looked up. Meeting new people during lockdown was an unusual, even illegal, occurrence.

Jeannette met her gaze defensively. "They were walking past the gate when I was weeding down at the bottom of the drive," she explained.

"Obvious, when you explain it," smiled Theo. "Who were they?"

"A clergyman from Oxford and his teenage son—Remy and Mike Swanson were the names, I think. They're house-sitting for Cedric. I've seen them before in the last few weeks but never had the chance to speak to them. I think there are younger children with them too, who weren't out with the dogs. But no mention was made of their mother."

But Theo was not particularly interested in Jeannette's speculations about the Swanson family scenario. "The spaniels will be enjoying having a decent walk," he observed.

"True. Even in lockdown, I should think they're getting more exercise than Cedric ever manages to give them."

Olivia finished her plateful and pushed back her chair. "I'm going to my room, but I'll come back and help Theo with the washing up later."

There was a silence after she had gone. Then Jeannette went on, as though nothing had been said, "I invited the Swansons to tea when it's allowed. The whole family."

Theo regarded her gravely. "Why did you do that?"

His tone was neutral and courteous, but she found herself squirming slightly as though caught out in something unexpected or incorrect. What was it about this encounter that was causing her family to put her under such uncomfortable scrutiny? Or was she imagining things?

"I don't really know. They seemed nice. And I am getting rather tired of social isolation." She hesitated. "Have you mentioned to Olivia about Marcus coming?"

"I've hardly had the chance, Jeannette. Besides, I don't want to make too big a thing of it yet. The opportunity will come up naturally if I wait."

This sounded to Jeannette like evading the issue, but perhaps Theo himself was worried about Marcus's arrival, and the implications that might have for all of them. If so, she would have to be careful how she broached the subject again.

~ * ~

Marcus himself, oblivious to the cross-currents his letter was causing at Tresayne, was standing at the open window of his flat, looking out over the Thames at the tall buildings of Canary Wharf, as he had done every day since lockdown measures had been announced. The quietness of the river—usually so full of busy commercial traffic and now so silent— oppressed him, and he wondered whether he would ever sail on it again. The Thames itself still flowed quietly and steadily towards the estuary, and the boats rocked gently on their moorings with the swell, while the city air was clear and fresh and no planes marked their passage from London's airports with jet streams. Nothing had changed in the weeks since lockdown began. But still he looked out, as though each day he was searching for a way out—an escape not only from his flat and the pandemic, but also from the stagnation of his personal life.

While there had been work to do in an office, and people around to distract him, the flat had offered him peace and space to heal, and the gated community had seemed like a refuge—a haven from a busy life in the cut-throat world of publishing, and from his personal problems. Now, it seemed like a prison. Without colleagues and the hectic flow of work, he had too much time to think of his failures.

Like many others, he had tried to fill up the emptiness and silence with creativity. Thinking it would help him understand the writer's mentality, and thus improve his relationships with the authors whose work he published, he had tried his hand at novel-writing. But he-soon had to admit defeat. He didn't have a glimmer of that creative spark. The story moved on leaden feet and the characters were made of cardboard. He'd known, without showing anyone the chapters he'd drafted, that it was no good. You either had that ability or you didn't, and he definitely did not.

The worst failures, though, he thought as he turned away from the window, were not professional but personal—first the breakdown of his long-term relationship with his girlfriend—a work colleague who had never lived with him, but whose affection had supported him through several turbulent years, before she abruptly emigrated to Australia without a word of farewell—with someone else, as he later discovered; and then the estrangement from his mother. She had been for so long the only parent in his life, but her marriage to an American tycoon possessing neither heart nor ethics had separated them when she went to live with her new husband in New York, and when she returned, the relationship had lost something essential. He told himself he had grown up and must not expect to have the same closeness with her, but the explanation felt false.

Yet most of all, since lockdown began, he had been aware of the empty place in his life where his father should have been. He wondered whether his letter had been received, and what the response would be.

Osborne House, Friday October 29th 1915

Poor Maudie is in disgrace. She has been carrying on a desperate flirtation with one of the staff here, but Mother tells me Gerald Booker, the young gardener she has been walking out with, has gone back to the Front now—fortunately before the affair could go any further. With any luck, he won't get any more leave for ages. But Mother says they went as far as saying they wanted to get married, which is beyond a joke. The young upstart actually made a point of asking for her hand in form! He came to me, as I am the head of the family since Lionel was killed—not that I would dare to oppose Mother in anything involving the family.

I suppose young Booker believes that, even though he started in the ranks, now he's been made a junior officer he's socially on a level with us, which is ridiculous. Has he forgotten his sister is still working as a housemaid here? How on earth he thinks such a marriage would work in peacetime, I can't imagine. Where would they live? What would they live on? But Mother and I have stood firm, and we must hope that as far as Maudie is concerned, now that he is out of sight, he'll be out of mind.

But what a silly girl my sister is. I try to make excuses for her and remember she's young and romantic, and there's no one of our own sort around now that most of the young men are at the Front. When the war's over, she's sure to meet someone much more suitable—though with so many being killed at the moment, I wonder how much more difficult it will be. The attrition rate for junior officers at the Front is terrible, though of course nothing's being said officially about that. I hope Freddie will continue to stay out of trouble.

There's a possibility our house here may be taken over as a military hospital, and Maudie will no doubt be kept busy looking after the wounded. Mother too, I hope. That must be better than waiting for news from the Front, though it will play havoc with our everyday routines. Perhaps I will get a benefice soon, and I can move out and go somewhere else—that is, if I don't apply to be an Army chaplain.

How long can this war possibly go on? We hear such contradictory things that I feel sure the newspapers must get the wrong end of the stick half the time. And Freddie always writes cheerfully, especially to Mother, and says the war is going well. But reading between the lines, I don't think he's very optimistic of an early victory.

Four

Theo had already finished the washing up by the time Olivia came downstairs, and was preparing a meal for the cat while the coffee machine burbled in the background. The cat sat waiting, his pink tongue fastidiously ridding his paws of any faint traces of soil that might have adhered to them while he was in the garden.

"Here you are, Kato. Tuna. Your favourite." Theo put the bowl of food down in the corner, and the cat instantly gave it his undivided attention.

Olivia laughed. "I've kept meaning to ask you, Theo. How on earth did you come to call him that? As a pun, 'Cato' isn't worthy of you, and you say it with a long 'a' not a short one, anyway. Is it after the Roman author?"

"God, no. Nothing so erudite," he replied. "I had very little to do with it, anyway. It isn't a pun. We called him 'Ben' when he first arrived. He only became Kato to reflect his penchant for jumping out from behind the coats in the hall or lying in wait for us on the stairs. It was your mother's idea."

Olivia looked puzzled.

"Inspector Clouseau," Theo reminded her. "The Peter Sellers films. Jeannette's favourites."

Her face cleared. "Oh, I remember. Kato was his assistant. The one who was supposed to take him by surprise."

"That's the one." Theo smiled. "Though usually poor Kato came off worse in their encounters, which always seemed rather unfair to me. That can hardly be said for our friend the cat here. I feel sorry for the mice, even though it is useful to have vermin kept under control in an old house like this. His human family are not altogether safe, either. Has he never attacked you?"

She laughed. "Not unless you count batting my foot with a paw as I pass."

"I expect he will, in the end," replied Theo darkly. "When he's got used to you. He likes to try out his teeth on my ankles in the morning when I'm in my dressing-gown." He looked at the coffee machine, which was showing a green light. "Do you want some coffee? I'm just going to take a cup to your mother."

Olivia hesitated.

"I'm not joining her this evening," he reassured her. "She'll be watching the *Great British Sewing Bee* tonight, and if there's one thing I can't stand, it's a lot of amateurs sitting in front of sewing machines and making outlandish garments. And I can't bear that Joe Lycett, either. He gets right up my nose."

"Yes," agreed Olivia, who had never watched the programme in her life. "I can imagine that wouldn't appeal, though I don't mind Joe myself—he's quite funny sometimes."

"We can take our coffee in the music room," he suggested.

"Well... if you're not in the middle of something, that would be nice." She was trying to sound nonchalant, but Theo was not deceived.

"Help yourself to some milk if you want it," he said, pouring coffee into a small, delicate porcelain mug. "I'll have mine black. If you take our cups through, I'll join you in a minute."

Olivia added some milk to her mug, picked up the small tray, and walked slowly along through the old hall, to the rear of the house, where in Victorian times a billiard room had been added to the ground floor. Out of this, when she married Theo, Jeannette had created a music room for her husband. The wall that divided the rooms from the hall was thick and more or less sound-proof, so he could play the piano or turn the hi-fi amplifier up high if he wanted to without disturbing anyone else. It was not unusual for Jeannette to join him there to listen to Radio Three in the evenings, or for him to play the piano to her while she read or sewed, but nevertheless it was viewed as Theo's room, to which no one came without invitation.

Olivia set the tray on the big glass-topped coffee table that stood in front of the sofa. There was barely room for the tray among the litter of books and papers that covered the table, but she daren't move anything for fear of disordering his work. It had been made clear to her long ago that however haphazard Theo's organisation of his materials appeared to be, there was a method in it that neither she nor her mother understood, but with which they were well advised not to meddle.

She looked around with appreciation at the book-lined walls and the decorated alcove that housed Theo's desk, where his laptop sat waiting for him. The all-important hi-fi system, with separate amplifier, several record and CD players, and two large loudspeakers, stood in the centre of one wall. A sofa—for visitors—and his own big upright leather armchair, a little shabby from long use, took up the centre of the floor, the chair carefully positioned in relation to the loudspeakers, so the sound came to him in precise stereophony.

In one corner stood his grand piano, a venerable Bechstein, which reminded her of childhood music lessons with him when he had first come to live at Tresayne. Olivia had proved to have no real talent for music, much to his disappointment, but she had enjoyed the privilege of being taught by him, of being allowed to come to the music room every day after school to practise, and the joy of spending time with this wonderful person who had come into her lonely life with such serendipity. The close relationship between them had been formed then, and it had continued throughout her teenage years, although she had given up learning the piano completely by the time she joined the Sixth Form. When she was with Theo, the dark corners of her personality seemed to disappear, and her anger died away. The relationship had gone on to sustain her through both her prolonged grief at the loss of her father, and her anger at her mother's refusal to let her see him before he died—both of which still haunted her. Without Theo, she would have been bereft indeed.

She touched one of the ivory keys reflectively and felt the memories rushing back. For a moment, she was again a child struggling with the misery of her parents' break-up, with the pain of rejection when her father left without a word, with the hatred and resentment she had felt towards her mother for driving him away, and then with her despair when she was told he had died. Yet somehow, looking back, her early life suddenly seemed more real, more authentic, than her grown-up years, even though the trade-off had been greater emotional comfort, an acceptance of her parents' separation, and a career of her own with its own kind of satisfaction.

Lockdown had found her between jobs, but she had to admit that her contentment with her work had been failing for years. The excitement of her role, organising the working life of her boss behind the scenes, often travelling with him abroad to conferences and meetings—and almost as often spicing up the experience with clandestine visits to his bedroom when the meetings were over for the day—had begun to fade, and over the years had become routine and even boring, the sexual spicing-up in the end becoming more important than the professional efficiency. Her final job, with a minister in the Scottish parliament, had concluded with a career-ending quarrel in a Tokyo hotel bedroom last December that had resulted in her flying home early and alone. She did not regret the quarrel—the man had treated her abominably and she valued the position he brought her less than her own sense of inviolate self-worth—but it had shown her how much she had changed. Once, she would have responded to the coarseness of his approach with charm, with allure—even with bravura, and taught him greater sophistication in the process. This time, when it came to it, she wasn't interested enough to bother. It was easier to quarrel, to quit, and to come home to the quietness of her London flat, where she had first taken on Findom clients to make ends meet while she tried to work out what she wanted to do next. Something different, she'd thought, something less dependent on men and their needs and desires, organisational and otherwise—but what? As well as a lack of direction, there had been a sense of personal emptiness, which pandemic restrictions had only exacerbated.

Drifting, still uncertain of her future, she had already given notice on her flat when lockdown was announced, and when her mother invited her to join them, she had accepted. She knew it wouldn't be easy to live at Tresayne House again, that there would be awkwardness—perhaps even conflict—but she couldn't think of an alternative. And there was always Theo, who had transformed her teenage years from misery to contentment—who perhaps had spoiled her for other men and made them all seem tawdry and undistinguished in comparison. For where was his equal?

The paragon entered the room, quietly, just as she reached this point in her reflections. "Thinking of playing again?" he asked, seeing her standing by the piano. "You might enjoy it more now. You studied for long enough to retain your basic skills, you know."

There was a hopeful note in his voice that she didn't want to disappoint, but she had to be honest. "No, Theo. I enjoyed it when I was a child, and I loved learning with you, but I don't want to go back."

He sat down in his big armchair and sipped his coffee, accepting her decision without comment. The cat strolled in and leapt lightly on to his knee, paws stretched out to knead his chest, and he stroked it absently, but his thoughts seemed far away.

Olivia settled herself on the sofa, half-facing him, and picked up her own mug, holding it between her hands as though for warmth. "Do either of your children play an instrument?" she asked.

Theo's first family were rarely mentioned, and normally she respected his reserve about them, but his obvious disappointment at her refusal to take up playing the piano again had aroused her curiosity. Had Marcus and Danielle done the same as she had, and abandoned music for other pursuits?

There was a slight pause, as if for thought. "I have no idea," he admitted at last. "They both did as children—Marcus played the violin and Danielle the piano. But whether they went on with their music, I just don't know." There was a note of infinite regret in his voice. "I didn't see much of them after Helen and I separated."

Olivia said nothing for a moment. "Why was that?" she asked tentatively.

She had never dared ask him such a question and expected him to change the subject. But to her surprise he did not. It was almost, she thought, as though he had been waiting for an opportunity like this.

"I made a complete mess of my first marriage," he told her, his gaze directed at the blank wall opposite, but his mind focusing on the past. "Music and my work were far too important to me—I see that now—and Helen, my wife, felt neglected. She shared my interests to some extent, but not enough. So she concentrated on the children, and I felt excluded in my turn. By the time I became aware of what was happening, it was too late. She had decided to leave and take the children with her. I was left with a big flat in London and my own selfish company." He shrugged slightly as if to lessen the impact of that bald statement.

Olivia was touched. "I'm sure it wasn't as black and white as that, Theo! The fault is never only on one side when a marriage breaks down." *Easy for me to say that*, she thought wryly, when she'd never made an attempt at any kind of long-term relationship, never mind taking on the commitment of marriage.

"I suppose I resented her jealousy of my work, her failure to appreciate music as I did. When we were first married, she would come to concerts with me, but after a while she found excuses not to. With young children to look after, that was fairly easy. But I couldn't understand why she had changed. Now I can see that perhaps she wasn't ever as keen as I thought she was. She tried to support me, but I fear I never showed much interest in the things she wanted to do, as I should have done." He sighed. "Maybe we were just too different. Maybe it could never have worked."

"And the children haven't tried to make contact with you since then?"

"For years they made no attempt to do so, and I'm sure Helen didn't encourage them to—probably exactly the reverse. But I don't think I'd given them enough of my time even when they were small and we were all living together. I hadn't built enough of a relationship with them, so I couldn't blame them if there was no real attachment on their part."

He paused, and she thought he was going to say something more; but the silence lengthened, and she did not pursue it.

"Was that why you made so much time for me," she asked instead, suddenly enlightened, "when you first came to live here?"

He turned to her eagerly. "Yes, absolutely! I didn't want to waste another opportunity. I wanted to create a real family this time, and Jeannette was keen for me to take on a father's role for you."

He stopped. Her reaction to this explanation must have shown in her face. "Livi, you know I have always loved you for yourself, as a person, not just as Jeannette's daughter."

She nodded, her face half-turned from him to hide her emotion. "I was never angry with *you* about losing my real father, only with Mother."

"None of what happened was her fault, my dear." His voice was gentle.

"It was. *It was.* She drove Dad away, and I never saw him again. He died far away from me, and I wasn't even allowed to go to see him, even when he was ill. You've been a wonderful stepfather, Theo. But it doesn't change that... that sense of loss I have still."

His face showed sympathy, but he made no attempt to comfort her. "Your mother had good reasons for what she did. Always."

"What reasons? She never gave me any."

"I think she felt you were too young to understand. She wasn't able to tell you the truth. And then..."

"Then he died, and it was too late."

"Perhaps." Theo stroked his beard thoughtfully. "But also, perhaps, you never asked her."

She had been too angry with her mother to ask; too sure Jeannette was in the wrong; too firm in her belief that her mother had blighted Olivia's life deliberately by quarrelling with her father. "So what were these reasons?"

"You will have to ask her yourself, Livi," replied Theo quietly. "It's not for me to tell you."

But Olivia told herself this was something she would never do. Was it pride—because she didn't want to let go of her anger in order to find out her mother's side of the story? Or was it merely that she found it too painful even to consider asking for more details? She would rather just try to forget.

But I haven't forgotten, she admitted to herself. *That's just the problem. Maybe I have to ask her, soon, or I never will. It will always be there, even if it's buried deep, that sense of loss and mystery that haunts me.*

Osborne House, Thursday November 4th 1915

I'm not so keen to move out and go elsewhere now, even to have an incumbency of my own—however difficult it may be if they turn the house into a hospital. For something wonderful happened yesterday night, and it's made me see everything differently.

Gerald's sister, Mary (oh, Mary—even your name sends me into a kind of ecstasy now!) came to see me yesterday morning and asked for a private interview. To my amazement, she wanted to ask me not to stand in the way of her brother's courtship of Maudie, and to begin with I stood firm and told her not to get involved. But then she came close to me, and I really looked at her for the first time. Up until then, I'd just thought of her as the new housemaid who came into service with us this spring. I'd hardly noticed anything about her, fool that I was.

How can I find the words to describe her? I suppose she is about fifteen or sixteen—that is the age they usually come to us, though we have had no need of any new women servants for a few years so she may be older. She's tall and strongly made—a true farmer's daughter—but graceful as well, with a wonderful curvy figure, womanly without being voluptuous. Her hair is a massive coil of dark auburn, like the copper beech leaves in early spring, and her face is heart-shaped, with straight, dark eyebrows above eyes of a deep, deep blue, full of light and life— I've never seen eyes that express a personality so clearly. When she stood close to me, and those eyes gazed at me so directly, I felt weak, as though my legs might give way under me. I could not refuse her anything, and she promised to come to my bedroom that night and reward me for agreeing to her request. I tried to stop her, to say that it wasn't necessary. I didn't want her to offer herself to me for that kind of reason. But I waited for her just the same until late that night, not knowing whether to hope or fear that she would keep her promise.

It was after midnight when she came. I suppose she-had to wait for the rest of the household to be asleep. In her white cotton nightshift and with her hair loose around her shoulders, she had come straight from her bed to mine. I can't write down what happened between us—it is too precious, too magical to be reduced to words. But I'll always remember that she was a virgin, and yet not virginal; there was no shrinking, no fear of what was unknown to her. Just a trust in me, and a delight in our lovemaking that made the whole night an ecstasy. She will come again when she can, I hope—I pray, though surely it must be wrong to pray for such a thing.

Five

There was no one to be seen on the beach at Trebarwith Strand. Its golden sand stretched in pristine tranquillity from one rocky outcrop to another, while the pools left by the receding tide glistened undisturbed in the sunshine. Hardly a breath of wind ruffled the bay, and the sea was as quiet as Olivia had ever seen it, with only the smallest of ripples showing where waves were finding their gentle way up the sand. The azure blue reflection of the sky stretched to the horizon, and where a few stretches of high cloud paled the water to white, the intensity of the afternoon sunlight was blinding. It was a famed venue for surfers, who rode the enormous breakers that thundered against the shore when any kind of breeze was blowing. But today only the tiniest of waves shush-shushed on the sand, and the surfers, many of whom used to travel long distances to enjoy their sport, were presumably locked down in their household units like everyone else.

Olivia had hurried down the hill from the car park, leaving her mother to follow with her normal encumbrances—a beach bag containing a sandwich for each of them, a flask of coffee, a towel to sit on and a book to read. She stood at the entrance to the cove, her feet planted carefully on the slippery slate that formed the natural walkway from the road and marvelled at the emptiness. She had often come to the beach with her mother in school holidays, and sometimes after school during the summer term, to dig sandcastles or paddle in the shallows and the rock pools while Jeannette sat reading with her back propped against a rock. Her father had come with them a few times, in her earliest memories, his tall rather lean figure deftly wielding a plastic spade to fill her castle-shaped bucket, patting the sand down firmly before turning it out to fashion a section of battlement, or carrying water from the stream or the edge of the breaking surf to fill a moat. But mostly mother and daughter had come alone, bringing a picnic lunch or tea to sustain them. After her father's departure, they had come more seldom, the two of them locked in the painful silence that still separated them, in which information was neither asked nor given, but his loss was the elephant in the room.

When Jeannette remarried, their visits to the beach had gradually ceased, because Theo was not interested in sitting by the sea, and Jeannette preferred to spend time with him at home. But today she had suggested it, and Olivia had accepted the invitation to join her. It was the first time they had come to Trebarwith together since her early teens, and Olivia had not originally planned to revisit the beach or the memories it evoked. But somehow, when restrictions eased a little, and a short trip in the car to a beauty spot became permitted, it had been an obvious place to go. When that morning her mother had come up with the idea of an outing, Olivia had suppressed her instinctive reluctance, dimly aware that, even against her better judgement, she wanted to spend time with Jeannette, perhaps even to have the chance at last to ask those questions about her father that Theo had suggested she should. Who knew when there might be another chance? So they checked the tide times, and set off after lunch together, with the intention, on Jeannette's part at least, to sit and enjoy the early June sunshine that beat down on the west-facing rocks.

There had been two other cars in the car park, but so far Olivia had not caught sight of their owners. However, it was a big beach, with many nooks and crannies, and even a cave or two, so they might be hidden away somewhere out of her sight. Perhaps if she lingered long enough, they would emerge.

Her mother quickly found some rocks to sit on and got out her book. What did she expect Olivia to do, her daughter wondered. Play sandcastles and paddle? Irritated, unwilling—now the opportunity was there—to talk to her mother about the ghost that lay between them, she began to wander along the edge of the rocks, her eyes on the waves breaking on the shore halfway down the beach. The tide was coming in, but there should be a couple of hours before it brought the water near enough to matter—though it would be wise to watch out for it. The beach at Trebarwith was notorious for the speed with which parts of it were submerged by the incoming tide, regularly stranding unwary tourists, who had to climb the rocks above the beach to avoid inundation. It was impossible to escape until the tide fell again, for at high water the sea covered the whole beach as far as the entrance to the cove, and, on occasion, the waves even came right up to the road. It was the northern end of the beach where the ground dipped and the tide rose fastest, and Olivia saw that her mother had picked a place to sit near the entrance, where there was no chance of the tide catching her unawares.

As she wandered along the soft sand, skirting the sea edge where the tiny waves broke into bubbly ripples on the shore, she heard voices from the far side of a group of large rocks. As she moved towards them, she saw it was a family group—a middle-aged man and three children, the younger two paddling in the shallow surf, while the older, a girl perhaps in her mid-teens, walked beside her father, the two apparently deep in conversation. Further off were two dogs, intent on their own business.

Father and daughter stopped when they saw Olivia, but the younger children took no notice, absorbed in their game.

"Hi!" called the girl in a friendly fashion.

Olivia walked a little closer, careful to keep more than the required two metres' distance. She felt unaccountably tongue-tied.

"What a lovely beach," the girl went on. "Do you live near?"

"I live in London usually. But I was staying with my parents when lockdown began, so here I still am."

Could the strangers be tourists? It had been rumoured that cars would be stopped on the A30 at the Devon/Cornwall border to discourage people from breaking the law and driving long distances to enjoy the seaside. Had this family run the gauntlet of such prohibitions, or found back roads to avoid the risk?

"We've been here since mid-March," the girl told her, answering her unspoken question. "We're house-sitting for someone in a place called Trebartha, near North Hill. Do you know it?"

Olivia's eyes opened wider. "That's not far from where I'm staying, at Tresayne House."

The girl's father looked surprised in his turn. "We walk past there with the dogs most days," he said. "I think we have spoken to your mother. But today we thought we'd have a change of scene, now we're allowed to. How strange to meet you here."

Olivia thought of her mother's description of the two men she'd spoken to at the gate a few days ago. The man could well be the same, but where was his son? She turned to call her mother for confirmation. But as she did so, a voice called from further up the beach. "Dad! Dad! Come over here, quickly."

Olivia turned. A tall young figure had emerged from behind the rocks and was running in their direction. This must be the son her mother had mentioned.

"There's a cave," he called breathlessly. "And a man."

His father's attention sharpened. "A man?"

The boy immediately turned back to lead them in the other direction. "He's ill," he explained over his shoulder. "Or perhaps dead."

Dead? Olivia recoiled, but then she saw that father and daughter were about to follow the boy, apparently unmindful of any danger, and without regard for the younger children and the dogs for whom they were presumably responsible. What kind of family was this?

"He isn't moving," the boy went on, casually. "But I touched him, and he didn't feel really cold."

He began to run again, his sister close behind him.

"Excuse me," said the father to her briefly, good manners seemingly intact even in an emergency. "I must see if we can help."

"Of course." She watched helplessly as they sped away from her, then began, slowly, to follow them, reluctant but compelled by curiosity as much as anything else. She looked back towards her mother, but Jeannette, oblivious to events at the far end of the beach, was still reading placidly.

~ * ~

Jeremy hurried after his impulsive son, aware that if this turned out to be a crime scene, nothing should be touched. And if the man were alive, urgent medical help should be sought, restrictions or not. He had seen the young woman they had met pulling her phone out of her jeans pocket as he turned to follow Mike, and he hoped she was summoning the emergency services. There probably wouldn't be much signal inside the cave.

The man was lying near the entrance, curled like a bundle of dirty clothing on the rocky floor.

"Mike! We shouldn't touch anything," Jeremy warned. Apart from the crime-scene aspect, there was always the danger of contact with coronavirus, in such an unknown situation. Supposing Mike was exposing them to that and all it might mean?

To his horror, Mike took no notice, but approached the body briskly and, before his father could stop him, shook the nearest shoulder.

There was a growl from the huddled shape on the ground, which unrolled itself to reveal a middle-aged man, unshaven and tousle-haired, his face rimed with salt and sand. But not a stranger, Jeremy realised, as he stared down at a face which a few years ago had been quite familiar to him. In spite of the man's dishevelled state, he could not be mistaken.

"Clive?"

A haggard face stared back at him, and a grimy hand rubbed the creased and dirty forehead. He didn't seem to recognise Jeremy.

"Are you sure, Dad?" Mike asked him. "Clive Althorpe—Rose's husband?"

Jeremy nodded. When he had last seen Clive, the man had been well groomed and wearing a suit, as befitted a successful senior manager in a big company. He knew that soon afterwards Clive had left his family and his job and taken a completely different direction in life, but nevertheless it was hard to believe he had ended up like this.

He looked more closely at Clive's face and said sharply to Mike, "Stand back. He has a fever."

"I suppose, seeing that he's alive after all," his son remarked, "we'd better get him to a hospital."

Jeremy hesitated. Hospitals were associated in his mind, as in most people's just then, with the horror of pandemic wards taken up with Covid patients. All other NHS activities had ground to a halt. In any case, he knew the nearest hospital was in Plymouth, nearly fifty miles away, and ambulance coverage would be poor, unless the air ambulance was available. He didn't know how far paramedics would have to come to reach them, but he'd rather not put Clive in his car with the children if there was any risk of his having Covid.

"I've rung the emergency services," said a voice behind them. "They said to keep our distance and an ambulance will come."

Jeremy looked round. It was the young woman they'd met outside the cave. "We ought to cover him up and keep him warm," he said. "I can't remember if we have any blankets in the car." His mind felt woolly and blank. Why should there be blankets in the car, anyway?

"There's the picnic rug," his daughter reminded him. "I'll go and fetch it."

She ran off, and the young woman came a step or two closer, even as Jeremy and Mike moved away. "I don't know how long it will be till the ambulance arrives," she said. "Perhaps I should stay and wait for them. I can keep well away from him, just in case. You won't want to take risks with the children."

"That's good of you. I'm Remy Swanson, by the way. This is my son Mike, and my daughter Lorna has gone for the blanket. God, we've the twins with us somewhere too." He looked round rather wildly. "Mike, you'd better go and find them. And the dogs."

Mike nodded and went out of the cave, leaving Jeremy with the young woman.

"My name's Olivia Landry," she told him.

The name rang a bell, though he was sure he'd never met her. He couldn't believe he would have forgotten; she was striking, even in a simple T-shirt and jeans, with the strong bones in her tanned face, deep blue eyes and thick fair hair pulled back into a ponytail. But before she could say anything more, there was an interruption from the fever patient on the floor.

"Olivia?"

She looked down and froze. Jeremy thought she might faint, but then she rallied.

"Clive?" She swallowed. "What on earth are you doing here, in this condition?"

"I wondered the same thing myself," observed Jeremy. "He used to be one of my parishioners, when I was a parish priest in Hampshire. How do you know him?"

"He used to be my boss, some years ago." She hesitated, and Jeremy guessed there must have been more than a manager–subordinate relationship. No wonder she had been shaken by seeing Clive like this.

"Seems he's come on hard times. He was in pretty good fettle when I knew him in Hampshire."

"Things had started to go wrong for him when I last saw him." Olivia spoke slowly, as though the words were being dragged out of her. "He wasn't the same person after his son went missing, even though they found the boy safe and sound. Some sort of breakdown, I think." Her voice tailed off as though she had thought better of what she was going to say.

Suddenly, Jeremy realised who she was, and why her name had sounded so familiar. He had been right about the relationship between her and Clive—he remembered Rose, Clive's wife, telling him about it, in much distress. Olivia had been Clive's PA, and at least partly responsible for the breakup of his marriage.

"I moved from Hampshire quite soon after that business with his young son," he said, and without intending it, an austere note crept into his voice. "I lost touch with him after that, though we know Rose and her son Robert quite well—they're living in Oxford now, not far from us. But nothing that happened then would have made me expect him to end up like this."

Olivia shrugged, her face becoming closed and uncommunicative. "I haven't seen him for ages, not since I stopped working with him."

"He's not well enough to ask him what went wrong," said Jeremy. "That will have to wait. He'll need to have somewhere safe to go, though, when the paramedics have seen him—they won't want to take him to hospital unless they must, with things as they are."

He didn't need to say any more. Olivia would know as well as he did why hospitals wouldn't want to admit anyone they didn't have to. "Could you take him in?" he asked. Tresayne House had looked pretty large to him, what he'd seen of it from the lane; quite big enough to accommodate someone extra with plenty of social distancing.

Olivia stared at him. "You must be out of your mind! My parents are elderly. I can't take a risk like that."

"On the contrary," came a quiet, firm voice from behind her. "Of course we must take him in, if he's in need."

Olivia swung round. Her mother was standing just inside the mouth of the cave and had obviously heard at least the end of the conversation.

"Mother," she hissed furiously. "If I don't feel any responsibility for him, why should you? What about Theo? Anyway, aren't tramps being put up in hotels, while there are no tourists?"

"Yes, they are," put in Jeremy quickly, hoping that mother and daughter were not going to quarrel in front of him. He smiled at Jeannette, who looked vaguely familiar, though he couldn't remember for the moment where he had met her. "I wonder why he's here. Did a hotel throw him out, do you think, because he was ill? Surely not."

"You wouldn't find me in one of those hotels," snarled Clive, sitting up suddenly. "They offered me a room, weeks back, but I wouldn't take it. No, I'm happier on the road—or I was until I started to feel ill." He coughed deep in his chest and Olivia and Jeremy, who were closest to him, instinctively took a pace backwards. He laughed rather grimly at them. "A pilgrim, that's what I am. A wandering soul."

"It's no good wandering," Jeannette told him firmly, kneeling beside him, "when you are ill. That's when pilgrims must take their rest and accept others' help."

He turned away from her and rolled himself up again into an uncooperative ball.

His would-be rescuers looked at each other over his uncommunicative form.

"I met Mike outside," said Olivia's mother. "He said to tell you that he's taken the rest of the family back to your car. And the dogs."

Light dawned suddenly on Jeremy. "Of course, you're Jeannette. We met at your gate, when Mike and I were out walking, a week or two back."

She nodded. "And this is my daughter, Olivia."

Olivia and Jeremy stared at each other. Jeremy thought better of telling her he knew just who she was and quite a lot about her connection with Clive. It wasn't the time or the place.

"I'd better go and take the family home, I suppose," he said instead.

Jeannette nodded. "Olivia and I will wait for the paramedics. And if the paramedics take him to hospital, as they probably will, and Clive then needs somewhere to stay when he is discharged, I will personally go down to Derriford Hospital and bring him home."

"That's very good of you, Mrs Landry," Jeremy told her. "He's in a strange state of mind just now, but I'm sure in time he'll appreciate it."

He saw that Olivia was about to argue further with her mother, and apostrophising himself as a coward, hurried away to find his offspring before the hard words began to fly.

Osborne House, Monday November 15th 1915

Three times this week, Mary has come to my room after everyone is asleep and given herself to me with such generosity as I have never known before in any woman. Words cannot describe the ecstasy she brings me with her soft, yielding flesh and her eager lips, the beauty of her face and her wonderful hair, the joy of her body warm against mine. There was never a woman like her, and yet, she has known no other man. I am truly blessed.

She tells me she cannot always come when she wants. She is afraid the maid she shares a room with, up in the attics, will wake and see her creeping out, or she will not get back to her own bed before the girl wakes in the morning, though always she leaves me long before dawn, even when I beg her to stay. I am afraid, too, afraid for her—if we are found out she will lose everything, her job, her reputation—even her family may throw her out. I am no great lord to install her in a flat somewhere for me to visit her when I'm in town. If we are discovered, all will be lost.

I have not made any effort to look for a clerical vacancy. But soon Mother will find me a living somewhere—she does not want me kicking my heels here any longer, she says—and then what will we do? I should tell Mary not to come to me again; but I cannot give her up, not yet, not now, while our joy is so fresh, and she so willing to risk everything to be with me. I am selfish—I know it, I confess it. I am in agonies of guilt. But I cannot let her go.

Six

After Jeremy had gone, Olivia rounded on her mother.

"Are you mad, suggesting Clive comes to stay with us?" she demanded. "What about Theo? What about the risk of him catching the coronavirus?"

"I will ask Theo," replied Jeannette calmly. "But I'm sure he will agree with me. And they will test Clive for the virus at the hospital, so there will be no particular risk. This man has nowhere to go, and he is an old friend of yours, Olivia. I can't understand why you want to turn your back on him."

Olivia turned away, unable to explain to her mother just why this 'old friend' was someone she was only too happy to abandon. She was not even sure she could make sense of it herself, but the gut feeling was very strong. Perhaps he reminded her of the self she had been when they had been together, when sexual adventures had been a way of keeping her demons at bay; the self she had striven so hard to bolster and shield since then; the self that, more recently, she had begun to want to leave behind.

Clive had always seemed tough-minded, a successful manager who took no prisoners, and she had enjoyed matching his competence, making their relationship a vibrant partnership that married efficiency and pleasure, in both the boardroom and the bedroom. It had lasted for seven years. In the end, she had made the mistake of believing that, if she asked him, he would leave his dead-end marriage and his tedious family, and start a new life with her beside him. She had been so sure of her power over him. But when she did ask, he had rejected her, and she had never forgiven him for it, because that rejection had fatally damaged her belief in her own power over the men she associated with, and from that moment her enjoyment of her career as a high-flying PA had drained away. She might have come to see since then that the career had been a dangerous drug, addictive and damaging to her as a person, but still she hated Clive for taking it away. Worse still, after his young son disappeared soon afterwards, his sudden vulnerability—taking weeks off work and clearly unable to cope with the demands of the job when he returned—had startled and appalled her. That fall from grace had been the catalyst that had set her on the road away from the corporate highjinks and jet-setting lifestyle she had up till then enjoyed. It had been like a contagion that had infected her and destroyed her confidence from within.

But that train of events was too irrational and too complicated to explain to Jeannette, even if she had wanted to. Her mother had never understood her, and it was useless to expect she ever would. Their lives were too different, and the older woman lacked the imagination to cross the gap. The gulf between them, which had narrowed briefly as they set out together this afternoon, seemed wider than ever. Olivia wondered why on earth she had thought, even for a moment, that the time might be right to ask her mother for details of her father's defection, and why he had died alone so far from home.

~ * ~

Lorna reached the car just ahead of Mike and the twins, with the two dogs running close behind them. She waited while Mike operated the central unlocking system, then dug the picnic rug out of the boot before the dogs jumped in.

"I'm just taking this for the corpse," she said. "The corpse that turned out to be alive, that is."

Mike grinned. "I'll amuse the kids till you and Dad get back."

Lorna wished him luck at that. Bethan and Chris, at twelve, were leaving behind their earlier hero worship of Mike and starting to demand equal rights with their siblings.

She ran off down the strip of tarmac road, over the slippery slate entrance to the cove and across the sand, jumping the small rocks as she came to them.

Her father met her half-way to the cave.

"Mike has the dogs and the twins safe," she told him, slowing briefly. "I'll take this down and come back, if you're ready to go."

Her father nodded rather absent-mindedly. Occasional inattention to what was said to him was not unusual, however, so she paid it no heed but went on her way.

In the cave, the two women were standing some distance apart, the sick man between them. He was lying down again, curled up as he had been when they first found him. He was probably cold, Lorna thought compassionately, as she wrapped the rug around him carefully. Although the sun was warm outside, in the cave it was damp and chilly.

"Lorna, be careful," the younger woman warned her. "He may have Coronavirus."

Lorna stepped back. "He still needs to be warm."

She wondered suddenly whether they would ever get the picnic rug back. Probably the hospital would burn it in case of infection. She sighed. It had been an expensive one, a gift from one of her grandparents.

She looked across at the older woman and found she was smiling. "Thanks for bringing your blanket."

The younger, by contrast, made an impatient movement and then left the cave abruptly, almost tripping over a rock embedded in the floor as she did so. Lorna wondered what was wrong.

"I'm sorry about Olivia," said the older woman. "She used to know this man years ago, and finding him in this condition has upset her."

Lorna smiled at her, glad to know why Olivia had reacted so badly, even though it didn't explain the deeper hostility she had sensed between the two women.

"I'm Jeannette Landry," the older woman went on. "I live at Tresayne House, quite near the cottage where you're staying."

Lorna nodded. "Dad told me about you. He said you had a lovely garden."

"And I hope," Jeannette went on warmly, "that when we are allowed to have visitors again, you will all come and have tea with us."

Lorna wondered privately whether that would be possible before they all had to go back to Oxford, but she answered politely. "That would be lovely. I'm not any good at gardens, but Mike and I are both interested in houses."

"Ours is ancient, though it isn't a really big house like some of the great Cornish mansions. But it has quite an interesting history. My husband is researching it as a kind of lockdown project, so he might have some things to tell us by the time you come."

"I'd better go now. The others are waiting for me." Lorna hesitated, looking down at the curled figure on the floor of the cave. "I hope he will be all right. I didn't ever know him very well when he lived near us, but he was always very smart, very organised— except when his son went missing. He rather went to pieces then. It's strange to see him like this."

"Yes, I think that was what Olivia felt. Perhaps when he is better, we'll learn what happened to him."

Lorna nodded. "Goodbye, Mrs Landry. It was nice to meet you, and I do hope we can come and have tea sometime."

She rode home in the back of the car rather thoughtfully, tuning out the twins' lively prattle. Her happy childhood, loved by both her parents and enjoying good relationships with them, seemed in danger of being lost among all the challenges of the pandemic, and she was beginning to see it more clearly, and value it more highly in the light of the experience of others who had not had the same good fortune. Today, there was the unease between Olivia and her mother. But yesterday, there had been something far more serious and disturbing, which she was still processing.

She had gone out for a run, up the hill from their cottage past Stonaford and up on to the moors. Running was new to her, a discovery of being stuck in Cornwall with her family for the past few weeks, with few activities open to her apart from the exercise time that fortunately a wise government had decided to allow. An hour didn't give her time to run anywhere very exciting, but it had felt good to keep up her fitness, and the hills were a physical challenge. At the same time, she found herself appreciating the natural beauty around her. In Oxford, over the last year or so, she had started to get interested in environmental issues, and suddenly here she was in the midst of the most wonderful landscapes. She had lived in a semi-rural area before they moved to Oxford, but she had not really noticed it much. Her world had been bounded by school buses and trips in the car to the local town to shop for clothes or gifts, and like the rest of her generation, after she'd done her homework, internet surfing and social media had filled up the rest. The countryside was there, but it hadn't really mattered. Now she knew how fragile it all was, how deep were the problems of global warming, plastic pollution, marine contamination, and air quality.

Last week, without telling anyone, she had joined Extinction Rebellion, full of zeal to save the planet, though she was sure her parents wouldn't approve. It was unlike her to be secretive, and she rationalised it by reminding herself that both her parents were preoccupied with the events of the pandemic and with their own separation from each other. At sixteen, it was the first personal act of teenage independence she had ever undertaken, and she was ready for more when the time came, when XR called on her to take action.

But just now, the Cornish banks and verges displayed a wealth of wildflowers, the streams ran clear in their rocky beds, and some fields were full of healthy-looking cattle and sheep, while others showed green shoots of wheat and barley. The air was pure, and there was no traffic, even though the holiday season would normally be in full swing. It was all a long way from the city streets of Oxford, and she meant to enjoy every second of it while she could.

In the last week or so, she had fallen in love with the moors. Since the restrictions had eased, and slightly longer spells away from home had been allowed, she had discovered the upland heaths and rocky outcrops, interspersed with rough grazing, that covered the high ground a few miles from the cottage where they were staying. If you ran to the top of the hill they called Ridge, where the sky seemed enormous and on a clear day you could see for miles, it was like entering another world.

But it was another world in a different sense, too. For up there on the moors she had met Jude, and Jude was one more secret she hadn't yet dared to tell her parents.

Lorna thought of herself as a modern teenager, in spite of her rectory upbringing, but Jude had been a shock, even to her. Abused, isolated, different; vulnerable yet defiant; scared yet courageous. It was hard to find words to describe Jude, never mind the dilemma Jude was facing, trapped in an abyss between two worlds and uncertain how to escape.

Lorna had been pushing herself up the hill, feeling the lactic acid in her thigh muscles in spite of the weeks of running but eager to reach the top and see whether the day was clear enough to get the best of the views. She had been told you could sometimes see Lundy Island off the north coast of Devon, in one direction, and the nearer slopes of Dartmoor in the other, which sounded marvellous. But just as she was nearing the top, where the hill flattened out into a high plateau, and the view of Dartmoor was already in sight to her right, she was brought to an abrupt stop by the sight of a tall, bulky figure crouched behind a rock, as though trying to avoid being seen.

She stared at the apparition, not sure whether to feel threatened. Cornwall seemed generally a very safe place to be, compared to the city life she'd been living for the past three years, or even the semi-rural Hampshire village she'd grown up in. But the moor was even emptier of walkers than usual, under lockdown restrictions, and if the figure she'd seen did pose a threat, there would be no one within call. On the other hand, if she caught her breath for a minute or two, she could probably outrun a possible assailant. She hesitated, but curiosity got the better of fear.

"Who are you? And why are you hiding?"

Osborne House, Wednesday December 1st 1915

I have been corresponding with pacifists in London who are opposing the War. I believe the National Peace Council has split irrevocably on the issue, for some oppose all wars, and feel that we should never have become involved with this one, while others say, as I do, that this country had to guarantee Belgian neutrality, as a matter of honour, but that the war is now being conducted badly and with no regard for the men's lives or the conditions they are fighting in. They want negotiations opened with Germany as soon as possible, in a spirit of reconciliation. Everyone I've heard from in the FCR, however, agrees that the real danger for us as a group is the prospect of conscription, which the government is now considering introducing. I pray that ways may be found to respect the consciences of those who believe that killing is wrong, even as a soldier under orders. But in any case, conscription must be a mistake. How can men fight well if they are being forced to do so? I suppose our losses have been so great that they are running out of volunteers, even with Kitchener's efforts to recruit.

Some of my Cambridge pacifist friends who have gone into the professions are being treated abominably by their clients and colleagues because of their beliefs. I must admit I have not said much about my views here in the village, particularly now that I am surrounded by wounded soldiers in the hospital that our home has become. And with my brothers and Maudie's fiancé at the Front, it seems invidious to be ineligible to fight and then criticise those who do. Perhaps I am being a coward, yet again.

I have said nothing to Mary about my beliefs. I don't know whether she would understand, or even whether she would turn from me with abhorrence—and I could not bear that. Besides, we do not talk much when she comes to my room. The time for lovemaking is too precious, too exquisite, to spend in speech, other than that of passion. Our conversation is of the body, of touch and sensation and deep ecstasy. God bless her now and always.

Seven

The figure uncurled itself from its hiding place and proved to be bulky mainly because of a bunchy oversized jacket and loose jogging pants. He or she was certainly tall and broad-shouldered, and, Lorna thought, about her own age, but she was at a loss to work out whether the teenager was male or female—the head of close-cropped curls, the big broad face and firm chin, the medium-sized feet in their ragged trainers with broken laces, could have belonged to either. But there was a softness in the face that made her opt for a girl, at least until informed otherwise. Cornish girls, she'd noticed, were often tall and well built, especially the farmers' daughters. Fear, already overcome by a desire to find out more, retreated another step. She could not believe this person—male or female—would do anything to harm her. The teenager looked like a fugitive, and more scared of Lorna than a threat to her.

"I won't hurt you," she said quickly, holding out her hand. "Why are you frightened? Can I help?"

There was silence, and the figure seemed to shrink behind the rock again.

Lorna felt in her pocket for the cereal bar she carried in case she felt hungry on the run. She held it out silently, like a lure to a wild animal.

After a moment, the wild creature moved forward quickly, grabbed the snack, and retired behind the rock again, tearing the wrapper off and biting into it hungrily.

Lorna moved a few paces away and found a smaller rock to sit on. Could this be someone living rough? And if so, why? What had happened to drive her from home? In this strange period, when families were isolated from each other, and no social contact outside the household was permitted except for the most basic activities of shopping or exercise, the problem must surely be at home.

After finishing every crumb of the cereal bar, the vagrant crept warily from behind the rock and found a seat a little nearer to Lorna's, near enough for conversation, but far enough to be able to move away quickly if any attempt at capture was made. Lorna sat very still.

"What's your name? Mine is Lorna."

There was no reply for a minute or two.

"Why are you frightened?" Lorna asked again when the silence persisted. "I know you're scared of something—someone."

"Jude." It was a hoarse whisper, as though the voice hadn't been used for a while. "M'name is Jude."

Lorna waited.

"M'father," the voice went on. "I be hiding from 'un. He'll likely take the strap to me if'n he find me."

The Cornish accent was very strong, and Lorna struggled to understand her.

"The strap? D'you mean he'll beat you?"

Jude nodded. "Allus has." Again the hesitation. "And other things."

Lorna frowned. "What other things?"

There was a shake of the head. The other things were clearly too bad to voice. Lorna began to feel anxious. There were matters here far beyond her experience, and she wished her father were with her.

"How can I help?" Practical assistance seemed more important than understanding the situation completely. If the teenager's father was physically abusing her, and to the point that she'd run away, then clearly action was needed.

There was another silence, while the fugitive clearly struggled to trust this stranger far enough to ask for help.

Lorna looked at her watch. "I have to go home," she said. "But tomorrow I could bring you anything you need. Are you living rough?" She gestured to the bare moorland of gorse and stones and unfurling bracken. "Where are you living?"

Jude seemed to make up her mind. "There be a rock shelter—up near the top o' Ridge. Works well enough while the weather be fine."

"You need food, though," Lorna persisted. "I'll bring you food."

"Please." Another pause. "And—pads. Sanitary pads, tampons—anything you have."

"Oh, you poor thing." That was the gender doubt sorted, anyway.

Lorna hesitated. "Will you cope until tomorrow? I'm sure I can get here in the morning."

"I'll manage. Won't be the first night I've gone hungry. I can maybe sneak back to t'farm and steal some food."

"Is the farm where you've run away from?" Lorna had only passed one farmhouse on the way up the hill, a rough-looking place with a couple of barking collies chained in a kennel by the gate, but there might be others further along the road. There were plenty of smallholdings on the edge of the moor, with their rough pasture fields grazed by sheep and moorland cattle. "No—don't tell me," she added, as Jude shrank away from her. "I promise I wouldn't give you away, but if I don't know anything, then you'll feel safer." Even her father, in whom she confided most things, had better not know about this. Not until she could find out more, or she'd had a chance to think what was best to do.

She got up. "Be careful—stay out of sight. I'll be back in the morning." She started to walk carefully down the hill, not looking back, anxious not to scare the fugitive any further.

The next day she returned as she had promised, armed with cold meat taken from the cottage fridge, a couple of apples and as many slices of bread as she thought she could remove without their loss being noticed. With perpetually hungry gannets around like her brother and the twins, who were used to snacking when they felt like it, she thought it was unlikely her depredations would arouse suspicions. She'd filled a large Cola bottle with tap water as well, rather concerned that Jude might be drinking from streams or ponds on the moor—it had been so dry lately that no water up there would be very fresh.

She looked for Jude near the path where she had met her the day before, and then climbed up to the rock shelter Jude had mentioned, where there were certainly signs of occupation, including an old blanket rolled up under the rock shelf that formed a kind of roof, and an old travel cup. But of Jude there was no sign at all.

Olivia left the food and the bottle of water on top of the blanket, hoping Jude would come back and find them, and then hung around miserably for a while wondering what else she should do. On the way back, she slowed to a walk as she passed the farmhouse, set back from the road with its wooden gates firmly roped shut and its barking collies still in the yard. But if Jude were there, she was well hidden.

She jogged on. There was nothing more that she could do that day. She didn't feel she could talk to the family about Jude, not even to Mike. She simply didn't know enough, didn't understand what Jude was dealing with, or what she was keeping secret that perhaps needed to be secret. Worst of all, she had no idea how to help.

That afternoon they had gone to the beach and met Jeannette and Olivia and found Clive in the cave. It had been too late to go back to the moor that evening, and she couldn't have thought of a good excuse, anyway. But she promised herself she would go in the morning, straight after breakfast.

"You seem very keen to go running these days, Lorna," her father observed as she ate her cereal. "You don't usually run every day, do you?" He smiled, but there was still a question to be answered.

She looked up, surprised he had noticed her exercise regime at all, given his preoccupation lately with all matters related to the pandemic. "It's so lovely on the moors," she explained glibly. "And I think this wonderful weather won't last much longer. I want to make the most of it." The likelihood that the fine weather would break was one of the things that worried her about Jude's situation. It was one thing living outdoors in a rough rock shelter when the weather was warm, dry and settled as it had been. What would happen if it became cold and wet?

He nodded, accepting her explanation. "How long will you be? Mike and I have been invited to have coffee with the Landrys this morning, and I don't want to risk taking the twins."

"Are we allowed?"

"The regulations have just changed. Two households and no more than six people, I think. They're calling it the Rule of Six. Outside only—it's supposed to be parks and public spaces rather than home gardens, but Jeannette reckons their garden is so big it would count as public rather than private space—they even open it a few times a year, for the National Garden Scheme."

"I don't know how long I'll be—it takes an hour or so to get up to Ridge and back again, usually. What time are you invited for?"

"Eleven-ish." He looked at his watch. "It's only eight now, so you'll be back, surely?"

"I guess so." *I'll just have to be, whatever's happening with Jude.*

"And Mum texted me to say she wants you and the children to go home soon. Term's pretty much over, with no exams to invigilate, and the Year 12s out of school anyway. She wants to spend some time with you."

I can't possibly go home just now. How can I help Jude if I'm back in Oxford? "I thought we had to stay put."

"Mum reckons you can change households as long as you then stay where you are. You still can't go and stay, and then come back again, though I think that will change in the next few weeks. Mum just meant we should go home as soon as we can."

Lorna digested this. "So are we all going home?"

"I suppose so. I expect Cedric will want to come back for the summer vacation. He usually spends summer in Cornwall, so if he's allowed to come, I expect he will. But I haven't heard from him yet."

Lorna relaxed. There was still time. *I never thought I'd be glad of lockdown regulations!*

~ * ~

Marcus opened the door of his flat, breathing hard after climbing the stairs two at a time, and bent to remove his running shoes. It had been good to go out jogging, and he had stayed out a little longer than usual, making the most of the slight relaxation in regulations. He'd enjoyed the feeling of fresh air in his lungs and on his face, and the endorphins his body released in response to vigorous exercise. But it wouldn't take long for those to disperse, and his breathing was already returning to normal. The day stretched out in front of him, empty of both physical and social activity, and publishing seemed to have ground to a halt, so there wasn't even any work to do. He had plenty of savings, and there was the government furlough scheme to fall back on if necessary, but for the moment, the firm were still paying his salary. He wasn't anxious about his finances, even with a big mortgage on the flat. But the social emptiness was another matter.

He turned on the coffee machine and stood beside it while the water heated and the coffee brewed. He loved the way his environment fed his physical senses: the aroma of freshly ground coffee, the touch of water on his skin in the shower or outside in the rain, the sight of the river and the sky or flowers and trees, the sound of music or children laughing. Lockdown had been so limiting to opportunities for sensual enjoyment, and it had made him especially miss the closeness of another human being, even though he knew now that Anna had never really cared very much for him, that she would certainly not have stayed with him forever.

He was over Anna now, he knew that. Her abrupt and unheralded defection had shown him the shallowness of their relationship, and although he felt angry and betrayed, it was a temporary emotion which went no deeper than hurt pride. But that didn't stop him feeling lonely, or longing for the permanent relationship that had eluded him so far, for a woman who would share his life with him—someone whom he could love deeply and who would love him wholeheartedly in return. But where was he to find her?

Osborne House, Friday December 10th 1915

I heard today that I have the offer of a living in Cornwall. We have a family connection with the patron, and a little manor house that belongs to us in the parish has been used in the past as the rectory, so there is a house for me to live in. The current incumbent has recently offered himself as an Army chaplain, so the offer can be taken up immediately. It is a tiny place—two or three hamlets and a little church built fifty years ago at the behest of an ambitious patron. The stipend is low, but I have money of my own, and it will be a start.

The difficulty is that my mother, now she has the opportunity to get rid of me, has begged me to stay here. She is heavily involved with the military hospital and has suggested I become its chaplain— such is the level of casualties now coming in. Indeed, I have been trying to help the men as best I can in an unofficial capacity. But I have always thought that when I had the opportunity, I would rather go away and try making a life on my own. Mother's low opinion of me is hard to live with, though much of the time I feel it may be justified.

And now I have another dilemma. What should I do about Mary? She has not come to my bedroom so often recently, though when she does, she is as loving and generous toward me as at the beginning. It is becoming more difficult to come, she says. The maid with whom she shares a room has become suspicious and she fears she may be discovered leaving or returning—and how shall she answer any questions the girl may ask? Our liaison might come to the notice of the housekeeper, and that will be the end of it. If we are found out, my mother will have Mary dismissed.

Perhaps this move of mine may prove to be a blessing in disguise. I do not want to abandon Mary, but perhaps it will be better, for both of us, if the temptation is removed, though God knows it would tear my heart out to leave her. If I am not here, Mary will not be able to come and lie with me. She would be safer thus, and how else can I resolve this? Any permanent arrangement would be impossible in the circumstances. I could not take my mistress to my parish, even if she wanted to leave her family and her position here and go with me. And marriage is out of the question, for I need to marry well, someone who will help me in my parish work and be able to maintain the social position of a vicar's wife among the big houses of the area. Mary was not brought up in that world, and she would not be accepted by them. In a country parish that is important, and it is the parish—and my ministry—that must come first.

Eight

"I've written to Marcus," Jeannette told Theo as they cleared the breakfast table next morning. "I invited him to come as soon as he can."

"I don't think we'll be allowed to have him to sleep here, not for a few weeks longer. I notice the latest regulations are still forbidding overnight stays."

"Well at least he's invited. We can put dates in the diary when we know."

"True. And I gather you've invited the Swansons to coffee this morning?"

Jeannette nodded. "Isn't it wonderful to be able to be hospitable again? Even if it's only in the garden, and socially distanced. I've taken some scones out of the freezer. I don't know whether they'll feel able to eat them, but at least they'll be on offer."

Theo smiled at her. "Shall I join you and be sociable?"

"I hope you will! And Olivia, too—I'll speak to her about it. We've had so little chance to talk to anyone over the last couple of months. We must make the most of it."

Jeannette found herself humming as she put some coffee mugs ready on a tray and filled the big percolator. Singing was another thing she missed. Before lockdown she had belonged to a local choir which practised weekly, but all that had stopped abruptly in March, and she wondered when it would be allowed again. *Allowed, permitted.* Regulations, she tutted to herself with annoyance. *Where have all our freedoms disappeared to?*

By eleven, the coffee was burbling cheerfully in the percolator, the scones were buttered, and a table was laid outside with the pretty porcelain mugs, matching plates, and a jug of milk. She had set the garden chairs out in two groups, well separated, with the table between them. Her guests could collect their food and mugs from the table, to avoid any cross-contamination, though it all seemed slightly unnecessary. Technically, she wasn't sure whether she was even allowed to provide the mugs or the drinks, though it seemed accepted that food itself didn't carry any risk. Jeremy had offered to bring a flask of his own coffee for himself and Mike, but she had refused to countenance that. She simply could not believe that, even if she or Theo were harbouring Covid unbeknown, the virus would be carried on clean mugs straight out of the cupboard and handled carefully with plastic gloves to be on the safe side. Fortunately, he had seemed to agree.

Theo was sitting outside and had promised to greet the guests and come and fetch her when they arrived. She felt extraordinarily excited, like a girl at her first grown-up party. Which was ridiculous. But lockdown is like this, she thought. *We're all living a different life, with no guarantee that anything will ever be the same again.* Just to have a few guests to coffee seemed like a celebration, a return to social life.

"Jeannette!" Theo was calling from the garden. "They're here."

She picked up the percolator carefully and walked out into the hall.

"Olivia!" she called. "The Swansons are here, if you want to see them." She wondered whether her daughter would respond. She had been rather silent when they had come back from the beach the previous evening. It must have been a shock to her to see Clive in the state he was. The paramedics had taken him to hospital and said he would have to stay there for a few days, at least. He would be tested for Covid-19, and the test results would take some time to come through. He was clearly ill, anyway, even if it was only exposure and general self-neglect. She wondered how long he'd been homeless. It sounded as though it had initially been from choice rather than necessity, which made no sense.

Jeremy and Mike both rose to greet her when she arrived. She could sense a slight constraint still, as though talking to strangers was a skill they had all forgotten. She saw Jeremy moving towards her as though to take the heavy percolator from her, but it seemed he remembered just in time that such close contact was not permitted. He sank back into his chair and watched Theo make space for the coffee pot on the table.

Jeannette poured some liquid into the cups and then stepped back.

"I'll let you help yourself to milk," she said. "And sugar if you want it. And scones."

Mike came forward readily and loaded his plate with scones and his mug of coffee with several spoons of sugar. "I used to hate the stuff," he said cheerfully. "Coffee, I mean. But sugar makes a big difference."

"Most young people find coffee rather bitter, I think. What you'd call an acquired taste."

"But once acquired," observed Jeremy, helping himself to milk and half a scone in his turn, "irresistible. This smells wonderful. Thank you so much, Jeannette."

He was aware of a great lifting of the heart. The news on the pandemic was, as Liz had reminded him earlier in the week, getting better, and there seemed some prospect of the virus coming under control before too long. But more than anything, he was responding to the social occasion, to the experience of meeting with others in person. Social distancing took away some of the pleasure, but by no means all. He could not only hear their voices but see their faces, watch their body language, and unconsciously read the signs those gave. He was back in his own milieu, no longer shut away like a hermit.

Theo waited until Jeremy and Mike had seated themselves again and then took some coffee and a scone for himself. "Feels terribly unnatural, all this, doesn't it?" he commented. "Like acting out a scene in a play, but badly."

Jeremy laughed.

"It can't last long, though, surely?" said Mike optimistically. "I've been following the progress of the Oxford vaccine. They're getting some really good early results."

"Vaccines will take a while to come through," Jeremy reminded him. "The government will have to keep quite a few restrictions until then."

"They're recommending everyone wears face masks in public places," agreed Theo. "It seems that some scientists at least think that cuts down the risk of infection—that and this 'social distancing'. One more hoop for us to jump through, but I guess we must go along with it."

Jeannette leaned forward and put her mug on the tray. "Personally, I can't stand wearing a mask. I feel as though I can't breathe."

"Do you have asthma?" Jeremy asked her, interested.

"No—not since I was a child, anyway. I had an inhaler for a while then. No, it's more that it just feels... claustrophobic, somehow."

"But worth it, surely, if it saves someone's life," Theo suggested gently.

"Oh, put that way, of course. If they become mandatory, I will wear one."

"But not until then?" asked Jeremy.

"Probably not." She bristled but saw the twinkle in his eye just in time. "You're teasing me."

"He does," Mike told her. "Everyone."

"*Mea culpa*," said his father. "But only family and friends," he added quickly. "Not in my pastoral work."

Jeannette remembered suddenly the sad, weary expression he had worn when she first met him and was glad to see him looking more cheerful. Perhaps there was good news of Clive. "Have you heard from Derriford?" she asked.

"About Clive? No, and I don't suppose we will. We aren't next of kin, after all."

"I wonder who is."

"His wife, I should think."

"I didn't realise he had one."

"They used to be my parishioners. Rose, his wife, lives in Oxford now, and we see her from time to time. I don't think there's been a divorce, though they've been separated for three years or more. I wonder whether I should let her know about Clive," he added. "It's not as though she can go and see him in hospital, even if she wanted to." He reflected, sadly, that not even the relatives of the dying were permitted to do that.

"Olivia used to work for Clive," Jeannette told him, to fill the uncomfortable silence that followed his last remark. "As you know, I think." She paused. "Speaking of Olivia, I wonder where she is. I did tell her that you were here."

Theo's eyes turned her way. "I'm sure Olivia will join us if she wants to."

Was there something admonitory in the glance? Jeremy wondered. The words were calm and neutral enough.

Theo turned back towards him. "How have you enjoyed Cornwall in these strange times, Jeremy?"

Jeremy hesitated, determined to be honest but recognising the question was probably no more than a conversational gambit— Theo didn't really want to know the answer. "I guess the circumstances have been odd, even a bit depressing. I gather it's much quieter than usual, but the weather has been lovely, the countryside is beautiful, and the Coronavirus incidence has been quite low, which makes it feel a safe place for the children. A bit like evacuating them from London in 1939!"

"But no bombs fell, and most of them went home in time for the Blitz," Theo said wryly. "Odd how this feels like a wartime situation."

"Mum has suggested we come home as soon as possible," put in Mike. "I don't suppose there'll be much more danger in Oxford than there is here, once restrictions are lifted."

"Especially not if they ease stay-over regulations in time for the summer holidays," said Jeannette. "Cornwall can get really crowded in July and August. And with people not being able to go abroad, I think it'll be busier than usual."

"One of the most noticeable things about the past weeks," Theo agreed, "has been the emptiness of the A30."

"We've never come to Cornwall before," Mike told him. "So I suppose we just thought it was always like this."

"Out of season, it's not too busy normally— though it's never as quiet as it is now. But I noticed it particularly the Spring Bank Holiday weekend—it's usually half term then, and the cars are nose to tail all the way from Launceston to Truro. You have to wait for ages to turn right on to the dual carriageway at Plusha. This year— nothing."

There was silence. No one, it appeared, had anything else to say about the A30 either in or out of season.

"This is a lovely garden," Jeremy remarked.

"Thank you," said Jeannette.

Glancing around, she felt a sense of pride. The last of the rhododendrons were in bloom, the rose garden was approaching its best, and colour was creeping into the hydrangea flowers, for the warm weather had moved everything along faster than normal. Even the extensive herbaceous borders were flourishing, with the early summer plants already coming into flower. And the two copper beech trees that shaded the lawn were in full leaf, the brilliant dark colour of their leaves setting off the green of the grass below.

"All Jeannette's work," Theo told him. "I'm afraid I do nothing except enjoy it from my chair when the weather is fine."

"I have a jobbing gardener who comes two days a week," Jeannette explained quickly. "I didn't create the garden. It was my grandparents who first did the landscaping, after the First War. And then my own parents continued and developed it, although it wasn't a full-time occupation for them. I just keep it going, refresh a border here and there with new planting when they need it. So you could say we're a family of gardeners!"

"And yet," suggested Jeremy quietly, "It doesn't feel like a happy house."

Jeannette looked at him sharply, wondering what had occasioned this remark.

"There was a tragedy behind it all," Theo told him, before she could ask the question. "Jeannette's grandmother inherited because all her three elder brothers had died young."

"In the First War?"

Jeannette shook her head, wishing she had not been asked about the family, but unwilling to turn the question aside rudely. "Only two of them were killed in France; the third was a clergyman. He was using this house as a vicarage in 1916. He went out during a terrible rainstorm one night to visit a dying man and was swept away crossing the River Lynher on the way back."

"How extraordinary." But that, Jeremy thought, could certainly explain the sense he'd had, as he walked up the drive, of some deep shadow of tragedy hanging over the house, in spite of the loveliness of the garden, and the bright late-spring sunshine. Always sensitive to spiritual darkness, in spite of his professional commitment to focus on the light, and always fascinated—though not without qualms of conscience about it—by bizarre and tragic events, especially if there was an element of mystery about them, Jeremy opened his mouth to ask for more details. But at that moment, Jeannette heard Olivia calling from the house door.

"Phone for you, Mother."

Jeannette got up and went towards her. "Come and talk to our guests, Olivia, while I see what it is."

Olivia gave her the handset. "It's Derriford."

Osborne House, Sunday December 12th 1915

Freddie writes that he is out of the front line for a couple of weeks on a bombing course, though they will be back in their billets for Christmas. This in a letter to Mother, not me. She is much happier when he is away from the Front, though it gives her more time to pay attention to other things, such as Maudie's engagement. I've told Maudie I'm no longer opposed to her marrying Gerald, though I think she could do much better for herself. But Gerald seems to be doing well as an officer now that he has been promoted, so perhaps he will be able to make a career in the Army and rise to her level socially in time. During wartime, sadly there are a lot of dead men's shoes to fill, and social barriers are weakening all around us. The older generation like Mother try to keep them up—indeed, I don't think Mother sees that everything is changing as a result of the War. She just expects that when it is all over, we will live as before. But it will not be so, I know it will not.

Of course, instead of gaining promotion from the natural wastage of war, Gerald might be a casualty himself. He is at the Front, like Freddie, and the life of a junior officer does seem very perilous, as they share the dangers faced by the men as well as meeting the extra demands of leading a platoon in those conditions. Mary would be terribly distressed, I know, if he were killed or maimed. After all, she loved her brother enough to offer herself to me to help him gain Maudie's hand, even though it wasn't necessary! Truly, it was a terrible thing to do, but I cannot bring myself to regret that she did, even though I know my time with her cannot last.

Nine

When Jeannette had gone back into the house with the handset, Olivia helped herself to coffee and sat down silently beside Theo, her face closed, clearly unwilling to take part in the conversation.

"Are you retired, Theo?" asked Jeremy, to give her time. "How has lockdown affected you?"

"Not too badly overall. I have a long-standing book project I'm working on, about the work of Benjamin Britten, so being here is allowing me to get on with that, among other things. But I work in London normally, because I'm lucky enough to attend concerts for a living." He smiled. "And review CDs, and sometimes present TV programmes."

"I thought I recognised you, sir!" Mike put in. "But it wasn't a programme about music I saw—it was about an old house, here in Cornwall, surely? It was interesting, at least I thought it was." He grinned. "But I'm interested in anything to do with old houses."

Theo's eyes sparkled. "I'm glad you enjoyed it. I'm a musicologist by profession, but once the TV companies find you can front a programme, they're liable to ask you to go well outside your subject. I, too, am very interested in old houses. In fact, during lockdown, one of the things I've been doing is some research on this house. We have lots of archive material, but most of the papers haven't been read for years, if ever. They've just been sitting in a trunk, of no interest to the family at all, for some reason."

"It isn't a very important house, Theo," Olivia pointed out. "Not like some of the great Cornish houses and gardens that people come to visit."

"But it's quite old, isn't it?" asked Jeremy.

Theo nodded. "Built at the very beginning of the Jacobean period, with the Victorian wing added on later. There's nothing particularly remarkable about it architecturally. But it has a priest hole."

"A priest hole?" repeated Mike with awe.

"I never knew that." Olivia was indignant. "I lived here for twenty-one years, and no one ever told me."

"I'm sure your mother knows about it," Theo answered her smoothly. "Maybe she thought it wouldn't interest you."

"I suppose it is quite likely a house like this would have one," put in Jeremy. "Lots of Cornish families resisted the Reformation, didn't they? And if a priest passed through the area and came to say Mass for them, they would have to have somewhere to hide him at need."

Theo nodded. "The Tresaynes were a recusant family."

"What does 'recusant' mean?" enquired Mike, frowning. "Oh – I remember! Is it people who stuck to Catholicism when the country turned Protestant?"

"Got it in one, Mike." Jeremy smiled.

Olivia's indignation increased. It was her house, her family. What business was it of theirs? And why had she not been told these things when she was younger? How many more secrets had her mother kept from her?

"Where is this priest hole?" she demanded.

"No one knows," replied her stepfather. "I think Maudie, your great-grandmother, spoke of it once to Jeannette when she lived here, so you could ask your mother what she said. But perhaps even she didn't know its location. It can't have been used since the seventeenth century, after all."

Olivia froze, and all the small hairs on her neck seemed to rise. Suddenly, the house seemed alien and unfriendly, with some undiscovered corner hidden away. *It's only a piece of history*, she told herself stoutly. Theirs was an old house, and bound to have mysteries, but until now she had avoided thinking much about them. But she was reminded of the bedroom next door to hers. Hadn't there always been something odd about that room?

She saw Jeremy looking at her enquiringly. "Do you have an inkling of where the priest hole might be?"

"I haven't a clue." Not for anything was she going to admit to the fears that had beset her since childhood and even kept her away from home in adulthood. Certainly not in this company. The priest hole didn't have anything to do with her fears, anyway. She hadn't known it existed until now.

Just then, Jeremy's mobile phone began to ring in his pocket. "Excuse me—I'll just see if it's important." He pulled it out and looked at the screen. "It's an unknown number, but... Hallo? Jeremy Swanson here... I see. Thanks for letting us know."

He put the phone back in his pocket and looked across at Theo. "That was Derriford. Apparently, Clive has tested positive for Covid."

There was a little silence.

"That means a fortnight in self-isolation for all of us, doesn't it?" Mike's voice was rather small.

"Yes," said Jeremy, who had got to his feet.

"But surely," suggested Theo, remaining in his seat, "if we are all in isolation for the same contact—you and your family, and Jeannette and ours—we shouldn't have to be in isolation from each other."

"You weren't with us at the cave yesterday," countered Jeremy. The current regulations were not at all clear on this kind of detail, and his instinct was to proceed with caution.

"Nor were the twins," Mike pointed out. "But I guess they're going to have to be isolated with the rest of us."

"I suppose we shall have to keep away from them as much as possible."

"That goes for you too, Theo," Olivia pointed out. "We'll have to shut you away in the music room." If this was an attempt at a joke, a lightening of the atmosphere, Jeremy did not feel it succeeded.

"None of us has actually contracted the virus, though," said Mike. "I don't think you need to isolate from each other if no one catches it."

"But we can't know, can we?" Jeremy frowned. "The most infectious period is at the beginning, before the symptoms start— or so they say."

"Half-an-hour surely isn't going to make any difference," Theo asserted. "Sit down and finish your coffee, both of you—please. Jeannette has been so much looking forward to this, and I don't want this to spoil it for her."

Jeannette reached them too late to hear him, and full of her own preoccupations. "Derriford say Clive has Covid-19."

"They phoned me too," Jeremy told her. "So we were just debating whether we can isolate together. At least while we drink our coffee."

Jeannette had been looking anxious, but her face relaxed a little at this. "I expect we can," she said. "Is it a fortnight, Theo? I can't remember."

"I believe so. Sit down, my dear. You haven't had a sip of that coffee yet. It'll be cold."

The coffee was drunk, but conversation faltered and died. They were each thinking through the implications of fourteen days' isolation. Jeremy wondered whether any supermarket delivery slots would be available. With four hungry children in Cedric's cottage, and their stay only temporary, he had not been able to stock up for every eventuality.

Olivia had taken leave of them and gone back into the house, leaving half her coffee in her mug, but no one commented on her departure.

"Ready, Mike?" Jeremy rose to his feet again, and this time no one tried to stop him. Jeannette walked along with them to the gate, keeping her distance and feeling rather sad, as Theo had feared, that her first social event for months had to end this way.

In their abstraction, no one noticed the person limping towards them up the lane from the clapper bridge.

"Mrs Landry! Mrs Landry—please help me!"

Jeannette turned. "Why, it's Jude! What are you doing here? Are you all right?"

"Clearly not." Jeremy halted in the gateway. He watched the figure stumble nearer, revealing a bloodstained face with a heavy bruise over one cheekbone. Knowing their new Covid status, he wondered what Jeannette would do.

But Jeannette didn't hesitate. Someone in need of help always aroused her ready compassion, and Covid rules and regulations were instantly forgotten. "Come in, come in. What happened? Did you fall?"

A headshake. Jude looked at Mike and Jeremy warily.

"These are friends, Jude. Jeremy and Mike Swanson from Oxford. They're staying just down the road, and they've been having coffee with me. Come in and let me attend to that cheek. Don't go just yet," she added to Jeremy. "We may need you." Quite why she felt this, she didn't know, but instinct told her that Jeremy would be a useful man to have at hand in a crisis.

She took Jude's arm and led the teenager to one of the garden seats that Jeremy and Mike had just vacated. "Stay there while I go and get the first-aid kit."

Jude gave Theo a scared look.

"That's just my husband," Jeannette told her. "Do you remember him? Maybe you two never met. Theo, this is Jude Laurence who lives up on Ridge. We know each other from when I was a school governor, years ago, don't we, Jude? But you've certainly grown up since then! Fifteen, is it? Sixteen?"

Jude didn't answer.

"Would you rather I went inside?" Theo asked gently.

"And it's time we went home," said Jeremy.

"Don't leave me alone," the fugitive muttered suddenly, with a sidelong glance at the drive. "He might come looking."

Jeannette turned back. "Who might come?"

There was silence.

"Your dad? Did he do this?" Jeannette wasn't sure why she had immediately jumped to this conclusion, but in her days as school governor she had come across the Laurence family a number of times and had suspected Jude's father of being a violent man. His wife often looked cowed at school events, and Jude had never had much to say for herself. But there had been nothing overt, no visible bruising, nothing the school could act on, even if the authorities had wanted to.

Jude nodded. "He's been angry all through lockdown, 'cos of somethin' I told 'un. I ran away in the end. Been living rough on moor."

Jeannette was shocked. "Jude, how awful!"

She went away to get the first aid box, leaving Jude sitting uncomfortably surrounded by the men. Poor Jude. She mustn't leave her for long. Perhaps Olivia would come and help if she called her—but then again, Olivia's reactions to someone in trouble were unpredictable, and Jeannette, having seen her leave the garden abruptly as she was returning from the Derriford phone call, thought she might be upset about Clive's illness. Better not to trouble her over this.

Left in the garden, Jeremy's mind, always quickly tuned in to anything mysterious, was turning over possibilities. Everyone knew that domestic abuse had increased during lockdown, particularly in families where there were already problems. That part of Jude's story was perfectly credible. But what did one do in a situation like this? Would social services come to see a child in difficulties, as they would have done in the past, and take that child to a place of safety? Would the police arrest the father if abuse were reported? He didn't even know whether Childline was operating. So many people were working from home, but getting the technology set up for volunteers might be challenging.

He looked carefully at the hunched figure sitting on the edge of the chair. A strange girl—but was Jude a girl? Suddenly, he wasn't sure; the bulky hoodie and loose-fitting jogging pants hid the teenager's body very successfully, and he couldn't see much of the face. Even the voice had been indeterminate, neither high nor low. It almost seemed as though she/he—perhaps he had better use 'they', in the modern parlance—were hiding their very identity. Jeannette would know, but he could hardly ask the question in front of Jude, and he wasn't likely to get a private word with Jeannette.

A thought occurred to him, and without further consideration he put it into words. "Jude, did you meet my daughter Lorna when you were living on the moors? She goes jogging up on Ridge, I know."

Jude sat up, and the bruised face gained the travesty of a smile. "Yes! Lorna, she were so kind to me—she were going to bring me food and stuff."

Was she, indeed? Robbing the cottage larder, I suppose. Just like Lorna to get involved. Though who am I to criticise that?

"But then Dad came and found me and took me home, and I couldn't get out to see her." There was a stifled sob, and the Cornish accent grew thicker. "Tell Lorna I couldn't come—I were anxious she'd feel I'd lied to her, or summat."

"Yes, I'll tell her. Don't worry. She won't think that." Jeremy wondered why on earth Lorna hadn't told him anything of this meeting with Jude. When she was younger, she would certainly have enlisted his help. *She's growing up and doesn't think she needs me anymore. I guess that's natural, even if it hurts.*

Jeannette, returning with a bowl of water and some dressings, heard the last of this exchange. "Did you say you'd met Lorna?"

Jude nodded. "She were so kind."

Jeannette smiled at Jeremy, as if congratulating him on his daughter's kindness, and he instantly felt better.

"I think you should stay here with us, Jude," Jeannette went on. "At least until we've worked out what to do for the best. You can't live on the moors, and you can't go back to the farm, either, if your dad is going to hit you. You'll be safe here while we sort somewhere else for you to go."

She knelt beside Jude's chair and started to bathe the teenager's face gently.

"I think it's time we went home," began Jeremy again. "Lorna..."

"Would you stay a little while longer? Please?" Jeannette asked him. "Perhaps Mike can go home and help Lorna with your other children. Or maybe Jude would like to see Lorna, if she would be good enough to come over here." She looked at Jude for confirmation.

"Yes, I would. Please."

"Jeremy is a clergyman, Jude, a vicar. You can trust him, and I expect he can give us good advice about what we should do next to help you."

Jude looked anxious. "My dad's a Christian. He b'lieves in hellfire and damnation for anyone who's wicked or doesn't live a Christian life." There was another sob. "I'm going to hell, he says."

"But I'm not that kind of Christian," Jeremy hastened to reassure her. "I believe Christianity is about love—God's love for us and ours for each other. And forgiveness if we don't match up to the high standards He sets us," he added. Then, more gently, he observed, "I don't think you've had much experience of that kind of love, have you?"

There were tears on the bruised face.

Jeannette smiled at Jeremy. "That's just the kind of help I was looking for, Remy. Thank you. Now if Mike…"

Mike had risen to his feet. "I'll send Lorna over for Jude. I can look after the twins until you get back, Dad." He hesitated. "We don't have to worry about self-isolation, do we? I mean—is it all right for Lorna to come here and help look after Jude?"

Jeremy said at once: "One thing I do know about all these regulations is that there are exceptions if you are helping a vulnerable person. I don't think there's any question here but that we're dealing with someone extremely vulnerable."

Osborne House, Thursday December 16th 1915

I will be going to Cornwall at the end of January, it seems. Tresayne House is being made ready for me, and the housekeeper is employing more servants. I have not told anyone yet that I will be leaving in a few weeks. My mother and Maudie still hope I will stay, and Mary knows nothing of the matter at all. I have not yet found the right opportunity to tell her it must end between us— her lovemaking raises me to heaven, God forgive me, and when I try to tell her I am leaving, my tongue fails. But before long I must speak with her. It is not a light love to be easily abandoned, but it cannot continue. God give me the courage and the firmness to stop it before we come to disaster. I must use some of our precious time together to tell her that our affair must end, and soon. But I shrink from it still. Oh, Mary! How can I bear to part myself from you?

Ten

Jeannette decided to make up a bed for Jude in the small twin room next door to Olivia's.

"I chose the room because it has two beds," she explained, sensing that Olivia was far from happy with the arrangement. "I thought we might ask if Lorna would like to stay. Jude may need company, and she obviously has confidence in Lorna. We don't know how long she will have to stay, and I'll need the main guest-room for Marcus in due course."

Olivia ignored this. "Why didn't you tell me about the priest hole?"

Jeannette looked surprised. "What on earth has that to do with anything? You never asked, for one thing. I didn't think of your wanting to know about it—goodness, Olivia, I haven't thought about it myself for years. It's just a bit of the house's history. I don't even know where in the house it is."

"It may have escaped your notice, Mother, but this is my home, too, or at least I grew up here. Didn't you think I'd want to know about something like that?" Olivia decided it wasn't the moment to say anything more about the peculiarities of the room

89

next door to her bedroom, the vague feeling she had that odd sounds came from it, that the atmosphere in there was creepy. If the two young people were to occupy it, then these things were better not said—or at least, not immediately. She must just hope they wouldn't notice anything. And why should they, if it was all her imagination—as it must be? "Theo says your grandmother told you about it. Why didn't you tell me?"

Her mother looked at her with some irritation. "Granny talked to me about it when I was a child, long before you were born. Besides, whenever I've tried to tell you anything of the family history, you've actually shown a singular lack of interest. How was I to know this was different?"

Her voice softened suddenly. "But I'm sorry, if I've disappointed you."

Olivia hastened to take advantage of this momentary weakening. "I'm fairly used to it by now. You have a long record of it, after all."

Jeannette recoiled as if stung. "Oh, that's very unfair, darling."

"Is it? Is it really?"

"Olivia, if we need to talk about this, now isn't the time. I need to get Jude's room sorted and work out which authorities we should inform about the situation. And I can see Lorna coming up the drive."

She waited until Olivia had retreated into her own quarters next door, and then let out a long breath. What had got into Olivia? The longer they had been under lockdown regulations, the more brittle she had become, and just as there was some hope of an easing of restrictions, they had to go into this period of self-isolation for a fortnight. It was very frustrating.

She heard voices outside on the landing and went out to meet Lorna, who had found Jude in the hall below. As Jeannette left the bedroom, Kato rose from the corner by the stairs, hissing loudly. Lorna and Jude both recoiled, but Jeannette saw that the cat's ire seemed to be directed mainly at Jude. She picked him up and held him firmly.

"I do apologise for the cat. His manners are atrocious. Hallo, Lorna. Welcome to Tresayne."

"Thank you, Mrs Landry. I'm so glad to be here. And thank you for taking care of Jude. She's had a horrible time."

Jude stood hunched into the big shapeless hoodie, not looking at Jeannette, and clearly very uncomfortable with the situation.

"Everything's ready," Jeannette said briskly. "I've put you both in this room here, so Jude isn't alone. I'll leave you to get settled in. Do you have everything you need, Lorna?"

The girl nodded. She looked up at Jude. "I brought some pyjamas for you. Mike said he didn't think you'd brought much with you."

A mute headshake.

"I'm afraid they're Mike's—the pyjamas, I mean. Mine would be far too small."

Jeannette looked curiously at Jude, wondering how she would react to this comment. Some girls would be sensitive about being so tall and broad in the shoulder, and possibly even about borrowing a young man's pyjamas. But in Cornwall, big strong young women were two a penny. She saw no sign of chagrin on Jude's face.

"Thanks, Lorna." Jude spoke at last. "That were kind of Mike. Must be nice to have a brother."

"Well yes, it is. I don't suppose all brothers are like him, though."

The cat wriggled in Jeannette's arms, and she put him down at the top of the stairs as Jude and Lorna went into their bedroom, hoping his hostility to Jude would be short-lived. She watched him for a moment, just in case he was planning to renew it, but he stalked down the stairs in front of her, his long black tail held high. He knew what he knew, and if the humans were too stupid to sense it, he would leave them to it.

~ * ~

"I didn't get a chance to say this earlier," said Jeannette to Theo, unscrewing her earrings at her dressing-table that evening after everyone had gone to bed. "I heard yesterday from Marcus—he's going to come as soon as he can."

Theo was buttoning up his pyjama jacket. "He emailed me too. He seems really pleased. Thanks, Jeannette—I do really appreciate your being so welcoming to him, and I'm sure he does too."

"Have you talked to Olivia about it?"

Theo raised an eyebrow. "I informed her he was coming to stay, if that's what you mean. She didn't say much, but I don't see why she should have a problem with it. I haven't had much chance to talk to her about it today, though, I must admit."

Jeannette put her watch on the chest of drawers beside her bed and plugged her mobile phone into the wall socket. "She's close to you, and she's been with us in isolation all these weeks. Maybe she will feel threatened by Marcus's arrival?"

"Surely not. She can't possibly believe he will want to sideline her or rob her of my affection, even if he could, which is ridiculous. She has been my beloved daughter for over twenty years."

"I know." Jeannette closed the carved lid of her jewellery box. "But she seems rather unhappy just now. She was odd about poor Jude sleeping next door to her, even though Lorna is there, too." She sighed. "I'm not sure what she's frightened of."

"I shouldn't think she's frightened of anything. She rarely is. Perhaps she doesn't want strangers so close. She's used to living alone, after all." He paused. "I did wonder whether she was upset about Clive being ill, or even worried about him. But she hasn't said anything."

"No. I thought, when we went to the beach, that she was going to talk to me about the past, about her father. But then we met the Swansons, and Clive, and somehow it didn't happen."

"Be patient," advised Theo. "I think she's nearly ready."

~ * ~

Olivia would have been surprised to hear him say this, for what she was feeling more than anything was completely at odds with herself and with all the situations in which she currently found herself. Her career was on hold, and she didn't want to return to it anyway. Her relationship with her mother was no better than it had ever been, perhaps rather worse, and she had no idea how to deal with that or even if she wanted to make the effort. And Theo's son Marcus was coming to stay. She wanted to meet him—anyone connected with Theo was of interest to her; in this, if in nothing else, she was at one with her mother. But at the same time, he was Theo's real son, his biological son, and she was only adopted. Until now, knowing that there was no contact between Theo and the children of his first marriage, she had felt no sense of threat, no need to compete with them. She had grown used to being the apple of Theo's eye ever since she was ten. But this might change everything. Marcus was her brother, legally, even though they had never met—but he had also been in Theo's life long before she had, and it was clear Theo was thrilled he was coming to stay. In doing so, he was coming back into a life that it seemed had not been whole without him, whatever Theo had said in the past. She admitted that she felt apprehensive, even a bit jealous, and she wasn't sure, either, how it would look from Marcus's point of view. Would he see her as an interloper, someone who might threaten his rights, even his inheritance? Theo had told her once that he had changed his will to divide his possessions among the three of them, that she would inherit a share along with Marcus and Danielle. She wondered whether they knew about this; she could imagine how she would feel about it if she were one of his biological children.

As always when inner conflict beset her, she took it out on the paypigs. Her Findomme business had flourished during lockdown, when the men she serviced were mainly working at home or on furlough, and missing outside distractions—though some of them had to use more stratagems than usual to keep their online activities secret from their wives and live-in partners. They had money and nothing much else to spend it on, and Olivia had no hesitation about making the most of it while she too had nothing else to do. She did not plan to carry the work on indefinitely. Sooner or later, when life got back to normal, she expected to go back to London and get a job in an office as before, though perhaps not exactly as before. She needed to look around. But for the moment, Findomme was keeping her in pocket money, not to mention exotic clothes that at present she had no occasion to wear. Stung yet fulfilled by her sarcastic comments and her put-downs and lured on by the provocative photographs she posted of herself wearing lingerie and thigh-high boots with stiletto heels, the pigs seemed happy to pay up.

To be successful was always a good feeling. But somehow, she wished the success had been in a different field of action. No doubt her mother would be shocked if she knew how Olivia was earning a living during lockdown. She wondered again what Theo would think. Would he reject her, too? She didn't think so, but it was impossible to be sure, and it was a prospect she preferred not to entertain. *It's no use speculating*, she told herself as she drifted off to sleep.

~ * ~

Marcus looked out of the window. The Thames looked the same, and so did the buildings across the river. The boats were still moored along the jetties and only police launches plied the water. But with a flash of wry humour, Marcus saw Canary Wharf suddenly as an outsize Lego project, with different types of plastic bricks and moulded sections fitted together onto an enormous board, like a kit from a box. An unreal creation, the product of a toymaker's imagination, rather than the hub of an important industry. For presumably it was empty just now, its workers hunched over computers at home, enjoying (or hating) the solitude and quiet.

In the last week, his heart had lifted a little above the loneliness of lockdown, for both his father and Jeannette had written. His father had emailed, and he'd known for certain that he was forgiven for his failure to keep in contact over the years since he'd become an adult and could have jettisoned his mother's emotional influence. And today he'd received a letter from Jeannette—in her own hand, with an envelope and a stamp, which made it seem so much more personal—and in such welcoming terms that he had almost wept. Forgiveness and welcome. What more could you ask? It would be a few weeks yet before he could go to see them, weeks in which he would need to continue watching the empty Thames and making the most of what work there was. But sometime soon, he would be able to make the trip to Cornwall to meet Jeannette and Olivia, and see his father again. He couldn't wait.

Osborne House, Saturday December 25th 1915

It is early on Christmas morning, and I have told Mary I am leaving.

It was after we had made love—I could not bear to say anything before, since she was so beautiful in her self-giving, so eager to do everything to please me and give me fulfilment. I could not stop her to say that our time was coming to an end; that I must go, and she must stay here without me.

But when I did, she wept with such abandon that I was alarmed. I have never seen such distress. She pleaded with me to take her with me. She did not want to hold me back from my career, she said. We could be as discreet as we had been here—it would be easier, she told me. I could be her housekeeper, and no one would know. She would be in charge of the maids and would see that there was no gossip.

I told her I already have a housekeeper at Tresayne House, an old retainer who cannot be dismissed or replaced. She would know what Mary was to me the minute she walked through the door. It could not be.

But still she wept, until my heart was ready to break.

At last, I promised her we would continue to meet until I actually leave Osborne House at the end of January. A whole four weeks more of loving! God knows I do not want to stop her from coming to me. My body aches from wanting her on those few nights when she has not been able to come, and sleep eludes me. I do not know how I will be able to live without her when I go to Cornwall. But I must. Scandal here if we were discovered would be bad enough—and it would ruin her. But scandal where I am going would be worse, for it would distress not only the family but also my parishioners, to whom I am supposed to give a good example. I could not be responsible for that.

I tried to explain, but she could not understand. She said she would do anything if only she could stay with me, if only our love could go on forever. And then she asked me why it could not! I had no answer to such wild questions, to such unreasoning passion. I kissed her and caressed her, and we made love again. And afterwards she slept, but I could not.

Eleven

In the darkness and the quiet of the ancient house, Lorna lay listening to Jude's breathing. It sounded regular enough, but she wasn't convinced Jude was asleep, not with the discomfort of a badly bruised face and the two cuts that Jeannette had reluctantly agreed probably did not need stitches. She would, Lorna knew, have preferred to take Jude to the local minor injuries unit at Launceston—if indeed it proved to be open when so many places were closed. But Jude had refused point blank to go anywhere to have the hurts seen to.

"If we leave here," Jude had cried in terror, "Dad will find me and take me home. And God knows what he'll do to me then."

Theo and Jeannette's attempts to make it clear that in this situation the abusive father had no rights had fallen on deaf ears, and reluctantly Jeannette gave in.

"Well, we'll keep an eye on those cuts," she said. "And you must rest as much as possible. You'll need it, after all this."

Jude nodded agreement. "Will you come with me, Lorna?"

"Of course I will."

For the rest of the day, Jude had lain quietly on the bed, apart from thanking Lorna again and again for her support. "I know I can trust you. And Mrs Landry."

"How do you know her, Jude?" Lorna had asked. "Mrs Landry, I mean."

"She were a school governor when I were a little tacker at the primary school down in the village, years ago. She used to come and hear us read. I were a slow learner in them days, and she were always so patient and kind."

"I can imagine she would be."

"And I seen her since, at the village fair, and such like. She judges the dog show sometimes, and hands out prizes. She'm gentry, like. Far above me and such as me."

Lorna was uncomfortable with this view. "She doesn't think of herself as better than you, Jude. She'd think she was privileged, not superior. I expect that's why she helped at the school." This was the way she herself had been brought up to think, that privilege meant taking responsibility for helping those who hadn't had your advantages. And it seemed to be the way Jeannette thought, too. There was an open-hearted generosity in her towards others that made Lorna feel comfortable with her, even though she hadn't met her until a few days ago. Look at how she'd have given even Clive a bed if he'd needed it—though perhaps that was because he and Olivia had once worked together? Anyway, it wasn't right for Jude to run herself down like this.

"I know," Jude agreed. "And I knew where she lives, see, and it isn't far from the farm. I pass this way coming down to catch the school bus of a morning. Sometimes I used t'see her over the gate. So when I were in such trouble, I thought of her. I reckoned she'd help me if she could. She never did think much of m'father—I could see that, though she'd never say anything. And with her being gentry, he wouldn't dare trespass on her land. I knew I'd be safe here."

Jude said nothing more. Lorna phoned her father after dinner and updated him as much as she could, then joined Jude upstairs in the room they were to share. Jude, apparently comfortable in Mike's pyjamas, was already in bed, and seemed to be asleep, but Lorna was not convinced, as she still was not, two hours later.

So she wasn't in the least surprised when Jude turned towards her in the darkness, and said, "I haven't told you everything, Lorna, and I should."

"You don't need to tell me anything," Lorna said quickly. "Not unless you want to."

"But I do."

"Is it about your father?"

"Some. Dad took exception, see, to what I told him when the lockdown started. He'd always taken the strap to me if'n I spoke back or didn't do what I were told. It's his way. But never anything more, though I think perhaps with my sister..." The sentence trailed off. "She's more like a girl, and so he'd think of her that way. Used to tell me I were a tomboy and should wear skirts and stuff."

Lorna was silent, wondering what was coming next.

"But then I told him I didn't want to be a girl. I thought, if I'm going to be around the farm for weeks, with no school, an' nowhere to go, he'd better know. Otherwise, he'd have gone on and on about it. That's what I thought, anyhow."

"I don't quite see what you mean," ventured Lorna cautiously.

"It's always been the same. From when I were little, I've always felt like a boy. It's a strange thing—I don't quite know how to explain it." She shrugged. "I didn't manage to explain to Dad, that's for sure."

"You're trans?" Lorna felt excited. She had never had a transgender friend. At once, she felt ashamed of her reaction and its self-centredness. This wasn't exciting for Jude, but terrifying.

"Yep. That's what they do call it. But Dad, he don't believe in such things. For him I were born a girl, and a girl is what I got to be. So first of all he tried to beat it out o' me."

"Oh, Jude!"

"But that didn't work. I told him nothing would change it. So..."

Jude broke off and said no more. Lorna realised her friend had finished confiding, that perhaps what had been about to emerge was more than Jude was yet ready to tell her. But what could it be? What could be worse than your father beating you to punish you for something you couldn't even help? At length she accepted that no more revelations would be made that night, and let herself fall asleep.

For the next two nights, Jude slept peacefully, while Lorna kept watch. She dozed, off and on, but she was very conscious how fragile Jude's mental state seemed to be, and how much her friend needed unremitting care. During the daytime, Jeannette encouraged Jude to come down and sit in the garden while she weeded the flower beds, or to keep her company in the kitchen while she was baking or preparing a meal, but Jude remained silent and withdrawn throughout, even with Lorna.

It was on the third night that the wailing was heard.

Lorna had fallen into quite a deep sleep, since for two nights her watchfulness appeared to have been quite unnecessary. The unaccustomed sleep deprivation had begun to make her feel jaded, and her young body, when her mind at length allowed it, took what it needed. She drifted off, dreamlessly, into oblivion.

She woke abruptly to find Jude staring at the wall in terror.

"Jude! What is it? Were you dreaming?" Lorna rubbed the sleep out of her eyes and sat up, trying to subdue an inward groan at being disturbed.

"I dunno," Jude replied. "I heard summat. Don't know what it was. Someone crying—wailing, more like."

Lorna frowned. "Where? Was it outside or inside?" Could Olivia be upset about something, and her crying have been heard through the wall? It seemed unlikely. For one thing, Olivia seemed to her just about as hard and unfeeling a person as anyone could be, apparently completely unmoved by poor Jude's situation and resentful of having them in the room next to hers—though you could always be mistaken in a person, she reminded herself.

"I dunno. Seemed like it came from that wall," Jude said, pointing at the chimney breast.

"That's just a chimney, Jude. I suppose it may be open in the room below, but the fireplace is all blocked up here, see? Unless you heard the wind in the chimney, I suppose."

She pushed back her quilt and went over to the window, drawing back the curtains to reveal a quiet, starry night. No sign of any wind, certainly nothing like a gale that might set up wind noises in or around the chimney.

"Someone was crying, I tell you. I heard 'em. Crying fit to break their heart."

Goodness, I hope Jude's not going mad. But she didn't seem hysterical; more matter of fact than anything else—which was doubly disturbing. It made it easy to believe that there had actually been something to hear.

But what could it have been?

"Can you hear anything now?" she asked.

"No. But I did, I tell you. It woke me, see."

"I expect you were dreaming." Lorna tried to sound soothing. For surely whatever Jude had heard must have been just that, a dream. "Go back to sleep. I'm sure you won't hear it again, but if you do, then wake me."

But nothing more was heard that night, by either of them, and both slept quietly until morning.

Osborne House, Wednesday January 5th 1916

Nineteen-sixteen has dawned, and the government has enacted a law to make service in the armed forces compulsory for every man under the age of forty-five except for those in occupations they see as necessary or conferring exception. Being in Holy Orders is one of those occupations, though many of my colleagues have volunteered as chaplains. I have not heard of any pacifist ordinands who have done so, but perhaps some have been able to face the task of encouraging the troops to see those in the German army as enemies to be killed. I know I could not.

I have been thinking about what society may be like when the War is over, and whether it will be more possible for different classes to marry, like Maudie and her Gerald. Please God, peace at least must be of more value to us all in the future than it has been. I can't believe that even after more than a year of war there are still plenty of people—including those in command—who see it as a glorious and justified endeavour. Even the officer-poets like Rupert Brooke, God rest his soul, described war in those terms, though they must have seen some of the horrors that Freddie so carefully doesn't describe to Mother.

My friends in London tell me that Philip and Ottoline Morrell have decided to open Garsington House to pacifists as a kind of haven. They will be officially farm workers, which is another reserved occupation, but in reality, they will just be given the opportunity to stay away from the fighting, as their conscience bids them. I'm sure they will have a wonderful time together. I wish I could join them—I met Lady Ottoline once in Cambridge, and she is an exciting and vibrant person.

Mary continues to beg me to take her with me when I go to Tresayne. She says she will find her own way there if I give her the money for it. There are carriers who go from here to Launceston, and she says I can then come and fetch her from the town, as it is only ten miles or so from there to Tresayne. I suppose it could be done. But although I long for it, my deep reservations remain. To pretend that we have just met and I have decided to make her my wife will hardly pass muster, even if it would sound plausible, for no one would believe I'd be likely to choose a former housemaid to marry. My family, at least, will know that it is not true, and my parishioners would lose all respect for me, I think—if Tresayne is as full of old-fashioned people as North Devon is.

Though my heart is very heavy at the prospect, I'm sure it is better for both of us to bid each other farewell and look to the future, and marriage with someone more of our own rank. I suspect the younger of our remaining footmen at Osborne House is quite enamoured of Mary, confound him. But if I am here, she will not look at anyone else.

Twelve

Jeremy was in the garden attempting to exercise the spaniels with the aid of a heavy rubber ball when his phone rang. They were six days into their fortnight's isolation, and no one was finding it easy, least of all the dogs. It was surprising how much even an hour's exercise out on the lanes could be missed when it was no longer permitted. Self-isolation was extraordinarily restrictive. Still, he told himself, it could have been worse. Supposing you were in self-isolation in a studio flat in a city, as many people were? It didn't bear thinking about.

His phone, as he opened it, showed him the call was from Lorna.

"Hi, darling. How are you getting on?"

"Dad, I think we need your help."

His attention sharpened. "What kind of help? It's a bit difficult, just now."

"Yes, I know that." Lorna sounded brisk and practical, as usual, and he relaxed slightly. It didn't seem that she herself was any trouble.

"What then?"

"It's Jude. And—this sounds odd, but bear with me—the house."

"The house?"

He listened while she explained that Jude was hearing sounds during the night. "Wailing, Jude said. Someone crying. There doesn't seem to be anything real happening. But there's something odd about it..."

He waited.

"I haven't heard anything myself," his daughter went on, "though Jude wakes me every time. But I'm wondering whether it's something to do with... I mean—maybe that's where the priest hole is that Theo told us about—do you remember?"

"Interesting."

"No one seems to know, but... could Jude be hearing ghosts?"

"On the face of it, you wouldn't think a priest hole would be associated with ghosts. Theo didn't give the impression that the family recusancy had ever caused any real disaster. And no one seems to know where the priest hole is—or was. Jeannette said it hadn't been used for centuries."

"True. It was just a thought."

"I think it's probably better to tackle it from the other end, as it were."

"What do you mean?"

"Well, Tresayne House doesn't seem to have a reputation for being haunted. Nothing was said by Jeannette and Theo. So why is Jude hearing these sounds?"

"You think she's imagining them."

"Not exactly. But if no one else is hearing them, then it must be something that's going on in her head, in some sense."

Lorna was silent. Then she said, "I see what you mean. Jude might be in need of psychiatric help."

"Quite likely, I should think. How long has her father been beating her?"

"I don't know exactly. I gather it has been bad during lockdown, but I think maybe he had always done it."

"The longer she's been living with that kind of stress, the more likely she is to have sustained some psychological damage. But there's not much we can do about all that at the moment, unless it's an emergency. The police won't want to investigate a girl hearing things in the night."

Lorna seemed to hesitate, and then think better of whatever she was going to say.

"Is there more to tell me?" Jeremy had always thought of Lorna as a naturally open and honest person, and valued the fact that he was usually in her confidence. But there was clearly something about Jude, and whatever Jude had shared with her, that was making her cagey.

"Not now," she answered. "Not yet. I don't think it has any bearing on what's been happening, but Jude told me a few things in confidence that make me feel that Jude might need some therapy, or help of some kind, anyway."

"Keep me posted," he said. "I can keep secrets, you know that."

"Oh Dad, of course I do. But it's Jude's secret, not mine. I'd have to ask, and I don't want to forfeit h-her confidence."

Jeremy heard the momentary hesitation and began to have an inkling of what the problem might be. "I'm here when you need me. Just don't forget that. Whatever it is."

"Yes. Thanks, Dad."

~ * ~

Jeannette had put Marcus's visit in the calendar for mid-July, when hospitality venues were to open up, and tourism would be permitted and—surely—staying overnight with friends and family might be allowed, too. They would be well past their isolation period by then, too, always supposing none of them actually contracted Covid. The arrangement didn't really have to go in the calendar, for there was nothing else in there for July, or any other month, for that matter, so it could hardly be overlooked, but it cheered her up to see it there, and she hoped it would make Theo feel sure his son was truly welcome. Over a week had passed since their contact with Clive, and none of them had shown any sign of illness, so she was beginning to feel optimistic that they would all escape it, at least for now—for who knew what the future might bring? Even Marcus's visit, she supposed, came with a health warning, although he had promised to self-isolate beforehand, then come by car and picnic on the way rather than stopping anywhere he might pick up the infection, which was thoughtful of him.

She sat at the kitchen table with a mug of coffee beside her and thought about arrangements for his visit. He would have the main guestroom, in the Victorian wing of the house, opposite their own room. The Victorian bedrooms were large, but only their own room had been fitted with an ensuite shower when she and Theo first lived here, while those who slept in the bedrooms above the old hall shared the family bathroom next to the kitchen, as Marcus would have to do too. Apart from that, there was just the little cloakroom off the scullery. She supposed the house was rather short of bathrooms—certainly in terms of the modern fashion for ensuites in almost every bedroom—but in an old house you had to be mindful of where the original plumbing was and then design bathrooms around that, and Tresayne House was no exception.

She hoped Olivia wasn't resenting sharing a bathroom with Jude and Lorna—she hadn't seemed very happy to have them up there with her. But it had seemed the best arrangement, so the two teenagers could share a twin-bedded room. She was sure Jude had wanted to share with Lorna, and the only other guestrooms were single ones, one of which Jeannette used as her sewing room and could not make it ready without a bit more notice, the other the little study downstairs in the old part of the house next to Theo's music room, which contained a single bed but was also an overspill space for any of Theo's books that wouldn't fit into the music room's capacious but already overcrowded shelves. It was much better for Lorna to stay and keep Jude company, for Jeannette could see that Lorna was doing her a lot of good.

Just as she was reflecting on this, Lorna put her head round the door. "Mrs Landry, do you have a moment? I'd like to talk to you about Jude."

"Of course, Lorna. Come in." Jeannette hung the calendar back on its hook. "Do you want some coffee? Or a cold drink?"

"No, thanks. I'm fine." Lorna came forward and took a chair at the kitchen table.

"Is Jude well? The bruises and cuts seem to be healing nicely."

"Yes, it's not that." Lorna paused as if she were seeking inspiration, even courage, and Jeannette waited. "Mrs Landry, she's hearing things at night."

Jeannette frowned. "What kind of things? It's so quiet here, and we've had no gales. It can get quite noisy when the wind blows, because the house is such an odd shape."

"I don't think it's anything like that, and I have to say I haven't heard anything myself. Maybe it's just a bad dream he—she's having. But she says she wakes up and hears someone crying—wailing, even. Someone in real distress." Another pause. "I'm not sure what to do."

Jeannette looked at her, possible solutions tumbling over each other in her mind. But what a terrible nuisance all these restrictions were! Social services out of action, and probably no access to any kind of talking therapy via the NHS or anywhere else, either. It was hard to know where to turn.

"I wondered...," Lorna suggested tentatively. "Would you be willing for my father to come over? As a clergyman, he's had a lot of experience with people in trouble, and with mysterious events, too. I think he would be a good person to help Jude if Jude would let him."

"That sounds a good idea," agreed Jeannette in relief. "I can't see why he shouldn't come, do you? We've had no Covid symptoms, and presumably neither have your family?"

"Not when I spoke to him yesterday, certainly. Would you talk to him? I think he'd want to be sure that the invitation came from you and not just from me. It's your house..."

"What about Jude? Will she be willing to talk to your father? It's not much good his coming unless she will."

"I think so." Lorna hesitated. "I have asked, and Jude seems to be willing to talk to Dad. I don't know what will happen when he's actually here, but we can only try."

Jeannette nodded. "Then try we will."

She picked up the landline receiver and began to dial.

Osborne House, Thursday 27th January 1916

I am getting ready to leave for Cornwall. The carrier is booked for Monday next, and Johnson is sorting out linen. Johnson will stay behind here, as he was Lionel's man and will be Freddie's when he comes home. I shan't need a manservant in my new job. There will be no clothes to look after as I shall wear my black clerical robes every day, and the housekeeper can arrange for them to be laundered when needed. I will even wear them on the journey, inconvenient though they are for travel, to remind myself of the vocation that awaits me. My Cornish parishioners shall not see me without them, or they might think of me as an ordinary man, with an ordinary man's failings—as indeed I am— instead of the divine representative I should be to them. I will try to live up to that calling, frail though I now know I am when it comes to things of the flesh.

I have told Mary that this Saturday must be our last night together. Sunday should be kept clean of sin, and I must make some effort to purify my soul before I go. Over these months, I have forgotten such matters and have fallen into such a pit of desire and lust that I wonder whether I will be able to haul myself out of it.

The Church would tell me I have been mired in sin, and I have thought of going to our local priest to confess it before I become a priest myself. I would wish to start my service in Truro diocese without a stain on my conscience. But our priest here would not, I fear, keep my story to himself, whatever the obligations of the confessional. He is so much a part of local society here, hunting with the local gentry and dining with their families. It would be too good a piece of gossip to resist, I suspect, especially when he's had a few glasses of port.

No, I must bear the burden of my sins myself, for now, at least. Perhaps the confessor I shall be allotted in Cornwall will be someone I can trust to hear and absolve me. God knows I need it.

Yet am I right to see our loving this way? Mary weeps every time she visits me now, and our lovemaking has become her only comfort. I cannot refuse her, and—God forgive me!—I do not wish to. It brings me solace too. How can such love be sin?

Thirteen

Jeannette, Jeremy, Lorna and Jude met in the big conservatory that had been added to the side of the house in the nineteen-thirties. The weather had turned showery, but Jeannette felt they should at least give lip-service to the regulations, so she had opened the doors and windows and placed some basket chairs around a low table, suitably distanced. They could each have a mug of coffee while they talked, but she wouldn't put out biscuits. It was as near outdoors as she could manage, and as Jeremy had been self-isolating like the inhabitants of Tresayne House, and for the same length of time, she felt it could be justified.

Jeremy, unaware of the thought that lay behind these preparations, listened carefully as Lorna described again what Jude had heard. Jude sat silent, contributing little to the conversation, and when Lorna had finished Jeremy asked, "Can you describe this crying, or wailing, Jude?"

"It sounded like someone who was desperate, and they didn't know what to do. Like they couldn't bear... whatever 'twas."

Jeremy passed his hand over his chin, an action that often unconsciously represented bafflement, but at the same time seemed to help him think more clearly. "And you're sure you didn't dream it?"

A definite headshake. "No. It weren't a dream. The first time, I thought maybe 'twas. But last night I were awake when it happened. Awake and thinking about m'father and whether he's worked out where I'm to. Worriting about it, I were. And then I heard her crying again."

"You think it's a woman's voice."

Jude nodded. "Definitely. A high voice, like. And the kind of crying women do when they're at their wit's end."

Jeremy noticed the phraseology, which clearly positioned women as different from the speaker, and thought it another clue to Jude's state of mind. He turned to Jeannette. "You've never heard of any hauntings here? Nothing that perhaps your parents or grandparents might have mentioned? I know you grew up here and knew your grandparents. It's an old house, after all, and there are often stories, village tales, that kind of thing."

Jeannette shook her head. "My grandfather died when I was very small, but I used to talk to my grandmother a great deal—she lived with us for several years when I was a child."

"Are your parents still alive? Perhaps they might remember something."

"They both died some years ago. I don't believe in hauntings, if I'm honest. I don't believe ghosts exist. It must have been some trick of the wind."

Jude looked upset by this disbelieving attitude but said nothing.

"'Ghosts' is an emotive word," said Jeremy. "But spiritual disturbances are well attested. Poltergeist activity has been studied. But that's not what I'm asking. Have there been any tales of such activity associated with the house?"

"Well, I've never heard of anything like that here, and surely my grandmother would have said something, even if my father didn't. She was a bit superstitious, especially in her old age. My father grew up here, as I did. I can't believe we wouldn't have known if there was something to be known."

Jeremy made an accepting gesture and tried to deal with the situation tactfully, though he found Jeannette's materialist obduracy slightly irritating, especially since she had asked him to help. But to help with Jude, clearly; for Jeannette the problem had nothing to do with the house. For his part, he wasn't quite so sure now that he had talked to Jude. "I do see what you mean. An idea I had…"

"Yes," said Lorna at once, eagerly. "What do you suggest, Dad?"

Her faith in him was clearly intact, which was heartwarming.

"How about moving Jude to another room?"

Jeannette pursed her lips. "We have Theo's son Marcus coming to stay soon, and he will have the main guestroom upstairs in our end of the house. But there is… there is a little single room downstairs, next to the music room. Theo uses it as an extra book room, but Jude could have that, if she didn't mind—and if you don't mind staying where you are, on your own, Lorna? Or you could go back to Cedric's with your father, I suppose. We are nearly at the end of our isolation period."

"I'd rather stay here, Mrs Landry, if that's okay with you. I don't want to leave Jude until things are sorted out. But I don't mind staying where I am. I'm not afraid of ghosts."

Jeannette smiled approvingly, but Jeremy was aware of undercurrents of defiant courage in his daughter. She was not quite sure, he suspected, however modern and robust and down to earth in her attitudes, that there was not something odd about the room they were sleeping in. He was proud to see this had not deterred her.

"How often is that room used?" he asked. "The one where Lorna and Jude have been sleeping?"

"Not often at all. In fact, I can't remember when we last used it for guests. Possibly not since Olivia was a teenager—if she had friends staying over, they used to sleep there. We don't usually have a houseful of guests now, and when Olivia is in London, I tend to use her rooms for extra guests, rather than the twin room, which I always feel is rather cold and unwelcoming, to be honest. It's just that it faces north and doesn't get much in the way of sunshine. But the twin beds seemed the best thing for Lorna and Jude—sharing, you see," she added, sounding slightly defensive. "I put a fan heater on in there to air it, and it's been a warm dry couple of months, so it didn't feel damp."

"It's been fine, Mrs Landry!" Lorna hastened to reassure her. "Apart from Jude hearing this person crying, we've been perfectly okay in there. Haven't we, Jude?"

Jude nodded, but Jeremy noticed the teenager had hunched up inside the hoodie, rather like on the first day, as though something in the conversation was troubling the poor kid.

"Are you okay with that idea, too?" he asked. "Sleeping on your own for a bit, I mean, in a different room?"

Jude nodded. "Maybe I won't hear her crying if I'm not in that room. But I didn't dream it—I know I didn't."

Jeremy thought of the way poltergeist activity could be set off by teenage girls as they went through puberty. That was a possibility, and if that were the problem it might be cured by moving Jude to a different room, or removing her from the house altogether. Then again, it might not. But all this didn't seem quite consistent with that kind of phenomenon, and in any case, if he'd guessed right about what Lorna hadn't told him about Jude, it wouldn't fit anyway. He had a gut feeling, an intuition, whatever Jeannette might think, that the problem was something to do with the house, and Jude just happened to be sensitive to it.

"Do you know," he went on, riding the hunch, "whether Olivia has ever heard any sounds coming from that room? Her room is next door, isn't it?"

Jeannette looked rather taken aback. "Well, she's never said anything, and she's slept there since she was a teenager. But I must admit I haven't asked her. Do you want me to?"

"It might be useful. If not, then we proceed as we've agreed. Jude should move anyway, I think, because it's clearly frightening her to sleep in that room at the moment, and we can't blame her for that. But if Olivia has heard something, or thinks she might have, even if it was long ago... well, that would be a different kettle of fish, wouldn't it?"

Jude straightened up. "I'll go and move my stuff into the other room."

"I'll come with you," said Lorna. "I know where it is, I think—next to the music room, off the big hall, you said?"

Jeannette nodded. "You pass the door on the way through to the kitchen. That bed won't be made up, Lorna. I'll come and get you some bedding so you can help Jude make it up. And we may need to tidy up a bit in there, too."

Jeremy watched them go, quite relieved, in spite of his compassion for Jude, that Lorna would henceforth sleep in a separate room. There was something brooding and morose about the teenager that troubled him. Sooner or later, they would have to find some way of helping Jude come to terms with what had happened in the past, and find some confidence in their identity, too. Being in a place of safety like this was unlikely to be enough to do that, unfortunately. And, like his daughter, he suspected there was more Jude needed to tell them before they could act.

"I'd love to know more about this house and your family history," he ventured to Jeannette as she put the coffee mugs on a tray, ready to carry back to the kitchen.

She looked up. "I can tell you about the family," she said, "but you need Theo for the house, really. He's been looking at its history as a sort of lockdown project, along with keeping track of all the Covid statistics—which is a depressing kind of exercise to my mind, but he will do it."

Jeremy nodded. "Maybe next time I'm here? Jude isn't telling us everything, I think, so with your permission I'd like to explore this further. Lorna probably knows more, but if it's in confidence I don't want to press her. Tell me about the family, anyway. You said your grandparents created the garden? Who lived here before that?"

Jeannette sat for a moment, trying to remember all the details. She had not thought much about the family's history for a long time. It hadn't seemed relevant to her day-to-day life with Theo, and Olivia had never shown much interest—in fact, she had, disturbingly, seemed keener to find out about her father's family, of which Jeannette knew very little and wanted very much to keep it that way. She felt vaguely apprehensive even about revisiting her own family's past, of reviving the memories of all her grandmother had told her long ago.

However, the earlier history of the family was unproblematic. She would begin there.

"The house was built in the early seventeenth century, most likely on the proceeds of piracy, or at least a bit of Elizabethan privateering. There were fortunes to be made then by preying on enemy shipping wherever you found it, and the Cornish have always been seafarers. The Tresaynes were in good company."

Jeremy nodded. He knew of the strong tradition of seafaring in Cornwall, whether it was fishing or commercial transport, naval action or illicit acts of piracy and smuggling—even wrecking, allegedly, when the situation lent itself to that. Partly because of the duchy's remoteness, the Cornish were a law unto themselves, though he wasn't going to speak that observation aloud to Jeannette.

"I've never understood why the Tresaynes decided to build here on the moor," Jeannette went on, "rather than on the coast, if they used to be sailors. But I suppose they had their reasons. The river runs along the bottom of the property here—you've crossed the clapper bridge that takes the footpath over to the other side, haven't you? Perhaps that was sufficient for them, though it's not much of a river here, so near the source."

"Perhaps they had had enough of the sea," suggested Jeremy.

"Maybe. Anyway, after the house was built, the family seem to have settled down to a fairly uneventful life, living off the rents. Trebartha owned most of the moorland, but we owned land in the valley then, where the farming is better and the rents would have been higher. The Tresaynes were gentry, but they never aspired to the nobility. They didn't take part in national politics, although one or two were MPs in the days of the rotten boroughs. Their daughters married local yeomen and gentlemen, and the younger sons became soldiers or naval officers or clergymen, but none of them seem to have become generals or admirals or bishops."

It all sounded very conventional in the end, Jeremy thought, however the family had made its money in the first place.

"Sometimes they married money and increased the family holdings—that's how they gained an estate in North Devon, which became their main home in the nineteenth century. There seem always to have been sons to carry on the line, which makes me doubly sad that I am the last of the Tresaynes. Olivia was adopted by Theo when I married him, and she has taken his name."

Jeremy pondered briefly the implications of this statement. Surely Olivia's maiden name would have been her father's rather than her mother's? Perhaps, he deduced, Jeannette had not been married to Olivia's father. There was a story here that Jeannette was not telling him. Not that there was any reason why she should, but he couldn't help being curious.

"My grandmother was in a similar situation," Jeannette continued, oblivious to Jeremy's shrewd speculations. "Her brothers all died young—two of them in action in the Great War, and the other in tragic circumstances not far from this house when he was serving as vicar of the parish here. I think Theo mentioned it the other day, didn't he? So their sister—she was my grandmother—inherited, and her husband took the name Tresayne. But they only had one son, and he only had one daughter—me."

"I remember a tragedy was mentioned," agreed Jeremy cautiously. He felt as though he were dealing with sensitive matters here, although it had all happened a long time ago.

"There were three brothers. Great-uncle Lionel was the eldest and the heir to the property—my great-grandfather was killed in South Africa in 1901, and Lionel inherited the estate when he was eleven, but my great-grandmother ran everything while he was a child. He joined the local regiment here, the Duke of Cornwall's Light Infantry, as a junior officer straight out of Sandhurst, and died on the retreat from Mons in 1914. I suppose he must have been in his early twenties. The youngest, Frederick, was killed at High Wood on the Somme at the age of nineteen. He was listed as missing in action at first, and his mother wouldn't believe he was dead for ages. It was very sad. My grandmother remembered that time very vividly. She was about seventeen, I believe, and the youngest of the siblings; I think she was very close to Freddie. It must have been dreadful for them all."

She paused. "The middle brother, Edwin, the clergyman, was some kind of conscientious objector. I didn't really understand what that was when my grandmother mentioned it, but it seems he had moral objections to the fighting. But he wasn't called up anyway because he was ordained sometime in 1915 and came here to be vicar."

"Not on the face of it a dangerous job," Jeremy commented with a wry smile.

"No, you'd think not, wouldn't you? He was killed in a fall from his horse, coming back very late one night in torrential rain from visiting a dying parishioner. No one really knew what happened, but it seems he tried to cross a rather rickety wooden bridge a couple of miles downriver when the water was high—if the moors are waterlogged, the river can get dangerously swollen and fast-flowing, even up here near the source. The bridge broke, and he and his horse were swept away in the torrent. His body was picked up further down the valley a few days later. So my poor great-grandmother lost all three of her sons in the space of two years."

Jeremy murmured sympathetically. It was a tragic story altogether. But the details she'd given only strengthened his first impression: that clouds of darkness—emotional, spiritual or both, he wasn't sure—swirled around the house and its inhabitants.

"Money became very tight after the War," Jeannette went on, "and my great-grandmother sold the North Devon estate to make ends meet. She lived here for a while after Edwin's death, but Tresayne was inherited by her daughter and son-in-law."

"Who developed the gardens."

"Yes. My grandfather had been a gardener on the North Devon estate before the War. I don't think the family wanted my grandmother to marry him, in fact, but he had a distinguished career as a 'ranker' officer in the War, and that seems to have changed their minds, especially as he was willing to change his name to Tresayne and carry on the family line."

"They had a son, I think you said. That would have been your father?"

"Yes, but that was quite a long time after their marriage. My grandmother didn't say much about it, but I think she may have had several miscarriages or stillbirths. They had a daughter, born back in 1919, not long after my grandfather left the armed forces, but she died young. My father wasn't born until 1928, which meant he wasn't old enough to fight in the Second War. Maybe that was a good thing, after the family's losses in the First... But you don't think, do you," she added, "that all this has anything to do with Jude's experiences?"

"I don't know. The house has seen a lot of family tragedy, one way and another, it seems, especially during the Great War period. Jude might just be in a very sensitive state right now, and able to sense things no one else can. Or, as you suggest, it may be all imagination. Only time will tell."

Osborne House, Saturday January 30th 2016

The clock has struck four, and Mary has left me. It must be the last time, and now I cannot sleep for grief.

She gave me everything in her sweet nature tonight—our few hours together were filled with tenderness and passion; but it was a requiem for all that we have meant to each other, and while my body is filled with exultation and languor, my heart is torn with despair, for there is no way out for us.

Yet, how can I live without her? Why am I putting an end to something that fills my heart with joy as nothing else has ever done?

She begged me to let her stay until morning, saying she did not care for danger of discovery, or even for scandal, if only we can be together. And when I told her it could not be, she begged me again to take her with me when I go to Cornwall next week, or to let her follow me when I am settled. This time I prevaricated—I could not bear to say 'no' to her definitely, after all the generosity of her lovemaking, the depth of her passion for me. But in my heart, I know I cannot see my way to this. The scandal would destroy us both, for my position will depend on good character and reputation, and I cannot marry her, even if I wanted to. It would break Mother's heart to see both her children make such mésalliances. If it were only myself... but I cannot ask Maudie to give up Gerald, now that I understand the depth of love she must feel for him. She is willing to face a life that will be so different, with none of the comforts she has grown up with. I cannot match that or turn against them now.

Surely when I have gone, Mary will forget me, or at least our lovemaking will become but an exquisite memory for both of us. It is for the best.

Fourteen

The following week, their isolation was at an end, much to everyone's relief, and although face masks had been made mandatory in shops and on public transport, the re-opening of what had been classed as 'non-essential' shops and other businesses was welcome, and more restrictions were due to be lifted in July, which was cheering.

"It feels like we're getting back to normal at last," Jeannette said to Lorna, as they loaded the dishwasher together one morning. She had been pleasantly surprised by Lorna's helpfulness, and more than happy to go on having her as a guest while Jude was with them. For, as she said to Theo, "I've lost the knack of having extra people in the house, what with Olivia and now Jude and Lorna. But it's good to have another pair of hands. Lorna seems to like helping me, and Jude obviously knows how to take her turn. I suppose Lorna, with three siblings and working parents, must be used to being helpful."

Theo made no reply. He would have been much happier if Jude had seemed more relaxed, rather than withdrawn and silent, though he didn't want to interfere with what Jeannette was trying to do to help. But as Jeremy had feared, it had turned out moving Jude to another room had not made much difference, except that as the teenager slept alone in a single room, the rest of the household were slower to hear about any further experiences.

Lorna asked anxiously every morning about any night-time visitations, but received only grunts in reply. To everyone's surprise, it was Olivia who opened the subject up again, several days after Jeremy had listened to Jeannette's account of Tresayne family history.

"Have you heard any more crying during the night?" she asked Jude one morning at breakfast before Lorna had had a chance to do so. "Don't be afraid to say if you have. I know no one else thinks there's anything to it, but I've always thought there was something odd about that room next door to mine. I can't help wondering whether that's where we might find the priest hole that I didn't know about."

There was a bite to the last sentence that Theo knew was directed at Jeannette. He sighed inwardly, while both Jeannette and Lorna gaped at Olivia, but Jude seemed to have no hesitation in answering.

"It's not so clear, see, because now it's coming from upstairs, from that room. But I can still hear it. Terrible wailing, lost and desperate. Summat awful, it is."

The silence that followed this statement was redolent of shock, dismay and guilt. Then they burst forth with a variety of reactions.

"Oh, Jude, you poor thing. *I* still haven't heard anything, and I'm sleeping up there!" Lorna put her arm round her friend.

Jeannette exchanged glances with Theo. "We should ask Jeremy to come back. He always thought there was something to it, not just your imagination, Jude. I'm so sorry we've put you through all this."

"Something must be done, certainly," said Theo. "But we still don't know what we're dealing with. If Lorna hasn't heard anything, sleeping in that room, how can it be that room where the problem is?"

Olivia alone sat silently, saying nothing but looking every bit as shocked as everyone else. After a few moments, she got up quietly and tiptoed away.

"I suppose," Lorna ventured hesitantly, "that maybe I just don't hear things and see things like that. My family always say that I have my feet too firmly on the ground, like my mum. She is always sceptical about anything supernatural—apart from Christian things, naturally. The idea that something —or someone—could be crying out to us in that room, from another time perhaps, seems quite mad to me. I can't get my head round it. So maybe if there is something, I just wouldn't hear it."

Theo smiled. A jumble of ideas and possibilities, but all of it very honest and open-minded. What a nice girl she was.

Jude was sitting silently, with an expressionless face. "Maybe I'd better leave this house. I'm just creating trouble—you'd none of you heard nothing till I came. It's all my fault, even though it is real. There is something there, someone who's frightened and desperate, or there was, once. But I didn't mean to bring her back to life."

"No, no," said Jeannette at once, reaching out to lay her hand on Jude's arm. "You mustn't feel it's your fault. Whatever we're dealing with, that isn't so. Would you speak to Remy again, if he comes? Tell him a bit more about yourself, and what happened with your dad? I know it doesn't seem to have much to do with all this, but who knows?"

Jude nodded. "He does seem a good guy, someone you can talk to, someone you can trust, like Lorna." Jude smiled at her friend across the table. "I'll talk to him, but I don't know as I can help, just the same. I don't know what it's all about either."

"Dad loves mysteries," said Lorna. "And he's good at solving them, too. At least we should let him try."

~ * ~

Jeremy was at that moment in the middle of a somewhat difficult conversation with his wife, who had phoned to suggest—

or was it to demand?—yet again that he send, or bring, the children home to Oxford as soon as possible.

"Oh, Liz," he groaned. "I don't know whether I can. I don't want to send them on the train, even with Lorna and Mike in charge. Public transport doesn't feel very safe at the moment, even when it's actually operating, and though Mike's got his licence, it's too much to ask him to drive them all that way. Besides, I need the car here."

"I'm sure Mike would cope perfectly well on the train," he heard her reply. "We just need to let him grow up a bit."

Jeremy sighed. It was so easy to overprotect your children and prevent them from growing up, even though they themselves were more than willing to have a go at new things. "I suppose if he has Lorna with him to look after Chris and Bethan... They're getting out of hand, Liz, and I'll be glad to hand them over, if I'm honest."

"But why can't you drive them back yourself, Remy? Mike could do some of the driving and give you a break, like you did going down. Surely, you could all come home now?"

"I can't just leave the dogs to their own devices. I haven't heard from Cedric when he's going to return. He usually takes the train, but I don't know whether he'll want to do that. If he does, I ought to go to Exeter, or at least to Liskeard, to pick him up."

"Let him get a taxi," urged Liz. "You're doing him a favour, dog-sitting and house-sitting all this time." There was a pause. "I'm not suggesting you all come back this minute, but soon. Please. I miss you all. It's getting lonely now that my work's finished for the summer. I can't come down to you—look at all the trouble Dominic Cummings has caused, driving about the country while he had Covid, and then saying he wasn't breaking the rules—but you five could come home soon, I'm sure. Certainly by the beginning of July."

"I'll talk to Cedric," promised Jeremy. He didn't want to embark on an explanation to Liz of what had been going on at Tresayne House, and admit how much he wanted to stay and solve the mystery. He knew what she would say. He also thought Lorna wouldn't want to leave Jude at present. But he could stall easily enough for a day or two, which would give him time to get something arranged with Cedric, talk to Lorna and try to sort that out, too. Unfortunately, he had the feeling that a few days weren't going to see an end to the strange events at Tresayne House, nor to the mystery surrounding them.

"Don't think I don't want to be home in Oxford, and back with you, Liz. I do, very much. That goes without saying. But there's something here I need to sort out, and I shan't feel happy until I've worked out what's going on, even if I'm not the one to fix it."

He paused, hoping for Liz's understanding. She must know what he meant. Sometimes there were mysteries he just had to get on top of, for his own peace of mind, and this was one of them. But she said nothing.

He tried another tack. "Are you sure you can't come down here to stay with us, instead, Liz? Surely the students aren't going to be back in college this term? Things are opening up a bit on the travel restrictions front, too."

"No can do," she replied. "I've got my Year 12s to consider. They've missed a lot of important work during lockdown. And anyway, there's a possibility the schools may re-open for kids in some years. Bethan and Chris ought to come home in case they can have a few weeks in school. No one seems to be recognising what an effect missing a whole term's schooling is going to have on our children, even with online lessons going on. All the teachers are doing their best, but it's not the same."

Jeremy sighed. "Okay. I'll organise for the kids to come home as soon as I can. If necessary, they can go on the train and keep away from everyone else. I don't suppose there'll be many passengers yet, with movement about the country still so restricted. We can take the chance if you think it's best."

"If you have to stay on there, the four of them can take up a set of table-seats on the train. That way they'll be the best part of two metres from everyone else even if there are any other passengers. And they can wear their masks. I'll bet people will instinctively keep plenty of space between themselves and strangers for the moment, for their own sake if not for anyone else's."

"I expect you're right." Jeremy sighed. What did that say about the way society was changing—had to change if anything was ever to get back to normal? Masks and social distancing, and the feeling that everyone represented a potential health threat. How long would it take for people to respond normally to each other again?

Another thought came to him. "I meant to say this last time I spoke to you, Liz. Have you seen Rose lately?"

"'Seen' in what sense?" Liz asked. "I mean, I haven't bumped into her when I've been out jogging, if that's what you mean."

"No. Sorry. I meant—have you had any contact with her?"

"No. But I've no reason to, really."

"I've been a bit concerned about her with regard to Clive. I guess she may still be officially his next of kin. No one from Derriford has contacted us, and because we aren't relatives, I don't think they'll tell us anything about how he is. I thought..."

"We ought to warn Rose, in case he dies."

Jeremy sighed. That was Liz putting her finger on the nub of the problem, as usual. "I suppose that's about the size of it, yes. I hope and pray he won't, but supposing the first Rose knows is a phone call from them to say he's dead?"

"I expect they'll have contacted her already, won't they? I mean, hospitals do contact people if their relatives are admitted, surely."

"Maybe. Unusual times these, though. I mean, she wouldn't be allowed to visit him, even if she wanted to. Would they bother?"

"Well, if you don't know, I certainly don't. Why don't you phone her?"

"I could, I suppose. But..."

"You'd rather not be bearer of bad news."

"Oh, Liz. Put that way it sounds awful. I think I just feel it might come better from you."

There was a moment's silence. "Okay, if you think it would be better, I will."

"Thanks. I do, though I know it sounds weak and feeble of me."

"At least you and the kids are out of isolation now, with no harm done." Liz was obviously trying to cheer him. "I know that's very selfish of me, but that's what seems the most important thing. Surely things are getting better now? Infection rates and death rates are falling, and I hear the Oxford vaccine is coming along well. Once that's approved, we can all get back to normal."

Jeremy said nothing. He wished he thought it would be that simple. But it seemed to him that there was a very long way to go before there would be any kind of return to normality—if indeed it ever came.

~ * ~

Marcus stood with his back to the still static view of the river and read the letter from Jeannette again. It meant a great deal to him to have had a handwritten invitation from his hostess, whom he had never met, and who for all he knew might have resented his coming or felt jealous of his desire to reawaken his relationship with his father.

We are very much looking forward to your coming, she had written. *It seems so strange that Olivia and I have never met you in all the years I've been with your father, and I am happy that this can now be remedied. "Stay safe," as they say these days, and we will see you in July. My very kind regards, Jeannette.*

Embarrassed at his own emotion, he brought the letter to his lips. Jeannette had succeeded in making his father happy. He tried not to remember that his own mother had failed, for he longed to keep her in his mind in the role of innocent party, the one neglected and abandoned, which was the way she had always seen herself. Maybe his father had made mistakes in their relationship—*haven't we all?* he thought wryly—but Marcus was remembering what he had long willed into oblivion—those early years when he and his father had enjoyed each other's company, when his father had taken him to violin lessons and acted as his accompanist when he took part in junior music competitions, presented him with exciting construction kits at Christmas, and laid on trips to London pantomimes. When his mother had taken them away to live in another part of London, those memories had faded and been lost in adjusting to a new and different life, and she had encouraged that; in fact, she had done everything she could to make sure that when he grew up, he left his relationship with his father behind. It had suited her to do so, he saw now. She had not wanted any reminders of the past.

But for him the memories were still there, if he wanted to look them out and dust them off. He was going to do his best to start anew with his father and create an adult relationship with him; and it was good to remember that there had been a childhood relationship on which to build.

Tresayne House, Saturday February 5th 1916

I left Osborne House on Monday for Cornwall. Mother, Maudie and I made our farewells after an early breakfast, and I arrived here at Tresayne as darkness was falling. The carriers have been found accommodation with our stable lads in the garrets above the stables for the night, and they are hoping to pick up some business in Launceston on the way back. I wish them well, for the carrier and his young son have done everything we asked of them, with no grumbling. The horses too deserved their rest and feed in our stables. I am glad I paid the extra to have two horses and the large cart, even though I did not have many large items to bring with me.

It was a long ride, for I did not like to leave the carrier to manage the journey all alone in case he lost his way or was tempted to delay at one of the many hostelries we passed on our route. The lanes were bad after the interminable wet weather, and the mud and ruts made progress difficult for a wheeled vehicle. It reminded me a little of Freddie's accounts of the Front and the quagmire the trenches and battlefields are reduced to on occasion. At least we were not stuck in the mud, and the lanes are perfectly passable for a horse and rider.

I had not previously been to Cornwall, and it seems a bleak, unfriendly place. We are on the edge of the moors here at Tresayne—the major part stretches westwards for miles towards Bodmin. When we joined the coach road at Launceston, at first it seemed just like North Devon, with enclosed fields and undulating countryside. But as we grew nearer Tresayne, I could see the vast stretches of the moor ahead of us, treeless and stony, grazed only by sheep and small horned cattle, with a light mist hanging over it all. I am glad we did not have to venture out on to it. Even the coach road would be lonely, and a traveller would be vulnerable to bad weather and at the mercy of any lawless robber. There was little other traffic on the road and beyond Trewint, where we turned off the road, few other habitations before the great coaching stop at Jamaica Inn. Perhaps it will look better when spring comes, and I may feel like riding further afield. For now, I will be glad to stay on our own land. The estate is quite large, though smaller than it used to be, I believe, and there are a number of tenant farmers. I will have to remember I am squire here as well as rector and take the time to visit those who rent land from us.

Fifteen

"Are you okay, Jude?" Lorna asked anxiously. She and Jude were helping Jeannette that morning by making up the bed in the main spare room for Marcus, who was due to visit in a few days' time. Lorna had asked Jeannette if they could do the job to keep Jude busy. She was anxious about her new friend, who she feared was brooding not only about whatever strange haunting had been set off at Tresayne House, but also about what was going on at home on the farm.

There was a long pause. "I guess," said Jude at last.

"Don't lie to me," Lorna begged. "I know there's more stuff you haven't told me. I want to help, Jude. And you know I haven't said anything about what you told me, about being trans, I mean. Though I think my father guesses something. He isn't hard to fool."

Jude nodded slowly. "I'd feel able to talk to him if I need to. He's someone you can trust, I can see that. But what's the point? What can he do to help?"

"He thinks he might be able to contact someone who could find you somewhere safe to live."

"On my own? Where could I possibly go that would be safer than this?"

Lorna shut her mouth on what she had been going to reply to this. Jude couldn't possibly stay at Tresayne for all that much longer—it wouldn't be fair on Jeannette and Theo. And Olivia didn't want her there. Anyone could see that. Not to mention the cat, who spat at Jude and hissed whenever they met, though so far he had done nothing more drastic to indicate his displeasure. Lorna's family had never owned a cat, so she wasn't quite sure what to make of Kato's behaviour, but she could tell Theo and Jeannette were puzzled.

Jude suddenly seemed to make up his mind. "There is more, you'm right. More to tell, I mean."

Lorna held her breath.

"After I told him, 'bout being trans, he started doing… other things… He said I had to learn to be a woman." She looked away from Lorna, as though ashamed.

"Do you mean…?" Lorna faltered. She stopped. No. Surely no one could be as awful—as downright evil—as she was imagining.

Jude nodded, and his body hunched up as it had when he had first come to Tresayne House. "He'd done it when I were a little tacker, nine or ten. And then my sister grew up a little and she were more feminine, see. He liked that better, and he didn't take the strap to her, so that was something."

Lorna was aghast. "But didn't your mother do anything about it? Didn't you *tell* her?"

Jude gave a bitter laugh. "Mum's been on the bottle for years. 'Tis her way of coping with Dad's temper, maybe. If she'm drunk, she don't feel it as much if he beats her. Or else she just don't want to notice what's going on—easier that way. I cann't blame her."

Lorna was almost in tears.

"But during lockdown it all got worse, see? We was all stuck in the farmhouse together—Dad still had to deal with the animals, and we went on selling eggs to the local shops. Megan and I helped, as usual. But with no school, and nowhere for Mum to go either, it was just... awful."

"Jude, we have to tell someone about this—the police would arrest him. We can't let your mother and Megan go on trying to cope with him, even if you've escaped."

Jude sighed. "I see what you'm sayin', I do. But what would Mum do without Dad to run the farm? She and Megan wouldn't be able to stay there on their own. They couldn't cope. And where else would they go?"

"If he wasn't there, then you could go back," suggested Lorna eagerly. "The three of you could manage, surely?"

"No! For one thing, I bain't never going back there. Beastly place at the back of beyond. I don't want to bury meself there, nor Megan. And Mum will never pull out of it. The drink's everything to her now. I cann't see that changing. It would be me and Megan trying to look after everything on our own. That's no life, even if we could do it, and we cann't."

"Social services will find somewhere for Megan to go that's safe. We can't leave her there, Jude."

"Mebbe you're right. But I cann't face the police, not yet. It's hard enough telling you about it. You understand. Don't know that they will."

Lorna opened her mouth to say the police would be modern in their outlook and would know about inclusivity. They wouldn't make any judgements. And then she shut it again, because she wasn't quite sure they would be, down here in Cornwall so far from the centres of liberal thought. Cornwall was not a very progressive place to live in, from what she'd heard, however beautiful it might be as a holiday destination. And making Jude talk to the police might be detrimental to his mental health. Besides no one else could help Megan, if he refused to.

She could only hope and pray that Jude's father would focus on Jude's defection, rather than taking it out on the rest of the family. But she would tell Dad if Jude said she could. His advice was always worth having. She wondered now why she had found it so difficult to tell him about Jude when they'd first met up on the moors.

As it happened, Jeremy arrived that morning, apparently intent on finding out more about the house and its history. She saw him out of the window as she and Jude finished getting the room ready for Marcus. Theo met him on the terrace, and the two of them walked along the front of the house, then turned the corner of the Victorian wing out of sight. She wondered what they were doing. Her father clearly thought the hauntings had more to do with the house than with Jude himself, and she was glad of that. But she must catch him before he left.

"Jude, will you talk to my father if I go and find him? Right now, I mean. I've just seen him in the garden with Theo. I think someone needs to know what's been going on at the farm. I know he'll help you if he possibly can. And he can keep a secret—it's part of being a vicar, you know. They have to, if someone tells them something in confidence."

Jude looked wary. "Teachers don't, not if it's what they call a safeguarding issue. They have to tell the authorities. I'm not sure as I want that. You can't trust the social services. Once they know about my dad, they'll do what they think best, and none of us will be able to stop them."

"I don't think it's the same for vicars," Lorna told her, hoping she'd got her facts straight. She knew her father took confidences very seriously, even if the person were confessing to a crime. Surely what Jude had to tell wouldn't come under that category? "You can't leave Megan to cope with what you've run away from, Jude. You simply can't."

There was silence for a minute or two. Then Jude said, "Okay. But tell him it's got to be a secret. No exceptions."

Lorna ran down the stairs. In the main hall, she encountered Jeannette, who was arranging some garden flowers in a vase on the round table by the door. "Do you know where Dad is? I think I saw him in the garden."

Jeannette looked surprised. "I haven't seen him, Lorna."

"He was talking to Theo."

"Go and look for them if you want to. Is Jude still upstairs?"

Lorna nodded. "We've finished making up the bed."

"Thanks so much. You are a treasure. I'll put some flowers in there tomorrow morning, so they'll still be fresh."

Lorna ran out into the garden. She found her father and Theo in the old stableyard, apparently pacing out the length of the house wall that formed one side of it.

"I make it about five metres," she heard her father say as she reached him.

"Yes, I agree." Theo made a note. "We'll need to check that against the inside width."

"It may be only a few feet out each way. The priest hole may be quite small."

This sounded intriguing, but she didn't want to be distracted by it. "Dad, Jude wants to talk to you."

Her father looked up. "Are you sure?"

"Yes. There's much more than I've been able to tell you. Are you able to keep everything a secret? I think Jude's afraid of what social services may do—breaking the family up and so on. I said you were bound by the seal of the confessional. Is that right?"

He smiled. "It's the right phrase, yes. I think if there are serious safeguarding issues, I might have to pass information on to the relevant authorities, but it would be under Church of England rules, not local council ones, so I've got much more discretion."

Lorna sighed with relief. "That's okay then. When can you come and talk to Jude?"

"I'm just in the middle of doing something with Theo."

"Measuring. I saw. Is it to do with the priest hole?"

He smiled. "Maybe. Can we do some measuring in your room?"

"Of course." *Heavens. So they think the priest hole is in there.* "How long will you be? I don't want Jude to think better of talking to you."

"Not long. But I wanted to have a word with you, anyway. Mum thinks all of you kids should go home. She might make an exception for Mike, but not for the rest of you."

"Oh, Dad. That is so unfair. Why does it have to be me travelling home with the kids?" She thought quickly. "Can't Mike take them? I've done an awful lot of babysitting while we've been here, while you and Mike were out with the dogs, and Mike taking photos, and you working on your article." She tried not to sound pleading, but she could hear her voice rising slightly plaintively.

It was all true, what she'd said, though in fact, as Dad knew quite well, she didn't mind looking after the twins, who were fun to be around even if they didn't always do as she told them. But you could have too much of a good thing; she really had spent a lot of their time in Cornwall minding the twins in one way or another. Mike had got off relatively lightly.

"I don't want to leave Jude while everything is so uncertain," she continued, mustering the best arguments she could. "And anyway, it's my turn to do something with you, Dad. Mike always seems to be the one who helps with your mysteries. Look at that time he ended up being threatened by the Mad Monk! Why should he have all the fun?"

Jeremy grinned. "I'm not sure the Mad Monk incident was all that much fun at the time, but I see what you mean."

"Jude still needs me, though. You must see that."

"Jude needs official help if we could but get the kid to accept it. Still, we'll see what Mum says about you staying and Mike taking the twins home. I'll phone her tonight. As for myself, I'm not sure what Cedric's immediate plans are, but I can't just leave the dogs. And Jeannette and Theo want me to stay around, I think, until we get to the bottom of all this supernatural activity, whatever it is. I don't think there's likely to be any physical danger involved, this time. But I can't argue with Mum about the others going home if she feels that's best."

Lorna smiled. What Mum said usually carried the day. But in this case, Mum would understand about Jude. And she wouldn't see danger where there wasn't any. Ghosts wouldn't faze Mum.

~ * ~

"It seems to me there is a discrepancy, as we thought," Theo observed as Jeremy followed him into the house.

"Lorna's fine with us measuring in her room. It won't take long, will it? Because apparently Jude wants to talk to me. That might be important for Jude, as well as for our investigations."

Theo led the way into the bedroom, and Jeremy felt the sudden drop in temperature—a penetrating cold even in the warmth of the early summer day, not just because he was in a stone building and the room faced north, but with that particular coldness he knew from the past indicated some spiritual disturbance. He shivered.

Theo, apparently impervious to the ambience of the room, was wielding the long measuring tape. "Take this end, will you, Remy? Let's see what we've got."

Jeremy read off the measurement from the side wall to the chimney breast, and Theo wrote it down. They looked at each other.

"Either there's a space at your end," said Jeremy. "Or it's in the chimney breast."

"A false chimney?"

"I think that would be too obvious. Searchers would notice if the fireplace didn't work. And isn't this the chimney that runs up between the old hall and the kitchen?"

"It's a double chimney," Theo told him. "Open both sides, though we rarely use either of them. But if the priest hole is here, it couldn't be actually in the chimney. Your priest would be in deadly danger every time a fire was lit in the hall below."

"If the hiding place was built into the house," suggested Jeremy, "perhaps the chimney breast is just deeper than it needed to be."

He tapped the wall gently, listening for any change in the sound. If there were a wooden panel, the sound of his tapping knuckle would be quite different. But the sound was what you'd expect of a stone wall, which was interesting. Most seventeenth-century builders lined the walls with wooden panelling for insulation as well as decoration, often making the rooms dark. "Was there originally panelling in this room?"

"Quite likely, I should think. But it was probably all stripped off in the nineteenth century when there was a lot of building work done, around the time when the family built on the main wing, and the wall was re-plastered. The original builders must have thought up some way to hide the fugitive more securely than just to cover the priest hole with a panel, even if they'd then decorated it to look like a wall."

Jeremy nodded. There had probably been a lot of wall-tapping when the soldiers were searching for a priest hole. He supposed even Elizabethan soldiers would be wise to that one.

"In fact..." began Theo, and stopped.

Jeremy looked at him. "In fact, what?"

"Well, I think it works against the idea of the priest hole being here, really. In the seventeenth century, the old hall was open right up into the roof, which sloped down a long way on each side, as it does still. There was a gallery around it, possibly somewhere for musicians to play when the family were dining—though I expect they just hired them for special occasions. The Tresaynes weren't grand enough to employ minstrels on a permanent basis."

"So when did these rooms get built?"

"That's the odd thing. This room was created at gallery level during the alterations made in the late seventeenth century. But

Olivia's set of rooms, on the other side, weren't built until the early nineteen-seventies."

"So do we think the priest hole was in place in the original house?"

"It seems likely, doesn't it? Later on it wouldn't have been needed, surely. Most priest holes were in use early in the Jacobean period, not later."

Jeremy thought about this. "I think we've done all we can this morning. I'd better go and talk to Jude. But I don't think it all was just imagination. What troubles me is that Jude is still hearing these voices even from the room downstairs."

Theo looked worried. "Maybe she shouldn't be sleeping there either. It's still in the old part of the house. I'll talk to Jeannette. I'm sorry, Remy. I had no idea there could be a problem. I haven't been in this room for years, and whatever Olivia is saying now, she never mentioned hearing anything when she was living at home."

"Lorna has to go back to Oxford with the others, anyway. Liz wants them all home as soon as possible. We had a talk last night, and I don't think I can oppose her in this. I've told Lorna, but she doesn't want to leave Jude. Anyway, one way or another, they won't be with you much longer. We must find somewhere else for Jude to go, though how we're to do that in the present circumstances I don't know."

"I'll talk to Jeannette," Theo repeated. "You go and speak to Jude."

Tresayne House, Thursday February 10th 1916

I will meet my parishioners on Sunday when I take my first communion service after my inauguration. But already my churchwarden and his wife have called and made me welcome. There are not many great houses in the district where I may find friends of my own class, but to be truthful (which I seek to be in this journal, however much I may dissemble in company) I do not feel the need of such companionship. At present, much of what I feel is loss and longing. Osborne House, with the sea so close and the fresh breezes of the north coast ever present, was my home from childhood, and I miss it here among the river mists and the cloud hanging over the moorland that I can see from my bedroom window. The chill is more penetrating than I expected, and this old stone house seems never warm, although I have insisted that fires are kept burning in my study and bedroom to try to banish the damp and cold at least from where I work and sleep.

All this I could bear if the loss of my childhood home and comforts were all. But it is not. Of course it is not. However warm and comfortable the house was, it would seem desolate because Mary is not here. Although at Osborne House I did not always see her during the day, for she was busy about her housemaid tasks, and we dared not have much contact in front of others, at any moment I might pass her in the corridor, or catch sight of her through an open door. And at night, she came as often as she could and brought my body ecstasy and my heart an overflowing joy. Now there is nothing, and it is a more profound emptiness even than I expected.

My servants here are still shadowy characters whose names I barely know, and whose attributes I have yet to discover. I have no family to share my life. Oh Mary, was I wrong to leave you behind when you begged me to bring you with me? What have I done?

Sixteen

That evening, Jeremy confided the whole situation to Liz. If ever he'd needed counsel, he did now, and she was the only person he trusted to listen, and quite possibly to come up with some insight he had failed to find. It would not be the first time.

"So you see," he concluded, "we have a real problem on our hands. What to do with Jude, or *for* him, and how to resolve the issue of the priest hole, and whatever happened there. We can't just leave that now, even if the manifestations stop when Jude goes elsewhere, because Theo and Jeannette will always know there's a possibility they may return. And if I'm not much mistaken, Olivia has some fear of that room, however much she has hidden it."

There was a pause while Liz thought about this. "I see what you mean. But that's your job, Remy. Concentrated prayer, or something. I don't suppose you can enlist the local clergy? Or the diocese must have an exorcist, presumably."

"They call it deliverance ministry now, Liz. Truro will have someone competent, I'm sure. But I expect it all has to be arranged through the local incumbent, and whether anything can be done at the moment I doubt."

"I suppose they've gone all psychological about things like demon possession these days," observed Liz. "Probably a good thing in general."

"I agree. But not everything can be explained in scientific and medical terms. Sometimes prayer is the only way, and this isn't about demon possession anyway. Something really dreadful has happened in that house, Liz. I can feel it. Even walking up the drive I was conscious of it, before I ever went inside, even before I learned about the family history. Jude seems somehow to have disturbed the memory of it, and it has to be dealt with."

"M'm."

Jeremy could hear the scepticism in his wife's voice. She was a convinced and committed Christian and had always supported him in his ministry. But when he ventured into the byways of telepathy or spiritual deliverance, he had to proceed alone. She simply couldn't follow him, though she respected his sensitivity to the supernatural and tried to take account of it.

"Well, I think I can help you with Jude," she volunteered. "That can be my part in this."

Jeremy frowned. "How do you mean?"

"We've agreed the children should come home."

"Lorna isn't very happy about that. She asked me if you'd let her stay—she said all kinds of things about Mike always being the one to help me with mysteries and it was her turn. Plus, she doesn't want to leave Jude."

He heard her sigh. "Mike's the eldest, but I suppose that shouldn't really matter. I don't want either of them mixed up with whatever it is you're dealing with, Jeremy. I had quite enough of that when it was Whitehill Abbey and their librarian—the Polish one."

"Yes, I see what you mean. But I didn't mean to involve Mike in that, you know. You could say he involved himself."

"And had to be rescued," she reminded him sharply. "Anyway, let's leave that. My suggestion is, why not invite Jude to come back here with our kids? He's been staying with Lorna at Tresayne, so there's no question of Covid infection, and these pesky restrictions allow you to change household for your own safety, anyway. Social services won't be able to do anything for him at the moment except put him in a children's home—and I'm not sure they'll even do that. Send him to us, if he'd like to come, and we'll sort it all out officially later. He must be at an age when he can leave home if he wants to."

"What about his sister? Lorna seems to feel Jude shouldn't leave his little sister behind to deal with whatever's going on—especially if there's some possibility their father is sexually abusing her."

"I can see what she means. But what does Jude feel?"

"According to Lorna, if the father is arrested, then mother and sister won't be able to cope with the farm by themselves, so it would just be exchanging one problem for another. And Jude himself refuses to go back there whatever happens. It isn't what he wants for either himself or Megan."

"Maybe that is something that's going to have to wait until the restrictions lift. I can't really see we're going to help by getting involved. Megan is too young and the law won't be on our side if you go muscling in without authority, however tempting that is. It would be different if Megan had run away as well."

"Yes, I think you're right. It's hard, though, and I can understand why Lorna is unhappy about it."

"Send them all back here, and I'll see what I can do to persuade them we've done the right thing. I think we've fundamentally got to go with Jude's wishes. He obviously needs to escape from the situation completely, and if he moves to Oxford, we can get him into school here, or maybe find an apprenticeship."

"He's a farm boy," Jeremy reminded her. "I'm not sure he'll want an apprenticeship or a home in the city."

"Invite him, anyway. Then we'll decide what to do. When he's ready, I can ask Diane to examine him, and we can consult confidentially with Mitch too, if we want."

"That's a good idea." Diane was a doctor, and Mitch a police officer—and they were both members of the Swansons' local church in South Oxford. They were to be trusted and would not hesitate to help.

"But get on with it, Remy," added Liz. "Our children need to come home."

~ * ~

"Did you ever hear anything untoward from that room?" Jeannette asked her daughter, as she passed her a cup of tea. It must seem a strange thing to ask out of the blue, she realised, but she had only just remembered Jeremy's request for the information. "You said—when we talked about it with Jude at breakfast yesterday—you'd always thought there was something odd about the room, but not whether you'd actually heard this wailing that Jude speaks of."

They were sitting in the garden, under the copper beech tree on the lawn, as on the day she had first met Jeremy and Mike. How long ago that seemed, though in truth it was only a few weeks. The weather had turned cooler and more showery, but they were expecting Jeremy to join them at any moment, and it was still warm enough to be sitting outside. Jeannette was determined to keep to the lockdown rules wherever she could, and even entertaining someone from another household in the garden was pushing the boundaries. But the garden was so large that it was, she supposed, as big as some small town parks; and the main point about the Rule of Six was that they were to be outside, where scientists had decided the risk of infection was much less. She knew Theo had invited Jeremy inside earlier when they were investigating the dimensions of the room where Lorna was staying, though she disapproved of it. Still, Jeremy and the children were arguably almost part of their household, they had met so often, and had been in self-isolation at the same time after their contact with Clive, so perhaps it was all right, even if technically against the rules. In Wales, she had heard, two households were now allowed to link for socialising, even though other regulations were stricter there. A very good idea, she thought. Better than the support bubbles that had recently been announced for the benefit of single people.

She became aware that Olivia had not replied to her question. "Olivia?"

"I'm not sure. Is Remy coming over to discuss all this? Because if he is, I'd rather talk about it when we're all here."

"He should be here in a minute. He phoned to say he had news about the children going back to Oxford. Could you go and give Theo a shout? He's in the house somewhere."

"Prowling about in that room next to mine, the last I saw him."

"Jeremy and he were measuring it yesterday. I suppose they are working on the theory that the priest hole is in that room."

"Do you really not know where it is, Mother? Surely Great-grandma must have said something."

"I honestly don't think she did. I've been trying to remember."

"Didn't you ever wonder about it yourself?"

Jeannette pondered. "Something was said about a priest hole once, when I was at school, I think. There was a TV researcher going round Cornwall finding out about them for a BBC programme. But my parents told her they didn't know where ours was, so that came to nothing. The twin room was my bedroom for a few years, when I was small, before my parents built your bedroom and sitting room for my grandmother, but I didn't notice anything. I'm sure my grandmother didn't mention it. But then, why should she?"

She thought about all the years she'd lived in the house, at first sleeping in the dressing room off her parents' bedroom, then in the north-facing room, until the other bedrooms had been built above the old hall for her grandmother to use as a suite, and she had been able to move into the small bedroom above the kitchen that was now her sewing room. The room was certainly cold and looked out only onto the yard, and she had been glad to move out of it again when the new rooms were built, but there had never been anything creepy about it that she recalled. Even now, she didn't feel the frisson there that others seemed to. Perhaps, as she'd said to Jeremy earlier, she just didn't have the capacity to sense these things. After all, Lorna seemed not to have experienced anything either.

Memory took her onwards. In her twenties, after going away to university, she had returned to Tresayne. Her parents decided to retire to a cottage they'd bought years before on the south coast, so Olivia's father, James, whom Jeannette had met at university, joined her, and they settled at Tresayne together. Happy years, those had been to begin with, before disillusion set in and betrayal parted them. She had never given the priest hole a thought, either then or since, until Jude came to confront them all with the problem. The hiding place was simply a part of the house's long history, closed up, or even lost perhaps when the Victorian wing was built. She had never expected to give it any consideration again, never mind be actively trying to find it. In any case, she was still not convinced that the house had anything to do with Jude's troubles. That was another dilemma—poor girl, what were they to do about her when Lorna went home?

"Mrs Landry." It was Lorna, who had crossed the lawn from the house while she was lost in thought. "Do you mind if Jude and I go out for a walk?"

She turned to the girl, smiling. "No, of course not. Anywhere nice?"

"Not sure yet. But it's the first time Jude has wanted to go out, so I thought it would be good to go along with the idea. We won't go far, I expect."

"You can have a cup of tea when you come back if you'd like to. I can always make some fresh."

"Thanks." Lorna hesitated. "Tell Dad we'd like to see him when we come back, before he goes back to the cottage."

"I'll do that. He said he had some news about you all going back to Oxford, so I'm sure he'll want to see you anyway." Was it her imagination, or did Lorna look wary all of a sudden? "We'll see you later. Have fun on your walk."

~ * ~

"She's hiding something," said Olivia, when the two teenagers had run off down the drive together.

Jeannette stared at her. "Why on earth do you say that?"

"I don't know. I'll bet you she is, though."

"Olivia!" exclaimed Jeannette in exasperation. "You're so hard on those two girls. It's clear you don't want Lorna here, or Jude for that matter. Have you no compassion?"

"The truth is, Mother, you're a pushover. What do we really know about Jude, or her situation? Why on earth should we breaking all the Covid rules—and probably the law about care for minors as well—to have her staying here, not to mention Remy 'investigating' these sounds Jude says she hears at night? We only have her word for it, after all."

"Which brings us back to the question I asked you about whether you'd ever heard anything from that room. Remy said we needed to know, but I wish he'd just asked you himself. I might have known you'd be difficult about it if I broached the subject with you."

"Did I hear my name mentioned?"

Jeannette turned to find Jeremy half-way up the drive, already within earshot. He had clearly heard at least some of her exchange with her daughter, but she decided to react as though he had not, which was her preferred response to such situations. It would be embarrassing to acknowledge, and impossible to explain.

"You certainly did," she replied, smiling. "I was just asking Olivia whether she'd ever heard anything untoward from that bedroom you are investigating, but it seems she didn't. Or at least, she's suggesting Jude is making it all up."

Jeremy looked at Olivia. "Is that correct? You know, I had the feeling that you'd heard, or sensed, something."

"It's... it's so nebulous," she answered after a moment. "I've never liked going in there—that room has a sort of cold unhappy feeling about it—but how subjective that is! I can't really give you anything concrete to back it up. Occasionally, I've thought I might have heard weird sounds, but it was always a bit vague, so I've told myself it must just be the wind, which really does make strange noises round that corner of the house sometimes. I never said anything to anyone because there wasn't really anything to tell. If all this hadn't happened, I wouldn't have thought any more about it. I don't really believe in ghosts, or the paranormal. Could Jude just be being neurotic?"

"Yes, that's possible. But I myself can also sense something spiritually troubled in that room, and I would take that seriously, even if it's a memory, like a footprint, left from some trauma of the past. If so, I suspect that whatever happened was probably something very nasty."

He paused, but neither Jeannette nor Olivia said anything.

He looked at Jeannette. "Do you really not know of anything traumatic in the house's history? I'm not accusing you of holding anything back, it's just that you maybe didn't take much notice when you were told about it, whatever it was."

"I couldn't forget anything that bad, could I? But I don't know a great deal of the house's history—even my knowledge of the family is a tad sketchy, as I told you. My grandmother talked a great deal about the garden, but I think her memories of her family were painful, and she avoided speaking of them very much." She hesitated. "If anyone would haunt this house, I should think it would be my poor great-grandmother, who lost three sons within two years during the First World War. But why she should start doing so now..."

She got up. "Where is Theo? He knows far more about the house than I do, and he's got all the records and the family papers.

Perhaps there's something in those that would be helpful." She set off for the house, leaving Jeremy with Olivia.

~ * ~

Meet us on Ridge, by the cattle-grid, said the text from Lorna. *Bring the car and the dogs—and the twins if you have to.*

Mike frowned. What on earth was she up to now? His sister was getting out of hand, that was the trouble. And what did she mean by "if you have to"? Dad had gone over to Tresayne House, and he, Mike, was on twin duty, as he couldn't help feeling he had been far too often lately, when he would have liked to join his father in investigating the priest hole instead. He had developed his own theory about where it might be found, and thought Jeremy and Theo were taking Jude's 'hearings' too literally. It seemed to him that a priest hole would be more likely to be downstairs, possibly with access to the garden, so a hidden priest could escape more easily. He hadn't been inside the house yet, but possibly the Victorian builders, knowingly or not, had covered the entrance up when they constructed the front wing along the wall of the old kitchen and hall.

Oh well. He'd better go and meet Lorna and see what was going on. She might need help, he thought suddenly. Rescuing, even. His eyes brightened at the idea. Where were those twins?

"Chris! Beth!" he shouted up the stairs. "We're going out for a bit. Get your shoes on. Quick!"

Tresayne House, Tuesday, February 15th, 1916

I have had a letter from Maudie. From what she says, I think Mother is being impossible. Maudie is continuing to describe herself as engaged to be married, although Mother insists nothing is to be decided until after the War. Gerald is now a first lieutenant and seems much respected by his colleagues in the battalion, and I think Freddie has always been pleasant to him anyway for Maudie's sake. But Freddie is always careless of keeping up appearances socially, and I believe he turned a blind eye to Maudie's friendship with Gerald from the beginning. He knew about it before anyone else, Maudie says, even before Gerald joined the Duke of Cornwall's this time last year. None of this makes Mother able to accept Gerald as Maudie's fiancé, however, and I think it will be a long time until she feels she can. I have written back to Maudie encouraging her to wait and be patient. It will not achieve anything to quarrel with Mother about it. Perhaps, as head of the family now that Lionel is gone, my word may carry some weight?

I wonder whether Gerald and Maudie... No, this is something I should not speculate about. The thought of them lying together revolts me, though I am a hypocrite to feel so. Perhaps they would be as loving together as Mary and I were, though Maudie has never struck me as a passionate woman. She is steadfast, however. She will not give Gerald up as I have felt I must give Mary up.

But what if she is right, and I am wrong?

Seventeen

Lorna and Jude were hiding on the nearer side of the cattle grid, among the trees.

"Dad never comes over the grid unless he'm going out somewhere off the moor," Jude had said. "All our grazing land be on the moor, see, and if the animals need any care, then that's where he'll be to. The farm's further up the hill, so we'll be safe enough in the woods."

It had taken them more than half-an-hour to reach this spot on foot, and Lorna had texted Mike soon after they set out, so she hoped he would not be long in joining them. She didn't like to think what might happen if Jude's father saw them, whatever Jude might say about the unlikelihood of this as long as they were this side of the cattle-grid. He might frogmarch Jude away, and there would be nothing at all she could do about it. Not only would Mike's presence be a comfort in the circumstances, but the car was really necessary for their idea to work. Mike wouldn't like the plan, she knew, but she was confident that she could talk him round. He usually welcomed adventure, and lockdown restrictions had precluded anything but the most mundane activity for weeks. He would be ready to take his part in this.

She spotted the family car nosing its way slowly up the steep lane and stepped out of the woodland to signal. Mike stopped, and she opened the back door of the car for Jude to get in next to the twins, then hopped smartly into the front passenger seat beside Mike. He set the car in motion again, still slowly, as they climbed higher, while on their right the open moor rose in a wide green swathe, pockmarked with great stone outcrops, against a vast blue sky barred with cirrus clouds.

"Thanks, Mike." She felt slightly breathless, as though she'd been running, when all she had done for the last ten minutes or so was stand in the woodland waiting.

"So what's the plan? Something impulsive, I'm guessing. I hope not dangerous, too?"

"Not really. Just I haven't seen you in the last couple of days, and I haven't been able to be sure of getting you on your own even for a phone call. Jude and I have been planning this since yesterday, when we got the text from Megan, Jude's sister."

"And what exactly have you been planning? Jude's home is up here somewhere, isn't it? You aren't going to beard her father in his den or anything, I hope?"

"I wouldn't dare. No, like I said, it's Megan." She explained briefly why Jude's sister needed rescuing, and Mike's eyebrows rose to meet his hairline.

"Jeez. Are you sure about this? Sounds a bit risky to me. I suppose that's why you wanted me to bring a getaway car. But what are you going to do with her, even if you rescue her?" He wondered briefly what the twins would be making of this tale of sexual abuse, but it was too late to worry about that now. Lorna had spilled the beans, and he'd have to leave any fallout to Mum to sort out when they got home.

"Jude is going to text Megan to slip out and meet us, and then we'll hide her in the car and drive away." It did sound a bit mad, when she described it to Mike, but Jude had been sure they could do it.

"I can see why you want to rescue your sister, Jude," said Mike, meeting Jude's eyes briefly in the driving mirror as he spoke. "But are you sure she wants to be rescued? It'll mean leaving your mum, too. Will she be willing to stay on her own?"

"I had a text from Megan." Jude's voice was gruff. "I've sent her one or two messages, just so's she'd know I be safe. Yesterday she said Dad had been pestering round her again, and Mum was out of it with the drink. She asked if she could come and join me. Lorna said I couldn't leave her here and go to Oxford without her, and she's right. I cann't. Not now she's asked us to help her. So we thought this'd be the best way."

Mike drove past the farm and up on to the edge of Twelve Men's Moor. "Where on earth can we stop? We'll stick out like a sore thumb up here."

"No, we won't," averred Lorna confidently. "The twins and I are going to pretend we're out walking our dogs, like local people do. Jude will stay here in the car and text me when Megan comes out. Then you drive them back along the lane, and the twins and I will walk down with the dogs and meet you at the Trebartha crossroads. You can wait there, and no one will think anything of it. Or park at the other end of Trebartha village, where the track to West Castick goes off, if you like."

"No one will think anything of a car parked at the crossroads," Jude corroborated. "We'll be quite safe."

"If Jude's father does follow you," added Lorna, keen to show Mike that she and Jude had planned for all eventualities, "you drive on to Tresayne. He won't dare go there, I shouldn't think."

Mike had parked by the side of the road, out of sight of the farm. "I'm not sure about this, Lorna. Jude escaping is one thing. She's of an age to make up her own mind. But Megan is still a child, and you're taking her away from her legal guardians."

"If the police come, I'll tell them everything," Jude told him. "My parents bain't fit to look after a child."

"But what then?" persisted Mike, struggling with all the implications and wishing his father were there to back him up. "Won't Megan be put in care? I mean, even in lockdown there must be children's homes operating, and social services...."

"Mum will let us take Megan to Oxford," Lorna interrupted firmly. "Bethan and Chris are going to have their own rooms when we get home, and Bethan will share with Megan, won't you, Beth?"

"Yes," responded Bethan, clearly stirred by the story she had heard about Megan's situation. "We can put another bed in for her—my room's big enough for that."

Mike smiled. *Clever Lorna.* She knew Bethan wanted to stay in the twins' existing bedroom, which would mean Chris would have to sleep in the attic box room. The twins had been arguing over it for weeks, an unusual occurrence in their childhood, but now that they were growing up such altercations were becoming more frequent, and the twin-bond between them was only to be seen when they had to present a united front towards others. The presence of Megan would ensure that Beth would get her way, and Lorna had obviously calculated that it would be worth it to Beth to agree to sharing with Megan. What Mum would say about the plan was not so certain.

"Have you even *asked* Mum?"

"Let's rescue Megan first, and then we'll talk to Mum. She offered to have Jude, after all."

A *fait accompli.* "Well, rather you than me."

Lorna lifted her chin in determination. "We'll make it work. I know we will. Mum won't turn away someone in real need, like this. She's a teacher. Come on, Mike. We need to get on."

She pushed open the passenger door and got out, then let the dogs out of the back of the car. "Hurry up, you two. Let's get going."

Unwontedly obedient, clearly imbued with the spirit of adventure, the twins climbed out of the car and set off across the moor, following the dogs.

"Text me the minute you see Megan," Lorna reminded Jude. "And don't hang around waiting for us, Mike."

Her brother was silent. He was far from happy with the situation, but clearly Lorna had the bit between her teeth and there was nothing he could do but go with her plans and hope to pick up the pieces later.

~ * ~

Olivia and Jeremy sat together in silence for a few moments after Jeannette had gone. Then Olivia said, "Have you heard anything about Clive?"

"No. And I don't expect to if I'm honest. We only heard he had Covid because we all had to self-isolate. Derriford aren't going to give us any information about how he is, I'm afraid."

"I suppose you're right." She hesitated. "Remy, you know, don't you, that Clive and I... once worked together?"

"Yes. I was Rose's parish priest, remember. And my wife Liz is a close friend of hers."

Olivia looked at the rough grass beneath the tree intently, as though counting every blade, but in fact she saw nothing. She knew only too well in what light she must have appeared to Jeremy, if Rose had been the sole source of his information. "I regret what happened, now."

"With Clive?"

"Yes. He was a rotten boss, you know, driven and disloyal, and although I managed his diary and kept up with the office side of things all right, I can see our relationship outside of working hours was toxic. I didn't realise at the time—I suppose I thought having an affair with him was a way to manage him; I'd done it before, with other men in powerful positions. But when we were an item, which was mostly on working trips, it was a two-way thing. I guess you could say we used each other. But I wasn't married, and he was. I'm not sure whether that makes me more to blame, or less."

"It probably isn't all that helpful to apportion blame," Jeremy suggested. She looked up and found he was smiling at her kindly.

"I did a lot of harm to Rose." It was a painful admission, and Olivia couldn't understand why she was making it. But something in Jeremy's reaction to what she had said was prompting unwonted honesty.

"On the other hand," Jeremy pointed out fairly, "Rose's reaction to Clive's adultery led her to find someone else to love, and she has been very much happier for it. I don't think you should feel too bad about Rose."

"She wasn't the first, though. I don't know how much damage I'd done to others before her. I remember having a kind of regime of keeping my bosses' wives in their place, especially when I was screwing their men on the side—one at a time, don't get me wrong. I didn't sleep around." She was silent for a moment. "But I despised the wives, generally. I'm not sure why."

"Because you didn't want to be one, perhaps?"

"I was a career woman, certainly, though I think I always knew those hothouse affairs that seem to bedevil office life weren't going to satisfy me in the end." She sighed. "I don't seem to have the knack of loving someone properly. It was all sex and power games to me. But I don't suppose you'd know about that kind of affair, would you?"

"No, not really, I'm afraid. For one thing, I've never worked in an office—I was a scientist before I was a clergyman. And though I haven't forgotten what it was like to be young, I met Liz in my early twenties, and after that there was never anyone else for me."

"You're lucky." She heard the wistful note in her voice and felt suddenly angry with him. "I didn't mean this to be a confession!" she stormed at him. "You don't know anything about why I behaved as I did. Just because you've come here and got to know my parents..."

"I'm not judging you. And I didn't ask you to tell me anything, you know."

She felt both soothed and rebuked at the same time, an odd sensation. And what he said was true. She had volunteered the confidence. She shouldn't complain that he couldn't enter into her experience.

Beside him on the garden table, Jeremy's phone began to ring. He picked it up and looked at the screen. "Would you mind if I take this?"

"Of course not." She got up, checking her phone was in her pocket. She would go to her room and leave him to take his call in peace.

"Wait a minute, Olivia," Jeremy said, as she turned to go. "It's Liz, and she has news about Clive I think you'll want to hear."

Baffled, Olivia sat down again. How on earth would Jeremy's wife know anything about Clive? Then she remembered. Liz was a friend of Rose, Clive's wife.

"Thanks for letting me know, Liz. I've booked the kids on a train the day after tomorrow. I'll take them up to Exeter and you can meet them at Oxford station, if you're happy for them to do the change at Reading on their own. I'm sure they'll be okay, yes."

He put the phone down and looked across at Olivia. "It's bad news, I'm afraid. Derriford phoned Rose this morning to say Clive is on a ventilator and it's touch and go whether he'll live."

Olivia put her hand to her mouth. Her heart was beating faster, with a painful squeezing motion. "How awful," she managed to say.

Jeremy nodded, his eyes full of sympathy. "He's the first person I've known who's been hospitalised with the virus."

She took a deep breath, pushing the emotion away. "I don't know why I feel so upset. Honestly, Clive isn't anything to me now. Though something about the wreck he was when we found him in that cave... that did disturb me. Clive used to be one of the ruthless ones, the men who got what they wanted, who seemed to be able to brush off any difficulties, whatever they were, and whoever he damaged in the process. You didn't mess with Clive. But he'd started to lose it even before we split."

She wasn't being entirely honest with Jeremy. The truth was that Clive had rejected her because she'd wanted to get closer, because she'd expected him to leave Rose for her. He had done the dumping. There had been nothing amicable about it. Indeed, she had been very angry at the time. But she didn't want to share that with Jeremy. "I left the company and went elsewhere, after that, but I felt Clive was… diminished, somehow. It wasn't to do with Rose, I don't think. Wasn't there something about his son disappearing?"

Jeremy nodded. "That's right. But in fact Robert turned up safe and sound."

"Clive wasn't the same afterwards, even so. He had weeks off work, and when he came back, he just wasn't functioning. It bothered me. I'd thought of him as invincible, and suddenly… he wasn't."

"You were worried that something similar might happen to you."

"I guess that's true." She wasn't going to admit him to her present soul-searching about where her career should go after lockdown, and whether she would ever find a more permanent relationship. The man saw too damned much already. With relief, she saw her mother and Theo approaching. She had had enough of this tête à tête with Jeremy.

~ * ~

Marcus dug his suitcase out of the cupboard and put it on the bed. It was quite a large suitcase, but the only other option was the backpack he'd taken to Asia on his gap year, nearly twenty years ago. The suitcase had four wheels and was designed to trail through airports and up cruise liner gangplanks behind its owner. A holiday suitcase with locks. It would have to do.

It was several days before he was due to drive to Cornwall, but packing would give him something to do, and there was little else demanding his attention. He opened the case and put in a couple of pairs of jeans and a lightweight suit. Would he need the suit?

Presumably they would be staying close to home, perhaps going to a pub occasionally, or doing a bit of shopping. But Cornwall was a very rural place, and the house was a long way from Truro and Plymouth. The government were still encouraging everyone to stay at home as much as possible. Even by travelling to stay with them, he was possibly contravening the spirit, if not the letter, of the current regulations. But the invitation had been sent and accepted and nothing would stop him taking it up. No date had been suggested for him to return home, so it could be thought of as a change of household. But how long did he want to stay, anyway? There was always the possibility that it might be a disaster, this attempt to rebuild a relationship with his father and his new family.

He decided to pack enough clothes for a week, and include plenty of underclothes, in case his visit was successful, and he wanted to stay longer. And several extra shirts. He would hate to have to ask Jeannette if he could use the washing machine. But he didn't want to stay forever. The flat was his home, and however well he got on with the folk at Tresayne, he would be coming back here.

He thought about them for a minute. Both Jeannette's letter and Theo's email had welcomed him unreservedly. But what about Olivia? She had, he knew, been adopted by Theo when he married Jeannette. Theo had written to him and Debs at the time, although they hadn't been invited to the wedding—that would have been too much for Mum to take. So Olivia wasn't a stepsister so much as a sister, legally at least. When the adoption went through, Theo had told his children he'd altered his will and Olivia would inherit a share of his estate along with them. Marcus had resented this at the time, especially as presumably Olivia was her mother's heir as well, but he no longer did. His mother had quite deliberately prevented Theo from having any contact with his natural children, he saw that now. It was hardly surprising he'd wanted to adopt Olivia as his own, in their absence.

He wondered what she was like, this younger sister of his that he had never met—a grown woman who had no blood relationship with him, but whom Theo clearly loved as a daughter. And what did she think about his re-entering her adopted father's life at this point? It would be interesting to find out.

Tresayne House, Friday 18th February 1916

Freddie, I'm glad to say, has received my new address. In his latest letter, he tells me the brigades and divisions at the front have been reorganised, but this doesn't seem to have made much difference to his battalion, because they are part of the 95th brigade, which has stayed with the 5th Division in France. I'm sure Mother would have preferred it if that were not so. Freddie would be safer going off to Italy, as Gerald, in the 2nd battalion, has done.

Most of his letter was about the frivolity they enjoyed at Christmas, which seems to have included getting drunk illicitly with the 1st Devonshires, who are in the same sector, though more recently the battalion have clearly also spent some time in the front line trenches being shelled. He seems to be positively enjoying the experience of crawling through No Man's Land to throw bombs into enemy trenches, which sounds horribly dangerous to me. But he was always a bit of a daredevil. He makes light of the horrors I know he must have seen, even in a fairly quiet sector. But that's his way. Perhaps when I see him, he will share more.

It seems he may be able to take some leave soon, as everything is quiet at the Front for the moment. I hope he will have time to come down here—it will take him long enough to get across to North Devon from Southampton, and I can hardly leave my parish to go up to see him, so soon after arriving here. Still, a visit from Freddie will be a comfort to Mother, who seemed very unhappy to let me go when I set off for Cornwall, rather to my surprise. She is clearly still suffering from the loss of Lionel. Time does not seem to ease her distress, in spite of all her work at the hospital with Maudie. But perhaps, in the end, that work will help and distract her.

As for me, I have not yet grown accustomed to my own loneliness. During the day I can keep my sense of loss at bay, as I busy myself with settling into my new home and riding around the district learning the bounds of my parish and the temper of my parishioners. But at night... Oh, Mary. That is when I miss you most.

Eighteen

Mike sat uncomfortably at the wheel of the car, watching Jude approach the farmhouse cautiously. When she reached the outside wall of the yard, she ducked down, out of sight, and he spent an anxious couple of minutes wondering where she had gone. Then she emerged again, with a smaller figure beside her. So Megan had avoided surveillance long enough to escape. Awful to think of having to run away from home like that, as though the farmhouse were a prison from which the two youngsters had fled. But how else was one to see it, given the circumstances?

He turned the key in the ignition and sat gently revving the old engine as Jude and Megan ran towards him, Megan with a light backpack over her shoulder. They slid into the seat behind him and pulled the door closed as he set the car in motion down the hill. A quick glance in the rear-view mirror reassured him there was no pursuit. Trying to resist the temptation to gun the engine and get away as fast as possible, he kept the car in low gear as he drove down the slope to the cattle grid and into the woods. It was a narrow winding road, and steep, and he didn't dare pick up speed yet, but he saw no sign that anyone was following him. No other vehicles had been parked at the side of the road, and he'd seen no one else out with dogs apart from Lorna and the twins, who must by now be somewhere on their way down on foot, so any vehicle that followed him would probably have come from the farm.

He heard a sound from the back seat and saw in the mirror that Megan had buried her head in her arms, her shoulders shaking with sobs. Jude was patting her on the back gently, trying to soothe her. Poor kid. She hadn't brought much in the backpack, by the look of it. She must have left home with virtually nothing. But there was nothing he could say or do, except help them both to safety.

Down at the crossroads, he pulled in at the side of the road, with the nose of the car turned towards Tresayne. He switched off the engine and sat half-turned in his seat, watching for anything—vehicle or pedestrian—approaching the junction. It would be a while before the others could catch up; meanwhile, he was worried Megan's father might discover her disappearance, or even see Lorna and the twins walking along the edge of the moor. He wished he hadn't had to leave them behind so near the farm, hostages to any hostile action the farmer might decide upon. He could only hope their youth and the presence of the two dogs would protect them. Jude's father had never met Lorna, so surely she and the twins wouldn't come under suspicion? That had been Lorna's assumption, but she wasn't as street-wise as she thought she was, and he wouldn't be happy until the three of them came back safe and sound. God! What would Mum and Dad say if they found he'd taken the kids into danger?

To his relief, at that moment he caught sight of Lorna and the twins coming at speed up the incline as the lane approached the crossroads. But the relief was short-lived. Why were they running? They stopped at the crossroads, and there seemed to be a brief discussion, before the twins, each with a dog on its lead, set off down the lane towards Tresayne.

Lorna turned and hurried over to the car. "Don't get out!" she shouted to Mike, as he opened the driver's door. "There's a farm vehicle after us. Just drive. Away from Tresayne—we mustn't lead them there."

She ran round to the passenger side of the car and climbed in, just as a big SUV nosed its way up to the crossroads.

Mike started the engine, his foot on the clutch to engage gear as quickly as possible. "Where are we going?" he asked, deciding it was best to wait for an explanation until the immediate crisis, whatever it was, was over.

"That's Dad!" came a muttered exclamation from Jude in the back of the car.

"Don't go to the cottage or Tresayne," Lorna said again. "He might follow us."

Mike pulled out in front of the SUV and took the turn for Congdons Shop. He hadn't done a lot of driving around the area, except to accompany his father into Launceston occasionally for groceries, but he and Jeremy had walked miles with the dogs. He reckoned he knew the back lanes pretty well.

"He's following us," Lorna reported. "Jude and Megan, keep your heads down. He mustn't know you're in the car."

"I think he saw me," faltered Megan. "Just now."

"Keep your heads down, anyway," Mike told her. "And hold on. I'm going to try to lose him."

~ * ~

Jeremy waited quietly while Theo and Jeannette sat down together on the bench under the tree. He hoped Theo was going to have something useful to contribute to the problem of the priest hole and whether it had anything to do with the mystery they were trying to solve. He was finding it unusually difficult to focus on logical deduction. On the one hand, he was acutely conscious of Olivia's inner conflict, and unhappy that he had been unable to do anything to help. On the other, he was aware of grave psychological trauma in Jude; although pastoral listening was part of a clergyman's training, more professional counselling seemed almost certain to be required, and how were they to access that in the midst of a pandemic? Added to his own deep sorrow and angst about the suffering that in his view was only just beginning to make itself felt across the globe, it all seemed rather overwhelming. Yet he could see that Jeannette, at least, was relying on him to find a way through the thicket.

"I've brought my notes." Theo laid a cardboard folder on the wooden table beside him. "What is it you think might be useful information, Remy?"

Jeremy considered. "What materials have you got? Is it letters? Diaries?"

"Both. And less personal stuff, too, like building plans for the Victorian extensions and the twentieth-century bedrooms above the old hall, and layouts for the development of the gardens."

"I remember my mother showing me those," Jeannette put in. "Not all their plans were put into effect, partly because of the Second War." She smiled briefly. "Gardens take a long time to mature, and in the Second War, like the First, they lost most of their help, and were under pressure to dig large areas of the garden up to grow vegetables as well."

Jeremy was interested. "And did they?"

"My grandmother drew the line at digging up half-matured trees. But the herbaceous borders had to go and be replaced after the War. We fed the local village for years."

"With Land Girls to help grow the veg?"

She nodded. "Exactly. Most of the men came back afterwards, but only one of them decided to stay on as a gardener. The others left Cornwall for work upcountry. That was before I was born, but my father told me a lot about it. Cornwall became even more of a backwater then, with the mines all closed and only the farms and fishing fleets still operating. That was before fishing quotas, and cheap food from abroad. Even the farmers and the fishermen are struggling now."

Perhaps Jeannette was a supporter of Brexit, thought Jeremy, along with many Cornish people who believed their livelihoods had been damaged by competition from their European counterparts. An issue that for many on the Remain side, like himself, was still unresolved, in spite of the recent election victory which Boris Johnson was claiming would settle it once and for all. The pandemic had pulled the two sides together temporarily, and given the government something else to think about, but he wondered how long it would be before the divisions began to tear the country apart again, especially when the full economic fallout of Brexit—along with the pandemic itself—began to bite. He hoped people would not forget too quickly how they had needed each other in these dark days.

"I've found a number of letters from Jeannette's grandfather to her grandmother, mostly while he was on active service," offered Theo. "She must have kept them all, I think, even though he survived the War and came back to her."

"Theirs is a lovely story," Jeannette told him. "Whatever the tragedy that's behind our ghostly wailings—if that's what they are—it has nothing to do with my grandparents. They fell in love when they were teenagers; she was the daughter of the Big House, he one of the under-gardeners, and their commitment to each other eventually overcame parental opposition and disapproval, though they weren't officially engaged until after my great-grandmother died in 1917. My grandfather was in France to begin with, and then went out to the Mediterranean with his regiment, where he saw a lot of heavy fighting, though it wasn't as bad as being in the trenches. He was just an ordinary soldier at the beginning—one of Kitchener's 1915 volunteers, I think, but he was promoted through the ranks and ended the war as a captain. My grandmother was very proud of his war service, I remember."

"After the Tresaynes bought the North Devon mansion in the nineteenth century, this house was used as a rectory by Victorian incumbents of the local parish," Theo went on. "It was a tiny living and can't have paid much in the way of a stipend, but I suppose they had other sources of money. After the First War, the parish was absorbed by North Hill and doesn't exist any longer, but most of the Victorian and Edwardian incumbents were Tresayne family members."

Jeremy smiled. "Those were the days when a career in the Church was what the youngest son of a gentry family was expected to take up, after the eldest had inherited the estate, and the second son had gone in for an Army or Navy career."

"That's true, but ours wasn't a typical family. We were an Indian Army family in the Victorian period," Jeannette explained. "My grandmother was born in India when her father was serving there. The officers were British, and the other ranks were Indian. They took the distinctions very seriously."

Jeremy nodded. "Sounds odd to us now, doesn't it?"

"Yes, very odd. But it seemed quite normal then. My grandmother was sent home with her mother and brother when the children were old enough for prep school, and my great-grandfather came home on leave as often as he could. Which wasn't that often, by all accounts. It wasn't family life as we know it today. He was killed in the Boer War when my grandmother was small, and they stayed on in Devon after that. Maybe I told you that already? I'm sorry—I can't remember what we've discussed and what we haven't."

"It doesn't matter," smiled Jeremy. He thought about what family life at Tresayne House would have been like when Jeannette was young and doubted whether it had much resembled his and Liz's experience, with four children tumbling around an oversized Victorian rectory in Hampshire, when time for themselves as a couple had to be carved carefully out of the available, always insufficient, leisure. Warm, open, perhaps too busy sometimes— Liz had always tried to protect him from over-demanding parishioners, he remembered—but full of life and love. Something told him that Olivia and Jeannette's troubled relationship had a long history and deep roots.

He looked up, to see—almost as though he had inadvertently summoned them—Chris and Bethan running pellmell round the corner of the driveway towards him, Cedric's two dogs pulling energetically on their leashes ahead of them.

Jeannette jumped to her feet in surprise. "What on earth?"

"It's all right," he reassured her quickly. "This is the part of my family you haven't yet met."

The twins slid to a halt in front of him, clearly full of urgent news. His heart sank slightly. What had they been up to this time? And where was Mike, who was supposed to be looking after them? Maybe he asked too much of Lorna and Mike. The children were his responsibility, after all. Had they run away from Mike? But if so, why were they here, apparently running to him?

Tresayne House, Wednesday March 8th 1916

Now that I am living here, the history of this house has begun to interest me, especially the earlier years. It is an unusual building, dating from the Jacobean period, though I know nothing of whatever Tresaynes lived here then. Small gentry, I would imagine, without many pretensions. But this was the original home of the family—we only acquired the house and estate in North Devon fifty years ago or so, in the time of my grandfather.

The original house was built square and fairly squat, facing south-east at right-angles to the prevailing wind, with the stableyard protecting it to the north. There is a kitchen and scullery in the old part of the house, with a galleried hall, which must have served as a living room, which had one small bedroom built above it, and two bedrooms above the kitchen, one opening out of the other. The servants sleep in these rooms now. My great-uncle, who lived in the house when his brother—my grandfather—had taken his family to Devon to live, contrived to make a bathroom out of the scullery, and this is still in use. But I would like to put in something more modern upstairs, perhaps in the newer wing, when the War is over, and one can get workmen to do such things again.

For the moment, I have been sleeping in the main bedroom in the more recently added wing, which I believe was built before my grandfather bought the Osborne House estate. It was probably part of an attempt to enlarge the house when he first married my grandmother. She was Devon-born and brought money into the family. I expect she wanted to move back to be nearer her own family, and that is why they bought the estate there. I must remember to ask Mother about it—I'm sure she knows.

Nineteen

Mike drove as fast as he could up the narrow lane, aware from quick glances in the rear-view mirror that the SUV was close behind him. His mind was racing ahead, trying to decide where they could get far enough ahead to turn off without being followed. Was Jude's father the type to try to rough-house him off the road? He told himself to calm down, not to let Jude and Megan's fear infect him, and definitely not to dream up Hollywood-style car chase scenarios.

At the top of the lane, he slid out onto the B-road as fast as he dared, with only a quick glance over his shoulder to check that there was no traffic. It was rather a blind turn, and he mentally crossed his fingers as he turned out. But when he reached the T-junction at the Congdon's Shop crossroads, where there was a stop sign, the SUV drew up behind him.

"Stay down," he muttered over his shoulder. He couldn't see Jude and Megan in the mirror, so presumably their father couldn't see them either, although his vehicle was sitting close to their car's rear bumper.

He waited for a car coming up from Coads Green, then swung out left onto the road towards Plusha, but there was nothing else coming to hinder the SUV, which quickly slipped in behind him. The car ahead drove slowly and carefully through a narrow winding section of the road, which at times was only single car width, before turning off right towards Lewannick village. Mike rounded the left-hand bend and put his foot down as much as he dared, for ahead of him there were more narrow bends to negotiate.

"Lorry coming," Lorna warned him urgently as he came up to a small turn that led down towards a farm.

He braked hard and tucked into the side of the road to let the lorry pass. Behind him the SUV did the same, but as he set off again, he saw a tractor lumbering towards him. There was just time to nip into a tiny layby before the tractor and its trailer was upon him, but it occurred to him, as he let it pass, that this was his opportunity. In the rear-view mirror he could see that the SUV had had to back up to the top of the farm lane they'd passed. It would have to wait for the tractor, and with any luck on the next section, they would be out of sight behind the head-high Cornish banks that lined the ancient lane on each side.

There was nothing following the tractor, and he put his foot down, relying on Lorna to warn him if she saw a vehicle ahead on one of the blind right-hand bends, where her view from the passenger seat was better than his. But they were in luck. Nothing was approaching in the other direction, and as they came out into a faster, two-way section he could see nothing following him either.

There was a choice now, either to speed up along the faster section of the road as it went down the long hill towards the junction with the A30, or to turn off quickly while they were still out of sight of the SUV. He worked out that if he could go faster on the double-track road, so probably could the SUV. And even if they reached the dual carriageway well ahead, they would be visible, and Jude's father would know where they had gone. On the other hand, if he turned off, it would all depend on whether the farmer took the obvious route and went straight on, and how long it took for him to realise they were no longer in front of him. But even if he guessed they had turned off, this wasn't an easy road to turn round on, and by the time he was sure he'd missed them and turned back, there was a choice of two turnings they might have taken. Even if Jude's father guessed the right one, they would be well on their way down towards Tresayne, which is where Mike must take them for safety in the end. At least, if the twins had let the Landrys know what was happening, the people at Tresayne would be ready.

He had only fifty metres or so to make up his mind, but in the end, it was an easy choice. He brought the estate car up to the turn, braked hard, changing down as he did so, and swung sharply into the narrow lane. He accelerated down the steep hill, eyes watching the banks carefully to make sure he didn't take the car too close to either of them—both the hedge and bank looked benign enough, but in Cornish banks, he'd been told, there were rocks under the soil, and he had no wish to tangle with them. Fortunately, the lane was fairly straight, and the sight lines ahead were good. They met nothing coming in the other direction—for which he was thankful, as there was little in the way of passing places.

Glancing quickly in the rear-view mirror, he saw the SUV flash by on the B-road above him, and trusted the driver was focusing on the road ahead and not glancing down the lane in case they had turned off. So far so good.

At the bottom of the hill, he took the turn towards Tresayne, and then the tiny lane that led down to the house itself, and the clapper bridge beyond it, where they had often walked the dogs.

Lorna stirred beside him. "Well done, Mike," she said quietly. "I think we've lost him."

"Keep your heads down till we get there," he told the passengers behind him. "Just in case."

As they reached the turn to Tresayne House itself, he slowed down to let Lorna get out and open the driveway gate, but to his surprise it was already latched back waiting for them, Jeannette standing beside it waving them through; and then they were inside, and he was driving on towards the house, eager to get the car out of sight of the lane. He saw Theo ahead, beckoning him to drive round into the courtyard behind the house. With a sigh of relief, he parked beside Jeannette's little car and turned the engine off.

~ * ~

Jeannette closed the gate and stood by it, thoughtfully, watching for any sign of pursuit. From the quick-fire conversation Jeremy had had with the twins, she had gathered little of what had been going on, other than that Mike and Lorna might be arriving in the Swanson family car any minute, and that it had something to do with Jude. It had all sounded very urgent, not to mention dramatic, and Jeremy had at once asked her to open the gate for them to save time.

"We need to get the car out of sight as quickly as possible, just in case," he had said.

In case of what? she wondered. She looked back towards the house. The estate car had disappeared into the courtyard, followed by Jeremy and the twins. She fitted the chain round the gatepost and closed the padlock. It hadn't been used for many months, but it locked with a satisfying click, and she made her way round the house to join the others.

The courtyard seemed very crowded. Olivia had vanished into the house, but everyone else was in evidence, Lorna and Mike providing their father with voluble and in different ways self-exculpatory explanations, the twins keeping the dogs carefully under control, and Theo looking on with a kind of benign amusement. *Dear Theo,* she thought. He seemed to take everything in his stride, as he always had. *What a man to have with you in a crisis. What a man to have with you at any time!* Her heart swelled with love and affection for him.

Looking more closely, she saw that beside Jude's tall figure was a smaller, slighter one. A girl about Bethan's age, she judged. Who was this? The protective arm Jude held about the newcomer's shoulder suggested relationship. Hadn't mention been made of a sister? But what on earth was she doing here?

Whatever it was, she looked both frightened and shocked. Jeannette hurried towards her.

"Jude, are you all right? You and..." She looked enquiringly at the younger girl.

"This is my sister, Megan." Jude squeezed the girl's shoulder slightly. "Megan, you remember Mrs Landry."

The girl nodded, tongue-tied.

"What happened, Jude?"

Jude moved a little away from the animated and slightly argumentative conversation being held within the Swanson family. "Megan texted me," he explained. "To say she needed to run away. So Lorna and I went to fetch her."

Jeannette felt her eyebrows rise—indeed, she felt as though quite a lot of the rest of her was rising as well, including the hair on her head. But she tried not to let her feelings show. The poor child must be scared enough already, for all kinds of reasons.

"You're safe here," she told Megan firmly. "Let's take you inside. Do you have a bag or anything?"

"It's in the car," replied a muffled little voice.

"Jude will bring it in a minute, then," Jeannette reassured her. "You come into the kitchen with me."

Here I am again, she thought, *inviting people inside, against all the regulations. But Megan seems just as much in need as Jude was. I'm sure that will cover it. And anyway, she must have been shut away with her family for all these weeks—there can't be much risk.*

She led the way through the hallway and into the kitchen beyond. The sun was westering and the kitchen, whose window faced east, was fairly dim, but it always looked warm and welcoming. It was definitely the place Megan would like to be, she felt.

She switched on the lights. "Would you like some tea, or some juice, Megan? And there are some homemade flapjacks in the tin there." She had made them in honour of Marcus's arrival tomorrow, but if necessary, he would have to have something else instead. There was a sponge cake in the freezer, she was sure. She could get that out and put some icing on it.

She saw that Jude had followed them, whether for Megan's security and wellbeing, or for her own, she wasn't sure. "Are they still arguing out there?" She tried to sound lighthearted, though she had been slightly perturbed by the sheer vehemence of the exchanges between Jeremy and his offspring. The twins, she noticed, had kept out of the way. *I must give the dogs a drink*, she thought suddenly, trying to remember where a suitably sized bowl might be.

To her surprise, Jude grinned. "It'll be okay. I don't think Lorna's had a chance to talk to her mum about Megan, and the reverend is worried they're asking too much. I haven't met Mrs Swanson, but from what Lorna says, I reckon she's pretty much equal to anything."

"Er... Just what are they asking?"

"Lorna seems to think Megan and I should both go back to Oxford with them, and we'd be safe then. Dad would never know where we were to, see?"

"Goodness," exclaimed Jeannette rather faintly. "I see why Remy might be worried."

But what other solution was there? She and Theo couldn't keep Jude and Megan forever, and if they did, their father would be sure to find out eventually, and there would be hell to pay, and maybe even danger if he became violent, though she thought it unlikely. But Theo wouldn't be able to fight back, and they couldn't possibly involve Marcus in any fracas. The whole thing would be a nightmare. She thought Lorna's solution was probably the best one available and therefore resolved to give her some assistance. *Perhaps if I talk to Liz myself it would help. I could fill her in a bit more with the situation,* she thought—although she doubted whether she knew nearly as much as Lorna, or indeed Jeremy himself, in whom Jude had confided. But another woman's perspective might prove be useful, just the same.

She left Jude and Megan eating flapjacks at the kitchen table and went back into the courtyard. The heated discussion had died down, and Jeremy was loading the dogs, the twins and Mike into the car. Lorna, she saw, was standing to one side, a bag, presumably Megan's, in her hand.

"Megan can stay here," Jeannette told Jeremy. "You can't take her back to Cedric's."

"For tonight, that would be best," he agreed. "Thanks, Jeannette. That's very good of you. But tomorrow, the kids are going back to Oxford on the train, and Megan wants to go with them. I'll clear it with Liz."

"I could speak with Liz myself," she suggested. "I know we've never met, but one woman to another, perhaps…"

Jeremy's face relaxed suddenly, and he grinned. "Oh, I think we can cope, thanks. Lorna is the one who made the plan, and she can explain it all to her mother. As Mike has just said, rather her than me. My job is to book the train tickets and get them to Exeter."

"Will you have enough space in the car for all the children?" she asked anxiously. There were six of them altogether, if she'd counted correctly, which seemed an impossible number to fit even in the Swansons' big estate car. "If it weren't for Marcus coming tomorrow, I'd suggest we could provide a car and driver, but I don't think that will be possible in the circumstances. Still, I could get insurance for my car so that you could borrow it, and Mike could drive yours, if that would help?"

"That's such a kind thought. But there are folding seats in the boot of the car, when we don't need it for the dogs. We quite often have to transport four children and their baggage, not to mention sundry friends. So there's plenty of room, and if necessary, the kids can travel light with a bag each and something small on their knees, and I can take the rest on later."

He was obviously quite used to dealing with and organising such numbers, and she subsided, not without a sense of relief. It felt so important that they should have time and no outside distractions when Marcus arrived, and there was a chance that perhaps if Jude went with the Swansons to Oxford, there would be an end to whatever these 'paranormal' manifestations were, too. They could settle down for a week or two to create a new family for the future.

She had expected Olivia to go back to London as soon as restrictions were lifted, but so far at least her daughter had made no effort to do so, nor even mentioned the possibility. Finding a new flat would probably be difficult, under current circumstances, but estate agents were functioning, as people still needed to move house. It looked as though Olivia wanted to meet her stepbrother and wasn't going to leave Cornwall until she had.

Tresayne House, Monday March 20th 1916

Freddie rode over to see me on Friday, to my delight, and stayed a couple of days. Mother was beside herself about his leaving her so soon, but he insisted. I think a night or two being fussed over at Osborne House by Mother and Maudie was enough. I'm not sure I would have coped any better myself, and Freddie was always an outdoor boy who liked activity and the company of other boys, rather than the cloying attention Mother likes to give him. I don't suppose much has changed now that he's a man. He brought a letter for me from Maudie about her intention to marry Gerald as soon as possible, whenever he can arrange some leave, in fact. I read it in private, lest Freddie might warn Mother to be on her guard.

Freddie and I stayed up talking—and drinking, I confess— every night till the small hours. My younger brother has certainly had an adventurous time in France and seems quite unworried by the possibility of death or injury, even though quite a few of his men have been killed or maimed by shells while in the front line. His battalion has not seen much in the way of battle action yet, so I suppose some of the horror of trench warfare has passed him by for the moment. Or perhaps he is not telling me everything. Because of my pacifist inclinations, Freddie may not want to admit to me that war is not as glorious as he thought when he joined up, in case that allows me to believe I have won the argument—he would not relish that at all. Just as in his letters, he told me more of his off-duty times and the highjinks the officers get up to than of the deadly, interminable watches in the trenches, waiting for the silent advent of gas or the shrill whining of shells in the mud and rain. He thinks a major offensive is on the cards but doesn't know (obviously) whether his battalion will be involved or not.

Freddie left this morning. We rode down to the station, and he took a train to Southampton to embark again for the Front. I brought his horse back here, and Mother will send a groom over for it sometime when she can spare someone—though I wonder when that will be, with all she has to occupy her at the moment.

While Freddie was here, we made an exciting discovery at Tresayne. I had heard tell of a priest hole from Mother but had discounted the story as the product of a fevered female imagination. However, she is quite right. Tresayne House does have a priest hole, and I have found it. I imagine it was put in when the house was built, making it far more secure than one added later would have been.

We found it after one of the maids complained to the housekeeper that she heard strange tapping noises from the north-facing room upstairs in the old part of the house, where she was sleeping, and the housekeeper reported it to me. She does not credit the girl with any sense, and says she despises such superstitious nonsense, as of course do I. But I thought I should at least investigate. It occurred to me to ask Freddie to give me his aid, and together we searched, tapping the walls, and poking about, but all seemed secure. We looked downstairs in my study, too, where there is a big cupboard next to the door. It turns out the hiding place was quite small—only about six feet long and five feet wide—hardly big enough to lie down in. We found a wooden chair and table there, presumably for the priest's use, but they were crumbling away with worm and rot and the gardener has burnt them. The priest hole had clearly been closed for two hundred years, unused, and there was nothing there that could possibly have caused any hauntings.

I have told the housekeeper that none of the maids are to set foot in my study except to clean it and lay the fire for me each morning, and I keep it locked it up to make sure. It would not be difficult for a curious maid to find the way into the priest hole, if she knew how. I don't want anyone trapped there.

Twenty

Jeremy unloaded his passengers at the cottage and asked Mike to start preparing something to eat. Lorna, he knew, was intending to talk to her mother as soon as possible, but he wanted to prepare the ground for her if he could. He had joked about it with Jeannette, unwilling to involve a near-stranger in their family affairs, but he did, in fact, feel that Lorna was taking a lot for granted. On the other hand, he could see why the kids had felt Megan should be rescued, and what other option was there?

Mike was not all that interested in cooking, but since Lorna had been staying at Tresayne, he had learned how to create basic meals and seemed to enjoy it well enough so long as someone gave him assistance with preparing vegetables and setting the table. But the twins, tired after their long walk and all the excitement they had enjoyed during the afternoon, seemed unwilling to take on any extra tasks, so Jeremy agreed that fish and chips from the freezer with frozen vegetables to go with them would meet the bill for that evening.

"It'll use up some frozen stuff ahead of you lot going back to Oxford," he commented. "I'm going to have a lot of trouble finishing it all off before I join you."

"Do we have any idea when that'll be, Dad? I mean, Mum won't want to have the whole lot of us under her feet all summer without you, will she?" Mike paused. "I don't suppose you'd let me stay after all, would you? I've got a few ideas about that priest hole you're investigating. That *is* why you aren't coming back with us, isn't it? To find out about the priest hole?"

Jeremy smiled, wondering how far to take his son into his confidence. "Not entirely. I can't just leave the cottage and the dogs while Cedric's away, can I? But I'm hoping it won't take long. I have the feeling the Landrys would like to get us all out of their hair as soon as possible. They have Theo's son Marcus coming to stay, and that's obviously a big deal for them."

"So we might not be able to do much detecting for a week or two, then?"

"It's not 'we', Mike. Plus I love the idea of it being called 'detecting'."

"Well, you know what I mean. Mystery solving, if you like that better. And I strongly recommend it is 'we'."

Jeremy punched his son gently on the shoulder. "Get on with the fish and chips, Mike, and I'll go and see if I can catch Mum before Lorna does."

Mike grinned. "I would love to listen in to that conversation. I wonder what scheme Lorna has up her sleeve to convince Mum we can fit Megan in as well as Jude. She said something about her sharing with Beth. I hope that won't mean I've got to share with Chris."

"Beth and Chris were going to have separate rooms sometime this year anyway, weren't they? They're too old to share with each other now they're nearly teenagers, twins or not. I expect it will all work out somehow. Chris can have the box room. Would you mind sharing with Jude? I think that may turn out to be more sensible."

Mike stared at him. "You know, then. About Jude being trans? Lorna let on to me accidentally, but I didn't know she'd told you."

"I wondered from the start, to be honest, but Lorna confirmed it, with Jude's permission, and I've checked with Jude himself. I think it is genuine. He'd probably love to have your company, if we can get an extra bed in your room."

"That won't be necessary," Mike told him. "I'm planning to stay here and help you with the priest hole investigation, remember?"

Jeremy abandoned the argument and made for Cedric's study where he could talk to Liz in privacy. Mike would do as he was told if he and Liz stuck to their guns, he knew. He didn't blame the boy for wanting to stay and see the investigation through, and was only glad that Lorna seemed to have given up her aspirations to do the same. Maybe, on reflection, it might be easier for Jude not to have to share a room with Mike. Liz might even think it more appropriate.

In the bedroom they were sharing at the cottage, Bethan and Rob were engaged in a debrief.

"That was fun," said Rob, his eyes glinting.

"It was scary," retorted his sister.

"Oh well, you're a girl."

"That's got nothing to do with it. It was scary. I thought any minute Jude and Megan's Dad would catch up with us, and we would be in dead trouble."

"It was exciting," persisted Rob.

"Well... now it's all over, yes. It was exciting—but a bit scary, too."

Rob relented. "I was planning where to hide if we heard the SUV coming," he admitted.

Bethan punched his shoulder. "I knew you were scared."

He grinned. "I wonder how Lorna's getting on, trying to get Mum to agree to Megan coming back to Oxford as well as Jude. The house'll explode, it'll be so full."

"You'll get to sleep in the boxroom in peace, remember. I shall have to have Megan in my room. I hope she won't hear voices, like Jude. I like my sleep."

"D'you reckon Mum will agree?"

"Lorna thinks so."

"Mike isn't so sure, though. It's odd…" He paused.

"What is?"

"Lorna and Mike always think Mum can cope with everything."

"Supermum."

"Exactly. But she isn't, is she?"

"You mean, we don't always do what she tells us."

"Like we don't do what anyone tells us," grinned Rob, "unless we think we will."

"I guess that's because we're twins," suggested Bethan wisely. "Twins are different."

"It won't be the same," Rob said, "when we don't share a room."

"I know."

"I think I might be a bit lonely in the box-room, especially if you're best friends with Megan."

"I'll always be best friends with you, Rob."

"Will you, Beth? I know we have to grow up, and all that. But I'd hate to lose you. It would be like losing a bit of myself.

"You won't lose me," she reassured him. "Not ever."

~ * ~

In the study below them, the landline extension was winking, indicating there was a message on the answerphone. This had been a rare event during lockdown, but Jeremy decided he had better check it before phoning Liz, just in case.

To his surprise, the voice that spoke loudly and cheerfully from the answerphone belonged to Cedric himself.

"Hi there, Remy! Sorry to leave you messages on my own machine, but I seemed to have mislaid your mobile number somehow. Hope you're still having a good time down there in lovely Cornwall. I saw your lady wife the other day, and she said everything was good and the dogs were fine. I told her I knew you'd let me know if there were any problems. Anyway, the long and the short of it is, now the restrictions are easing, I think I should come down and check out the old estate and so on. When would it suit you to bring the brood home? Liz seemed to be saying that was going to be fairly soon, so I suppose we should try to arrange it so that I get down the same day you leave, to look after the dogs. I can get a taxi from Exeter or come on to Plymouth or Liskeard and get one from there. You don't need to come and fetch me. I don't suppose the boarding kennels are functioning yet, though. Give me a bell and let me know what you'd like to do."

"Damn!" Jeremy found himself saying and was immediately repentant. *If I'm needed here in order to solve this business of the priest hole*, he told himself severely, *then there'll be a way for me to stay, Cedric or no.* Technically he oughtn't to remain in the cottage when Cedric came home, under Covid regulations, even if Cedric were willing to let him do so, but he felt that his observance of the current rules, what with all the comings and goings between themselves and Tresayne, already left much to be desired. Anything might be possible, therefore, in the circumstances. But not if it was a danger to Cedric, who was well into his seventies and had an unreliable heart. He would have to think.

~ * ~

Lorna sat in the small armchair in Jude's little ground-floor bedroom at Tresayne and clicked on her mother's number in her mobile. The ringing tone went on for a few seconds, making her wonder whether she was going to have to leave voicemail. Not the easiest subject for that, she couldn't help thinking. But they were leaving Cornwall tomorrow morning, so it was now or never. Jude would never consent to leaving Megan behind, now she had escaped, even at Tresayne. For the first time, she wondered uneasily whether she had been right to embark on rescuing Megan and taking them both back to Oxford. She knew too little about what social services would do, or how legal the whole operation was. But Mum would take it all in her stride, that was for sure. If

Lorna had made a mistake, Mum would find some way of putting it right.

She smiled to herself. All the family had this view of their mother, except perhaps the twins, who took their own line on everything and backed themselves to get their own way even with Mum. To Lorna, she was wonder woman; the wisest, bravest, strongest person imaginable, the linchpin of the family, but her own person at the same time. No one else would ever be the same, and it wasn't any use wishing to emulate her. Besides, she knew Mum would say it was wrong—Lorna should be the very best person she could be, not try to be like anyone else, even her mother, however admired.

"Hi, Lorna." At the last moment, before the voicemail message began, her mother had answered. "How's it all going? Are you ready to come home?"

"Yes, I really am. We're all looking forward to it, except Mike, because he wants to stay and help Dad investigate the priest hole at Tresayne."

"I heard something about that," remarked Liz non-committally. "I don't mind if Dad doesn't."

"I suppose Dad thought you'd need Mike as well as me, with these extra people coming with us to Oxford. It's a lot to ask."

"People, you said? It was only one person—Jude—when I last heard. Sounds like it might be you really are about to ask a lot. Spit it out."

Lorna's heart sank. Mum was too quick. "Well, Mum. It's like this." She gave her mother a quick snapshot of the day's events, and the conclusion she'd come to, that Megan needed to come back with them to stay in Oxford as well as Jude. "For safety, Mum. Because their father sounds scary, and he chased us in his car when we rescued Megan. I was quite frightened he'd catch us, but Mike lost him in the lanes, and we got away. Mike was brilliant. Megan's father doesn't know where she is at the moment, but I'm worried what would happen if he found her and Jude. The Landrys might not be safe, for a start."

"M'm. And I suppose there isn't time to contact social services?"

"Dad said he would do it after we've gone, and tell them what's been happening, if he can get hold of them. They might want us to tell the police. I haven't been able to tell you everything about why Jude and Megan needed to get away, but it's bad, Mum. Really bad."

"Being in care isn't much fun, either," Liz observed.

"No, that's right." In both their minds, Lorna suspected, were two of her school friends who lived in children's homes, and who'd spent a lot of time with the Swansons because they hated it so much. She had had little contact with them while she'd been in Cornwall and wondered how they had fared. Being locked down in such a place would not be a happy experience.

"What do you say, Mum? Could we manage to have both of them to stay? Beth says she'll share with Megan, and there's the air bed she could sleep on until we can get something better. She can use my nice sleeping bag I bought for the Duke of Edinburgh award trip last year."

"That sounds a good plan." Liz sounded quite accepting of the idea, much to Lorna's amazement. Perhaps Dad had primed her after all. "We'll have to put Chris in the boxroom, but that might have been necessary anyway, if we're giving him and Beth their own rooms. I've done some decorating in there during lockdown, so we only have to move his bed. But in that case, where are we going to put Jude?"

"In Mike's room?"

"Would Mike mind, do you think? Would Jude mind, come to that?"

"I'm sure Jude wouldn't mind, but I can ask." Lorna clicked on the loudspeaker button so Jude could hear her mother's side of the conversation. She looked across at him enquiringly. "Would you mind sharing with Mike?"

"I don't mind. But it's a bit of an ask, for your brother, isn't it? I mean, he hardly knows me, and there I'd be invading his space—and he might be uncomfortable with my being trans, too."

"Mike takes people as they come. He wouldn't care about that."

"There's also the matter of beds, Lorna," said her mother. "The shops are opening up now, but I'm not sure I want to actually buy another bed unless either Jude or Megan is staying long term. It's one thing to put Megan on an airbed for a few nights, but I'm not sure Jude would be comfortable, even if we had a second one."

Lorna looked at Jude. Her mother had a point. He had seemed very big when she thought him a girl, but even as a boy he was quite sizeable. "What do we do then?" she asked rather helplessly.

"Why don't we suggest Mike stays in Cornwall?" suggested Liz. "He'd be pleased, your father won't have a problem with it, and Jude can borrow Mike's bed until he gets back, by which time we'll know more what the future will be for Jude and Megan. Clearly, they want to stay together, but that might not be easy to arrange in the current circumstances. This way it won't be a problem for them to stay for a bit with us."

Lorna smiled. That was just like Mum. You brought a problem to her, thinking it was completely insuperable, or that you were asking too much of her, and then she came up with an idea that solved everything in one go. "Oh, that sounds marvellous, Mum. If you're sure?"

"I talked it over with Dad when he phoned just now."

So you did already know about Megan. Sneaky Mum!

"We've agreed it's the best thing, but it means you won't have Mike with you on the train. Is that okay?"

"We can cope," Lorna asserted eagerly. "Jude will help with the younger ones, so it won't all fall on me. Mike has been brilliant over all this. He deserves to stay if that's what he wants. And perhaps..." she faltered, catching Jude's eye across the room, "it might be best for Jude to have a bedroom to himself, for now."

To her relief, Jude's face relaxed into a grin. "In case I hear voices, you mean? Nay, Lorna, there'll be no voices in your house in Oxford. It's something here that I heard. They'll find out, you'll see, your dad and Mike. Your dad believes me. He won't give up until he discovers what's causing it."

Having slept in the same room with him for several nights, Lorna thought Jude had nightmares, too, whatever else was going on. But that could be dealt with if it happened again. At least he and Megan would be safe.

"How much luggage will you have?" asked Liz. "Do you want me to bring my car to the station? I can take the bags and you kids can walk."

"Not much luggage, I think, because of getting it all in Dad's car, though I suppose if Mike stays here, there'll be a bit more space for bags. Jude and Megan have almost nothing—a backpack each was all they were able to carry when they left home."

"Just as well the shops are open again, then. We'll have to go out and buy them some clothes as soon as we can."

"Mum, you're the best. I'll text you when we're on the train at Reading. There's only the one change, if Dad takes us to Exeter."

"I'll be around all day. But I guess it'll be early afternoon before you get here."

"I'm not sure which train Dad has booked, but we'll let you know."

"That sounds good. Tell Dad from me to look after Mike, will you? I don't want to have any mad monks to deal with, especially from a distance."

Lorna laughed. "I don't think there's any danger attached to this mystery, Mum. Not physical danger, anyway."

"I'm not going to worry about the other kind. Have a safe journey, sweetheart, and just phone me if you're concerned about anything."

"Thanks, Mum." Lorna finished the call and put the phone back in her jeans pocket.

"She sounds great, your mum."

"Oh, she is. Like I said, she's the best."

"I don't think," replied Jude slowly, "she can possibly be better than her daughter. *You're* the best, Lorna."

Lorna looked up. There was something in Jude's expression that made her feel suddenly hot, as though she were blushing—something that had nothing to do with friendship; something warmer and more disturbing. And she thought, for the first time, *Jude is a boy and I'm a girl.* She had never been interested in relationships with boys at school and had positively rebuffed any advances they made. She wasn't sure whether she might feel differently about Jude, sometime in the future. But just now she didn't want things to get complicated, especially with him staying in her home, and with his being trans—she supposed that shouldn't really make a difference, but somehow it did. She smiled at him tentatively and resolved not to be anxious about it. Mum would be there. Mum would help her to handle it, if there turned out to be something to handle.

~ * ~

Jeannette stood by the front door the next morning and watched them pack their belongings into Remy's car and settle themselves into their seats for the hour's journey up to the station at Exeter St David's. Jeremy had put Jude beside him in the front passenger seat, she noticed, where the big teenager would be most likely to be comfortable, and Lorna and Megan in the back with the smaller of Lorna's two suitcases, while the twins rode in the fold-up seats in the car boot, with the rest of the luggage tucked in around them. It was just as well, she thought, that neither Jude nor Megan had much in the way of baggage, but no doubt Jeremy would have managed to fit everything and everyone in somehow.

She went down the steps to say goodbye to them all, and receive their thanks for her help, reflecting that in her own eyes, at least, she really hadn't done very much. She had given Jude sanctuary, it was true, and Megan too, more briefly, but it was the Swansons, and particularly Lorna, who had done the rest. It was fitting the youngsters should go back to Oxford under her care to make a new life there.

She watched as the big, baggy, androgynous figure of Jude helped Megan to climb into the back seat beside Lorna, and wondered what secrets were still hidden behind that ambiguous exterior. Even Jude's gender felt suddenly uncertain, switching from the timid little girl Jeannette had known to someone who seemed almost masculine. Perhaps Lorna knew the truth, but Jeannette found she didn't want to enquire further. This wife of Jeremy's sounded a sensible woman. She and Lorna between them would cope with Jude's issues, whatever they turned out to be. This was one burden she could lay at the feet of someone else and move on with her own.

She went back upstairs to strip the sheets from the beds Lorna, Jude and latterly Megan had slept in, and clean the room. She always hated to leave tasks undone, but this one especially she wanted to complete before Marcus came. She tried not to analyse why she felt this, because the implications were uncomfortable. Was there really something about this old, north-facing bedroom that was uncanny and needed sanitising, or was it just the prevailing sense that others had about it that was affecting her?

She pushed the thoughts aside and bent to her task. With luck, she could get the sheets through the machine and outside on the line before lunchtime and come back to vacuum and dust afterwards. The washing line was at the back of the house, in the walled garden, so Marcus would not see it. *He's family*, she told herself. *He doesn't need to be treated as a guest and have the workings of the household hidden from him.* But somehow, at least for now, Marcus didn't quite feel like family. The guest protocols she had developed for herself over the years must continue.

She opened the window before she left the room, reflecting that fresh air would help to make the room feel cleaner and more wholesome. As she passed along the landing, the cat, who had been sitting on the deep windowsill, jumped down from his place and preceded her down the staircase. She wondered suddenly why Kato so often seemed to spend time on this landing. The sunshine was a draw to any cat, but there was no morning sun in that window. No, there was something more to it, for here he was accompanying her back to the safety of the main house, as attentive as any dog might be. *Don't be fanciful*, she said to herself. Yet she couldn't quite shake off the feeling that Kato was trying to protect her from something. But what?

Tresayne House, Thursday March 30th 1916

I had another letter from Maudie this week. There has been a spate of casualties brought in to Osborne House, she says, and she and Mother have been very busy looking after them. So far, Maudie's intended has not been among them. I cannot wish any harm to come to him, for he is Mary's brother. But I still hope the marriage will come to nothing, mis-match that it is, even if Gerald turns out as good an officer as Maudie thinks he will. For a while, when Mary and I were lovers, I thought such a relationship might bring happiness, but now that I can reflect on it without the passion she evoked in me, I can see it was a good thing I had to come away. Nothing but misery could have come of our affair. Disappointment and regret for me, and disgrace for her. It is better as it is, though I confess I have not yet learned to discipline my body as a priest should. Some nights I still long for her and the joy of our physical union with every fibre of my being.

But no doubt it will pass, in time, and I have much to occupy me here in the parish, though I have not yet met many people of social standing. It is a bleak, uncivilised place with few folk I could see becoming my friends, never mind any woman suitable for me to marry. I tell myself that I have only been here two months, and there is plenty of time to look around when my passion for Mary has faded a little. It would certainly not be right to marry another woman when my heart still longs for her, however futile that yearning may be, and I tell myself I must possess my soul in patience.

Twenty-one

Marcus loaded his suitcase carefully into the back of his convertible and set off through the gates of the apartment complex and along the eerily quiet streets on to the M25, which was also unusually empty for July. Even though restrictions had been eased, it seemed most people were still staying away from their offices, and with so many working from home, rush hour traffic seemed a distant memory. It was shaping up to be a fine summer day, and he had lowered the roof of the car to get the benefit of the fresh breeze as he drove along. He had decided on a more scenic route than the recommended motorway one via the M4 and M5, and so turned the car southwards on to the M3. As he left London behind and green fields began to appear on both sides of the road, he felt his heart lifting. It was as though this journey represented a new start, and with every mile he was putting behind him the miseries of lockdown and starting to come alive again. There was a future in prospect, and he was driving towards it. The gentle undulations of the Hampshire countryside soothed him, and with a sense of excitement he took the A303 and headed westwards into Wiltshire.

He stopped for coffee in a big layby near Stonehenge and sat with his thermos and travel cup looking idly across the bleak plain at the ancient site. It was empty of visitors and wore an unaccustomed air of monumental mystery, so different from the busy throng of sightseers that so often surrounded it like a swarm of flies. He had visited the place with Anna, he remembered, one midsummer morning long ago, when there was still a magic in their relationship, and a craving for closeness. They had stood, arms around each other, under the spell of the great stones, as the sun rose. This year there had been no summer solstice ceremony, but instead his imagination peopled it with long-dead shamans whose relationship with the stones could now only be guessed at.

Just before Exeter, he stopped in another layby to check on the directions to his father's home he'd put into his phone earlier. While it loaded, he flicked through the pictures, looking for the photographs of Jeannette and Olivia his father had sent him. That of Jeannette was clearly a snapshot, taken on a stretch of moorland. She was sitting on a rock against a background of wildflowers and a blue sky flecked with cloud, with her hair blowing back from her face in the wind. It was, he thought, a classic Celtic face, strong-boned and olive-skinned, not much lined and with a lovely quirk to the smile, while her short, curly hair was still dark, with threads of grey running through it. He wondered how long ago it had been taken. He had looked at this one first, and when he clicked on the photo of Olivia below it, he was very surprised to see she had hardly a look of Jeannette at all.

This photo was a studio portrait. Olivia's face was beautifully made up, her long blonde hair tied up in a French plait and her lips curved in a cool half-smile. Her expression gave nothing away, and he had the impression of a woman who was used to hiding herself and her thoughts behind a polished exterior, which made him feel the woman in the picture was shutting him out. She was not his type at all, but then, he reflected, that was just as well, because she was his sister. All he needed to do was to get along with her while he was in Cornwall. There was no necessity for them to see much of each other after that.

Yet he found himself feeling quite sad about this. Danielle and her mother were very close, and when he quarrelled with his mother, he felt he had lost his sister as well. It had become quite important to him that the renewal of his relationship with his father should bring about a place in a new family. Jeannette, he could tell, was ready to offer him that. But Olivia?

He shrugged and put the car into gear. What would be would be, and he could only do his best. If he couldn't make Olivia think of him as a brother, it wouldn't be his fault.

"Starting route to Tresayne," the automated iMaps voice began, as he swung out again into the traffic, which grew heavier the nearer he came to his destination, though the road was nothing like as busy as he had expected. The estimated time of this section of the journey was now an hour, but at least, everything was moving at a reasonable pace. The A30 was dualled all the way to his turn-off, so unless an accident or some other untoward event occurred ahead of him, it shouldn't be too slow a drive. It didn't matter, anyway. He was going to meet his family, and even the thought of delays along the way had no power to deflect him from the pleasure of that.

A brief rain shower as he turned off the M5 on to the A30 at Exeter made him stop again and put up the roof. So much for the sunny West Country. But his mood lifted again as the road climbed the edge of the moor, and the landscape opened up around him. The wastes of Dartmoor, treeless and bleak like Salisbury Plain, accompanied him on one side, while on the other a patchwork of small fields, multi-coloured with different crops and punctuated by green pasture and isolated copses, presented a picturesque and domestic scene. Down the road swooped towards the Tamar, and the sun came out again as he passed the sign welcoming him to Cornwall. Up the hill he went again, and through the outskirts of

Launceston, before finding himself out in the countryside again, with the hills of Bodmin Moor beckoning ahead of him.

"In three miles, turn left on to the B3259," said iMaps. He was nearly there.

~ * ~

Olivia stepped out of the shower, pulled on her towelling robe and swept her hair up into a towel. She paused in front of the mirror above the wash basin, and her face, bare of make-up, looked back at her, expressionless. What would Marcus think of her, she wondered. She looked back across the lonely years of her childhood in this house. She had made friends at school, had even been quite popular among her own crowd, often the one who came up with ideas for group activities, and led the dancing at birthday parties. But she always came back to a house where she had no peers, where she was an only child. Her mother had been an only child too, and she had never met any of her father's family, so there were no cousins to share experiences with. The chance to have a brother, now, in her thirties, seemed almost too good to be true.

Was she setting too much store by it? Probably. Marcus might come this once and go away again, and they might see no more of him. Or he might want to build a relationship with Theo and her mother, but not with her. He had a perfectly good sister already, after all. And why did it seem to matter so much, anyway? Why did she feel the need of a brother? It was foolish, and she couldn't think why she had let herself get into this needy state of mind.

But deep down, she knew the reason. Without siblings, in the end there was no one of her own generation she could rely on. The friends of her schooldays had all left Cornwall, as she had, and scattered to the four winds. She had not kept in touch with any of them, and if they met by accident, they barely knew each other and had little in common. University friends had gone the same way, and as she had told Jeremy, she had not allowed any of her relationships with colleagues and bosses to become more than passing distractions. It had been quite deliberate. Although Clive had dumped her rather than the other way round, she knew in her heart that the relationship would have had no long-term future. None of the husbands she had enjoyed secret liaisons with would ever, if it came to a choice, leave their wives for her. And beyond the feeling of power that defection would have given her, she hadn't truly wanted them to. The temporary nature of those relationships was part of the fun, part of the sense of dizzy headlong excitement that had no place for a future settling-down to contented humdrum everyday life. Perhaps, she thought, she had simply not met the right man, not least because she had not been looking for him. But a brother was a different matter. Biological brothers were permanent. They would always be there if you needed them, or at least so she had always believed. Perhaps that was a fantasy. But even a legal brother might give a good prospect of permanence, if played the right way.

Back in her bedroom, she rubbed her hair dry with the towel and brushed it out, letting it flow freely around her shoulders, blonde, fine and flyaway. Then she opened the wardrobe doors and ran her eyes over the contents. This wasn't a job interview, she reminded herself. But the right clothes for the occasion were important, just the same. She pulled out her favourite pair of casual jeans, slightly worn with use but still smart enough. She hesitated longer over a choice of top, before finding a pretty short-sleeved blouse with a square-cut neckline—slightly old-fashioned, perhaps, but there was no harm in that. Marcus must be at least as old as she was, she thought, and he wouldn't want her to look like a teenager. The turquoise shade set off her fair colouring and complemented the white jeans nicely. It would do.

She selected a pair of sandals and stepped out on to the quiet landing. It was pleasant to have the older part of the house to herself again. Jude, Megan, and Lorna had been picked up by Jeremy just before ten o'clock, and she had managed to say a civil farewell to them before heading for the shower. Lorna was a pleasant girl, she thought, but Jude was... something else. Too big, for a start, and too secretive, with a permanently closed-in expression. And the clothes she wore were horrific: cheap, nondescript and baggy. Olivia hoped Lorna's mother would be able to do something about that. As for the sounds she said she had heard.... Olivia shivered. It was true there was something odd about that room—her eyes flicked involuntarily down the corridor towards the door that led to it—but surely Jude had made too much of it?

She thrust those thoughts from her and turned towards the head of the staircase. Kato sat waiting for her on the top step and led her down in stately fashion into the old hall. Ahead of her was the door to the little study where Jude had latterly slept, and from where she had claimed still to hear a voice crying. Perhaps there would be no respite from these hauntings after all, even if, with Jude's departure to Oxford, they were only memories from her own childhood. But she didn't want to be tormented by her sense of something strange and forbidding in that room, nor continue to feel reluctant to enter it, conscious every time she walked along the corridor from her room that something brooded there which, Jeremy seemed to think, needed to be exorcised.

She turned away from the old house and made for the sitting room at the front, overlooking the drive, where she knew Theo and her mother would be watching for Marcus's car. It couldn't be here for a long time yet, if he had only left London that morning, however early. But they would all be waiting when he came.

~ * ~

Jeannette looked up from her book as her daughter entered the room, and thought how pretty she was looking, and how much she preferred the more casual clothes and hairstyle that Olivia had affected during lockdown over her more formal office wardrobe. She was glad Olivia hadn't thought it necessary to "dress up" for Marcus. She herself was wearing a practical denim skirt and one of her favourite cotton blouses, attire which would allow her to get on with her household chores while they awaited their guest.

As it happened, Jeannette was more conscious than her daughter realised of the lonely childhood Olivia had spent here at Tresayne, for it was very much like her own. She too had lacked cousins and had not made many local friends; and those she had made at university had drifted away unnoticed and unlamented when she began living with James. By the time she realised how far from perfect James was, and how much she might need her friends, it was too late. They had formed other friendships, many of them were married with children, and they had no time for her, by then raising a child on her own, nor, it seemed, any inclination to make an effort to reanimate the closeness they had enjoyed at university. A few of them still sent Christmas cards, and her local acquaintances had shown as much sympathy as they could find in the intervals of their own busy lives, but until she met Theo, she had felt more alone than Olivia could imagine.

She hoped desperately that Marcus and Olivia would get on well. But she knew so little about him that it was impossible to do more than hope. The letter she had received accepting their invitation had been slightly formal, though he was clearly pleased at their response to his overtures. Theo could only tell her what he had been like as a small boy, because he had seen little of Marcus since his teenage years. In a sense, Theo would be getting to know his son just as much as they all would. She wasn't sure whether to be apprehensive or excited, and with her normal commonsense decided that neither was appropriate. It was better just to take things as they came.

Meanwhile, the clouds were clearing and the sun just peeping out. Good weather for Marcus's first introduction to Cornwall, she thought. Even though holiday-makers persistently remembered the coastal sunshine, here on the moors, even in the summer, the weather was too often grey and wet. She was pleased the duchy was putting on a shining face for him.

She marked her place carefully and put down the book on the glass coffee table. "I'm going to do a bit of dead-heading in the garden," she said. "Marcus can't possibly be here before lunch—he told us not to expect him till the afternoon." It would depend on the traffic, as visitor arrivals usually did.

She smiled at them both and went out. A few minutes later, they saw her pass the window with a basket over her arm to carry the dead flowers, and a pair of secateurs in her hand.

"Nothing keeps your mother out of the garden for long," Theo commented with a smile. "But on this occasion, I envy her the occupation."

Olivia looked at him in surprise. "Theo, are you nervous?"

"A little, perhaps. It's quite a big deal for me, this, you know."

"I can see it might be. But after all, Marcus wanted to come. I mean, he made contact with you, not the other way round. All we have to do is follow his lead, surely?"

"I hope so. But you know, Livi, I don't really know my son now, and I don't know why he wanted to come."

"You mean, it might not be for the reasons he said?"

"Exactly. After all, how many of us always tell the strict truth about anything, especially if we want something badly?"

"I hadn't thought of it like that," admitted Olivia. "I suppose I just thought he'd been lonely during lockdown and so he wanted to rebuild his relationship with you, like he said."

"I truly hope it is like that. But I can't help wondering—and perhaps this is paranoid of me—whether his mother put him up to it."

Olivia blinked. "But why should she?"

"I don't know. And maybe I'm being unfair to her. I know she had much to put up with when we were married, as I told you. But she did tend to be a bit manipulative, and when we were trying to agree on a divorce settlement, she was greedy, and I felt guilty and didn't want to fight her over money. I just think she might have found in Marcus a willing tool. But we shall see."

Olivia said nothing, but suddenly her vision of the big brother who would be her friend faded a little. Perhaps he wasn't to be trusted after all. She got up and went back to her room and her laptop, where the paypigs needed some attention.

Tresayne House, Friday April 21st 1916

I read an amazing poem in The Cambridge Gazette *this week. It is called "The Redeemer" and was written by Siegfried Sassoon, whose war poems so far have always glorified conflict and the sacrifices of the men. Sassoon is a serving officer, so what he says will carry weight with public opinion. But it seems he is beginning to be tired of watching the suffering and is questioning the uncritical acceptance by most people that it is necessary, even glorious. This is a wonderful development, and desperately needed if we are to see a change of heart on the part of the people in charge of the conduct of the war. Oh, that they would listen to those of us who are trying to tell them it is time to negotiate, to accept that we cannot win this war without enormous numbers of casualties, and the legacy that will leave to the next generation.*

I expect Sasson's Cambridge associations made it easier for him to persuade the Gazette to publish, but I wonder whether any other papers will be so daring. The poem will ruffle some people, including many of my ordained colleagues, I expect, because it compares the soldier to Christ, which some will see as close to blasphemy, though it has been done before. Down here in my backwater, I shall not have to take any notice of that. To me, it makes Sasson's description of the hell that is now the front line even more stark and biting and identifies Christ with those who suffer.

It is Good Friday today, and the darkness of that day, expressed in the bare altar in my church, and the liturgy for the day, still oppresses me. I suppose the poem is part of that, even though the fact of its publication cheers me. It makes grim reading, but at least it is a sign that not everyone is prepared to glorify the fighting. It has become so easy to despair as the War drags on, apparently indefinitely.

But more than anything, it makes me think of Freddie. How dreadful that he should have not only to endure such horrors, but be responsible, like Sassoon, for the men who suffer them. And his 19th birthday isn't until next month.

Twenty-two

It was just after half-past twelve when Marcus's black convertible slid up to the gate. Jeannette, dead-heading in the herbaceous border along the driveway, looked up in surprise, and put down her basket and secateurs in haste to open the gate for him.

He drove through and waited while she closed it again behind him. "Thanks," he said, leaning across to push the passenger door open. "Do you want to hop in? You can show me where to park."

Slightly flustered, she stripped off her gardening gloves and got into the passenger seat, hoping there was no mud on her shoes to transfer itself to the immaculate mat beneath her feet. She looked across at him curiously as he put the car in motion again, recognising immediately how much he resembled his father when she had first met him. He was a little younger than Theo had been, his hair still a dark blonde with no grey, though receding slightly at the temples, and he had a deeper tan to his skin. Theo was a pale-skinned indoor person, where Marcus had clearly used to good effect the hour of daily exercise permitted during lockdown, and the arms emerging from his short-sleeved cotton shirt sported a good set of muscles.

"We didn't expect you so soon," Jeannette found herself saying, as though explaining the reason for her gardening attire.

"The traffic wasn't too bad. And I left early." He flicked a glance across at her. "I couldn't wait. Not too early, am I?"

He seemed so relaxed, as though this visit were a regular occurrence, as though he knew her and liked her even though they had never met, that any misgivings she had had died away. "Of course not. We've been looking forward to seeing you so very much."

"It was good of you to invite me," he responded.

She opened her mouth to say Theo had wanted him to come, and that was enough for her, but that seemed ungracious, so she swallowed the comment. The car purred smoothly up to the front door and stopped. "Why not decant your luggage here," she suggested, "and we can show you where to put the car after that. There's a courtyard at the back of the house where we keep ours, and there's room for this one as well."

He nodded and she climbed out, holding her gardening gloves slightly awkwardly in her hand. She dumped them beside the front door, heeled off her gardening brogues and ushered him and his suitcase inside just as Theo came out of the living room to greet him.

"Dad!" Marcus smiled, but to her eye it was a slightly anxious smile. "Thanks so much for inviting me."

"It's a pleasure," Jeannette put in quickly, not waiting for Theo to respond.

"We aren't allowed to shake hands," Theo said. "And I don't know about you, but this fashion for bumping elbows seems ludicrous to me. So I'll just say, 'Welcome, son.'"

There was a constraint between them, Jeannette thought, but that was understandable, perhaps inevitable. She was sure it would pass.

"Shall I show you to your room?" she asked, the old hostessly rituals coming to the surface. "It's up these stairs. Then perhaps Theo will pour you a drink while I get some lunch for everyone. Unless you'd prefer coffee at this hour?"

"Livi is somewhere around," Theo told her. "Maybe in her room? I'll see if I can find her."

Jeannette hoped Marcus wouldn't feel that Olivia wasn't interested in his arrival, or worse still hadn't wanted him to come at all. But she couldn't immediately think how to reassure him without making too much of it. Apart from anything else, Jeannette really didn't know how Olivia was likely to behave with him. Theo had told her that she was keen to meet her brother, but for her part, Jeannette was aware of more complexity in her daughter's emotions.

"I'd love a glass of beer, if there is one," she heard Marcus reply to Theo's suggestion. "A nice cool lager would be good. I'm sorry if I'm earlier than you expected." He still sounded slightly uncertain of his welcome. "Don't bother Olivia if she's busy. I'm sure I'll see her later."

"Yes, she'll be down for lunch," Theo replied. "As for me, you couldn't get here early enough. I've been twiddling my thumbs in the sitting room all morning, where I could see the drive."

~ * ~

They are an interesting bunch, Marcus thought to himself as they sat around the dining room table, where Jeannette had set out salad dishes to await his arrival. After the warmth of his father's greeting, and Jeannette's obvious pleasure that he had been able to visit them, he had felt able to relax and let his normal powers of observation have full rein. People fascinated him, especially the dynamics between and among them, and there were tensions and power games going on in this family he couldn't fail to be aware of, especially having experienced similar problems in his own.

Theo and Jeannette seemed at ease with each other, and moved in harmony about their different tasks as Jeannette brought the last of the food in from the kitchen refrigerator while Theo poured wine and settled them round the table. But Olivia—who had joined them fairly promptly once she realised he had arrived—was less comfortable, particularly with her mother. She greeted him civilly enough, although it seemed with some reservations, which he had half-expected, but when her mother made a mild criticism of her absence at the time of his arrival, she was impatient and defensive, and then fell silent, picking at the food without much appetite and contributing little to the conversation. It was a pity she seemed to have no social graces, he thought, because even unsmiling and withdrawn there was no question about her beauty. He thought her much more attractive in a simple top with her hair on her shoulders than in the formal photograph Theo had sent him.

Marcus turned his attention to his father. "Dad, I've kept up with your professional activities as far as I could recently. I've watched your TV programmes, and I've read your book on Delius. Did you know I work for the firm who published it?"

Theo looked amazed. "I had no idea. I knew that you were working as an editor, but not where."

"Which is your subject area?" asked Jeannette.

"English literature. I deal with the academic stuff, mostly, but occasionally they ask me to deal with the fiction authors. We don't commission much fiction, but we have a professional relationship with some individuals. It's all literary stuff we publish, no commercial fiction."

"Jeannette works freelance as a copyeditor," Theo told him. "English is one of the subjects they send her."

Marcus turned to her with real interest. "I'd no idea. Is it academic or educational manuscripts you work on?"

"Academic, for the most part, though I'm semi-retired now—I haven't done much at all for the last few months, which is hardly surprising, I suppose. Which publisher is it you work for?" She glanced across at her husband. "I'm sorry, Theo. I ought to know, if they publish your books, but I'm afraid I don't."

Marcus gave her the name, but apparently it was not one she had freelanced for. "These days most of my work goes through a big company that puts publishers and freelances in touch with each other. They pay the fees and, I presume, are reimbursed by the publishers. It seems to be the new trend."

"How did you get into copyediting?" he asked. "It isn't an obvious career progression unless you've worked in-house."

"No, by the time I started doing it, everyone was working freelance. When Olivia was small it was very useful to be able to work from home, and I had a humanities degree. Olivia and I were living here on our own then, and I needed whatever work I could find."

This shed a new light on Jeannette's life before his father came along. So she hadn't always been the privileged and comfortably off woman she now appeared. He wondered why not, since it seemed she was the only heir to what had obviously been quite a big estate. The curse of inheritance tax, perhaps? That could cripple an estate of any size.

"But I like the work," Jeannette went on. "Every job is different, too, and I thrive on variety. So I stuck with it, even after Olivia grew up."

"Fair enough," he said, to encourage her. It had been a surprise to find that she worked in the same field as he did, although with a different role. She seemed an interesting person, someone who had made a life for herself out of what sounded like quite difficult circumstances. And his father clearly loved her and was happy with her. That counted for a lot. He smiled at her, waiting to see if she had more to say.

"I suppose it's rather a backwater, Cornwall, so I wouldn't have found it easy to find a suitable job here—and to be honest, I'm a bit of a home-bird, and there's always plenty I want to get on with in the garden if I have an hour or two to spare."

Olivia said nothing, but her face was looking sulkier than ever. What on earth was the matter with her? Was she jealous of her mother's share in the conversation? He decided to ignore her, at least for the moment, and give her a chance to sort herself out.

"Your garden looked really lovely, what I saw of it. You must be very proud of it."

Jeannette seemed about to embark on a detailed description of the garden and its glories, but an impatient movement from her daughter stopped her in her tracks. "I am, it's true. And if you would like me to, I'll take you round and show it to you while you're here. But I mustn't bore you with it now. Once I get going on the garden and its history, I'm hard to stop!"

He smiled at her, liking the way she had dealt with her daughter's rudeness. His eyes flicked over to Olivia, and he was surprised to see her looking not only shamefaced, but unhappy. Perhaps there was more to her reaction than simple boorishness.

For her part, Olivia sat miserably listening to the conversation—light and social and affectionate—going on around her and thought how well Marcus was fitting in already. She watched him across the table as he looked from Theo to Jeannette and back, skilfully keeping the small talk going, both showing an interest in their lives and sharing something of his own with them.

"And you, Olivia?" His face had turned to her at last. "What do you get up to when you're not in lockdown in Cornwall?"

Was his tone a shade patronising? She supposed that for her to sit silently at the table, taking no part in the conversation as it sparkled its way around the participants, must seem wayward, like a child in the sulks, and he had spoken to her accordingly. She looked up, desperate to correct the impression, and met his eyes— and they were Theo's eyes, the same blue-grey, set deep beneath thick brows. His gaze was kind and full of understanding, even sympathy. He wasn't being patronising. He was just trying to help her.

"I was a PA, in financial services, mainly," she answered, smiling for the first time. "But I don't think I'll go back to it when everything gets back to normal. I feel I need a change." She felt her chin go up rather defiantly, and saw her mother exchange glances with Theo.

"Do you have any idea what kind of change?" His voice was still neutral, interested but not prying, even slightly detached. But his eyes met hers again, encouraging her to be positive.

Reading that look, she wanted so much to live up to his expectations. But sadly, there was nothing positive to say, and she felt her face fall back into sullenness. "I don't know yet. Something will turn up."

Tresayne House, Friday May 5th 1916

Maudie writes with news that has thrown my thoughts into turmoil. She tells me Mary has been dismissed because she is pregnant. The second footman has been blamed, and he has also been dismissed—largely, it seems, because he has denied paternity and refused to marry her. I remember thinking he had an eye for her and would perhaps make her a good husband when she had recovered from my leaving, but this is terrible. She must have swiftly taken up with him after I came away, and become pregnant almost immediately, which seems odd because she did not conceive a child with me through all the weeks we made love so often, and I had wondered if she was barren. I admit I had not thought her so wanton as to transfer her affections so quickly. But what kind of a cad must he be to get her with child and then abandon her? I'm sure my mother would have kept them both on and found them a cottage on the estate to live on, if he had stood by her.

Mother is very upset, Maudie says, because Mary is Gerald's sister and it throws a very bad light on him. Maudie has written to him, but as he is in Salonika, he will probably not receive the letter for weeks. She says Mother will write to me for my views, but the truth is I have always left the management of the household to her, as Lionel did, and I would not like to interfere. In any case, I could not command her to keep on a housemaid who has fallen from grace, even for Gerald and Maudie's sake, never mind my own, which I cannot divulge.

Perhaps when I have recovered from the shock, I will feel more kindly towards Mary. I must write back to Maudie asking her to do her best for the girl, for Gerald's sake. But just now, all I feel is anger, hurt and betrayal. I thought her an innocent and loving girl—and indeed she was a virgin when she first came to me. But to part from me with such distress and apparent devotion, and then take up so quickly with a servant—it spoils all my love for her. I can only be glad I left her when I did and did not listen to her importunities. If I had brought her here, what havoc might she have wrought?

Twenty-three

After lunch, Marcus and his father went away to Theo's music room to chat, and Jeannette donned her gardening shoes again and returned to her deadheading. She had tacitly left Olivia to clear up after the meal, which was, Olivia acknowledged grudgingly, fair enough. Jeannette had prepared the food, and it was natural that Theo should want to have a private conversation with his long-lost son. For a moment, resenting that no one wanted to spend time helping her, she was tempted to dump the dishes in the sink and let her mother sort them out later, but good sense prevailed, and she stacked the plates neatly in the dishwasher, threw away the plastic cartons that had held supermarket-prepared coleslaw and pasta salad, and tidied up the kitchen. Feeling virtuous and much more worthy of Marcus's brotherhood-—and laughing at herself wryly as a result—she went back upstairs to her sitting-room.

The cat, who disliked visitors at the best of times and had clearly hoped that with the departure of Lorna, Megan and Jude he had seen the last of them for a while, was sitting on the landing, keeping an eye on the door to the twin spare room. Olivia glanced at him, and then at the door to the room, which was firmly closed.

Her mother, she knew, would be hoping fervently that no ghostly visitations would beset them while Marcus was here. But shutting the door wouldn't make any difference, even if Jude's experiences had after all been just the product of a hysterical imagination and emotional trauma, which she doubted–although it would be a great outcome if it turned out to be true.

She wondered what Marcus would make of it all.

~ * ~

"I can't tell you how good it is to see you again, Marcus." Theo poured coffee and handed his son a cup. "Help yourself to milk and sugar."

"No, thanks. I gave them both up years ago. Just black for me, please."

There was silence for a moment. Then he added: "I'm sorry it's been so long since we've had much contact."

"So am I." It was a simple statement, but full of regret. "Perhaps I should have tried harder."

"No, you're not to blame yourself, Dad. It was my fault, and perhaps Mum's." Marcus was finding this conversation unexpectedly difficult. He hadn't wanted to mention his mother, but how could he let his father take the blame for losing contact with his children?

"Believe me," said Theo, "I don't blame your mother for anything. How is she?"

Marcus hesitated. "I don't really know."

"I realise you haven't seen her during lockdown, but ..."

"We had a right royal quarrel at New Year." It was out, and Marcus felt a sense of relief that it could be shared. "I haven't spoken to her since."

"Oh, Marcus, I'm so sorry. That must have been awful for you, especially during lockdown."

Marcus nodded and hoped the tears he felt behind his eyes would stay there. He hadn't come to visit his father just to break down right at the beginning. "I saw a lot of things more clearly then. About her—and about you." He looked across at Theo. "It was as though all the early part of my life, before she left you and took us with her, had been covered over, and I didn't know how to find it again. And I'm afraid Mum had encouraged us to forget. After I quarrelled with her, I remembered things I hadn't thought of for years."

"I know she was very much hurt, not to mention angry, about my preoccupation with my work. I expect that pretending the relationship had never existed was the easiest way to deal with the fallout of our separation."

Marcus agreed and was grateful for his father's understanding. "I think that's true. But she acted as though we'd never had a father. Debs was older, and it might have been easier for her to keep her memories of you fresh, but she was so partisan I think she just chose to let them go. It wasn't quite the same for me."

"But Debbie did ask me to her wedding," Theo pointed out. "I was so grateful for that—and quite surprised, as well."

"Yes, I wondered initially whether she would, and Mum certainly didn't want her to, but I think in the end she felt you shouldn't be left out. Debs is very strong on right and wrong." Marcus saw his father's face contract and wished he hadn't explained so much. "Dad, I'm sorry. I don't know what her motivation was, really. That's just my speculation."

"You're probably right," said Theo. "She always was keen to do everything correctly, even when she was a small child. Too keen, perhaps. I used to worry she would never rebel enough to find independence. People don't really change, not essentially, so I suppose it isn't surprising if she wanted to make her wedding day perfect for everyone."

Marcus laughed. "It was certainly that! Cost a bomb, too. Did you have to pay? I never dared ask."

Theo smiled. "I did play my part, yes. Your mother and I shared the cost, and I think your stepfather chipped in too. I gathered he's very fond of Debbie."

"He doesn't have any children, so he enjoyed being a dad to us whenever he was around. But we were pretty much grown up before he came along, so he hasn't had all that much to do." Marcus heard the reservation in his own voice. "Sorry. I don't mean to be nasty about him. He did his best."

"I'm sure he did. Was he party to this quarrel you had?"

"No, he and Mum went their separate ways just before Christmas. That was part of the problem." He paused, but Theo said nothing, giving him time. "When Saul told her the marriage was over, she went to pieces, and she turned to me to look after everything and solve all her problems. It was 'Marcus, this' and 'Marcus, that' all the time. I was sorry for her—truly, I was—but in the end, it was too much. I couldn't let her be dependent on me like that. She wanted me to buy a house for us both to live in, but I knew it wouldn't work, and when I refused point blank even to consider it, she threw the most enormous tantrum."

"No fun for either of you."

"No. But fortunately, Debs has picked up the pieces, and Mum's been living with her and the children during lockdown. I think they're going to look for a bigger house to buy together, but that's on hold for the moment. Debs still talks to me occasionally, but she and Mum are thick as thieves, and to Mum I'm Public Enemy Number One." Marcus tried to sound nonchalant and laconic about it, and to hide the hurt he'd felt at their attitude.

Theo's face was full of sympathy. "I really am so sad to hear all this. Sorry for your mother, too, being left alone again. But at the same time, I'm glad you made contact with us. I've missed you. Very much."

"You've found a treasure in Jeannette, anyway." It was a slight effort to say this, because it sounded disloyal to his own mother, but Marcus felt his stepmother deserved it.

"You like her? I'm so glad. She is such a support to me."

"You don't live here all the time, though, do you?"

"This has been Jeannette's family home through three generations, and the garden is important to her, so she makes Tresayne her base, and I come whenever I'm free. We've spent Lockdown here. But I have a flat in London, and she comes up to stay with me there quite often or has done in the past. It works for us."

Marcus nodded. "Sometimes it's best not to be on top of each other the whole time."

He thought suddenly of Anna, and her insistence that they spent every available leisure minute together, even though she wouldn't live with him. That hadn't, in the end, worked out too well either. He wondered still why she had suddenly left him. Surely, she hadn't been with the Australian guy for months, stringing Marcus along while she decided between them? The question had haunted him ever since she emigrated nearly a year ago.

He hesitated. "Dad, can I ask you something?"

"Of course. What's on your mind?"

"Olivia. Does she resent my coming? I can see it might be difficult for her..."

"If you're thinking about what happened at lunch, that had nothing to do with you. How can I put this?" Theo paused, considering. "There are some longstanding issues between Olivia and her mother that have perhaps come to the fore again during lockdown. Olivia hasn't lived with us since she left university, but I think these past few weeks have been a catalyst. It's all coming to a head, I think—and not before time."

Marcus looked an enquiry, but Theo shook his head. "It is between the two of them, and nothing to do with either of us. Though I suppose she might talk to you, as you are someone outside the situation but connected. Why don't you take her out somewhere tomorrow, or the next day? Whenever you feel ready. Even though most of the tourist places are only open in a limited way, with a lot of social distancing, there are some interesting spots she could show you. I think she very much wants to get to know you. I also think the idea of having a brother is quite attractive to her. Being an only child wasn't the best thing for her, I've always thought, and it threw her too much on to her own resources when she was young."

"That's a good idea, Dad. I'd like to get to know her, too. It seems strange to have a grown-up sister I've only just met."

"I believe you will get on well," Theo encouraged him. "Give it a try."

"I'd thought of suggesting we have a day out together, just her and me. It'll be easy enough in this fine weather to have the roof down on the car, and from a Covid point of view, I guess I'm part of your household for a time, anyway. Hard to know how to interpret all these rules sometimes."

Theo laughed. "I know what you mean. We've had lovely fun with that in the last few weeks with some waifs and strays Jeannette took in."

This time the enquiring look met with a slightly more positive response. "She'll tell you about it if you ask her, I expect. Some aspects of it are more difficult than others, but I'll leave it to her to pick and choose."

Marcus finished his coffee, feeling glad that his father had not said more. *It's good that Dad still keeps secrets and knows when to share things and when not. I'll remember that in case I have any confidences of my own to tell him.*

Tresayne House, Monday June 5th 1916

I am in a terrible dilemma. Mary appeared here yesterday, bedraggled and wretched, begging for sanctuary. She had walked all the way from North Devon, she told me, sleeping under bushes and in barns on the way. As Maudie had already informed me, she has been dismissed by my mother because the housekeeper discovered Mary is with child. She tried to hide it, she says, for as long as possible, but that busybody of a maid she shares an attic with nosed it out and told on her. But she says she cannot blame the footman for refusing to marry her. It was the maid whose room she shared who suggested he was the father, and it seems everyone believes it. But in fact, she tells me, she conceived just before I left Devon, and the child is mine. No one suspects this, I gather, but there can be no doubt that it is mine, if she is five months gone now, as she says. And indeed, I cannot help but believe her. Seeing her again, I know that she is no wanton. I am glad no one knows it is my child, but I am in no doubt that Mary is telling the truth.

But what should I do now? I cannot marry her, nor do I feel it would be for the best, even in these changed circumstances. A farmer's daughter is simply not a suitable wife for a clergyman, and Mary has little education, and no social graces. She would not know how to receive the gentry ladies of the district when they call, as call they undoubtedly would, if I were married. And how would the servants take to obeying instructions from someone they would see as a jumped-up housemaid, just because she is bearing a child to the vicar? Worst of all, what would my position here among my parishioners be if they guessed she had been my mistress back in Devon, as they would be sure to do in time, whatever we told them, for the old wives can count months perfectly well! The lies we would have to tell would be sure to find us out in time. Perhaps there is a way, but I cannot think of it yet.

Yet I can't turn her from my door. As the father of her child, I have a duty to provide for her and her baby. I have found a home for her for the moment with a widow who has a cottage in the village. She feels loyalty to our family, as a retired parlourmaid here, but she has few ties with the current staff at Tresayne House. I told her Mary had been turned off for her pregnancy, and that as a clergyman, and now head of the Tresayne family, I felt I should help her. Mary will not tell her the real situation, I am sure. She will bear her shame silently as well as bravely, for my sake, little as I deserve it.

But it will only serve for a short time. I will have to find something more permanent for her when her time draws near. The child is due in September, she thinks, but she has had no medical advice of any kind, so I suppose she may be wrong, and babies do not always wait until they are due to arrive. God, what on earth am I to do with her?

Twenty-four

In what she felt was fast becoming a tradition, Jeannette carried a tray of tea and scones out into the garden for afternoon tea under the beech tree. The weather was still fine, and the garden was full of perennials in bloom, while the annuals in the big earthenware pots on the terrace were flowering and at their best. The few roses she had nurtured in specially dug and mulched beds—Cornish soil being too light for roses to be over-comfortable in it—had finished their first flowering, brought on early by the warm sunny spring, but the new buds on their summer growth were beginning to open. She sat in her chair and looked around with pleasure.

"Would you take me round the garden after tea, Jeannette?" asked Marcus. "I'm no gardener, being a city dweller, but I always enjoy other people's, and yours is definitely worth a second look!"

How polite and thoughtful he was, Jeannette thought. Very like Theo, whose courtesy had been one of the first things she'd appreciated about him in the early days of their acquaintance.

"I'd love to," she responded. "But you will have to tell me when you've had enough. There's nearly three acres here, and it's all garden. No paddocks or wildflower meadows, except right down by the river where it's usually too wet to grow much, and we just have bog-garden and other moisture-loving plants taking over. My grandparents were enthusiasts, and my parents carried on the tradition, so I grew up with it, and I tend to forget not everyone is as keen as I am!"

"I'll tell you," he promised.

He was a good listener, she thought, as she introduced him to the different 'rooms' in the garden, each with its own character. He clearly knew very little either about garden design or plants, but he asked intelligent questions and was clearly willing to learn.

"Thank you so much," he said, as they finished their tour.

"It's a pleasure to show someone round who isn't bored, or at least who is as good at hiding it as you are. The garden is different in every season. I hope you'll come back and see it in the autumn, or better still, next spring. Spring is always the best time in a Cornish garden."

"I would love to. It looks pretty good now, so I'm not sure how it can be better in the spring. Still, I'll take your word for it."

"It's the azaleas and the rhododendrons," she explained. "They are truly spectacular, and unlike roses, they love the Cornish soil."

They wandered in via the courtyard, where Marcus's convertible stood parked next to her own little car in front of the old coach house. In the kitchen, they found Olivia washing vegetables at the sink, while Theo sliced meat beside the electric cooker.

"I'm cooking tonight," Theo told them, laying down his knife. "So why don't you pour Marcus a drink, Jeannette, and take it outside, or into the sitting room, whichever you prefer."

"Do you need any help?" asked Marcus. "I'm quite handy with the pots and pans, and I've got handier during lockdown while I've been cooking for myself."

"Olivia is helping me tonight," Theo reassured him. Olivia went on with the vegetables, apparently oblivious. Was it deliberate, Marcus wondered, or just a kind of natural boorishness? The latter seemed increasingly unlikely, in view of what his father had told him.

"Sherry or wine, Marcus?" asked Jeannette, ushering him out into the hall before he could say anything else. "Or we have some Scotch, I think."

"In the music room," Theo called after her. "The Scotch, I mean. And if you'd like to be really kind, you could bring me one, too."

~ * ~

Over dinner, Marcus managed to wangle into the conversation a suggestion that Olivia might show him some of the local sights. "I know most things won't be open properly, but surely we can find something we can do? Anything by the sea would be great. I haven't been to the seaside in I don't know how long."

Olivia looked at him across the table, clearly assessing his motivations, and he wondered why she was so suspicious.

"Charlestown," suggested Jeannette, as the pause became awkward. "It's where they film the tall ships for films and TV, Marcus. Did you watch *Poldark*?"

"The first couple of series," he answered. "Not more recently." It had been one of Anna's favourites, and he had avoided the final series because of the painful associations. "It must have been interesting for you, living close to the action."

"I think everyone in Cornwall must have watched *Poldark*," said Jeannette. "We all enjoyed trying to recognise the locations. A few people I know got work as extras on it, too, so we had to look out for them in the background."

"What do you think, Olivia?" he asked. "I love sailing, so Charlestown sounds great. But I'm happy to go somewhere else if you prefer."

He spoke truthfully, for the place sounded fascinating, yet he wished Jeannette had not been so quick with her suggestion. He would have liked Olivia to choose their destination. Otherwise, she might see him as too aligned with her mother—which he truly was not, although he liked his hostess and had enjoyed going round the garden with her. It was beginning to feel increasingly important to break through Olivia's rather hostile reserve and get to know her properly. Already he felt part of this family, if only in that he noticed their tensions and wanted to help them.

To his relief, Olivia smiled. "I've never done any sailing. Can you imagine Theo in a boat, Marcus? And my mother likes gardening and reading and not much else. Though, to be fair, she did take me to the beach when I was a child. I built sandcastles and guess what? She read a book."

Her tone was less barbed than previously, and although he heard Jeannette make a slight sound of protest, she didn't attempt a rebuttal, so Marcus suspected the charge was broadly true.

He laughed, taking her comment as the joke it might have been intended to be. "Tomorrow, or the next day? What would suit?"

"You've only just arrived today," Jeannette pointed out. "Take a day to relax and unwind after that journey, Marcus."

Immediately, Olivia's face changed, and Marcus said quickly, "I've had most of today to unwind, not to mention the whole of lockdown, so don't let that worry you. We can go tomorrow if you'd like."

Olivia smiled. "If you're sure, I think I would like. Let's see what the morning brings in the way of weather. You aren't used yet to Cornwall's way of changing quickly from sunshine to rain overnight, whatever the forecast may say. Plans have to change too."

"Do we have a visit from Jeremy arranged for tomorrow?" Theo asked Jeannette. "He was busy today taking the rest of the kids up to Exeter, but presumably he's back at Cedric's now."

Marcus waited for an explanation. This must be a reference to those 'waifs and strays' Theo had mentioned. He was clearly giving Jeannette a chance to provide more information, if she wished.

But it was Olivia who spoke, more lightly this time. "We have been having some exciting times the last couple of weeks, Marcus. And I suspect they aren't finished yet. Are you up for a bit of mystery-solving?"

"A mystery, is it? Sounds fascinating." Marcus turned to Jeannette. "Don't go solving it tomorrow while we're out at Charlestown, will you? I'd like to be in on this."

~ * ~

"So, tell me about this mystery." Marcus pulled out on to the A30 and set off westwards. The breeze became brisk as they picked up speed, and he was glad he'd warned Olivia to bring a headscarf to tie round her hair, much as he enjoyed the idea of the blonde mass of it lifted by the wind. "Dad mentioned your mum had taken in what he called 'waifs and strays.' What was that about?"

"It's part of the same thing, really." Olivia embarked on as much of an explanation as she felt he would want to hear, but when she finished, found herself being bombarded by questions.

"So it's only this Jude who has actually heard anything?"

"Y-yes. But Remy said something troubled him about the house from the very first time he came here."

Marcus made a sound expressing incredulity. "He's a priest, isn't he? I mean, it's his job to see the supernatural in everything."

Olivia frowned. "That's true, and I don't share his beliefs. But when I was living here as a teenager—don't laugh, Marcus, but I used to think I'd heard things, too. I always put it down to the wind, which does make a terrific racket round the side of the house there. But if I'm honest, I didn't want to believe it was anything else. I still don't like going in that room."

Marcus threw a quick glance at her. "If you're saying there's something untoward there, I'll believe it. You don't strike me as a credulous person."

"No, I don't think I am. But neither Mother nor Theo have ever heard or sensed anything, and Mother's lived here all her life. Surely, if it goes back to some ancient traumatic event, as Remy thinks, you'd think someone in the household would have commented on it in her hearing? Her father was born here at Tresayne, and her grandmother and grandfather came to live here after the First War, when they were young. I mean, it just doesn't seem likely that there'd be no family tradition about it, if there's really something. And yet..."

"Yes, it's the 'and yet' bit that's convincing, isn't it? Everything's against it, but you think there might be something in it—and you've no axe to grind." He thought for a moment. "Jeannette and Dad sleep in the Victorian part of the house, don't they?"

She nodded. "Yes, they always have. But Mother slept in that room next to mine when she was young, and she says she never heard anything. The rooms I have are in that wing of the house, but they were put in when she was a teenager. They don't date back even to the Victorian extensions. The house has a very complicated history, architecturally."

"Well, it'll be interesting to see what happens next. Do you think Dad and Jeannette will pursue it, now that Jude has gone?"

"I don't know. I think Mother has started to feel a bit unsettled by it all, and she was glad to get rid of Jude, though she was happy enough to take her in when she first came here for help, before all the ghostly stuff kicked off. Maybe she will want to try to find out what caused it, if Remy can help. He won't be here for much longer, I think, because he's only house-and dog-sitting for our neighbour Cedric and soon he and Mike will have to go home, because Cedric is coming back to Cornwall."

"Why Jude, I wonder? Apart from your mum—why do you call her 'Mother,' by the way? It sounds rather formal—presumably other people have stayed in that room over the years, when Dad and Jeannette have had a houseful of guests. Why should anyone hear anything now?"

"I haven't the least idea." Olivia ignored the question about her mother. "I suppose other people must have stayed there, but not when I've been around, certainly. We have six bedrooms in total—seven, if you count the one I use as a sitting room—so perhaps it wasn't necessary. Or perhaps guests wouldn't like to say, if they'd heard anything."

"Jude was quick to do so."

Olivia tried to be objective, and put aside her own private reservations about Jude, who she felt was certainly odd, and in a way that might possibly have something to do with the mystery. She was sure that she and her mother hadn't been told everything there was to know about Jude, which only added to her instinctive dislike. "That's true, but it was Lorna, Mike's sister, who made it seem real. Lorna's never heard anything herself, even though she slept in that room too, but she was sure Jude had—it wasn't just a dream. It was Lorna who told Mother about it. I think Jude would just have suffered in silence."

"Well, it all sounds very interesting. Dad has been studying the history of the house, he tells me. Maybe he will be writing a book about it for us to publish, if all this turns out to be connected!"

"Rather than just Jude being hysterical, you mean."

He shrugged. "Well, that's always a possibility, isn't it? I'm keen to meet your Remy, though. I'm not a great fan of the clergy, if I'm honest, or religion in general, but on the other hand there are things we can't explain in a scientific way, so I have an open mind. If he thinks there's something supernatural going on, I'll be listening."

Olivia was silent. She wasn't sure, herself, that being open-minded was altogether a good thing. And so often even people who thought they had an open mind turned out to be quite limited in what they would accept. Would Marcus freak out if she told him about her Findom activities, for example? Probably. She sighed. That was a secret she would be wiser to keep from everyone.

She looked across at him, noticing how relaxed he was at the controls of the car—his hands holding the steering wheel lightly but firmly, the movements of clutch, brake and gear stick neat and economical, the whole operation both graceful and confident. She couldn't help also noticing—even admiring—the strong biceps exposed by his short-sleeved shirt. Physical strength in a man didn't normally impress her—she preferred sophistication and social *nous*—but in a brother perhaps it was different? However, that might be, she felt safe with him. She relaxed into her seat, looking forward to the day out.

"Where's this turn-off?" he asked. "Don't let me go speeding past it, will you?"

Tresayne House, Friday June 9th 1916

I have been thinking about myself and Mary. I went to visit her yesterday, to check that she is settling in with Mrs Brown, who seems to have accepted the situation graciously, although I can tell she disapproves of Mary's situation and doesn't want her to stay for very long. She says she does not think the cottage suitable for a child, which is nonsense as I know she and her husband brought up three of their own there. But I will have to find somewhere else for Mary before long. Perhaps I will ask Mrs Brown if she can think of any young man of her own station in the local area who might be willing to marry Mary, if I find a dowry of sorts to go with her. There are cottages on the estate they might live in, and labouring work to be had on the local farms. That might be a possible solution, though my heart is torn at the thought, for it would separate us as surely as the miles between here and North Devon have done, and how could I bear to see her as the wife of another man, and watch the child that I know is mine growing up in the care of a stranger? At least if the footman back at home had married her, she and her child would not be in my sight tormenting me.

Yet how brave she is. And even now that her belly is swollen with the coming child, she is still beautiful, still desirable. I long to keep her with me. But even if I could have married her before, when no one knew of our liaison, I could not do so now that she is carrying a child. She says she could live with the disgrace and scandal, if only I will let her stay. She does not ask me to marry her. She would live privately, she says, where I could visit her secretly. But to my shame, I do not think I could face even this. To live a lie, to carry on an illicit affair while pastoring my parishioners, presiding over the Eucharist, preaching to them of a morality I would know nothing of. No, that is not a way I can countenance.

Twenty-five

Marcus and Olivia arrived at Charlestown just before noon and parked in the centre of the village. There were quite a few cars there, and a sprinkling of sightseers around the tiny harbour, though nothing much was happening. They stood for a while watching the tall ships rocking at anchor, their yards stripped of canvas and their decks bare, silent except for the slapping of the lines against the masts in the stiff breeze blowing off the sea.

"I hope it seems worth the drive?" Olivia asked, sounding slightly anxious.

Marcus turned to her quickly. "It's great. I'd love to go out on one of those ships."

"I think you have to hire them, and a crew to go with them. I don't know whether they do private hires, but they won't be open for business just now, anyway. I expect it's expensive, too! It's mainly film work they do, in normal times."

He grinned. "It's lovely to see the sea, anyway. I've missed that."

"I haven't seen much of it during lockdown," she admitted, thinking of the disastrous afternoon she'd spent at Trebarwith Strand in June. "And before that I had a flat in Dulwich."

Marcus stood in silence, breathing in deeply the unmistakable smell of the ocean. Here in the south-west of the peninsula, thrust out into the Atlantic like a gnarled finger, the sea was no longer a friendly presence but a being of awe. The tameness of the English and Bristol Channels, each side of it, were left behind here, as the straits gave way to the ocean. To the south was the Bay of Biscay, famous for its storms, to the north the turbulent Irish Sea, and to the south-west the Scilly Isles, where innumerable tall ships had been wrecked in centuries gone by.

"Well," he said at last. "I'm hungry. I'm looking forward to finding out what's in that picnic basket Jeannette packed for us."

"It'll be good," Olivia promised him. "One thing Mother is really good at is picnics."

"The basket itself is impressive. A real basket, for a start, not an insulated bag. I like that."

"I suppose the insulated bag would be better at keeping things fresh. But this is what we do, as a family. We keep up traditions, and we hold on to things from bygone eras, too. That picnic basket is decades old. I'm quite surprised it hasn't developed woodworm."

He smiled. "You don't sound too positive about it."

"Oh, it drives me mad sometimes, this tradition thing. We have far too much stuff in the attic that no one ever uses or will ever use. I don't mind so much about antique furniture, but some of it is just tat, honestly. But my mother's sense of family tradition is too strong to let any of it go."

He waited while they unpacked the basket from the boot of his car and found an empty bench to sit on while they ate the food. Olivia had been right. Jeannette's picnic was a splendid one, in a tradition that probably arose from days when the family had had servants to provide meals, and its members only had to relax and enjoy the fruits of their efforts. He wondered whether Jeannette's own childhood was too recent for servants. She must have grown up in the sixties and seventies, so it probably was. Biting into a piece of French bread spread with butter, cheese and pickle, and sipping a glass of white wine—a real glass, he noticed, not a plastic one, and held safely against the side of the basket with a leather strap made for the purpose—he considered how to raise the other topic he'd wanted to discuss with Olivia.

"I have the feeling," he began carefully, "that you sometimes don't get on all that well with your mother." He hesitated. "And before you tell me to mind my own business, let me explain that I've recently quarrelled with my own mother and at the moment we aren't speaking to each other." It was hard to say the words, just as it had been painful to admit the estrangement to his father the day before, but he thought it might give Olivia a sense of fellow-feeling and unlock her reserve.

She looked at him. "I'm really sad to hear that, Marcus. You're right, Mother and I don't always rub along together very well, especially when we're in the same house for long. But we've never been at odds with each other to the extent that I couldn't come home if I wanted to, or that we weren't speaking." She hesitated. "You asked me earlier why I call her 'Mother', and I don't know really. I think I started doing that when I was at boarding school. 'Mummy' sounded a bit precious and childish, and none of the other girls would have called their mothers 'Mum.'"

"You were at boarding school? That surprises me, though I don't know why it should."

"I think the Tresaynes have always have sent their children away to school. It's part of the gentry tradition, you know. I didn't go till I was thirteen. I expect part of the reason was that Theo and Mother wanted to have time together without me always being around. They liked to go back and forth to London, even then, and that made a day school difficult. In a way, it was good for me. Mother and I were already uncomfortable with each other, and at least I made friends there. I used to visit their houses during the holidays sometimes, too, instead of going home."

"At least your family home is available if you want to go there," he pointed out. "Apart from my flat, I don't have a home now." He heard the slight tone of self-pity in those words and retracted at once. "Sorry! That sounds plaintive, and I don't mean it that way. I'm not a child, after all. But my mother remarried many years ago, and for a while she lived in New York, so we didn't see much of each other, though we talked on the phone a lot. But New York was never home for me."

"You said you had a quarrel recently. What was it about?"

He smiled ruefully. For some reason, he hadn't anticipated the question. Inadvertently, he seemed to have placed himself in a position where he could be interrogated, instead of the other way round. "A lot of things, I suppose. Mostly that she wanted to live in my pocket."

"But what about your stepfather?"

"They aren't together anymore. Mum came back to this country in the autumn, and she wanted to live with me. Not in my flat, but in a house somewhere."

Olivia made a face. "Why on earth would she want to do that?"

"A fear of loneliness, I suspect. She has never been happy without someone around."

"I wonder..." Olivia stopped and then began again. "Theo told me that he was a workaholic when he was younger. I suppose he still is in a way, but he makes sure some of the work keeps him at home with Mother now. He learned something from losing you, you know. I was just wondering whether what you said—the fear of loneliness—was why your mother couldn't cope with him being so busy when you were children."

"I could believe that, except that when she left him and took us with her, she didn't actually run to anyone. She just ended up lonelier than ever."

"And leant on you and your sister."

He was surprised she had seen that possibility so quickly. "Correct."

"So what is she doing, now that you won't play ball?"

"She's gone to live with my sister."

"Who also won't talk to you, I'm guessing."

"Correct again. They're going to buy a bigger house so there's enough room for my mother to have an annex. Even Debs didn't fancy the idea of sharing a kitchen with her."

Olivia rubbed her chin. "You're well out of that. But I suppose you can't help feeling bad about it." She looked up at him. "It's funny how the guilty ones can make us feel bad, isn't it?"

"Sometimes," he agreed cautiously. "So what's Jeannette done that makes you feel bad? What on earth can she be guilty of?"

"It sounds mean, put that way. But... when she split up with my father, she wouldn't let me see him."

Marcus put his hand out to touch hers briefly in sympathy. "I can understand what that feels like, anyway."

"Yes. But my father left us, not the other way round. And I think from what Mother has said that she told him to go. It was her house, so I guess she had the right. He didn't want to leave, and when he said goodbye to me, he cried. That—I can't forget that. I was only seven at the time. To see an adult in tears like that, especially Dad, who always seemed so tough. He didn't give me many hugs—nor Mother, not that I saw anyway. But he was fun, and always laughing. I said I would find a way to see him, and he said that would be good. In fact, I never saw him again."

Marcus's hand found its way along the back of the bench to rest on her shoulder. It felt awkward, to be touching her after all these weeks when no one had been allowed to touch anyone, and he had to curb the feeling that someone might be watching and disapproving. But if anyone was looking, they would only think he and Olivia were a couple. No one would think anything of it if even he put his arms round her, though he didn't feel he knew her well enough for that. An arm tentatively around her shoulders would have to do.

"But that isn't really your mother's fault, is it?" He sensed her reaction through his fingertips and looked more closely at her. "You feel it was."

"Yes. She drove him away. I used to hear them quarrelling at night after I'd gone to bed. I couldn't hear the words, but she sounded angry, and he sounded sad and pleading. And then, a couple of years after he left us, he was ill. Mother told me that, but she wouldn't let me go and see him, even though I begged her. So he died, and I was far away. I was only nine then. The following year she married Theo. I don't even know where my father was when he died, or where he's buried. I've never forgiven her for that."

"Maybe," suggested Marcus tentatively, "he was abroad and you couldn't have gone to him."

"I s'pose. But there was something hidden about it. Something she didn't tell me, and still hasn't."

"Maybe you need to ask her?"

He saw her brush away a tear angrily. "Like that's easy to do." She sighed. "It's what Theo said, too, though. Maybe you're right, both of you. But suppose it's something I don't want to know? I'm afraid, Marcus. I loved him so much."

"Perhaps that's why Jeannette didn't tell you. Perhaps she knew it would spoil your memory of him."

Oliva frowned. "D'you know, I never thought of that. But I can't believe he would have done anything really dreadful. He loved playing with me and taking me places—he loved me. I know he did."

His arm tightened round her a little. "I'm sure he did. It must have been hard for him to leave like that. On the other hand—I don't know your mother all that well yet, but she doesn't seem like someone who would drive your father away for no reason. Not out of spite, or to be vindictive, even if they weren't getting on."

Olivia suddenly moved as though his arm were unwelcome, and he hurriedly withdrew it.

"That's what Theo said—have you been talking to him, Marcus? What has he said to you about this? Is that why you're asking all these questions?"

"Hey, don't turn on me. Dad didn't say a word. I can work things out for myself. I suppose I was just curious. You're prickly with Jeannette, and she's sad about it. Surely you can see that? I'm sorry if you'd rather I ignored it." He could have kicked himself. *Trying to act like one of the family before they were ready for it. How stupid could you get?*

"Being big brother, is that it?" The words might have been sarcastic, but the tone was not, and she smiled as she said it, glancing sideways at him.

He was grateful to her for trying to lighten the whole conversation and make the situation into a joke. "Can't help it," he said, following her lead. "I've only been a little brother before. Little brothers are annoying and get in their big sisters' way. Big brothers..."

"Yes?"

"I suppose..." he answered slowly, more seriously, "I suppose they try to support their little sister. They want to make things better for her. I really hadn't thought about it."

"I've been hoping for that," she told him softly. "I've never had a brother, big or small. Please do go on being my big brother, Marcus. I promise I will listen to you, even when you sound like Theo."

He laughed. "Sorry about that. But I'm telling you the truth. He didn't tell me anything confidential about you."

She turned on the bench and regarded him. "You look like him too."

He felt slightly uncomfortable. "Do I? I suppose I do. Without the grey hairs, hopefully."

"There's a photo of him when he first met Mum. It's in the sitting room. I'll show you. I suppose that would be about twenty-five years ago."

"He would have been nearly fifty, then. I'm not even forty yet!"

She laughed. "No, I know. But honestly, you have a real look of him in that photo."

"How did they meet?" he asked.

"At a concert in London, I think. Mother likes classical music, and we used to stay with friends there sometimes. I suppose he was in the audience as a critic for *Gramophone* or one of the broadsheet newspapers. It was quite soon after Dad left, though Theo and Mother didn't get together for several months after that, and they didn't get married until after Dad died. Mother never divorced him—I don't know why."

"Perhaps he wouldn't agree to it."

"That's a possibility. Suggests she felt guilty, though, don't you think?"

"Not necessarily. Olivia..." He hesitated. "Can I call you Livi, like Dad does? At the risk of being too much like Dad again, but I just love it as a name. Much better than Olivia. That sounds all stuffy and starchy, which you are definitely not."

She smiled at him, and his heart skipped a beat, which, he told himself, it really should not have done. She was his sister, dammit.

"I'd like that," she said. "It's Theo's name for me, and Theo is very special. But you're very special as well, and I can't help noticing how like him you are. You might as well go the whole hog and call me Livi, too."

He frowned, suddenly slightly disturbed at the turn the conversation had taken. She clearly had a close relationship with his father, and he didn't want to be seen as just a younger version. "I love it that you care so much about my dad. Just don't let it make you think of me in the same breath as him, will you? My name's Marcus, remember. Don't think of me as Young Theo. I'm your big brother, not your stepdad."

"I suppose it should make you a stepbrother, actually. But Theo adopted me, so we are really and truly brother and sister."

She sounded very happy about it, so why, Marcus asked himself, did a chill fall on his heart as she said it? Didn't he want to be her big brother after all? And if not, what the devil did he want?

Tresayne House, Sunday June 11th 1916

Mary came to me after church today and insisted on discussing her future. She has been thinking about the situation, she says, and she is convinced that Gerald, who is to be my brother-in-law, would want me to marry her, and that there is no reason why I should not, fallen woman though she is. She has obviously been considering how best to persuade me, and I suppose, apart from her pregnancy, the position between her and me is not so different from that of Maudie and Gerald—indeed in some ways, as she points out, marriage would be easier for us, for he will be marrying above him, and it is the man whose status his wife takes.

But there are differences, just the same. He did at least go to a respectable school, for his father spent as much as he could afford on his son's education. I remember Mary told me when we were in Devon that she was sent into service when she was fifteen to help pay her brother's school fees at Blundells. At the time I blessed God for it, because I would probably not have met her if she had not been on our staff. Now I curse the day I took her into my bed, to have this misfortune come upon me—upon us both. More fool me for agreeing to support her brother's suit in the first place. But as an officer, whatever his background, Gerald will be able to become a gentleman if he marries Maudie. Mary will never now be anything but a disgraced servant, poor girl, and must do the best she can in the circumstances.

I wonder even whether her brother will stand by her, as she hopes. If he wants to be accepted by the Tresayne family, it is possible he will not. Mother will certainly expect him to turn his back on her, and I do not feel I know him well enough as a person to judge what he will do. When he is next on leave, I must try to get him to come here with Maudie so we can discuss the situation, though of course without telling him whose child Mary is carrying. But there is so little time, and he is far away. He may not be given leave for months.

Twenty-six

Jeremy and Mike finished off the pasta supper that had been prepared by Mike, and took their coffee companionably into the cottage sitting room.

"It's a whole lot quieter without the kids," Mike observed, stretching out his long legs.

Jeremy smiled. Mike was only two years older than Lorna, but he clearly thought of himself as far more adult. Which was perhaps only fair, though in their father's opinion, Lorna was catching up fast. This whole business with Jude and Megan had shown that. He wondered whether the youngsters had reached home yet. It would be good to know they were safe. Lorna had promised to text him when they arrived at Oxford, and if she forgot then he knew Liz would do it.

"Now all we have to do is to get this Tresayne business sorted," said Mike.

Jeremy raised his eyebrows. "A bit easier said than done."

"I had a thought about the priest hole."

"What kind of thought?"

"About where it might be. Think of it this way, Dad." Mike leaned forward, the better to propound his theory. "Surely there would be downstairs access, so the priest could be got away easily when chance offered? It seems odd to me that the door to it would be in an upstairs room. Surely that would hide the occupant rather too securely? I mean, they wouldn't want him to get trapped there."

Jeremy thought about that. "I guess you could be right. There's no obvious sign of an entrance to it in that spare bedroom, anyway. I did a lot of wall-tapping. It all sounds like stone."

"There you are then. I don't believe all this will be sorted until we know where the priest hole is and what's in it."

"What do you mean, 'what's in it'?"

"I'm sure something terrible happened there, like you said. I don't have a sixth sense, as you do, Dad, but I can make deductions. And I don't see how we can work out what happened without finding the priest hole and opening it. There may be a body in it or something."

"Steady on, Mike. I agree something nasty must have happened, but it wasn't necessarily a murder."

"What a good place to hide a body, though, don't you think?"

Jeremy saw that Mike had got the bit between his teeth and was now bolting happily down the race track. A steadying hand on the rein was definitely necessary. "That could be true, but it's a big leap of deduction. Let's see whether we can find any linking evidence first."

"Okay. So we know Jude must have somehow activated the spiritual disturbances. What would you call it, Dad? We can't keep on saying dramatic things like 'ghostly wailings'."

"'Spiritual disturbances' might be a good way of putting it, I think. It's clearly not ordinary everyday stuff, if voices are being heard when there's no one there, even though only one person has heard them; but on the other hand, it isn't anything definitely supernatural. We just don't know."

"Is there a possibility Jude was imagining it? I mean, I believe Lorna absolutely when she said Jude was hearing something, but there are such things as nightmares, after all."

"I think it's significant that Olivia, who strikes me as quite a hard-boiled person emotionally, at least on the surface, remembers hearing something from that room when she was a teenager. She was probably more sensitive then—though she told me she put it down to the wind, which apparently can be really noisy around that end of the house; Jeannette confirmed that. But Olivia's clearly still not very comfortable about that room, and indeed, it seems everyone feels it's cold and unfriendly, and they don't use it very often."

"And you sensed something you didn't like when you first went to the house."

"Yes, I did. Hard to put my finger on what it was. A feeling of something tragic in its history, perhaps. But that doesn't prove anything."

"Except that you've got that sixth sense, haven't you? Premonitions, hunches, even a feeling of being prompted to do something. Remember that time when you sensed young Robert Althorpe was in danger? And you nearly went to the farm to see George when he was about to commit suicide."

"I ignored that prompting," admitted Jeremy. "And bitterly regretted it afterwards. I was very nearly too late that time. If it hadn't been for the paramedics coming quickly and realising he was still alive..."

"All the more reason to believe your own feelings now," Mike interrupted. "Taken along with the rest, surely it's more than enough evidence for us to do something."

"I suppose so," Jeremy agreed reluctantly. "But what?"

"Suggestions on the back of a five-pound note?"

"Absolutely," smiled Jeremy.

"Right. Let's make a list, like they do in the detective novels."

"Do they? Which detective novels?"

Mike waved a hand impatiently. "Never mind which ones, Dad. What shall we put first?" He took the top leaf from the telephone message pad and picked up the pen that went with it. "Number one. Find the priest hole. Number two, break into it and see what's there."

"If anything."

"Okay."

"I think those two should be further down the list. Number one ought to be finding out more about the history of the house and the family. We can't ask the Landrys to tear their house apart just to look for a priest hole."

"I suppose so." But Jeremy could see Mike was itching to do something physical, practical—and preferably dramatic.

"Theo has a lot of family records, and he's researching the history of the house."

"Yes, Dad! That's true. Diaries and letters and stuff. I remember him saying."

"Well, maybe that's where we should start. If, that is, the Landrys really want us to do any more. They've got Theo's son staying with them now, remember. They might not want us fiddling about all round them while he's there."

"The thing is," Mike pointed out, "if we don't do it now, we may be stuffed. Cedric will want rid of us once he's back to look after the dogs, won't he? Our chance will be over."

Jeremy nodded. "True. Well, one step at a time. Talking of the dogs, one of us had better take them out before we go to bed. Will you do that, or would you rather wash up?"

"I'll take the dogs," decided Mike at once. "You can sort out the dishes. I cooked, after all."

Jeremy scowled at him affectionately. "Fine. I'll phone the Landrys in the morning and see how they're placed. Even though neither of them really believes there's anything to discover, I don't think either Theo or Jeannette are a hundred per cent happy to leave things as they are."

~ * ~

Jeannette was enjoying a session of baking in the kitchen, reflecting happily while she cut out shortbread on the pastry board that so far Marcus's visit had been a great success, especially his obvious affection for Theo and his wish to build a new relationship with him. Even Olivia, after that first rather uncomfortable evening when she had been so prickly, seemed to have decided to give him the benefit of the doubt. Certainly, she had gone off in the car with him this morning quite happily, looking lovely in jeans and an orange-and-white T-shirt. It would be interesting to see whether they came back on as good terms as they left, but on the whole Jeannette felt quite optimistic about it.

When the phone rang, she brushed the flour from her hands and wiped them on a cloth, for it was she who normally answered the landline. There was an extension in the sitting room as well as the kitchen, but Theo, she knew, was in the music room, out of earshot, and he had always refused to have an extension in there. Anyone who needed him for a work-related query would use his mobile number or email, he had reasoned; almost anything that came in on the landline would be local and for Jeannette, and it would only be a nuisance if it disturbed a train of thought—or worse still, a passage of music he was listening to. She didn't mind. It was probably one of her friends ringing up for a chat.

"Tresayne House," she said.

"Hallo, Jeannette. It's Remy."

She blinked. There was no reason at all why Jeremy shouldn't phone her, but with the departure of Lorna and the others, she had, perhaps foolishly, not expected any further communication from him.

"Did the children get home safely?" she asked, fixing on the only possible reason she could think of for the call. "Lorna was a tiny bit apprehensive about the journey, though I told her it would be fine."

"Yes, the trains were on time and they got home by late afternoon. Liz seems to have settled them all in happily, so we shall hope everything will go well."

"Yes. You... you don't think Jude will have more nightmares or... or hear voices in a strange house again, do you?" *Why am I bringing this up?* she asked herself with irritation. Had she not told herself it was all over, that with Jude gone there would be no more hauntings—if that had indeed been what they were?

"I doubt it, but we shall hear, no doubt, if so. That brings me to what I phoned you about."

Her heart sank slightly, but she answered, as stoutly as she could. "What's that, Remy?"

"Theo said something about having lots of family papers which might throw light on anything that could have set off Jude's experiences. Mike and I probably won't be here much longer because Cedric is planning to return soon, so we wondered whether we could have a look at some of them, or maybe help Theo go through them, even? I know you have Marcus there, and won't want us in the way, but perhaps we could bring some stuff back here and sort it?"

"Theo isn't here at the moment," Jeannette told him, justifying the white lie by reckoning that Theo might be physically in the building but was almost certainly emotionally and mentally somewhere else altogether. She always tried not to disturb him when he was busy in the music room, and he'd had little enough time to concentrate on any of his current projects in the last few weeks. "Perhaps he could phone you back?"

"Or we could come by on our walk with the dogs, perhaps? We'll be going out a bit later, and we could drop in on the way back. If it's not inconvenient," he added.

Jeannette smiled to herself. *Men and their enthusiasms,* she thought. Theo probably wouldn't mind being disturbed later in the morning, and she knew he liked Jeremy and would enjoy showing him some of the Tresayne family papers he was working on.

"Olivia has taken Marcus out for the day," she told him. "Or at least, more accurately, he has taken her, in his car. They took a picnic lunch with them, so they clearly aren't planning to come back any time soon. You won't be interrupting any family get-togethers."

"Thanks. That would be great, Jeannette." She could hear relief in Jeremy's voice. She wondered whether it was his own enthusiasm, or Mike's, that he was fostering. Was this why Mike hadn't gone home with the others? But perhaps she was putting two and two together and making about seven.

"We'll see you later, then," she said." I'm just making some biscuits, so you can tell Mike there'll be something to eat when you come. And we can maybe have some coffee."

"Mike is always happy to eat," Jeremy said. "And he has great respect for you as a baker, I know. We shall look forward to it."

They arrived just after eleven, and as promised, she regaled them with coffee and biscuits under the beech tree. Mike made enthusiastic and gratifying inroads into the shortbread, and it turned out that Theo had been going through the family papers on his own account that morning and didn't mind at all being disturbed in his endeavours.

"It seemed to me we need to know more about both the house and its history," he explained. "I'm sorry, my dear," he added to Jeannette. "I know you'd much prefer us to let sleeping dogs lie now that Jude has gone, and it's possible no one else will hear anything. But whatever the reason for Jude setting this off, I doubt whether any of us will really be content to leave things as they are. Livi, for one, is quite troubled about it, you know."

Jeannette sighed. She knew he was right, even though she didn't want to admit it. "Well, you must do what you think best, Theo. Do you mind if I get on with my baking, rather than joining you? You can tell me anything you discover later on."

After Jeannette had gone back to the kitchen, Theo suggested they take the remains of their coffee inside.

"I'll show you what I've looked at so far," he said, leading the way into the music room. "I started at the beginning, as much as I could, and there's an early diary—it's seventeenth century and talks quite a bit about the family recusancy, so we could certainly have a look there for anything about the priest hole and its whereabouts. I haven't got all the way through that one. And then there's a diary written by Reverend Edwin, the one who was drowned one night coming back from visiting a parishioner. I haven't started looking at that, but I must say, so far I haven't seen anything in any of the papers about hauntings, or any particularly traumatic events from the time when the priest hole would have been active. As far as I can make out, the family had a resident priest, who also served as the local parish priest for the neighbourhood, where ordinary folk were as anti-reformation as the Tresaynes."

"Which, I suppose, suggests that whatever we're investigating happened later," said Jeremy. "It may not even have anything to do with the priest hole. Mike will be disappointed if that's the case!"

He glanced at his son, but Mike wasn't listening.

Mike was looking round the room, impressed by the high ceiling, the tall bookshelves, the shining hi-fi rack with its array of winking lights, not to mention the grand piano and the rest of the quietly luxurious furnishings. "This is a marvellous room, sir!" he couldn't help exclaiming.

Theo put his coffee mug down on the table and gestured to them to sit down. "I'm glad you like it, Mike. It was originally the Victorian house's billiard room, built on to the back of the old building when the bedrooms and reception rooms were added to the front. We converted it soon after Jeannette and I married, twenty-five years ago."

"So the old house is kind of in the middle?" Mike was interested in the way houses were laid out, especially historic ones. He hadn't told his parents yet, but he had half a mind to study architecture at some point, with a view to making a career designing houses.

"That's right. I'll show you the plans in a minute, and you'll see how it evolved from quite a small place in the early seventeenth century."

"Do you think they built a priest's hiding place into the original house?" asked Mike. "Or was it added during one of the later building phrases?"

"That's an interesting question. It's true that, according to family tradition, at some point there seems to have been a priest hole in the house. But I don't think any of the family priests was ever arrested, and no one was being burnt at the stake by the time the house was built, although one or two recusant priests had been executed in Cornwall during the Elizabethan period. There was a lot of anti-Catholic feeling after the attempted Guy Fawkes coup, but not here particularly, because the love of the old ways went on well into mid-century."

"I suppose the Tresaynes must have been Royalists during the Civil Wars," put in Mike.

"You mean they might have needed a priest hole to hide King Charles II on the run?" asked Jeremy whimsically.

Mike reddened slightly. "He didn't come here, though, did he?" he retorted, wishing Dad wouldn't disconcert him with teasing jokes when he was being earnest and serious. It wasn't as though the situation required humour. "He went off and hid in oak trees in Shropshire."

Jeremy put a hand on his son's arm. "Sorry, Mike. I didn't mean to laugh at you."

Theo smiled at them both, and the momentary tension dissolved. "In any case, this house was only a tiny place at that point, compared to its size now—just the old hall with its gallery, and the kitchen with a couple of bedrooms above. The main Tresayne estate was on the north coast then, and this was just somewhere to settle indigent relatives. It was only later in the century that this house and estate became their main seat, and they added the small bedroom where Jude heard those sounds, and the little room next door to this. In fact, I'm quite surprised they kept the priest hole, because by the end of the seventeenth century, Catholics weren't really persecuted any more, although being Catholic still involved exclusion from certain occupations. Perhaps that was when it was blocked up."

"So, the little study downstairs was built at the same time that bedroom was made out of the gallery?" asked Mike.

"I think we'd better get out the plans I've found. They show the way the house developed over the centuries. If you're still thinking about where the priest hole is, that would probably be best."

"That would be great, sir. I've had a few ideas of my own about where it might be, but...." His voice trailed away, and Jeremy frowned at him. "Sorry, Dad."

"The last thing we want to do is to be taking you on a wild goose chase," said Jeremy. "Mike has this idea that the entrance to the priest hole would be likely to be downstairs, not upstairs, because of easy escape routes, so a look at how the house evolved would be very useful, not to mention intrinsically interesting, if you're sure you've got the time, Theo."

Theo put his coffee mug down. "It's all to hand, because I've become so fascinated by the house's history that I've put the book I'm writing on Britten aside and am focusing on this. Apart from anything else, I definitely feel we need to find out what caused poor Jude to hear someone crying."

Tresayne House, Monday June 26th 1916

Freddie writes of a major battle in preparation, though he cannot say much because of the censor. Can such a major preparation be kept secret, I wonder? He describes the artillery being brought up behind their trenches, and much movement of troops in the area he is in. He also says morale is high among the men, and they are eager to go into action. How can this be? He writes of wet weather, in spite of the time of year, and surely that must make fighting in the open difficult, if that is what is planned? And the Germans will be able to see the troop movements and the artillery being set up, and surely they are not fools enough to ignore it? I suppose it depends on what their intelligence is on the heavy fighting the French army is involved in further south in the battle for Verdun. Perhaps they will think it is a feint—and perhaps it is.

But my heart misgives me about this action. It smacks of vainglory and over-confidence, yet again, on the part of the generals, and my dear young brother is there in the midst of the danger—although he himself seems quite unworried by it and writes instead of taking German prisoners, picking up souvenirs, and gassing their trenches. I am sickened to my soul by such talk. Are not Germans human beings like our own people?

But I know this is the pacifist in me talking. Most men would react to the situation as Freddie has, especially when they have waited so long to be involved in any major battle, and all the time have been encouraged to think of the German soldiers as simply 'the enemy'. And then our own troops have suffered from gas attacks, for the Germans used it first. I cannot condemn him too much.

For now, they are in reserve, I think. But if the battle does not go well, then they will be called into action. May God protect him.

Twenty-seven

They spread the plans on top of the grand piano, which was the only flat surface large enough, and ranged themselves around it, with Theo on one side and Jeremy and Mike on the other. Theo reached up and switched on the reading light that normally shone on the music when he was playing.

"The original Jacobean house was just this central portion." He indicated a sketch plan, with different coloured inks showing the walls of different periods. "This plan was prepared by the Victorian Tresaynes before they built on their extensions. I suppose it was helpful to the architects to see where the original load-bearing walls were and how the house had evolved in the seventeenth century."

Mike studied the plan. He could see a room marked where the kitchen now was, linked to the old hall by an archway, presumably the same one that still existed. Red ink showed where the gallery above the hall had been, while to the north, a small ground-floor chamber was shown leading off the hall.

"Is this the study, next door to this room we're in now?" he asked.

"That's right. It may have originally been the estate office, as it had an external door. That was blocked up when the music room was built, and it can only be accessed from the old hall now. Then when the upper floor was created to house extra bedchambers, it became a study. It shares a chimney with this room, which may have been there before the Victorian alterations."

Mike could see there had originally been a large cupboard to one side of the chimney in the study, next to the door that gave on to the hall. Perhaps this cupboard had acted as a priest hole? The door could have been camouflaged, he supposed.

"Was this the study Reverend Edwin would have used?" asked Jeremy suddenly, before Mike had a chance to say anything. "When he was rector here?"

"Yes, I believe so. Structurally, the house was much as it is now by that time, apart from the extra bedrooms above the old hall, but as is always the case, room use changed over the centuries to suit different lifestyles. In a rectory, I think that would be the natural room to use for private study and interviews with parishioners, who could enter through the old hall. The sitting room and dining room would be for entertaining, and guests would enter at the front of the house. Some of the Victorian bookshelves are still in place in the room next door—they contain some of my own books that I don't often use—so I think it's a fair bet that it was used as a study at least until Jeannette's grandparents came to live here in 1917, and maybe afterwards."

"Would it be okay for me to have a look at that room?" Mike asked quickly, ignoring his father's frown. "Given that Jude heard sounds even from there, it might be there's something odd about it. Especially if it was part of the original house."

"Certainly," Theo responded. "Do you want to do that now, before we look at the rest of the plans?"

Mike opened his mouth to agree, but Jeremy cut in. "Can we see the later plans first, Theo, to give us an idea of what might have been done by the Victorian builders?"

Theo unrolled several large sheets of paper. These looked more like the kind of plans Mike had seen before. They showed the Victorian extensions overlaid on the original house plan, and as Theo had said, these were clearly added both to the front and the rear of the house.

"But in fact, the concept of front and rear don't really work here," Theo pointed out. "In a sense these were side extensions, but they rotated the access points. The original entrance to the house was on the west, and there was also a door from the scullery/still-room into the courtyard to the north, which gave on to a number of outbuildings that were then demolished by the Victorian builders to make room for the walled kitchen garden. I think the kitchen and the hall may both originally have had windows facing south, as well, but these were blocked up when the Victorians created a new 'front' with the reception rooms either side of a new hallway. I think they must have enlarged the east window in the kitchen to make up for losing the light from the south."

He paused to allow Jeremy and Mike to follow this line of argument through the plans, then went on. "The billiard room was added to the east of the study, around the same time as the rest of the Victorian alterations, which made the house roughly rectangular, where it had once been nearer to an E-shape."

"So the priest hole was probably put into the original building, though it could have been added when they put in the bedroom," observed Mike.

"I would think so, yes. No point creating it after persecution had stopped, so we know the Victorian builders can't have had anything to do with it—although I suppose they may have removed it, and we are looking for something that no longer exists."

"Or they may have blocked it up permanently," suggested Jeremy.

"Indeed. I don't think the plans will get us much further. We need to look at some of the written material. And there's plenty of that. Boxes and boxes of it."

Mike, jiggling with impatience, felt impelled to ask again: "Do you mind if I take a look at the study?"

His father was frowning, but Theo smiled. "I'm sorry, Mike. Of course you can. Do you want to go and do that while your dad and I are sorting out some of the diaries and letters? I think those are the materials that are most likely to give us some clues to this mystery."

Mike jumped to his feet at once, and almost ran out of the music room into the old hall. The doorway to the old study was deep, as though it had been driven through the thick outside wall of the hall. Yet, this room had been part of the original building, he'd been told.

He went into the room and walked around it, wall tapping as his father had done in the bedroom upstairs. As Remy had reported of the upper room, the walls sounded as though they were solid stone. To one side of the door, in the corner where it backed on to the music room, there was a wide cupboard. He opened it, to find a hanging rail with a row of empty hangers. He pushed between these and tapped carefully around the back of the cupboard. Directly in front of him the wall sounded solid, though even if it hadn't, there wouldn't be enough room for much of a hiding place. Perhaps, after all, he was wrong about where the priest hole must be.

He tried to remember exactly what Dad had told him about the room off the landing above the old hall. Hadn't the measurements been odd? He went back into the music room. His father and Theo were sitting on opposite sides of the coffee table, each with a pile of documents in front of him.

"Dad, I'm sorry to disturb you, but can you remind me what you said about the difference in measurements in the room upstairs? Wasn't there a discrepancy or something?"

"That's right," Theo answered him at once. "We reckon the room is five feet narrower than it looks to be from the outside. Though it's difficult to be sure because of that massive chimney between the old hall and the kitchen."

Mike thought about this. In houses this old, he knew, chimneys were quite often bigger downstairs than upstairs, because of the flue narrowing, but often the chimney breast itself carried on at the same width all the way up. "Would it be okay if I went upstairs to look?"

Jeremy got up from his chair. "I'll come with you. Theo, don't feel you have to look after us. You look as though you've found some interesting stuff there."

"I'm reading some eighteenth-century letters," Theo told him. "Some of them are fascinating, others are tedious in the extreme. But so far, I've seen nothing about a priest hole, nor about anything terrible happening in the house. I'm not sure the family of that time even knew there was a priest hole, so perhaps it had already been closed off. Give me a shout if you need me."

Father and son climbed the stairs out of the old hall and went into the small north-facing room.

"This room was converted from a gallery, wasn't it?" said Mike. "I suppose this is how the access worked most easily, because they'd have to put in a sprung floor over the hall."

Jeremy nodded. "That makes sense. Did you find anything interesting in the study?"

"Nothing helpful," Mike admitted. "The walls are uneven in thickness in places, but in an old house that doesn't necessarily mean anything, does it? I mean, I was surprised at how deep the recesses are each side of the chimney breast, because I thought the plans showed that room as part of the original house, so they shouldn't have had to make a hole for the door."

"It's easy to argue anything from the plans, though, is it? As Theo said, they're only a sketch, rather than a proper blueprint, and they're probably based on what the Victorian owner of the house told them, to guide them when they were designing the new extensions, rather than on anything the original builders left behind."

Mike nodded, feeling his ideas yet again being squeezed out of contention by the uncertainties of the evidence. It was very frustrating.

"Theo and I worked out that the width of this room—I mean, from the chimney breast to the wall opposite—is less actually here in the room than it looks outside. This room look almost square, inside, but outside it is clearly rectangular. The chimney is enormous, but I wonder whether that altogether accounts for it."

Mike laid a hand on the chimney wall. There was a small grate, presumably used to heat the room for Victorian servants, but it was dwarfed by the chimney breast, which extended across the whole of the south wall of the room. "I suppose it's big because the hearth below it heated the whole of that big hall. But it doesn't taper, does it, which you might expect?"

Jeremy returned to his tapping, aware yet again of the cold and spiritual darkness of this room. He couldn't quite believe it was simply his over-active imagination, interpreting the phenomena much too dramatically. Yet, he couldn't help asking, what on earth could have happened here to cause it? He repressed a shiver, and returned his sense of doom to his subconscious, not denying its validity but choosing to focus instead on the practical search for empirical evidence.

"I'm wondering whether the late-seventeenth-century alterations included filling it in to make it look symmetrical. It might have tapered in the first place. It all sounds quite solid, though."

"So why is the chimney breast so deep and wide?" asked Mike.

"That is the question. If this is where the priest hole is, how on earth did they access it? And it couldn't be both sides of the fireplace, could it?"

"Camouflage, perhaps?"

"That would fit with it being built into the original house. You couldn't add a stone wall like that without strengthening the structure downstairs, and there's no evidence of that."

"Maybe it's just brick? That would sound solid. It does seem as though this is the most likely place, from what we know so far."

"But if there's no access," Jeremy pointed out, "it must have been blocked at some stage, and you'd think there'd be some sign of it, if only a change in the sound, although I suppose if was well plastered afterwards, it would be hard to be sure whether you're tapping on brick or stone."

Mike sighed. "We're not much further on, are we?"

Jeremy patted him on the shoulder. "We need to go back and look at the written evidence, I think, Mike. Archaeology will only get you so far."

Mike grinned. "I prefer it to going through dusty old documents, as you know, Dad."

"Have a break, then. Go and walk the dogs or something. We shouldn't leave them on their own too long."

"Yes, I think I will do that. Walking is good for thinking."

Jeremy went back to the music room and settled down again to reading the letters of long-gone and probably forgotten Tresayne ancestors. Theo had hardly moved. He was obviously deep in his own researches which at this point seemed to be in the family accounts. Jeremy could only assume Theo thought there might be some evidence to be found there of one of the ancestors actually adding a priest hole to the existing structure. Personally, he thought that unlikely. The hiding place must be somewhere in that massive chimney breast he and Mike had just been examining. But without finding the entrance to it, they couldn't be sure. Besides, the fact of its existence didn't prove anything. What they needed to know was what had caused Jude to hear voices in the night. They were no nearer working that out than they had been before.

When Mike returned, Jeannette set sandwiches and drinks on the table outside and listened politely while they told her what they had (and had not) discovered. She seemed most interested in Mike's theories about there being a hiding place somewhere in the big chimney breast above the old hall, but this was mainly, Jeremy suspected, because she actually believed in the possibility of a priest hole, since it had been mentioned by her grandparents, whereas she had no belief at all in any supernatural activity, whatever Jude might have heard.

"Come and show me," she said to Mike, as they finished their lunch and Theo and Jeremy headed back to the music room. "We could look at the other rooms upstairs, as well, the ones above the kitchen. One is a bathroom now, but the other is my sewing room—that's my winter hobby when there isn't much to do in the garden. That's on the other side of the big chimney, which served the kitchen below, as well as the old hall. If you ask me, they had much more idea then of keeping the house warm than the nineteenth-century builders did with their thin walls and small fireplaces."

But although Mike explained his theories in detail to Jeannette and showed her his reasoning, neither of them could find any sign of an entrance to the priest hole in either of the two rooms. "And I'm not tearing that big chimney breast apart looking for it, Mike. Besides Jude's hysterical ramblings, we don't have any evidence there's anything but a piece of history here."

Mike was rather disturbed by her strictures on Jude's experiences, but he was too polite to argue with her. Besides, in spite of her manifest kindness, he found her unquestioning certainties daunting. In her own way, she was certainly a formidable woman. He decided to leave Dad to do the arguing if it turned out necessary. He would back Dad on a mission to overcome even Jeannette's objections.

So Jeannette went back to her gardening, and Mike returned to the music room to have another look at the plans spread out on the top of the piano. His father and Theo seemed still engrossed in their own researches. Neither of them so much as looked up as he entered.

~ * ~

They were still there when Marcus and Olivia returned from their day out, Olivia with her cheeks softly pink from a day in the fresh air, Marcus as suave and assured as ever, and both clearly on good terms with the other. Jeannette, meeting them by the back door as they came in from parking the car in the courtyard, thought she had not seen Olivia look so happy in years.

"Any new discoveries?" asked Marcus, when she explained that Jeremy and Mike were in the music room helping Theo with his research on the house. "Livi told me something about the mystery, while we were out. It sounds fascinating."

Livi. No one but Theo has ever called her that. Presumably Olivia herself had given permission, but it suggested a rapid move towards sibling intimacy. Jeannette realised that part of her was very pleased that the brother–sister relationship was settling down so well. Yet, at the same time, another part was faintly anxious. She knew how much Olivia had wanted to build a relationship with her brother. But what did they really know of Marcus, after all?

Tresayne House, Tuesday July 4th 1916

There are reports in the newspapers of a great battle being fought on the Somme. I knew a major attack was being planned, from those guarded bits of information Freddie gave me in his letters, but it is taking place now. We have certainly gained some ground, it seems, but at great cost.

Freddie's battalion was not involved in the first attack, I think, though they are in that part of the line, and I suppose may well be mobilised for successive attacks in the weeks to come, as the immediate objectives have not been entirely met. I have written to Mother to try to comfort her. She will be so anxious for Freddie. Maudie must be glad Gerald is with the 2nd battalion in Greece, and perhaps is not in so much danger there.

The papers are full of patriotism and the heroic actions of our soldiers, but in reality, from what I hear from my pacifist friends, the attack has not been anything like the complete success that was required if we are to push on to victory. I do wish the Allies would at least begin negotiations with the Germans. Neither side has had the easy victory they first expected, and surely by now, two years on from the start of hostilities, the casualties both have suffered must give them pause? Surely it is time for a negotiated peace?

Twenty-eight

Olivia sat at the desk in her sitting room and opened her laptop. It was more than time to do her daily servicing of the paypigs. She answered their messages and depressed their egos as their fetishes demanded, but where normally there was a certain satisfaction about the activity, as though she were punishing these individuals for being men, however weak and needy, on behalf of all women who were oppressed by the stronger and more macho sex, today the whole operation seemed pointless. Why on earth— apart from the money, which wasn't peanuts and was the reason, at least ostensibly, for her taking up Findom in the first place—was she continuing to spend time and effort on these stupid, inadequate individuals?

Perhaps the root of her frustration was the contrast with the man with whom she had spent the day. She could imagine many of the men she had encountered in her business life—even some of those she had worked for and with whom she had had affairs— rather enjoying the perverted relationships she had with her paypigs. But not Marcus. Not in a million years would Marcus be attracted by such activity. More likely, he would be repelled by her involvement in it—a rather uncomfortable thought, in the circumstances.

After hearing his advice, what she most wanted to do was to talk to her mother, and find out the details about her father's death, and why he had left them. She remembered her conversation with Theo a few weeks ago, when he had pointed out to her that she had never asked her mother about the break-up and why it had happened. She had simply stuck with her notion that Jeannette had driven her father away; but there could indeed be reasons why her mother had felt she had to do so. She wondered why it had always seemed so important to her to side with her father. Perhaps he had seemed friendless and vulnerable, dying so far from home and without any of his family with him, and she had instinctively taken his part. But if Theo thought her mother had good reasons for her action, her respect for her stepfather meant that she should find out what they were.

The only problem was that with Jeremy and Mike in the house, and Marcus clearly interested in getting involved with the mystery of the priest hole, she didn't know whether her mother would have the time to sit down with her and have the kind of in-depth conversation the matter warranted.

She sighed and sent a few more messages to paypigs who wanted to give her money in exchange for her verbal humiliation of them. They might be fools, and unworthy of her notice, but it was their choice, after all.

Outside on the landing, she heard Kato hissing. It was a peculiar sound, quite unlike his normal plaint when he was hungry or the cat flap was closed, but not a cry of hurt or injury either. She had heard him hiss angrily once at another cat who ventured into the garden, but this sounded much more like fear. She got up and went over to the door.

The cat was standing with his back to her, hunched up into an arc. A terrible snake-like hiss came from his wide-open mouth. As she opened the door, he glanced round wildly, his eyes enormous, and fled down the stairs. Puzzled and rather worried, she walked down the corridor. Had another cat come into the house and threatened him? There was nothing to be seen. But she was sure Kato had been looking towards the other side of the landing, and as she walked towards it, she saw that the door of the twin room was slightly ajar. On impulse, she pushed it open and went in.

There was no one to be seen, either human or animal. The beds were stripped of linen, the flowers cleared from the chest of drawers, the windows slightly open. Perhaps her mother had been cleaning in there while she and Marcus were out. The breeze was blowing the curtains into the room, so perhaps Kato had heard something he hadn't understood and had panicked? But she had to admit that didn't sound at all like Kato, who became angry rather than timid under stress, and arrogant rather than anxious in his dealings with the humans of his household, never mind other cats. *Black cats are witches' cats,* she found herself thinking, whimsically, and then wished she hadn't.

But there was nothing in the room to feed into that instinctive unease that she had so often felt about it. She walked over to the window and looked down into the courtyard, where her mother's little car and Marcus's big convertible sat side by side. She tried to imagine the smell and bustle of the stables in the nineteenth and early twentieth centuries, when there were coaches in the coach-house, and the old barn was full of horses, standing in their individual stalls. The room she was in would, she supposed, have been a bedroom for a couple of servant women then, while the single men—just a coachman and a gardener, probably, for it had never been a grand enough house to have inside menservants such as footmen—slept above the coach-house. The men's quarters were still there but had been converted into storage space for tools by her grandparents during the Second World War, when a large proportion of the acreage had been put down to vegetables, many of which were stored over the winter in the coach-house. She remembered her grandfather talking about the Land Girls and the mischief they got into—"fun and larks" as he had called it. He had been away at school for much of the War, though, so he was probably remembering the lighter moments they had shared during his vacations.

And in all the reminiscences—those of her grandmother and her grandfather that she vaguely remembered, though they had only visited during her childhood, and she had not been close to them, those of her great-grandmother who had lived in the house when Olivia's own mother was young—there had been nothing about this room, or the rest of the house, being haunted.

She wondered how the men's research into the mystery was going. No doubt she and her mother would hear all about it over dinner.

"Olivia!" She heard Jeannette's voice calling from the old hall. "What on earth did you do to Kato? He's run off into the garden with his hair all standing on end. I've never seen him so upset."

"Not guilty, Mother. I found him in that state on the landing just now, hissing like mad at something. He seemed to be disturbed by something in the twin room," she added, finding herself unable to resist this small provocation. "But I can't for the life of me work out what it was. I went in there and couldn't see anything."

There was no reply.

~ * ~

In the music room, Mike was showing Marcus the plans and explaining to him his theory about the priest hole and the entrance to it.

"The original entrance to the study was to the east, you see? That made it separate from the main house, so I suppose the priest could go in and out without disturbing the family, though I think you could probably access it from the hall as you can now, as well. The builders blocked the entrance up when they built the billiard room, Theo says—the room that's now the music room. So I think the study must have been the priest's quarters, with the hiding place to go into just in case he needed it."

"Sounds plausible. But I don't see where the hiding place was."

That was just the problem, thought Mike. The cupboard itself clearly wasn't big enough for anyone to hide in for long, and he didn't have any other suggestions. He was slightly in awe of Marcus, who reminded him a little of his English teacher at school. Mr Hellyer had inspired him to study English Literature at university, and was a thoroughly heroic person, in Mike's opinion. He and Marcus must be about the same age, and they were physically much the same type, but Marcus was more worldly, more cosmopolitan, and clearly much richer. *London money,* thought Mike, with an inner smile. But then, the Tresaynes had been rich, too, you could tell, and Marcus's father was clearly helping Jeannette and Olivia to keep their living standards high. It was a different world, and one in which he felt slightly at a disadvantage. But, he told himself firmly, Dad would say we are all equal in the sight of God, and while he wasn't quite sure whether God existed or not, he was certain the equality idea was right.

Seated in their armchairs, Theo and Jeremy were studying diaries and letters respectively. A large box file lay open on the table between them, into which they put documents that might shed any light on the problem of the priest hole, but it was still almost empty. For the moment, the location of the priest hole was the sole focus of their search, but they had agreed that if there was any word of haunting or ghostly activity of any kind, all would immediately halt their own researches and take note.

Theo stretched and looked at his watch. "It's getting late," he observed, "and we've been at this pretty much all day. D'you want to call a halt for this evening?"

Mike waited on tenterhooks to hear his father's views on this. He himself was willing to go without food and continue the detective work indefinitely until they had found a proper lead. But

Dad, he knew, might feel that was taking advantage of Theo and Jeannette's hospitality.

"In fact, I've just come across an interesting letter from the Tresayne who had the seventeenth-century additions made to the house," Jeremy replied. "It's not that easy to decipher, but I think I've figured it out correctly."

Three pairs of eyes turned in his direction.

"What does it say?" asked Mike.

"Can you bring the sketch plan down and put it on the table where we can all see it, please, Mike? The one with the red colour on it showing the late-seventeenth century additions. It may help."

Mike laid the plan reverently on the coffee table beside the box file.

"I'm afraid this isn't any kind of instruction to the builders." Jeremy indicated the document in his hand. "It's a letter from Rupert Tresayne to his wife, who was upcountry somewhere, I'm not altogether sure why. It sounds as though she was in London. Maybe she had friends there. It doesn't say."

"Never mind about his wife!" exclaimed Mike. "What does the letter say about the priest hole?"

Jeremy smiled. "Hang on, Mike. I'll get to that in a minute."

He turned over the pages of what had obviously been a long letter, to find the paragraph he wanted. "As far as I can see, he says he's commissioned the builders to put in a priest's hiding place as part of the more general construction work they were doing."

"Rather as we thought," agreed Theo.

"That's right. It sounds as though it was an afterthought, and this is why he's writing to his wife about it. The building work had already begun, but something made him decide to increase the size of their safe place for the resident priest. Perhaps as Anglicanism was growing stronger politically, he feared that being Catholic might be about to become difficult again; it's clear the Tresaynes were quite determined to keep to the old faith, even after the departure of James II. Anyway, it seems there was a priest hole in the original Jacobean house, as we thought, but it was hardly more than a box hidden in the wall. The additions to the house were a good opportunity to improve it."

"I suppose," suggested Mike thoughtfully, "that *we* know persecution got less intense after the Civil War, and that eventually the government decided on Catholic Emancipation, but if the people here had had some bad experiences under Queen Elizabeth, they might think the bad times might come again. Especially when King William and Queen Mary were staunch Protestants."

"That's exactly the problem of looking at history with the benefit of hindsight," agreed Jeremy. "It's easy to forget the people who were living through those times didn't have that advantage."

"I suppose," went on Mike slowly, "it's a bit like not knowing how this pandemic will end. It could just fizzle out, with vaccines and treatments that will make it seem less serious. But we can't be sure that's how it will go. It might get worse and kill everyone. I guess that's why lots of people are frightened." His thoughts had taken him further than he had meant them to, and he stopped in confusion. After all, it seemed even his father had struggled to come to terms with the pandemic.

Jeremy said nothing, but Marcus smiled at him. "I think it's exactly like that. I don't blame Rupert Tresayne in the least for improving his priest hole. Remy, does it say where the original was?"

"That's the part I think Mike will be especially interested in." Jeremy looked up at him, and Mike realised his father had hardly heard what had been said about the pandemic. "The original Jacobean priest hole was in the dividing wall between the old hall and the study, with the entrance in the cupboard to the right of the chimney. It must be well camouflaged, because we didn't find it, but that was the point, I suppose."

"So that one *was* actually built into the original house." Mike sounded excited. "The wall seems to be the same thickness all the way along, but actually where the two rooms join it must be shallower."

"That's right."

"Can we go and look again?" Mike made for the door.

"Wait a minute, Mike. Don't you want to know where they built the extension, the one that must still be there now?"

Mike stopped. "But isn't it in the same place?"

"No. They re-used the entrance, but the priest hole itself was put upstairs, in the gallery room. The old priest hole became the stairs to it."

"Actually *in* the chimney breast."

"Yes, that must be why the chimney breast is so deep and wide in that room. Only a small part of it is actually chimney. The rest is camouflage. Let's have another look at the plans and see whether there's any indication of it. I think there must have been an entrance in the gallery bedroom, too."

They pored over the sketch plan but couldn't make much of it. "I don't think they ever put that detail in on the plans," concluded Theo at last. "It must have been just a verbal instruction from Rupert direct to the builder."

"That does make sense, I suppose," observed Jeremy. "Cover your tracks, and leave no evidence in the form of written instructions."

"Wow!" Mike straightened up. "Can we go and look for the entrance to the priest hole now? I *said* it would be downstairs."

Jeremy smiled at this. "You did indeed. Very clever of you."

Mike, not sure whether there was some reproof in the comment, hesitated before reiterating, "But can we go and look?"

Just at that moment, Jeannette came into the room bearing a tray of glasses. "Dinner is nearly ready. Can we offer you a drink, Marcus? You too, Jeremy, if you'd like one. And I've made enough food for you to stay and have a meal with us if you want to go on researching this evening."

Jeremy got up. "It's kind of you, Jeannette, but I think we should leave you to your evening. We've made some progress here, but there's more to do. May we come back tomorrow—whenever would be convenient? I'm sorry to press you, especially when you have Marcus staying, but I know Cedric will be turfing us out shortly, and Mike and I are both very keen to help you find this priest hole."

It was the only way he could think of to ask, but he knew that in truth Jeannette was not at all eager for this kind of help. She would rather the whole business was buried and forgotten. Unfortunately, he feared that was not going to be possible.

"Is the visitor permitted an opinion?" asked Marcus suddenly.

Jeannette looked at him. "Of course. And you mustn't think of yourself as a visitor any longer. A guest, yes, but a family guest."

"Thanks for that. I appreciate it. Well, I can only say that I would be enormously disappointed not to go on with this quest, wherever it leads us. Surely knowing where the priest hole is, especially if we can get into it, must be a useful step towards finding out what Jude heard?"

Jeannette looked at Theo, who nodded. "If you can bear it, my dear, I think another day or two may bring us to a conclusion, or at least to a knowledge of what, if anything, the priest hole has to do with Jude's experiences."

"In that case," she replied, smiling, "so be it. Coffee time tomorrow, Remy?"

"Perfect. Thank you, Jeannette."

Tresayne House, Wednesday July 28th 1916

Freddie's latest letter arrived this morning, which was reassuring as it means he is still safe. He writes of coming up through the old German positions that have been re-taken during the latest Big Push. His battalion was in trenches in the same area last year, so it must have been interesting to see how the area has changed. He says the Allied barrage flattened the German trenches completely, but from the amount of resistance it seems they have encountered, I fear the Germans had enough warning to have retreated out of harm's way before the barrage happened. I suppose he could not say more because of the censor. I'm sure he will not have written of military matters to Mother even as fully as he has to me. Indeed, I'm quite surprised he has had time to write letters at all!

He sounds as cheerful as ever, and even asks for more cigarettes and another Dawes' parcel. He seems to be enjoying the prospect of action. I think what he finds most difficult about trench warfare, in fact, is the boredom of simply sitting around waiting for something to happen, always knowing that 'something' might be enemy gas or shells but unable to do anything to prevent them. He is also focusing on capturing German rifles and helmets where he finds them, to keep as souvenirs. All the troops are doing it, he says, but I wonder whether an officer should? I suppose Freddie knows what would be frowned on—not that it would necessarily stop him doing what he wants to do! But direct orders I'm sure he will obey without question.

I am adding to this entry, for I have just received a cable from Maudie to say that Freddie is listed as Missing in Action. The presumption is that he was killed in the battle for High Wood, as his company was heavily involved in the fighting on the 23rd. But it's also possible he has been taken prisoner. The German authorities publish the names of those they have captured, so we shall know soon, but it will take a little time and is an uncertain process. My heart is heavy, for the most likely conclusion is that he is dead, and we will never see him again. All that youth and promise snuffed out like a candle, and for what? And my poor mother. If he is gone, what will she do?

Twenty-nine

Jeannette cleared breakfast away the following morning in a slightly frustrated frame of mind. Far from diverting Theo from the priest hole fixation that seemed to be afflicting not only him but also Jeremy and Mike, Marcus's arrival seemed to have exacerbated it. Why on earth Marcus should have become so interested in what was purely a Tresayne affair, she really couldn't fathom. She had expected him to spend a lot of time with his father and had resolved to make sure that he had the opportunity to do so. But instead, yesterday he had gone off for the day with Olivia, and then this morning had willingly accepted his father's invitation to join him in the music room, not, apparently, for in-depth father–son discussions, but for further researches into her family history.

It's not as though it's Landry family history, she thought with annoyance. If she and Olivia, the only Tresaynes remaining, had no great interest in finding their own house's priest hole, and no belief in any of the ghostly goings-on that Jude had sensed, then why had Marcus and Theo—never mind Jeremy and Mike, who had no connection even with the local area, never mind the family—become so fascinated by it? She sighed.

"Are you okay, Mother?"

She hadn't seen Olivia standing in the doorway. "I'm fine," she declared. "Just a bit frustrated with all this priest hole hunting, I must admit. I'd hoped we could all have taken Marcus out today, as a family outing."

"Another day, perhaps. I think he's planning to stay for a few weeks. He and I had fun yesterday. I like him a lot."

Something in her tone made Jeannette look at her more closely, but she decided to say nothing.

"Why don't you want to find this priest hole, Mother? Is it simply that you don't believe it has anything to do with what happened with Jude? Or are you afraid of what we might discover?"

"I'm not afraid of anything," Jeannette snapped. "I just think it's a waste of time, that's all. Now that Jude has gone, we probably won't have any more odd happenings."

"Kato hates that room," Olivia told her. "You saw him yourself yesterday. And in fact, I'm slightly spooked by it myself. I always have been."

"I suppose you told Remy that."

"Yes. You asked me to, remember?"

"What do you mean about Kato, anyway? He was in a very odd mood yesterday, but I thought you must have trodden on him or something."

Olivia told her what had happened. "I went in after he ran away. Had you been dusting in there? The windows were open."

"I thought it needed a bit of a spring clean," said Jeannette, sounding, even to her own ears, slightly defensive.

"You do feel something about that room!"

"It's a cold room, certainly, and not particularly cosy or welcoming. But we don't use it much, so I'm not sure that's a big deal, really. I don't get goose-bumps when I'm in there, or anything like that—though I know I'm not very sensitive to such things, so that means nothing. Anyway, the men have got the bit between their teeth, so we just have to go along with it."

"I agree. But that wasn't what I wanted to talk to you about," Olivia said.

Jeannette was surprised. It was so long since Olivia had wanted to talk to her about anything that the idea seemed quite alien, even alarming.

"What is it?" she asked. "I've got quite a lot to do before Remy and Mike come, and then they'll need feeding at lunchtime."

There was a pause.

"I'm sorry," Jeannette went on after a moment. "That didn't sound very inviting, did it? If you want to talk to me, Olivia, then of course I can find time. Do you want to help me clear the breakfast? Then we can have a cup of coffee and you can say anything you have a mind to."

Quite what Olivia was cooking up, she couldn't imagine, and the idea of having a deep conversation with her daughter was, she had to admit to herself, rather daunting. She wondered what new problem she was going to be asked to deal with, on top of all the rest. But if Olivia wanted to talk, the last thing she should do was to make it difficult for her. The vista of some improvement in their relationship opened up before her, full of hope and even a revival of affection. She mustn't risk shutting that down by mistake.

"I don't know why you let those lazy men get away with leaving all the cooking and clearing up to you," said Olivia. "You've enough to do looking after the house and the garden. Who does all the washing, changing beds, and so on? You. But I'm not always as helpful as I should be, I know."

"I think it's a generational thing," Jeannette told her briskly, ignoring the last comment. "Theo does wash up dinner if I've cooked it, and he feeds the cat, so he's not that lazy."

"The cat is Theo's," pointed out her daughter.

"Well, yes, that's true!" Jeannette laughed. "But Theo grew up in an era when it was women's work to look after the house, at least in middle-class families. And we had help, too, which I'll be glad to have again when we can. Theo would be very hurt if he knew you'd called him lazy. And Marcus is our guest, even if he is family."

"I'll bet Marcus would be more than happy to help. He seems very keen to be part of our family—I was surprised."

"Maybe he's had some problems with his own," suggested Jeannette.

"Yes, I think he has. But that's just made him appreciate Theo more. And I think he rather likes the idea of having me as a younger sister."

"And you?" asked Jeannette. "Do you like it, too?" She looked at her daughter as she spoke and was surprised to see her blush.

"I do, very much. You don't know how much I've minded being an only child."

Jeannette sighed. "It is a lonely old life, isn't it? I felt the same when I was young. It's probably why I took up with your father so quickly." *Now, why have I brought him up?* she asked herself. *There's been silence between us for long enough over him—not to mention antagonism.*

She looked at Olivia and found her staring at her. "That's what I wanted to talk to you about."

Jeannette said nothing. *Bite the bullet,* she told herself. *Seize the day. If Olivia is at last ready to raise this issue, then I must be too.*

"Mother?"

"Let's make some coffee and take it into the sitting room, shall we? I don't think the men will need us for a while."

Jeannette led the way through to the Victorian sitting-room, still the showpiece of the house with its high plaster ceilings, polished floorboards covered with a Persian rug, and matching chintz curtains and chair covers. It exuded comfort and luxury these days, but neither of the two women noticed.

They sat opposite each other—not too close, but near enough to allow for intimate conversation—Jeannette on one of the sofas, Olivia on a chair at right-angles to it, both unconsciously keeping some distance from each other without sending messages of rejection.

Jeannette crossed her legs slightly nervously and waited.

"It's about Dad, and what happened to him."

Jeannette met her daughter's determined, but rather hostile, gaze bravely, but her heart sank. She had known since Olivia's childhood that this day would come and had both feared and looked forward to it. The secrets she had kept—had had to keep, for Olivia's sake—and which, unfortunately, Olivia had resented her keeping, would have to be disclosed now, and who knew what effect that might have? Her daughter might turn tail and run, now that she could do so, back to her London life, and she might never see her again.

But in a way, even that would be better than the constant feeling of antagonism, even hatred, that she had sensed in her daughter for so long. Olivia had never understood why her mother had acted as she did, because she had never known the truth, but she had never tried to forgive her, either. And as the long years went on, they had moved further and further away from each other emotionally, until Olivia only came home, Jeannette knew, to see Theo. If she hadn't just happened to be between jobs and without accommodation when lockdown was put into effect, she would probably not have chosen to make her home at Tresayne for the duration.

That distancing had hurt and hurt badly. Yet Jeannette had no regrets about the decisions she had made, apart, perhaps, from the long delay in telling her daughter the truth. If only Olivia had asked her about all this when she was a teenager, she would have not have feared her daughter's anger, because when Olivia was younger, she would have found it easier to adjust. But the secrets had been kept for so long now, it was hard to predict how she would react to the truth.

She took a deep breath. "What do you want to know?"

"Why did you drive Dad away?"

Jeannette sighed. "It wasn't as simple as that. Nothing ever is, is it?"

Olivia said nothing.

"If you must know, he cheated me."

"Cheated on you?"

"That too, sadly, but I meant financially."

Olivia frowned. "How do you mean?"

"We were never married, only cohabiting—I'm not even sure that you knew that, did you, Olivia? We've never talked about it."

"I assumed you were married. So I am not only fatherless but also illegitimate." There was anger in her voice.

Jeannette sighed. "He didn't like the idea of marriage, and as you know, it was a time when lots of people our age just didn't bother. Either they didn't see marriage as a necessary institution or they wanted to remain free—which is not so different from today. I suppose I would have preferred to be married, especially when you came along, but at the time it didn't matter all that much to me."

"So I am really Olivia Tresayne."

"You were, though your father's name is on your birth certificate, as you know. But now you're Olivia Landry."

"Yes, that's true." Olivia paused to process this. "So how did he cheat you?"

"We had a joint bank account, and he siphoned money off it. He had quite a serious drug habit by the time he left me, and he found it hard to hold down a job, not that there were that many good jobs to be had down here even then. He was never very keen on Cornwall, and he started to spend more time away, mainly in London. I was stupid and didn't notice that money was leaving the account illicitly, and it took me a long time to guess that he'd found someone else to live with, too. I just thought we were spending more than I was earning, and I kept topping it up from a savings account where I'd put some money my grandmother left me. I got on with my life here and was glad to see him when he came."

"And then you found out."

"Yes. One day the joint account was cleared out. I closed it then, and that was it. I wouldn't have had him back, even if he'd wanted to come. I could never have trusted him again. Olivia, I'm so sorry. I know how you loved him."

Olivia thought for a moment. "I was a child then, and I just focused on the happy times we had when he was there. But looking back now, I can see there weren't that many of those, and I can understand why you wouldn't let me spend time with him, in the circumstances. But when he was ill, when he was dying, why wouldn't you let me see him then?"

Jeannette hesitated, but she had gone too far to stop now. "It turned out that he'd defrauded the company he went to work for when he left here. He was clever, when he could keep away from the drugs—and he only used them recreationally, at least to begin with. Anyway, the company found him out, and he was convicted of fraud."

Olivia gasped. "He was in prison?!"

Jeannette nodded. "I'm afraid so. And he died there, of an overdose. It seems drugs were as easy to get hold of in prison then as they are now. I couldn't take you to see him, Olivia. You were too young, and it would have been too traumatic for you. Besides, I didn't want to see him myself. I suppose... by then I didn't want to even try to forgive him."

There was silence between them for a long time. Then Olivia got up and went to sit beside her mother. "Mother—Mum, I'm so, so sorry. All these years I've blamed you, and it wasn't your fault. Why didn't you tell me before?"

Jeannette was at a loss as to how to answer this. "You didn't ask," she replied at last, "and after a bit I thought perhaps you didn't want to know. Maybe it was easier for you to go on believing in your father and seeing me as the villain. But I couldn't force the knowledge on you. It would have been too cruel."

To her amazement, she felt Olivia's arms round her, and the two of them embraced, both of them weeping. Jeannette had not seen her daughter cry for so long it felt awkward and embarrassing. But it was also cathartic, washing away much of the long-held misunderstanding and antagonism.

Too much emotion had always made Jeannette feel uncomfortable, and after a few moments she moved away. Olivia let go of her. "Poor you," she said. "How awful to have held on to this for so long with no relief."

"I did tell Theo," said Jeannette. "I felt I had to explain my actions to him."

"He told me to ask you about it, a few weeks ago. He said he couldn't tell me. It had to be you. I can see why now."

"He's good at keeping secrets," said Jeannette with a smile. "I'm sorry if it seems I'm comparing him with your father, but sometimes I can't help it. Until I met him, I had no idea what it was like to love someone and be loved in return."

Olivia sat very still, and Jeannette wondered whether perhaps her daughter's experience had also been lacking in this respect. She was tempted to tell Olivia it would happen for her sometime, to advise her to wait and be the best person she could be until that day, but the words stuck in her throat. It wasn't for her to judge her daughter or tell her how to live her life.

"Thanks for listening," she said at last, with an effort.

"Thanks for telling me. It can't have been easy." Olivia got up. "I think I'll go upstairs to my room for a bit. Wash my face and tidy up, for a start."

Jeannette looked at her. "I don't think anyone will notice."

"That I've been crying? Oh, I bet they will. I don't want to look all blotchy and be asked what's wrong."

"May I tell Theo that we've had this talk? Or would you rather tell him yourself?"

Olivia smiled. "You tell him if you want to. I think he's deserved that."

Tresayne House, Tuesday August 20th 1916

Maudie writes to say that Mother is distraught and will not believe that Freddie is dead. In the terrible fighting conditions many of the dead will not be identified for days if not weeks, and I gather some of the shell holes are enormous and half full of water. Mother's main horror seems to be that poor Freddie is wounded somewhere on the battlefield and has not been found, but I believe some of our men have been taken prisoner by the Germans, who will eventually publish a list of those they are holding, so we will know more then.

Mother now wishes to come down to Tresayne to stay with me for a few months. I can see why she might want to do that, for in Devon she will be surrounded by reminders of Freddie, while if she comes here, the change of scene may help—though if she is expecting any day to hear that he has been found, whether dead or alive, I would have thought she would prefer to stay where she is. Either way, I cannot refuse to have her, now that Maudie has her own duties in the hospital, for she has taken over from Mother in liaising with the military medical personnel in charge, a not inconsiderable job, from what I can gather.

But what am I to do about Mary? She has taken to coming almost every day to speak with me, and I have told the servants that she is in distress and comes to me for advice and counsel. I don't know whether they believe me, or what they make of her persistence, and can only hope they do not suspect the truth. But what is certain is that if Mother comes, she will recognize her at once, and will send her packing. I do not think she will guess the true state of affairs, but I cannot take the risk.

I should try to persuade Mary to go away from Tresayne and live somewhere else, at least while Mother is here. But her time is drawing nearer, and I must make sure she is safe and well-cared-for during her confinement. It is hard, for both of us have enjoyed our renewed contact, even though it is a chaste and proper relationship now. I had almost begun to consider the wild possibility that I might after all marry her and risk the scandal that might ensue here. But Mother's coming has put that idea to rest. All I can give my poor mother now is the consolation of my priestly calling. Mary must be found somewhere to go and must be made to go there. We cannot continue in this way.

Thirty

When the Swansons arrived later that morning, it was immediately obvious they had news to impart.

"Is everything all right?" Jeannette asked them anxiously, pouring coffee into mugs. "Is Jude okay? And Megan?"

"Yes, they're fine," Jeremy answered her. "Liz phoned last night to say that they're both settling in well."

"That is good to hear," said Jeannette. Having handed a mug to Marcus, she looked round for Theo, but he was nowhere to be seen. She stepped back to allow Jeremy and Mike to help themselves, thinking how ridiculous it was to go through the motions of social distancing when all day yesterday the two Swansons had been sitting with Theo in his music room. They were obeying the Rule of Six, just about, she supposed, though she wasn't sure they were supposed to be meeting inside, even now. But in the circumstances, she couldn't suggest everyone wore face masks.

The coffee jug stood on the table under the big copper beech tree, along with a plate of homemade flapjacks. Mike's eyes gleamed at the sight of these, she noticed. "Help yourself, Mike."

He smiled at her before quickly stuffing one into his mouth.

Jeremy looked round. "Is Olivia joining us?"

"She's upstairs," Jeannette explained. She knew that sounded slightly evasive but she didn't want to expose her daughter's distress to strangers. However much they'd seen of the Swansons in the last few weeks, somehow that was still what they were. Her instinct to keep her close family problems from outsiders was intact, she found, even though these particular strangers were walking all over the Tresaynes' family history.

"Is she okay?" asked Jeremy.

Damn it, do you have to know everything? "Yes, she's fine. We had a bit of a talk about the past, and I think she's feeling slightly upset." *And even that's more than you need to know.*

"Sorry," he said at once. "I didn't mean to pry."

The annoyance died, to be replaced by a slight feeling of dismay at her over-reaction. "No, I'm being too protective, I expect. I keep forgetting that you already know so much about our family it's natural you want to know more."

"Only if it's pertinent to our current mystery," he reassured her. "And Olivia hasn't confided in me anything about the family. We only talked about Clive, in fact, when I was here a few days ago. Which reminds me. Will you tell her Liz has heard from Rose, and Clive is now out of danger, though still in hospital?"

"I will tell her, but I expect she'll be down soon."

"How about if Livi and I take a walk down to the Tresayne cemetery?" suggested Marcus. "Olivia was saying yesterday I should see it. I can tell her about Clive."

Jeannette turned to him gratefully. "That's such a good idea. A walk will do her good. Shall I go and call her?"

"No, you finish your coffee. Her room is up the second staircase, isn't it? The one in the old hall?"

"Yes, that's right."

"Next to the priest hole room."

"Yes. But further down the corridor. I expect if you call up the stairs, she'll hear you."

Marcus strode away towards the house, leaving Jeannette with the Swansons.

"Quick, isn't he?" said Jeremy.

"Yes, and he seems to be being very kind to Olivia, which is nice."

"We do have something else to tell you."

She raised her eyebrows. "Mystery related?"

"Only indirectly. Cedric is returning tomorrow."

"Goodness. That is soon."

"He did tell me he wanted to come back, but I hadn't realised it was going to be this soon. Maybe he's worried the government may lock us down again before he gets here. Anything's possible. If Covid cases go up again, everything may change very quickly."

She nodded. "So today is your last day with us."

"Looks like it. And realistically, we'll have to go back and pack ourselves up this afternoon, because even though the others took quite a bit of their stuff with them, we all rather spread ourselves around the house over the weeks we've been here, and Lorna and the twins had to travel fairly light. We need to give the place a good clean and tidy up, too, which I haven't had any chance to do since the kids went home."

"Owing to your trying to help us with our family mystery."

"Owing, more like, to my terrible interfering inquisitiveness," he corrected, smiling.

She laughed. "Why don't you and Mike stay with us for a night or two after you've packed up Cedric's house? Then you all can go on investigating—Theo won't want you to leave before you've discovered the priest hole, that I'm sure of."

"What won't I want?" asked Theo, appearing from the house at that moment.

Jeannette explained.

"If it's all right with you, my dear, I absolutely concur. Stay until we've sorted the whole matter out, Remy. If you can bear to be away from home for a few days longer, that is. I'm sure you must want to see your wife."

"Please, Dad," put in Mike. "Could we?"

Jeannette watched Jeremy make up his mind. "If Mum is okay with it, then yes, we'll stay for a few days. And thank you, Jeannette, for your hospitality. I truly appreciate it."

"You're welcome. Do you mind sharing the twin room?"

Mike's face told her that this was the stuff of daydreams. "Can we really sleep there? That would be brilliant."

Jeremy smiled. "In fact, you'd actually like to be haunted, wouldn't you, Mike?"

"Dead right I would."

Jeremy drank the last of his coffee and put the mug back on the table. "We'll go and sort things out at the cottage first, in that case—pack up and so on. I told Cedric we would leave tomorrow morning, and he said he'd be back before evening for the dogs, so they will only have to be fed and given a walk, and they can stay in the house. We can always pop back and let them out if he gets delayed."

"That sounds fine. Bring the car, obviously, and it can go in the courtyard beside Marcus's. Your stuff will be safe there. I'll put my car away in the coach-house to make room."

"Before you go, Remy," put in Theo, "I've found a very interesting diary. Do you remember the vicar who went out to a parishioner and was drowned on the way back?"

"My great-uncle," Jeannette supplied.

"Yes. Reverend Edwin Tresayne. I've found his diary, and I think it might be really helpful. I haven't finished reading it yet, but he definitely says he found the priest hole. So it wasn't blocked up then. But he's rather cagey about how to get into it, I'm afraid."

"Shall I have a quick look now, or will it wait until tomorrow?"

"If I finish reading it today," suggested Theo, "you can see it later. Come back when you've finished packing if you like. You don't have to wait until tomorrow unless you want."

He turned to his wife. "I think you'll find it interesting too, Jeannette, though it doesn't make for comfortable reading. I'll show it to you when you have a minute. There's some family stuff you'll want to know about. It may not tell us much more about the priest hole than we know already, but I think there are some clues."

Tresayne House, September 16th 1916

Mother arrived last week after an arduous train journey. I went out to meet her with the gig at Launceston, which didn't please her at all, but how am I expected to keep a carriage here at Tresayne, a carriage I would never use? Perhaps, if Mother means to stay long, I shall have to do something about a covered vehicle. I have grown used to going out in all weathers on my horse, visiting in the parish, but Mother will expect more comfort. Fortunately, it was fine and dry this afternoon, but I can see she would be very discontented if rained upon. Indeed, I wonder whether I will be able to give her the creature comforts she explained to me, in great detail, that she needs in order to recover from Freddie's death. She seemed not to have any idea that I am grieving for Freddie too, but at least I am able to occupy myself with other things, rather than focusing on my grief. I do sincerely pity her and accept that it is right that she has come, but I confess I do not think happily of a long visit. Not least because I must keep Mary's presence in the district from her at all costs.

This is proving very difficult. Mary came this morning just before my mother emerged from her bedchamber, and I have hidden her in the priest hole. We were together in my study, talking, when one of the servants came to inform me that Mother was coming downstairs. I could think of nothing else, on the spur of the moment, but to put her inside the cupboard, for Mother will not be likely to open the door, even if she comes in here.

Mary had come to tell me that she will not go away. She cannot bear to live without me, she says, and will brave anything, even my mother's anger and the scandal of the district, in order to stay. She came close to me as she told me this, and kissed me, and—oh God!—my treacherous body remembered the lovemaking of the past. How can I send her away? for I know that I love her, that we belong together. She does not ask me to marry her, but I know to let her live with me without the benefit of marriage lines would eventually make my ministry here untenable. May God guide me, for I do not know what to do.

Thirty-one

Marcus and Olivia strolled down the lane towards the old cemetery, happy to be out together in the fine sunny morning and away from a mystery that seemed to be turning ever darker. Marcus was interested in discovering the whereabouts of the priest hole, certainly, but he was perfectly willing to leave the others to it and accompany Olivia to visit her ancestors. As they walked, the banks were full of campion and knotweed, while the odd stretch of wider verge was punctuated by tall clumps of willowherb. Above them a solitary buzzard drifted on the air currents, keeping an eye out for unwary rodents, while the hedgerow was alive with finches, flying in and out in search of food.

"It's a bit late for nesting, isn't it?" said Marcus, observing the bird activity.

"I'm a city girl," Olivia told him. "I believe you're right, but I haven't really been watching, I'm afraid."

"You grew up here, though," he pointed out. "Didn't you take an interest in country things when you were a child?"

"Not that I recall. Mother was very keen, but I think I just tuned it out. My dad didn't really take to country life, although he

284

did enjoy going to the beach occasionally. I think I just wanted to be like him.”

She hesitated, and Marcus looked down at her. “Did you talk to your mother about him?”

She nodded silently, trying to stop the tears. Enough of them had already fallen this morning.

He stopped and turned her towards him. “Was it bad?”

She nodded. He took her hand and walked on. “Is there a seat in this little cemetery of yours?”

She was confused by the change of subject, and very conscious of her hand in his. “I don’t know. I haven’t been there for years. Why?”

“I’d like you to feel able to tell me about it, and you won’t do that comfortably while walking along the road. Especially if you’re going to cry.”

“You hate women to cry, don’t you? I can tell.” Furiously, she tried to stem the tears before they fell. She didn’t want to disgust him, or even alienate him, by being upset. He himself always seemed to be so controlled, although she remembered he had spoken of crying when he was a child.

“Yes,” he admitted. “But don’t worry. My reason for that doesn’t apply to you.”

With relief, she returned the gentle pressure of his hand in hers. “Thanks. I’ll try not to.”

“Sometimes we all need to cry,” he said gently. “I don’t like women who cry to get their own way, that’s all. And I acquit you of that.”

The gate to the cemetery appeared on the right-hand side of the road, with the little Victorian chapel beside it. A fence divided the graveyard from the church, which had its own garden.

“The church has been turned into a house now,” she told him, feeling a little steadier. “The parish became part of North Hill a century or more ago. After my great-great-uncle died, I think—the one who was a vicar.”

"Reverend Edwin, who was drowned coming back from a parish visit?"

"That's him. The church itself continued to be a mission chapel for a few years, but then it was sold. There's a corner of the cemetery that's kept specially for the Tresaynes, and my grandparents and my great-grandmother are all buried there. The main burial ground for the parish now is the churchyard at North Hill. But we are still allowed to visit the cemetery here."

She led him over to a small wooden bench that stood on the far side of the cemetery from the gate. "The Tresaynes are over there, next to the chapel."

"Sit down first and tell me what your mother said."

She told the story baldly and as unemotionally as she could.

"God, that must have been devastating," was his response.

She smiled gratefully at him. "It sort of blew away everything I thought I knew about my dad, and left me with... nothing."

"He wasn't the person you thought he was."

"That's it exactly. I feel as though I didn't know him at all. I suppose when you're a young child, you only see what parents show you."

"I know from my own experience that it's easy to lose touch with your early relationships, too."

"You and Theo."

"Yes. I realised, when I had time to think about it during lockdown, that all I'd done was to take on board my mother's bitterness, forgetting my own experience of him when I was a small boy, which actually was quite positive."

"It's odd," she went on. "I'd have thought my mother would have been bitter, too, after all Dad did to her, but she isn't. I think I would hate him, but she doesn't seem to."

"She found Theo," Marcus reminded her. "That seems to have been very healing."

Olivia nodded. "I think you're right. What about your mother? It sounds as though she is still hostile to Theo."

"Yes, I'm afraid so. But really, I don't think she has much reason. Dad treated her fairly after she left him. We were never in need of anything financially. He paid my school fees, and Debs'. He would have continued to see Debs and me if Mum would have let him."

"I wonder what it was that went wrong between them. Theo says it was his fault, that he neglected you all, but I think that may not really be true."

"Who knows? There are always two sides to any quarrel. I'm just glad to have reconnected with him after all these years. It would be good if Mum would accept I've grown up and I make my own decisions, but if she refuses to, it's just too bad."

"And Debs? Do you see her?" Olivia asked the question tentatively, with an apprehensive heart. It must be as hard for Marcus to lose his sister as for her to have lost her father.

"She was always a bit jealous of me," he replied, sighing. "After she left Dad, Mum sort of treated me as the Man of the House, even though Debs was older." He laughed, but it wasn't a happy sound. "I was flattered, to begin with. I took a long time to see it for what it really was."

"A kind of control."

"Exactly. And I've never been married, though I did have a long-term girlfriend for a while."

Olivia wondered whether the girlfriend was still around. She wasn't living with Marcus, because he had talked of being alone during lockdown. And he had said 'did have', as though the relationship were in the past.

Marcus put his arm along the back of the bench, just as he had at Charlestown, and let his hand grip her shoulder gently. "We never lived together," he confirmed. "And she emigrated to Australia with someone else last year."

He paused, wondering why it seemed important to tell her about Anna, and that it was over. *Brothers and sisters share such things with each other,* he told himself. Not that he and Debs had ever shared any confidences that way.

Olivia leaned her head against his shoulder. "I've never experienced that kind of commitment."

He twisted to look at her. "Really? Someone like you, I'd have thought you'd have had men queueing up to be committed."

"I didn't encourage them," she replied simply. "It wasn't what I wanted—I don't know why. Because of Theo, in the end I had a very secure childhood. But I went on being angry with my mother because my father left us, even though it was only because I didn't fully know what had happened."

"Understandable, when your mother hadn't felt able to tell you."

"Yes, I suppose so. It's as though that anger has been with me ever since," she added, thoughtfully. "Like a cage, imprisoning me emotionally, stopping me from loving anyone."

Marcus thought for a moment about that piece of self-analysis. "But you love my dad."

"Oh yes, I always have. He's been so good to me. I suppose he's the only man I've ever really trusted. He at least has never let me down."

"Have other men let you down? Apart from your father, I mean?" Inside him a kind of rage welled up against these men. He wondered whether Clive was of their number. "That reminds me," he said quickly. "Your mother said to tell you Remy says Clive is out of danger."

"I'm glad to hear that."

"Livi... I have to ask. Was Clive one of those men you mentioned? Did he let you down?"

"Not really. We worked together, and we had an affair of sorts. But it wasn't love, what we shared. And he was married, anyway." She looked up at him, wondering whether he would be shocked, but his face showed nothing.

"It wasn't that any of the men I had affairs with let me down emotionally," she went on, "because I never let them get that close. They never matched up to the kind of man I wanted, though I wasn't really very sure what that was. And I didn't know Dad had let me down until today. I always thought it was my mother's fault."

"Like Debs and I were always encouraged to think it was Dad's fault their marriage failed," he said, steering her away from what might be perilous waters. "I think Debs will come round in time. Mum will marry again, eventually, I expect, and then Debs will probably see things differently. But she and I have never been particularly close, anyway."

"Strange, isn't it? We've both had a sea change in our relationships with our parents. You've seen your mother differently, and I've been told some things about my parents that have revolutionised completely how I think of both of them."

"It's a lot to take in," he agreed. "But I've had longer to process it. Take your time, Livi. I expect your dad had a point of view, too. But you never had a chance to hear it."

"Perhaps. Looking back, I can see that he was fun and very charming, and he liked to be loved. But I also remember that he wasn't here a great deal, even when I was very small, and he was supposed to be living with us at Tresayne. My mother was always busy, working in her study or doing the household chores, and when she was free, she liked to read, but at least she was always there if I needed her. And she's hardly gone out of her way to bad-mouth Dad to me as she could have done." She sighed. "Anyway, he's dead now. I mean to let him rest and move on."

"What are your plans for the future?" he asked. "Now that everything's opening up?"

She fidgeted slightly. "I don't know. I feel rather trapped by the past, I suppose. It isn't only that I don't really want to go back to my old type of work. I don't really want to be the person I've been, either."

"I like you the way you are," he said.

"But you don't really know me, do you, Marcus? Not yet."

Her words seemed to push him away a little. But he didn't move his arm from the back of the bench. It remained there, no longer touching her yet still registering a continued commitment to closeness. "That's true. But I mean to."

Olivia looked at him. Was it relief she felt? She wasn't sure. She did quite desperately want him to know her better, but she was also afraid. She sensed already that Marcus was determined and didn't give up easily when he wanted something. But what did he want of her? Would she be able to give it? And what would happen if she couldn't?

~ * ~

That night she had a vivid dream, in which she was shut in a stone prison with no windows. It was dark and cold and very frightening, and she began to scream: "Let me out! Let me out!" She awoke to the real darkness of the early hours, and wondered whether she had screamed in fact, or only in her dream. Since Theo, Jeannette and Marcus were all sleeping in the front of the house, divided from her by the thick stone walls of the older wing, she did not think anyone would have heard her, even if she had been screaming. Certainly no one came to comfort her, and she lay awake for a while, fearing to sleep again lest the nightmare come back, and wishing Marcus were there beside her. Eventually the first light appeared at the window, and she heard the birds singing in the garden. It was still very early, too early to get up, so she lay quietly, waiting for the household to wake, and at last she fell asleep. The dream did not recur, and she slept deeply, only waking well into the morning.

Outside on the drive, she heard a car arrive, and the voices of Jeremy and Mike, no doubt intent on more priest hole hunting. She lay for a while pondering on the meaning of the dream. Was it just her mind recognising that she was trapped, by all her past decisions and choices, into a life and a mindset she now wanted very much to escape? Perhaps that conversation with her mother yesterday had raised the possibility of change, and in her dream she was struggling to find a way. Perhaps talking to Marcus about her life as a PA had released some memories that she had buried.

Or was there some more sinister, supernatural explanation? Had she, like Jude, connected with someone who had once been trapped in the house? And if so, where was this person? She had so far kept in the background of the investigations, feeling no very great degree of interest, and also, she realised suddenly, out of a desire to evade those fears that had been with her since childhood, of the room along the corridor. Now she wondered whether she should get involved. It seemed to her that the room she had instinctively avoided for so long might have a message for her.

Tresayne House, Tuesday September 27th 1916

My mind is made up. Nothing but truth and honour will serve us, whatever scandal and distress that brings to my mother and to my parishioners. I cannot hide Mary any longer, nor can I bear to send her away, or marry her off to some man of her own station. She is Gerald's sister, and she is my love. Nothing else matters now. I cannot fathom why it took me so long to see it clearly, but now that I do, I cannot hold back.

Maudie will bear it, I feel sure, for Gerald's sake, but I fear for Mother, especially as she is here at Tresayne with me and will have to experience the scandal first hand rather than at a distance. Should I wait for her to return to Devon before I break the news? No, that would be cowardly, and Mary's situation will not wait, for her confinement cannot be far distant. And I must tell my mother to her face and apologise for the trouble I am bringing upon her. Truly, I fear for her reason, for she wanders the house murmuring to herself, but there is nothing I can do, for nothing will bring Freddie back. Please God she will not be driven further out of her mind by my revelations about Mary, for tomorrow I must make all plain.

Word has just come to me that old George Wells is dying, and I must go to give him some comfort in his passing. His cottage is not far, but the rain has been torrential all day, and the river is running high. The boy who brought the message says the man's breathing is laboured and he obviously does not have much time left, so I will go the quickest way I can, though it is a difficult path in the dark, and the moon will be hidden by the heavy clouds. But Denver is sure-footed and he knows the way. Mary is still in the priest hole, hiding from my mother, and it is best she stays there until I get back, for I cannot take the risk of Mother meeting her without explanation. Without me to support her, Mother might do her some harm. I have locked the door, and the way in from the gallery bedroom is nailed shut. She will take no hurt for a little while.

Thirty-two

Mike had packed his suitcase and found a carrier bag for all the other bits and pieces that wouldn't fit into it. While his father checked they hadn't missed anything, he loaded all the bags and boxes into the car. It was just as well, he thought, that they had the bulk of the car for luggage. He couldn't see how it could all have been fitted in if he'd had to leave seats for Lorna and the twins. When he'd finished, he gave the car keys back to his father and set off for a walk with the dogs. They'd agreed the spaniels should have some proper exercise while it was still cool, and then they would sleep happily for most of the day. If Cedric were delayed on the road, it would be easy enough to go back and let them out in the garden later. They could drop off the keys tomorrow when Cedric had returned.

Mike was excited that they were going to stay at Tresayne House, and in the haunted room itself, and he half-hoped, as his father had divined, that there might be some voices in the night. At present, not having stayed there, he felt annoyingly distanced from the heart of the mystery, which, for him, was the wailing Jude had heard. Jude and Lorna and perhaps Olivia were ranged on the side of Dad, who was convinced there was something spiritual (or supernatural) going on. On the other side, Theo Jeannette and presumably Marcus seemed to be against this view, believing in nothing but the rational and material; and instinctively he agreed with them, but at the same time, he recognised that what they were dealing with was something more than the tangible. Yet the rational search for the priest hole was so far the only avenue they had explored. He was sure Dad wanted to spend some time praying about the problem, and although prayer was rather alien to him, he felt in this case it was probably appropriate to approach the mystery from that angle, too. And it was always fun doing anything with Dad, whose outward seriousness hid a sense of the ridiculous that Mike enjoyed. Taking it all together, he looked forward to spending the night with his father in the twin room, whether it turned out to be haunted or not.

They left the car on the driveway in front of the house, to be unpacked later. Mike, who was at the wheel, remembered that it was quite awkward to park such a sizeable vehicle in the courtyard at the back, and was keen to check that Jeannette had moved her little car into the coach-house-garage first.

Jeannette let them in and offered them coffee. The weather had turned damp and chilly, and there was clearly going to be no sitting under beech trees in the open air this morning.

"Theo and Marcus are in the music room," she told them. "Why don't you go through? They have something to show you which we think is probably significant. Although it's rather sad from a family point of view."

Mike wondered where Olivia was. She seemed, he thought, curiously uninterested in something that concerned her family so nearly. But perhaps she just didn't show her feelings. Of all the Landrys, she was the one he felt he knew least. She was very attractive, even though clearly the wrong side of thirty, and he would rather have liked to see more of her. Perhaps now that they would actually be staying in the house, he might get the chance.

They found Theo and Marcus already drinking coffee, and Mike was glad to see there was another plate of flapjacks to tempt them. After an hour's walk with the dogs, breakfast seemed a long time ago.

"Remy!" Theo got up from his armchair. "Good to see you. We think we may have found a new lead, as I told you yesterday. In fact, now that we've all read it to the end, it seems even more significant than I thought then. But we haven't explored further because we wanted to see what you thought."

He waited until Jeremy and Mike had sat down—Mike choosing a seat as close as possible to the flapjacks—and then handed Jeremy a leather-bound book. "It's Edwin Tresayne's diary. The early entries are juvenilia, dating back beyond the First War. But it gets interesting later on, particularly when you get into 1916, when he came to be rector here."

"Be warned, though," said Jeannette, coming in with a small tray bearing two mugs of coffee for the new arrivals. "It's not comfortable reading. Or at least, it wasn't for me."

Mike moved away from the flapjacks and sat on the wide arm of his father's chair. "Can I look over your shoulder, Dad? It'll save time."

Jeremy smiled at his son's impatience. "If you like." He felt his jacket pocket in vain for his reading spectacles, a recent concession to middle age. "I'll just need to go out to the car and find my glasses first. Edwin's handwriting is not the clearest."

"I'll fetch them if you like, Dad," offered Mike, frustrated by the delay and convinced his younger legs would get out to the car and back much quicker.

"I'm not quite sure which bag I put them in. Better for me to go and look for myself."

Mike handed his father the car keys, and looked across at Theo, who smiled and without a word handed him the diary. He moved from the arm of his father's chair into the chair itself, which enveloped him comfortably. In the five minutes or more it would take his father to find his spectacles, he could have a quick look at this diary that had got everyone so excited.

He studied the book carefully, remembering the nineteenth-century facsimile of a medieval diary that he and his father had found on a secondhand bookstall a few years ago, and all the events that had flowed from that. This diary was a medium-sized book, the pages unlined, with a brass lock on the outside. He pressed the catch, which opened readily.

"Was it locked?" he asked.

Theo shook his head. "Someone clearly opened it long ago. I don't know what happened to the key."

Mike nodded and bent his head to read.

Outside on the front steps, Jeremy had stopped dead. Standing beside their car, looking murderous in the extreme, was a big, bulky, dark-haired man in dirty jeans and a tee-shirt. The tee-shirt rippled with heavy musculature on a barrel chest, though the unkempt dark hair and beard showed threads of grey.

The man looked round and saw him. "Where've you put my datters?" he asked in a thick Cornish accent. "I saw they in this car, both of 'un, and I reckon you was driving."

Out on the lane beyond the gate, Jeremy could see the outline of a battered SUV. This man must be Jude's father. How on earth had he found them? And why had he and Mike not thought to put their all-too-recognisable estate car out of sight of the lane? With Jude and Megan in Oxford, and the priest hole mystery occupying their thoughts, he supposed it hadn't seemed important.

"You must be Jude and Megan's father." His voice was quiet in an attempt to defuse the tension, stating the obvious but playing for time.

"That I be. Jake Laurence, and I'll thank you to tell me at once where my datters are. Abduction. Kidnapping. Who knows what kind of abuse? I'll have the police on you."

"By all means," returned Jeremy coolly. "The police have already been told about Jude and Megan. I informed them myself yesterday that we had taken them to a place of safety." He paused, wondering how far to push it. "I wouldn't be surprised if they pay you a visit soon. If we are to talk of abuse, it is you who may have to answer for it, not I."

Jake spat forth a stream of profanity. Jeremy found himself wondering, wryly, whether the man would have been more restrained if he, Jeremy, had been wearing his dog collar. But perhaps not. Behind him, in the house, he heard footsteps on the tiled hall floor. Someone had heard the raised voice and come to find out what was going on. He hoped it wasn't Mike, whose presence might inflame the situation.

"Mr Laurence," came Jeannette's clear tones from behind him. "You may not remember me, but we have met, at a school function I think, when Jude was younger." Her voice held its usual politeness, but there was a hint of disapproval beneath it.

Jeremy felt slightly anxious for her. This man looked aggressive and menacing, and as a livestock farmer, he was no doubt fit and strong as well. Jeremy was painfully uncertain whether he had the physical strength to protect a woman from attack. Where were Mike and Marcus? He turned towards the door to shout for help. But to his surprise, the man bowed his head submissively to Jeannette. As the chatelaine of Tresayne House and descendant of Tresaynes of the past, she would indeed command local respect. He was glad, now, to have her at his back. She clearly needed no protection from him.

"Mrs Landry, I seen Jude and Megan in this car, just a couple days ago. And the man driving it made it his business to lose me among the lanes. I've not found them, and they haven't come home. I'm fair out o' my mind with worry. D'ye know where they have been took?" He pointed an accusing finger at Jeremy. "Who's this man, anyhow? He'm an emmet, I reckon, and we all knows their ways. Where's my datters, that's what I want to know!"

His voice had grown even stronger and more belligerent as he spoke, but Jeremy saw no sign of discomfiture in Jeannette. She moved forward to stand beside him on the steps. "This is a good friend of mine," she told Jake firmly. "He is a vicar, Mr Laurence, and has nothing but concern for Jude and Megan's welfare. Which is more than can be said for you, by all I hear. As he says, we have acted on what Jude and Megan told us, and we have informed the authorities of the abuse they have been suffering at home during lockdown. It is up to those authorities what action to take. Your children are not here, or anywhere near here. But you may take my word that they are both safe and are being looked after."

The big man seemed to shrink into himself. "I never done them no hurt," he protested. "Twas all in love."

Jeremy stiffened at this, but Jeannette went on smoothly. "That is for the police to judge. We have acted on what the children told us, as we had to do. If we are asked questions, we shall answer them. No doubt you will be asked questions as well, and I suggest you too answer them truthfully. Lies will not help you." She paused, while her adversary absorbed her comments. "Now, Mr Laurence, I would like you to remove yourself from my land and go home."

For a second, Jeremy thought Jake might be thinking of defying her. He glared at her, and his hands balled into fists. But she met his gaze coolly and confidently, and his eyes dropped.

"If you say so, Mrs Landry," he said at last, and Jeremy saw that the fight had gone out of him. "I mun take your word for it, and I'll be on my way. But ye'll understand a father's anxiety. If I have spoke out of turn, I'd ask your pardon."

"Much that you've said and done is out of order," Jeannette told him, in a severe tone. "But we will overlook it if you go now."

"Tell Jude and Megan... Give 'em my love."

Neither Jeremy nor Jeannette said anything in reply to this, though Jeremy was holding his anger on a tight rein. Then the big man turned and walked away down the drive. They watched him get into his vehicle and drive away.

"Phew!" said Jeremy. He turned to his hostess with admiration. "Well done, Jeannette."

"I know his sort," she replied. "Most of his talk is bluster. He wouldn't dare touch me, you know."

"I'm glad you came," Jeremy told her with relief. "I think he might have done more than that to me. At least it wasn't Mike, who really was driving the car."

"Your children impress me, Remy," she said thoughtfully. "I don't know the twins well, but Lorna and Mike have the courage of their convictions, and they stick together. Those, I think, are two very worthy attributes."

Jeremy wasn't sure that either of his two older children would care to be described as 'worthy', but he let it pass. He admired those qualities in them himself. "I'd be careful, though," he warned her as they went back into the house. "Lock the front door, at least. If Jake Laurence knows the police are after him, he may become desperate. And desperate men are unpredictable. Even you and your family might not be safe."

"I don't think he'll do anything. But I'll bear what you say in mind." She led the way back to the music room, defiantly leaving the front door open. Her concern for keeping fresh air circulating in the house was clearly still greater than her fear of Jake Laurence.

"Everything okay?" asked Theo as they arrived. "Couldn't you find your glasses, Remy?" Clearly, in the music room, set right at the back of the house, they had heard nothing. Even cries for help might not have been answered.

Jeremy, discovering with annoyance that the glasses were in the breast pocket of his shirt, listened while Jeannette gave a brief explanation of what had happened. Mike, he knew, would regret that he had not been the one to face down Jake Laurence, but Theo took it all in his stride.

"Jeannette is equal to anything," was his bland observation to the room in general. "And she and the Tresayne family are held in great respect here. But we should perhaps tell the police he has been here. What do you think, Remy?"

"Yes, I would. Just to be on the safe side. This is quite an isolated spot, you know, and although he made no actual threats, there is always the chance he may think better of that."

"I think that's good advice, my dear," Theo said to Jeannette. "Will you phone or shall I?"

"I'll do it later. I want to hear Jeremy's view of Edwin's diary first." She smiled. "I know you're all enjoying the detective work. Even Marcus."

"Absolutely. After spending three months on my own in London, this is rather exciting!"

Mike moved back to the sofa and helped himself to a second flapjack. "It's hot stuff, that diary."

Marcus smiled. "You could say that."

There was silence in the room while Jeremy took the book in his hands and began to flick through it. The writing clearly came to an abrupt end not much more than half-way through the pages, with the last entry in a different hand. He turned back to 1915 and began to read. The entries were sparse, and quite widely spaced— Edwin had not found the time or inclination to write every day— but the story itself, told in little snatches, was clear. As he read, he felt himself becoming increasingly angry. What a rotten coward the man had been, especially considering he was a priest. Even the fact that he was only following the mores of his time hardly excused his behaviour. "I have to say," he said at one point, "and saving your presence, Jeannette, that this great-uncle of yours was not someone I would have wanted as a friend."

"Hardly the perfect gentleman," agreed Theo. "One can't help feeling for poor Mary."

Jeannette shrugged slightly, disclaiming any suggestion that she approved of the man and his actions. "He does seem to have been a bit of a cad," she agreed. "But read on. He meant to do the right thing in the end, even if events prevented him."

So Jeremy read on, through the last weak and vacillating months of Edwin Tresayne's life, through the ultimately tragic persistence of Mary Booker, to the final entry. And as he read the last few pages, the pieces of the jigsaw they had been trying to solve seemed at last to fall into place in his mind with an almost audible click.

Tresayne House, December 1st 1919

I, Maudie Tresayne, am writing the last entry in this diary. My brother, sadly, never returned from his errand of mercy to George Wells. The river was running very high, and the bridge collapsed under his horse as he rode back. The horse must have managed to clamber out, for he came back to his stable, but Edwin's body was washed up further down the river a few days later. I did not know he had written this diary and have only now discovered it among my mother's papers. So much I did not know about my brother, whom I thought my dearest friend! I wonder whether my mother read it too, or whether she simply kept it as a memento. The tiny key that opens it was in my brother's desk, but perhaps she did not know where it was kept. Or she may have felt it was private, and she should not pry. She might have preferred me to do the same, but I cannot regret that I have read it.

My husband and I took over this house after my mother died, two years ago. She was broken by the loss of all three of her sons in as many years. But now that Gerald is back home safe from the War, he and I are happy here, and have great plans for the garden.

One question remains, which I cannot answer. What happened to Gerald's sister, Mary? I have not shown my husband this diary, and I will keep it locked away, for it would cause him such pain to know that Edwin was the father of her child and the author of all her misfortunes. She must have run away from

Tresayne when Edwin was killed, but we have not heard from her again. I am so sad, for we would have welcomed her and her baby and taken care of them, for my brother's sake as well as her own. It is clear from the diary that in the end Edwin meant to marry her.

Poor Mary. Perhaps she has not yet heard that my mother is dead. If so, maybe she will still come back one day, and we will have a chance to make a fresh start. I truly hope so, for Gerald has been so worried on her behalf, knowing only that she is on her own with an illegitimate child.

Thirty-three

"We simply must get into that priest hole," declared Jeremy.

There was silence.

"Dad... you don't think... she's still there?"

"I must confess," said Theo, "the same thought had occurred to me, but I hoped I was just being fanciful."

"My God!" Marcus exclaimed in a low voice. "Surely not."

"I suppose it's possible she escaped," Jeremy acknowledged. "Maybe someone let her out when Mrs Tresayne wasn't looking. One of the servants must have known something, heard something."

"Yes." Mike's voice was brighter. "She'd have shouted and screamed, surely, if no one came to let her out."

There was another silence as they remembered what Jude had heard.

"It doesn't bear thinking about," said Marcus.

"No." Jeannette got up from her chair and left the room.

"Well," Jeremy said heavily. "We can't be sure until we've looked."

In sombre silence, the four men walked in single file into the old study next door. Now they knew where the entrance to the priest hole must be, it should have been easy to find it. But although they tapped assiduously all along the back wall of the cupboard, which being false, Jeremy reasoned, should have been hollow, the sound continued stubbornly solid, as of stone or brick.

"Stone was a much more usual building material than brick in seventeenth-century Cornwall," Theo remarked. "But as it was plastered, either by the Victorian builders or by one of their successors, there's no telling what lay behind it."

"They may have plastered it over deliberately," Marcus volunteered. "To hide the entrance to the priest hole, perhaps."

"Wouldn't that suggest they didn't want anyone to find the way in again?" asked Mike. "I mean, that means…"

"Guilty knowledge." Jeremy sighed. "Someone knew what the priest hole contained and didn't want anyone else to find it."

"But surely no one would deliberately leave someone to die there?" Marcus was incredulous.

"Let's hope not, for the sake of their immortal soul."

Mike shuddered slightly, understanding the implications of his father's comment. In his rectory upbringing, right and wrong had been seen as moral absolutes given by a higher power, to whom in the last resort all were accountable.

Theo and Marcus, free of such subconscious influences, returned to the cupboard.

"We've searched along the back," said Marcus. "Could the entrance be hidden in the side wall somehow?"

"I suppose the original priest hole may have been just a glorified cupboard, and the entrance may have been moved," observed Jeremy. "But the diary talks of a ladder, as though the cupboard led up to the priest hole somehow."

"In the chimney breast," said Mike, reviving. "In the twin room, Dad, remember? The chimney breast continues too far in this direction. Could there be a way over the top of the archway into a hiding place?"

"With the original entrance off the gallery? Or from the bedroom itself," mused Theo. "I suppose there could."

"This would be much more secure, though. And perhaps they bricked up the entrance in the upper floor later."

"Edwin wasn't the only Victorian clergyman to want to keep a mistress, I bet," observed Marcus, with humour. "A ladder up to the room above from his study would be very useful."

Jeremy ignored this piece of levity. "Let's try the back corner of the cupboard."

"Got it!" exclaimed Mike. "Listen!"

He tapped along the side wall, and they heard the sound change. "I think what they've done is to increase the width of the wall inside the cupboard, where it can't be seen. Look."

Theo and Jeremy peered in. "He's right," said Theo. "It's wider inside than outside."

"I wonder what the mechanism is."

Mike moved out of the way, but Jeremy made no move to go into the cupboard. "If it's plastered over, we won't be able to see it."

"I suppose it might be easier to access from the false chimney breast above," suggested Marcus.

"We'll do less damage from here," Theo pointed out.

"There's a keyhole." Mike had remained in the cupboard, feeling along the wall for any kind of catch or hidden handle. The wood looked smooth, and he couldn't believe the entrance had been permanently blocked. "No key, though."

"I'll go and find a chisel," said Theo. "And I'd better see where Jeannette is," he added. "There are some ancient keys somewhere, and one of those might be the key to this door—she'll know where they are. If not, we can't go destroying bits of her family house without asking her first."

There was silence after he'd left, as the other three men tried to process their own, decidedly uncomfortable thoughts. Marcus and Mike were still hopeful that nothing would be found, optimistic that some less tragic explanation must cover Mary Booker's mysterious disappearance. Jeremy had no such confidence. He had had much experience, in the varied and often secret life of the priesthood, of the darkness of the human soul, and its capability—if it could not face the consequences of more conventional alternatives—to stifle the voice of conscience and do the unthinkable. His strong sense of the clouds of darkness that gathered around this part of the house suggested that something tragic had happened here. Yet the possible events were beyond anything he had come across.

~ * ~

Jeannette was in her sewing room, surveying her great-uncle's kneehole desk, which her father had given her when she was a teenager to use for her homework. No laptops in those days, she thought. Just books and notebooks, pencils and pens. The desk had remained in the room when it had become her study, and she had used it when she was working as a copyeditor. Later, it became useful as a table for the sewing machine, and she had not thought of its connection with the family history for years. But now she had a vague sense it held something significant—yet another secret that had been lost, perhaps something she had known about once and then forgotten. Had it not seemed important at the time, or had she buried the memory, as she had buried so much else of the past?

She thought of her grandmother, sitting with her in this room when it was her bedroom, saying prayers with her before she slept. Her grandmother had always seemed sad, she recalled, as though some grief remained with her from the past; it was a strong impression, and one that dated from before the death of her grandfather, whom she remembered, although she had never known him very well.

She found she was still holding Edwin's diary in her hand. She had taken it back from Jeremy when he had read it, and then she had come here to this room, in answer to some inner prompting that—in spite of all her common sense and her rejection of fantasy—she had not been able to ignore. What was it that she remembered about the desk?

A hidden drawer. A picture came into her mind of a drawer beneath the desk. You couldn't see it from the front, and it was small enough to be hidden even when you sat at the desk with your knees tucked under it. It had had a key, years ago, but where was that now?

"Jeannette, my dear." Theo was standing in the doorway of the room. "We think we've found the entrance to the priest hole, in the study wardrobe cupboard, in the side wall, but it is locked or blocked up in some way. Do you know the whereabouts of those ancient keys we found? We sorted through them all, I recall, and only kept out the ones we knew fitted existing locks; but I don't know where we put the others. Do you remember? Otherwise, we'll have to take a chisel to it."

"I have no idea, Theo. It was a long time ago. I'd have to think where they might be."

"I don't think we should wait," he said. "Do you mind if we use force?"

~ * ~

Olivia, still in her dressing-gown, was sitting at the desk in her little sitting-room upstairs, when she became aware of a loud and insistent tapping from downstairs. An hour or so ago, there had been some kind of altercation on the drive, but she had been in the shower and had only heard the end of it. Her mother's calm tones seemed to have defused the situation, and whoever it was who had sounded so angry had gone away. She could see nothing of the driveway from her windows and was not inclined to go and get involved. There was too much else to think about.

The tapping, however, coming as it did from the old study, roused her from her abstraction. She dressed quickly and went down to the kitchen, where she found Kato partaking of a late breakfast. There was no one else to be seen, and she followed the sound of tapping, mixed now with cracking and splintering, into the old study. Much to her surprise, having licked his bowl clean, the cat followed her.

The single bed had been moved over to the far wall, and the coat-hangers from the cupboard piled upon it. A heap of broken and splintered panelling lay in front of the cupboard, while Marcus and Theo, by the light of a big flashlight, were taking apart the side wall, closely watched by Mike and his father.

"Good morning, Olivia." Her mother glanced at her, somewhat absently. "Events have moved on, as you see. It has been decided that we need to get into the priest hole."

"But why?"

"It's to do with the Reverend Edwin's diary," her mother explained vaguely. "Wait a minute, I'll get it for you."

She came back a few minutes later with the book in her hand. "Read it all, if you want, but it is the end that has worried us."

"But what are you looking for?" asked Olivia, perplexed.

"Read the diary."

Marcus had watched her come in, and seeing her bewilderment, he left his work in the cupboard to go over to her, leaving Jeremy to take his place. Mike, standing inside the room and wearing a pair of borrowed gauntlets, was taking the wood as it was removed and adding it to the pile.

"Morning, Livi. Sleep well?"

"I had an awful dream."

He looked sympathetic. "D' you want to tell me? We can sit on the bed. Mind those coat-hangers."

"But what is all this about, Marcus?"

"We found something in Edwin's diary—ah, I see you've got it there."

"Yes. Mother said I should read it." She looked round for her mother, but Jeannette was nowhere to be seen.

"Jeremy and Theo seem to think the last couple of entries are significant. Myself, I think they may be making too much of it, but I can see we can't just leave it. We have to know."

"But know what?" persisted Olivia.

"Whether there's a body in the priest hole."

At this bald statement, Olivia shrank, and the dream re-ran in her mind, with the voice screaming: "Let me out! Let me out!"

She felt Marcus's arms go round her, and his chin rested on her hair. "Ssh now."

The uprush of warmth she felt in her heart as he held her against him took her by surprise. She moved away a little, and immediately he let her go. "What's upsetting you, Livi? It isn't the possibility that there is something there, in the priest hole, is it?"

So she told him about the dream. "And now I don't know what it meant. I thought it was just about me and my feelings, but maybe it isn't."

From behind them came a shout from Jeremy. "We're through!"

Marcus turned. A gaping, rough-edged hole had appeared at the side of the cupboard. Kato, hissing and with his back arched, stood by the cupboard door as though to warn them not to go any further.

"There's a ladder," said Mike, looking through the hole.

"You should go first," Theo suggested, speaking to Jeremy and taking no notice of the cat. "Without you, we would never have got this far."

The other man hesitated. "No. It's been a team effort."

"Come on, Dad! You can't hold back now. I'll come with you." Mike slid past the cat, who hissed at him, pushed his way into the opening, and started up the ladder.

Jeremy grimaced at Theo and followed his son.

As they climbed, the air began to smell musty, with a strange stuffiness, mixed with a hint of decay and corruption, and it was bone-chillingly cold, even on a summer's day. The ladder emerged above the stone archway, which led into the false chimney breast beyond. It was almost pitch black, and Jeremy nearly collided with Mike, who had stopped just above him.

"Can I have the torch, Theo?" he called down.

Theo handed it to him, and Jeremy switched it on. "Take this, Mike." He passed the torch to his son, who moved up the last few runs into the priest hole.

Jeremy, following closely behind, took in the scene with a single glance and recoiled. The priest hole was a small space above the hall archway and inside the deep chimney breast, in all about seven feet long and four or five feet wide. At one end, there was a low armchair, its cover mottled with damp but its upholstery intact. Beside it lay a skeleton, still clad in the tattered remnants of a long dress.

He turned back towards the staircase and called down: "I'm sorry, but... we have found something. Only come if you are prepared for a shock. And one at a time, please. There's not much room up here."

There was an answering murmur from below. Whoever wanted to, would come. He hoped they would think about it first. He looked at Mike, whose face looked pale in the torchlight.

Mike stared down at the small skeleton, still curled up as though in pain, its mouth open in a scream of death, and his tender heart was wrung. This girl, he knew from the diary, had been younger than he was now, and had surely deserved protection and love where she had received only rejection. He felt a wave of fury towards those who had caused her death, especially Edwin, who had knowingly risked her life by leaving her in the priest hole without any means of escape, while he went out—no matter that it was on an errand of mercy, and he had made up his mind to stand by her after all.

But then he noticed something else. "That's odd. If she's been here ever since the Reverend Edwin left her that night, where is the baby?"

They both stared at the curled skeleton on the floor and the torch in Mike's hand wavered. The dark stain under the corpse spoke all too clearly of the manner of the woman's death. But the tiny foetal skeleton that should be with its mother, whether still within her body or beside it, was nowhere to be seen.

Jeremy blinked. "That is a very good question, Mike."

His son called down the ladder. "We're coming down."

Jeremy followed him. "We have found a body, I'm afraid, and we won't be able to get it down those stairs without damage. It's very dark, and there's a limit to what we can make out by torchlight."

Theo and Marcus looked horrified, and Olivia began to cry. Marcus put his arms round her again and seemed to be trying to comfort her.

"We will have to tell the police," Jeremy went on inexorably, "as it is an unexpected and unexplained death, however long ago it took place. And I imagine they will want to open up the priest hole, probably from the bedroom upstairs, and examine it very thoroughly."

"The strangest thing," Mike added, "is that there ought to be the skeleton of a baby. She was pregnant, wasn't she? But the baby isn't there."

"I think I can explain that," replied Jeannette, who had come into the room while he was speaking. "I found this in my desk—Edwin's desk—just now." She held up a folded sheet of thick writing paper, bearing words in faded ink in a tiny hand on both sides.

"When we read of Mary's disappearance," she explained, "and it was clear my grandmother didn't know where she had gone, I remembered this letter. I thought it might have a bearing on our mystery. I had seen it once, many years ago, when I was a young woman and my father first gave me the desk for my own. It was locked in a little hidden drawer, and I wasn't sure I should read it. In the end, I only looked at the first sentence before I put it back, for it was clear my great-grandmother had not meant anyone to find it, and I was still a child. I suppose I felt it was a secret I must respect. I don't know... It was a long time ago." She sighed. "But I have read it now."

She handed it to Theo, who looked through it quickly and gave it back to her.

"I would not have believed it," he said, shaking his head sadly, "if I had not seen this with my own eyes. God, Jeannette. The woman must have been mad."

"Can I see?" asked Marcus.

She passed the paper to him, and he read it, holding it so that Olivia, sitting close beside him, could see it, too. Neither of them said anything, but Olivia hid her face against him, and he bent his head over hers. This time she didn't try to move away.

Jeannette took the paper from him and handed it silently to Jeremy. He read it without a word. Then he took the torch from Mike, climbed the ladder again, and knelt by the skeleton to pray.

Tresayne House, January 25th, 1917

I am writing this privately, and will lock it into my son's desk, where I hope no one will ever discover it. But I know my days are numbered, and I find I cannot go to my grave without leaving a record of what really happened that night when my son went out to visit a dying parishioner and never returned. I do not believe in confession, nor in hell or punishment, so I feel no need to tell anyone of this, least of all a priest. But I cannot take the secret to my grave. My conscience, which I have abused so terribly, will not allow it. At the last, it must have the final word.

I heard that trollop crying and wailing. I heard her, and I knew where she was. I alone, for I had banished the servants from the house, except for Gladys, my old housekeeper, who came with me from Tresayne as my maid, and whom I knew I could trust. Gladys is going deaf and heard nothing. When I heard the wailing, I hardened my heart, for I guessed that girl—I cannot write her name—had come to Tresayne to bother Edwin with her importunities, though I did not then know why.

I know now.

I waited until the next day when Gladys was out visiting her cousin at Bodmin, and I knew I had the house to myself. I went into the priest hole, for I knew where the entrance was. The girl was dead, and horribly so, for she had birthed a child on her own in that place and bled out after it. I feel sick now just recalling it, but I have said I will write it down, and I must. But the priest hole must be her tomb, for I do not mean to tell a soul. I have had the opening from the hiding place into the upper room sealed up, and the secret door in the study is locked. I have thrown away the key.

Yet somehow, against all the odds, against all reason, the child had survived—weak and frail and silent, but alive. She must have bitten the cord with her teeth, after it was born, to save it from death. Then I fought a terrible battle with myself, for all my desire, may God forgive me, was to leave the child with its mother to die. If I did not, I risked discovery and with it all the scandal I had tried to avoid, together, perhaps, with questions about my own conduct which I would struggle to answer. But then the child—it was a boy—opened his eyes and looked at me, and suddenly, I could not leave him there. I wrapped him in a shawl and took him out to the stables, where I put him in the manger in the pony-stall. I knew Bill would find him when he came to check on the horses. I thought, even if the child does not survive, at least I have given him a chance.

I have heard that Bill found the child a home with his granddaughter, whose husband was killed on the Somme, like my Freddie. The young widow has recently miscarried their baby and is grieving. No one guesses where the child came from; he is assumed to be the bastard of a local girl who had abandoned him, which is not so very far from the truth. Who knows what that whore would have done if the birth had happened as expected? At least he will bring some joy to the young widow, for he brought none to his mother, nor to me. Judith Laurence, her name is, and her husband's family are incomers, though she herself is a

Cornish girl. Perhaps she will move away to live with her in-laws upcountry, and the baby's history will be forgotten.

It was the best I could do. I do not excuse myself by casting doubts on my sanity at the time I left that young woman to die. In spite of my grief at the loss of my sons, this was a deliberate choice, and I did what I knew was wrong, though for reasons I still stand by. I see now, from reading Edwin's diary, that this child was also a Tresayne, by blood at least, even though he was born the wrong side of the blanket. Ironic that we accused the footman of fathering Mary's child, when all along it was my son who was to blame.

And so I have condemned one of my own blood to a life as a Cornish peasant, to poverty and want and the life of those of low birth. It seems a fitting reward for my action, and perhaps he himself may be the happier for it. We Tresaynes have been an unlucky family in this generation. So I tell myself, and it is all the justification I can find. What is done is done and I will not waste time and energy on vain regrets. If there is a God—and how can I believe that, with all my sons dead in this War to End All Wars?—then He will deal with me as He sees fit. I am content.

Maria Tresayne

Thirty-four

Mike, dismayed by their various reactions, took the paper, and read it in his turn. "But surely this is good!" he exclaimed, his eyes shining. "It's terrible that she let poor Mary die, of course it is, but the baby, at least, survived."

"Judith Laurence." Theo repeated the name thoughtfully. "That's an odd coincidence."

Jeannette looked at him, her quick mind following his line of thought. "You mean... Jude may be the descendant of Mary's child? He was given to a widow of the name of Laurence, certainly. But we know no more than that from the letter. Though the Laurences have farmed up there on Ridge for generations," she added thoughtfully. "I suppose it could be so."

"It would explain everything, though, wouldn't it?" exclaimed Mike in excitement. "If Jude is a relation, wouldn't that make it more likely that..."

"That's a long shot," Marcus told him. "And we shall never know."

"We could at least ask Jude about the family connection, couldn't we?" Mike persisted.

There was a silence. Then they heard Jeremy descending the ladder again.

"Are we really going to tell Jude about this?" asked Olivia. "Won't it upset her all over again?"

"Jude isn't..." began Mike, impelled by an instinct for truthfulness which at that moment his father wished he hadn't developed.

"I think Jude should say what is to be known, not us, Mike," Jeremy interrupted. "And we will need to think carefully what Jude can cope with just at the moment."

"But if he asks..."

Too late, thought Jeremy. It was out.

"Sorry, Dad," said Mike at once, understanding his father's meaning at last. "But I don't think it is a secret, really. I mean, Mum knows, and the twins, as well as Lorna and me. And you had guessed, hadn't you?"

"Yes, I had, but then I'm used to keeping secrets. Something perhaps you should learn."

"What is this secret?" asked Marcus. "Or should I not be told?"

"I think I can guess," said Olivia, "though I must admit I hadn't until now. Had you, Mother?"

Jeannette nodded. "I wasn't sure, but it makes sense."

"Poor Jude." Olivia sighed. "I haven't been at all fair to her—him, I mean. I can see that. And now this. But I think you're right, Jeremy. We do have to be careful how much of this... truth... we tell him."

"Megan too," Jeannette added. "She shouldn't have to face this."

Jeremy drew a breath. "Well... I suppose it's all ancient history to them, apart from Jude's dreams, if dreams they were. Maybe we should say nothing."

Mike was indignant. "I know Lorna would say Jude should know," he asserted. "It was Jude who alerted us first to something,

Jude who heard poor Mary crying. Of course he should know what we've found."

"I'll talk to Mum, Mike. See what she says."

At this, Mike subsided, as his father had known he would. Mum's judgement would be wise.

"What really troubles me," Theo ventured, "is what we should do now."

"I think we should go and have a drink," was Jeannette's practical suggestion. "We probably all need it. And then we can decide what comes next."

Suddenly the room seemed uncomfortably full of people, all trying to process their own emotional responses to the tragedy. By unspoken consent, they trooped into the big sitting room at the front of the house, where Theo mixed drinks at the sideboard. It was not yet lunchtime, but no one questioned the wisdom of some alcohol to steady their nerves.

Olivia found herself sitting on the sofa with Marcus beside her, close enough for their arms to touch if they moved slightly. He had not moved more than a foot or two from her side since they realised the full extent of the horror her family history held, and his eyes had turned towards her again and again, checking whether she was upset, giving her wordless support. She could not imagine how this whole scenario would feel without him there; she realised suddenly that the scale and depth of his concern for her, and the physical expression of it, were new to her. It was loving without being sexual—brotherly, yet somehow there was something about it that went beyond brotherliness. Her responses disturbed her. But whatever it was, she welcomed it and felt comforted.

"How did the cat know?" she asked suddenly. Kato's reactions to the priest hole throughout their investigations seemed to her significant, though she didn't understand them. Perhaps Jeremy would have an answer.

But it was Jeannette who replied. "I'm not quite sure what you mean by his 'knowing'."

"He certainly sensed something." Theo was pouring scotch for himself and Jeremy.

"Cats are sensitive animals," Jeremy pointed out.

Theo nodded. "I suppose there was something in the atmosphere that spoke to him of fear and suffering, and he reacted to it."

He saw Marcus regarding him incredulously and added, "If this sounds rather weird, I am not an expert on the supernatural, and I cannot imagine what the mechanism is. That's more your field than mine, Remy."

"Well... there is a long tradition of people who have died by violence or misadventure leaving some imprint of their suffering on the atmosphere, particularly if they are unburied or their death is a mystery. I don't altogether understand it, but I recognise its validity. There can be a similar effect with long-term misery and abuse, you know. I've been asked to pray in houses where alcoholism or suicide have left a depressive atmosphere." He was silent for a moment. "So, in this case, my calling tells me to pray for the victim, to bury her, and to trust that God will restore the house to happiness."

"However we decide to proceed," Jeannette said to him, "please stay on for a few days as we planned. There will be much to do and to arrange, and much that we will not know how to manage for ourselves. I would really appreciate your help and support."

She looked across the room at Theo, and he nodded his agreement.

"May I take over the old study tonight?" asked Jeremy.

Jeannette looked shocked. "Is that what you want to do?"

He nodded. "Mike, you wouldn't mind, would you, sleeping in the twin room as we planned, but alone? As I've explained, I think the house needs prayer, if the spiritual disturbance caused by all this is to settle properly. The old study seems to me to be the right place for that, though I'll begin in the priest hole itself, while the body is still there. But I will be keeping vigil tonight, and I don't want to disturb you. You're young and need your sleep."

Mike opened his mouth to protest, to assert his determination to stay awake with his father for the sake of that poor young girl. But Jeremy met his gaze firmly, and he saw that it wasn't what his father wanted. "Okay, Dad. But you know I'll help with anything else."

"You can take some photographs of her, if you can bear it, Mike. The police will take some more, I expect, when they come, but I would like us to have some of our own."

Mike nodded.

"Should we not call the police right away?" asked Olivia.

"I don't think a night will make any difference after all these years," said Jeremy. "Besides, their processes do not always leave any room for spiritual matters."

Olivia looked at Marcus.

"I suppose now we've opened the room up," he said slowly, "the atmosphere may make things... deteriorate more quickly."

"Like keeping that Tudor ship damp," put in Mike eagerly. "So the timbers don't rot."

"The Mary Rose," supplied Theo.

Jeremy looked at him. "There isn't much need for the police to investigate immediately, is there? We can tell them what happened and why. Mike can take photographs of exactly where everything is, and we shan't move anything." He turned to Jeannette. "It is your house, and you must make the decision. Do you agree that we leave summoning the police until tomorrow?"

Olivia watched her mother turning it over in her mind and understood why she needed to. So many different things were involved, including family secrets that might put the house and its history in the public eye for all the wrong reasons. Yet in the end, the story would have to be told.

"I think we as a family owe this to Mary," she said at last. "Do what you feel is right, Remy. We will phone the police tomorrow."

That evening, with Marcus's help, Mike rigged up lights and took photographs of the skeleton and its exact position before they covered her reverently with a beautiful Victorian bedspread that Jeannette had dug out from a stock of such family items—things which she never used but could not bear to throw away. This seemed a very good use for it, she said.

Then they dispersed to grieve for the young girl each in their own way.

Mike, in spite of his deep sadness at her death, slept like a log in the twin room where Jude had heard a voice crying, and woke the next morning ready for anything. Jeannette and Theo stayed up together until after midnight in the music room, listening to funeral music and talking about Theo's history of Tresayne House, while Kato purred on Theo's knee, his extreme reactions to the week's events quite forgotten. Marcus read through Edwin's diary again before he slept. He lay awake for a while, and thought kind, sad thoughts of the girl who had been left to die in such circumstances, and then he slept soundly. But Olivia dreamed of nailed-down coffins and living skeletons and woke in the early hours to lie awake in a kind of dull, lonely misery that would not ease, wishing Marcus were beside her to comfort her. At last, the longing grew too much for her, and she crept down through the hall into the Victorian wing, and up the stairs.

There was silence on the landing, for Theo and Jeannette were already sound asleep. She tried the old latch on Marcus's bedroom door, and it lifted quietly. She pushed the door open. He lay on his stomach, spreadeagled across the double bed, the quilt lying across his hips. His torso was bare and even in the half-light she could see the ripple of muscles across his back and shoulders.

She stopped dead, as a wave of desire swept through her. What on earth was she feeling—and what did it mean? Her body burned hot and then froze, cold as ice, and she shivered in the warm night as though she had a fever. *I've been fooling myself these past few days. I looked for a brother, but instead I've found... what?* She didn't feel for Marcus anything remotely like the mixture of lust and adrenaline rush she had experienced with all those lovers of the past. But neither did she feel sisterly, calm and objective. All she knew was that the whole relationship had become enormously important to her. Being with him was a joy, and she desperately needed his love and the comfort his protectiveness towards her brought. If she woke him now and found he felt the same attraction she did... if he took her into his bed and made love to her, as deep down she wanted him to do... that might be the end of it. He might use her in the way men had always used her, and she had connived at it. He might enjoy a brief fling with her, slake her desire for him with great sex, kept secret from her family—for Theo and Jeannette would be shocked by such an incestuous relationship if they knew—and then move on. The fallout would mean she could never come home, if there were any chance of meeting him again. Worse still, she would lose him as a brother, as someone who would belong to her forever, whose affection she could count on.

She couldn't bear it.

She turned and closed the door behind her quietly, then fled away in haste on bare feet down the carpeted staircase, over the cool slate floor and into the old hall. Through the study door, as she passed it, she thought she heard a quiet voice praying—Jeremy keeping vigil for the dead woman. Ashamed, yet still haunted by her dream, she found her way up the stone staircase to her bedroom and lay down again. If she could not sleep, perhaps she too might bear her part in remembrance for this woman who also belonged to her family, for Mary Booker had been her great-grandfather's sister, after all, before she was Edwin's mistress.

~ * ~

Marcus stirred. The latch had made a faint click, and he was a light sleeper. He turned over and rubbed his eyes. The door was closed, and no one was to be seen. He could hear no footsteps on the stairs. But someone had been there, he was sure. He wasted no thought on the possibility that it was one more strange event in the catalogue of hauntings they had investigated. The priest hole had divulged its secrets at last, and he did not believe there would be any recurrence. Without any faith of his own, he trusted Jeremy to deal with the spiritual realm. No, a real person had opened his door, and had then run away.

It could only have been Livi, he thought. What terrors had afflicted her to make her come, and what had she wanted of him? He sat up, intending to follow her back to her room to find out. And then he lay down again. If she had wanted to stay with him, she would have woken him, surely? She would have been sure of her welcome.

Perhaps that was the problem.

He lay pondering their relationship for a long time. She had welcomed him as a brother, and clearly valued him as such. But he knew that wasn't enough for him and would never be. Did she feel some kind of sexual attraction in her turn? He wondered whether she had come for the kind of brotherly comfort he had given her earlier in the day, when she had told him of her dreams, and later when Mike and Jeremy had discovered the skeleton in the priest hole. But then, finding him asleep, had seen him as a man, as a potential lover, and feared it. He groaned slightly and turned over again. It dismayed him how much he desired her, but at the same time how deeply he wanted their relationship to be a permanent part of his life. If she had woken him, would he have been able to keep his desire within bounds so as to give her the quiet comfort she was looking for? How long would he have to wait for her to trust him as a lover as well as a brother? And, he wondered suddenly, would their legal relationship as brother and adopted sister complicate matters further?

These were questions to which he had no answer. Time only would bring him insight and, he hoped, some fulfilment. Jumping the gun would do nothing but frighten her away.

I love her, he thought, as he drifted off to sleep again. *And I always will.*

~ * ~

Jeremy spent the first part of the night in prayer beside the body in the priest hole before climbing down the ladder carefully and closing the cupboard on that scene of horror. He sat keeping vigil and praying in the old study until dawn banished the darkness from the room. At first the horror of what had happened came close to overwhelming him and he could not frame any words of prayer, struck mute and numb in the face of the depth of human folly, evil and selfishness, and what seemed like God's powerlessness in the face of it. Then, slowly, he became able to reconnect with his faith and all it meant, in his trust in God's presence in the midst of suffering, in the ultimate triumph of the good, the promised future renewal of the world and everything in it—and the Almighty's ability always to redeem and weave into the pattern of the grand scheme of things even the worst of human failures and sins. Even his deep disquiet at the onset of that new plague, Covid-19, and his pessimism about its power not only to kill in the short term but to damage human society in the longer, gradually faded away as he waited on God. Had not people learned to help each other again, and to have a new appreciation for the natural world? Not all its consequences were bad, nor had those of the tragedy of Mary Booker been. Her son, after all, had survived against all the odds and perhaps lived to have a family of his own. And he, Remy, could only see the small part of the picture that involved himself. Beyond that, he was blind and groping in the dark, waiting for the Light of the World to show the way.

Thirty-five

After breakfast next day—a quiet meal during which, it seemed to Jeannette, everyone kept their thoughts to themselves—she phoned the police.

"It's my house, and my family history," she said firmly to Jeremy. "I must take responsibility for this. But I'm sure the police will want to talk to you about what we have found. I will keep Edwin's diary and my great-grandmother's letter to hand. They will want to see those, I'm sure."

She turned to Olivia. "Darling,"—how sweet it was to use that word and know that it would not be rejected—"Why don't you show Marcus some more of Cornwall? Neither of you will need to talk to the police, I'm sure, and it may be noisy and unpleasant here."

Olivia looked at Marcus, still troubled by the dreams and wanderings of the night of which, she thought, he knew nothing.

"Where shall we go?" he asked lightly. "We've done the seaside."

"You wouldn't want to go to the coast now," Jeannette advised them. "The Emmets have arrived in droves, since staycations, as they call them, are all they are allowed this summer. The beaches will be teeming."

Olivia thought for a moment. "The moor?" she suggested.

"There's plenty of it," commented Theo with amusement. Tresayne was on the eastern edge of Bodmin Moor, and to the south and west it stretched for miles, much of it open grazing accessible for walking.

"The Hurlers," decided Olivia. "We can climb the Cheesewring."

"Don't forget to tell him about the area's mining heritage," Jeannette told her. "You'll see the mine chimneys while you're there."

"But I haven't got any suitable kit for climbing," objected Marcus, surmising that the Cheesewring must be a local mountain.

"Oh, it isn't a real climb," Olivia said. "It's just a gravel pathway, though it's quite steep. We don't even have to go to the top if you don't want to, but the view is amazing. Wear a pair of trainers, and you'll be fine."

"Take my little car, Olivia," Jeannette suggested. "The roads aren't suitable for that lovely convertible of Marcus's, never mind the car park at the Hurlers, full of boulders."

"That's a good idea," agreed Olivia. "Thanks. How long will you need to get ready, Marcus?"

"Not long." He looked down at the smart chinos and polished brogues he was wearing. "I'll go and find my trainers and a pair of jeans."

~ * ~

"So who or what are the Hurlers?" he asked a little later, as Olivia drove her mother's car down North Hill and out on to the Liskeard road. "And the Cheesewring, come to that."

"'The Hurlers' is a stone circle," she replied, waiting patiently for a car approaching in the other direction over the narrow bridge that crossed the Lynher river. "The Cheesewring is a hill just beyond the circle, with a pile of stones on top. Really big rocks—

they sort of balance, one on top of the other. It's hard to explain, but you'll see what I mean. We don't actually climb the stones at the top."

She drove slowly and carefully along the narrow B-road as it wound through the dark avenues of Middlewood and up the steep hill beyond. It was ages since she'd driven her mother's car, and she was out of practice on these contorted lanes. There was plenty of traffic, too, much of it driven by tourists— some scared by the roads, others over-confident and taking no account of the nature of them. She was glad when they reached Upton Cross and could turn off towards Minions and the Hurlers. She bumped into the rough car park at the edge of the moor and parked in the nearest space. The car park was busy, but there was plenty of moor, as Theo had said.

Marcus looked out of the window. "Wow."

"You wait," Olivia told him, opening the driver's door.

They walked slowly along the gravel paths, not speaking. It was, she thought as though neither of them knew what to say, although both were aware there was plenty to be said.

For his part, Marcus was content to look around him, enjoying the sense of space and freedom as the moor revealed itself, energised by the breeze that snatched at his clothes and flattened the long grass at the edges of the path. Sheep grazed not far from them, unmoved by the visitors unless they came too close. Some of the walkers had left the path and were striking out across the open moor, their dogs with them. Notices at the edge of the path appealed to them to keep their dogs under control, but some were running free, off the leash, and he wondered how much trouble the farmers had with dogs that chased the sheep.

"It's a big problem," Olivia said when he asked her. "But farmers can shoot a dog if it worries their sheep, so that's certainly a deterrent."

"Can they? I hadn't realised." He was conscious, suddenly, how little he knew of rural life and its ways. He had thought instinctively of Olivia as a Londoner, like himself, but of course she wasn't. She had been born and brought up here.

"But I'm not sure all the tourists know about it, unfortunately. In the spring, when there are lambs, the farmers are particularly twitchy about dogs, and every year there are losses. You have to see the dog to shoot it."

She pointed ahead and to their right. "There are the Hurlers, see? We have to leave the path and go across the moor. Watch out for very green bits of ground—they can be boggy. But there hasn't been much rain, so it should be okay."

He followed her, taking care as she had advised. He didn't want to lose a trainer to the bog. But the ground seemed firm enough, and after a while, he looked ahead of him and saw the stones, two circles close together, rough-hewn and incomplete, with gaps like missing teeth where stones were lost or fallen.

"These have been here about fifteen hundred years," said Olivia, as they reached them. "Nothing like Stonehenge, but they are interesting, and no one knows just what they were for."

"These ancient places are all a tad mysterious," he agreed.

"You have to go further west in Cornwall to see the really ancient sites," she said. "Maybe we can do that later in the week." She hesitated. "How long are you planning to stay, Marcus?"

He turned to look at her. "I'm not sure yet."

Their eyes met for a long moment. Then silently, each in their own bubble of thoughts and emotions that they feared to share, they walked on, close together like a couple but not touching, while around them he noticed how carefully others avoided them and each other, following the new norms of social distancing. Even the stones they climbed between, it seemed, were surfaces that visitors tried hard not to touch for fear of contamination.

After a few minutes, just as he was trying to find a way of telling her how he felt, Olivia began to talk, and she kept it up for the rest of their walk, dredging up for his enlightenment long-disused knowledge of the geology of the Cheesewring and the far distances they could see from the top of it because the day was fine. Then on the way back she regaled him with the history of the mining heritage exemplified by the old engine house, which stood, half-ruined, to one side of the route—in happier days a visitor centre, but just now barred and closed. They reached the car park again without having had the conversation he felt they desperately needed.

"Livi," he ventured at last, as they put on their seatbelts for the journey home. "We need to talk."

She looked at him, and he saw with dismay that there was fear in her eyes. "Do we?"

"You know we do. About the future. About us."

She swallowed and looked away. "Not yet," she implored him. "Please, Marcus. Not yet." She put the car into gear, and they bumped out of the car park in silence.

~ * ~

At Tresayne, the police had arrived around noon and set about making a hole in the wall of the false chimney breast to expose the scene of Mary Booker's death to the cruel light of day. It became clear that the doorway into that room from the priest hole had been bricked up—presumably on Maria Tresayne's instructions—which was why tapping it had given no clues as to the priest hole's whereabouts. Jeremy, watching the police at work, wondered how she had managed to seal the hiding place without the workman finding out what it contained. Had she stopped his mouth with money, he wondered, or relied on his loyalty? Perhaps she had some hold over him. One more detail they would never know.

The police photographed everything carefully and took the skeleton away for forensic examination; but in light of the diary entries and Maria Tresayne's letter, as explained to them by Jeremy, the evidence was clear, and in any case, there was no one left alive to be charged with any offence. But there were procedures that had to be followed, they told him, and he knew this was true.

When they had finished, the officer in charge apologised to Jeannette for the destruction they had wrought in her house and left her to deal with it. She only hoped she would be able to get a carpenter to come and make good the damage. It seemed the building trades were still dealing with a lockdown backlog of work, and it might take some time.

Preparing a late lunch for Theo and Jeremy–for Mike, armed with a sandwich, had gone to check that Cedric had returned as promised the night before, and take the dogs for a walk if they needed one, Jeannette found herself wondering how Marcus and Olivia were getting on. Olivia had looked unhappy, even tearful, at breakfast, which was partly why she had suggested the two of them escaped for the day. It seemed that, with the fresh understanding of the past she had found with her mother, Olivia was engaging with the family and its past in a new way, and in the current circumstances that was proving painful. She hoped, when the police had finished their investigations, they could all settle down into a period of peace and reflection and spend some proper time with Marcus before he had to go back to London. She supposed he would have to take up his job again sometime soon, even if it was remotely, from his flat. Olivia, too, would no doubt be looking for work. But she wanted to see her daughter in a happier frame of mind before she left home again.

~ * ~

When the police released the body a week or so later, Jeremy was allowed to bury her in the graveyard next to the old chapel with the family in discreet and socially distanced attendance. He was glad to be burying the body intact and where she could be remembered, rather than the ubiquitous cremation and scattering of ashes. The police had asked for it in case there were ever more questions to be answered for which they needed the physical body. But in any case, it seemed fitting.

That task accomplished, the next morning he and Mike put their bags back into the estate car and set off for Oxford to take up their normal lives again.

"Or as normal as anything can be," Mike said as they drove away. "How long will all this last, do you think, Dad?"

"The pandemic? Who knows?" Jeremy's mood was still sombre, and for once he found Mike's insouciant cheerfulness irritating. "Vaccines are on the way, but viruses are clever organisms. I don't suppose we're at the end of it by any means yet."

"Perhaps the End of the Beginning?" suggested Mike, thinking of Churchill's famous speech after El Alamein.

"Not even that, I suspect. Now be quiet, will you, Mike, while I drive? Save your energy for your own turn at the wheel later."

Mike subsided, and Jeremy was left to his own thoughts, which were not, in point of fact, about the pandemic, but about the conversation he had had with Jeannette earlier that morning, before he left Tresayne.

"I would like you to tell Jude about what we found, Remy," she said. "Jude will tell Megan when he thinks she's ready to hear. But also, I want no children's home for those two youngsters. They are my cousins, if we are right in our deductions. Theo says he will check via one of the ancestry websites, and we can verify it. But I think we are right, and that means I am responsible for them. Mary was greatly wronged by my family—first by my great-uncle Edwin in denying his paternity of her child, and then, more horrifically, by my great-grandmother in leaving her to die in that horrible way. I cannot right those wrongs. But I will not allow those youngsters to be dependent on the kindness of your family or the dubious provision of the welfare state. If Jude and Megan prefer to stay in Oxford, then I will support them financially."

Jeremy had opened his mouth to say it wasn't necessary, that he and Liz would take care of the Laurences. But she had forestalled him.

"I can tell, from what Lorna and Mike have said about their mother, that she is a wise woman. I know she will help Jude and Megan decide what is best for them. And if they want to come back to Cornwall, there will always be a home for them with us at

Tresayne. It is, after all, where they belong. At the very least, they should know that."

She sighed, and then patted his arm, in flagrant contravention, Jeremy thought with amusement, of the Covid regulations. "I owe you a great deal, Remy. My grandmother mourned the loss of her brothers all her long life, and I think my grandfather was always uncertain what had happened to his sister Mary and her child. I remember so well that my grandmother worried over it in her final illness, bedridden in this very house. I was at university then, so I only saw her in the vacations, but I recall sitting beside her listening to her talk about it. I thought then it was just ramblings, the confused half-memories of a dying woman. It embarrassed me, though I loved her dearly. But I think she knew more than she had told me. I think perhaps she had read that letter I found, written by her mother, and was afraid it was true. Yet she lived here all her life and did nothing. I wonder whether she told my grandfather—but I suspect she thought it would be too much for him to bear."

"We will never know," said Jeremy gently. "You mustn't dwell on it too much. It was all a long time ago."

She nodded. "But at least I can do something for Jude and Megan. It cannot take away my family's guilt, but it can be some recompense, I hope. And the truth has brought me some measure of peace, and some understanding of it all."

"It is to your credit," he assured her. "Leave it with me. I will tell you what they feel, when Liz and I have had a chance to talk to them."

"Thank you, Remy. Have a good journey home." She put out her hand to shake his in farewell, but this time she remembered, and took it back. "No, we can't shake hands. All I will say is, 'Take care, and God speed'."

She watched the Swansons drive away down the lane and shut the gate thoughtfully behind them. Then she walked back to the house and made her way upstairs to the twin room and into the priest hole, through the hole in the wall made by the police. She stood for a moment where the tragedy had had its culmination, and consciously and deliberately accepted the guilt the Tresaynes still bore for the enormity of it. She had not been able to find any understanding of her great-grandmother's actions, nor of the lack of contrition or remorse shown by the statement she had written afterwards. How could she, Jeannette, ever forgive those actions, or come to terms with the harm they had caused? The stain on her family history lay black, like the ancient bloodstain on the floor of the priest hole. It could never be expunged or expiated, whatever happened in the future. And it still tormented her, whether her grandmother had known what happened, in the end. Had she found the way into the priest hole, and seen that scene of horror for herself? All they had was the final diary entry she had written, at the end of Edwin's book. At that point, she clearly had not known, but had wondered still about Mary and her child and their whereabouts, and worried about her husband's fears for his sister. But later? When her grandmother had talked with Jeannette of the past, and the loss of her three brothers in the Great War, she had said nothing about the priest hole, or any tragedy connected with it. She had not mentioned Mary, or wondered what became of her—not until she was dying, and her mind began wandering unchecked. But perhaps, if she knew that behind the wall there lay a body, and that a death had come about because of her own mother's actions, it had been something she felt she could never mention—perhaps could not even face herself.

At least, Jeannette reflected, she and Olivia could now be open with each other about what had happened here, in their own family. There need no longer be any secrets to corrode their relationship or lie like a stain on their lives. History need not repeat itself. That was something.

She left the room and closed the door behind her, leaving the past where it lay. Some day she would arrange to have the debris cleared and the room replastered and repainted. She might close the priest hole off completely and seal it again. But on the other hand, the room lacked any proper clothes-hanging space. Perhaps she would turn the priest hole into a wardrobe, so that later generations could forget it had ever been a hiding-place and give it some proper, healthy use instead. Maybe that would be best.

Thirty-six

A few days after the Swansons had gone, Marcus requested an urgent interview with his father. Theo, surprised by this formality, at once brewed some coffee and took him into the privacy of his music room.

Marcus sat on the sofa and sipped thoughtfully. It had been agreed that he would return to London sometime in the next few days and leave the Landrys to themselves. He thought Jeannette and Theo at least would be glad of some time of quiet reflection after these weeks of tension and drama, and to resume their normal activities. Jeannette was already blanching a glut of beans and freezing them, making ratatouille with tomatoes and courgettes, and talking with anticipation about her daily cleaning lady returning to help her; and Theo must surely be wanting to concentrate on his work again.

Marcus thought about Olivia and all that the past few weeks had revealed to him about her, and about his feelings for her. "I'm in trouble, Dad," he confessed, at last. "And I don't know what to do about it."

"I'm listening," replied Theo gravely.

"I think I'm in love with Livi." He swallowed.

There was a long silence. "Only think?" asked Theo.

"No," admitted Marcus. "I *am* in love with her. It's just hard to believe it. This wasn't in the least what I expected to happen."

"Have you told her?"

"No! I haven't dared. Dad, she's my sister. And that's what she wants to be."

"What she wants is the only thing that matters," Theo agreed. "But as to her being your sister, that is only true legally, because I adopted her. In this country, at least, there is no barrier at all to you two getting together if you wanted to. You would even be free to marry."

"Would we?" Marriage came as a new idea to Marcus, but suddenly he liked it. If only Olivia would talk to him. But she was still putting him off, as though she feared where that conversation might lead.

"Certainly. I believe there are places in the world where it would be illegal, including some of the states in America. But not here. Here it is perfectly legal because there is no blood relationship."

Marcus leaned back in his chair in amazement and relief. Then doubt set in again, and horror at his own illicit feelings returned. "But isn't it incest?"

"Only if you had grown up together, and even then, legally it doesn't count."

"Because there is no blood relationship."

"Yes."

"How do you know all this?" Marcus demanded.

His father smiled. "You know, I had a feeling that something was going on, that you and Olivia were perhaps growing closer, and not as sister and brother. So I asked Jeremy before he went back to Oxford what the position was. I thought he'd be sure to know, being a clergyman. But I expect you could research it via Google if you wanted to."

"I must be more transparent than I realised," murmured Marcus ruefully. "If you guessed, what about Jeannette?"

"I haven't said anything to her, and she is… not always very observant about people," said Theo gently. "But she will accept what Jeremy says about the moral and legal implications."

"I'd rather she didn't know yet. There may never be any need for her to. Livi might not—ever—want that."

"Jeannette shall not know anything from me," Theo promised.

Marcus found his hands twisting together. He thrust them under his thighs to keep them still. "She won't talk to me, Dad."

"Olivia? About your future?"

"Yes."

There was a pause. Then Theo said: "Marcus, I think you may be misunderstanding Livi."

Marcus looked up, and his eyes brightened. "Really? You think so? You know her so much better than I do."

"Don't go too fast. It's just that I think she may be misreading her feelings because she has so much wanted to have a brother. I do not know that much about her life in London, but I think her experience of romantic entanglements, especially of the sexual variety, has not been altogether happy."

There was silence. It wasn't for him to say so to his father, but Marcus was sure, from what she had told him, that Olivia had never really learned how to love a man and be loved in return, with all that meant. But he would dedicate the rest of his life to teaching her if she would let him.

~ * ~

And so they sat together in her sitting room, later that evening, and Marcus invited Olivia to come and live with him. "You are planning to go back to London and find a job, aren't you? I have a flat, and it has plenty of room for two. We could form an official household, and if there are more lockdowns, we shall have each other for company."

"More lockdowns?!" She thought about this. "I suppose there may be. What an awful prospect."

"I wouldn't be surprised."

"Oh, Marcus, I can't bear it."

"Well... if there are, I don't want to be alone next time, bubbles or no bubbles."

"The bubbles are a good idea, aren't they?" she gabbled, hoping to stop the deeper conversation in its tracks. "For people who have no family and have to live alone. I must say I don't really want to be stuck here again, though I've been very glad to get on better terms with Mummy."

Mummy. The childhood word that had got lost somewhere long ago. It sounded awkward on her lips, but she had said it nevertheless, and that felt good.

"I'm glad too." Marcus hesitated. "What do you think of my idea?"

"You mean, we'd live together... as brother and sister?"

"Yes. But maybe..."

"Maybe what?"

He reached over and took her hands in his. "If what you want is to be my sister, I'd rather have you living with me on those terms than live without you. But in time—I have to be straight with you, Livi—if you could see it differently..."

"You want to sleep with me." The words were blunt, but there was a lost, hurt sound to her voice that went to his heart.

"No! I mean, yes, I do." He strove to be honest without frightening her away. "One day. But only if you wanted it too."

"I rather thought I'd give up having affairs," she said in a small voice. "I'd much rather have a brother and keep him forever."

"If we are ever more than brother and sister," Marcus told her firmly, "it will be forever. I love you, Livi, and I'm not going to stop. But that's why I don't want to press you. Why I promise I won't try to be anything but your brother until you say otherwise. I just thought you should know."

To his horror, she began to cry.

Marcus leapt to his feet. "God! I'm so sorry I've upset you! The last thing I meant to do."

She came and stood in front of him. "I'm just happy," she said quietly. "Happy that you love me, I mean. However you do."

His shoulders sagged with relief. "Livi, you had me worried then. I thought I'd blown it completely."

"No." Her eyes focused on his shirt, figuring out the chequered pattern on it in pink and blue and green, while she tried to find the words that would take them forward.

He put his hands on her shoulders tentatively, and at last she summoned the courage to look up at him. Grey eyes met blue and held.

"I've been so afraid, you see," she began, and once started, the words tumbled out of her in a rush. "I wanted a brother, but then I found I loved you in a different way, as though you weren't my brother, and I didn't know how to handle it. First, I thought it must be wrong, because Theo adopted me, and I'm his daughter just as much as you're his son, legally. Brothers and sisters aren't supposed to have sex, are they?"

"It's not incest," he put in quickly. "Not for us. We don't share any genes, and we didn't grow up together. I thought about that too, but it's okay. Dad asked Remy, and he said so."

She laughed at this and moved towards him. His arms went round her slowly, gathering her tightly against him.

"And then," she said, her muffled against his shoulder, "then I thought it might be like the relationships I've had before, that didn't last—that I didn't even want to last—and when it was over, I would have lost you completely. We wouldn't even be brother and sister. I couldn't face that. That's why I didn't want to talk about it. I didn't see how it could possibly work."

"I will never leave you, Livi," he promised, his mouth in her hair. "Brother and sister, lovers, even husband and wife. It's all possible. Whatever we want. Forever."

"Then I will come and live with you, Marcus." She took a breath, steadying herself. "I'm in love with you, too." She had said it at last, and as she did so the fear vanished. If Marcus loved her like that, with no reservations, she could trust him to do what he had promised.

He bent and kissed her, tasting the salt of her dried tears on her lips. But before he could take the kiss further, she spoke again, smiling.

"I'll need to find a job. I can't live off you."

"You can be my PA," he joked, "and travel to book fairs with me. Frankfurt is my favourite."

Her smile died. "That would be too like the way I once was, with all those bosses I travelled with on business. There was no love then, only lust and power games. It was part of the cage I was in, and now I'm trying to break free."

He kissed her again, reassuringly. "You should do something that doesn't depend on someone else. You have what it takes to be a businesswoman in your own right."

"A female dragon."

"Definitely. We'll wait for the right opportunity. As long as you'll come, Livi."

The yearning in his voice found an echo deep in her heart. She nodded, certain now. "I'll come."

After Marcus had gone downstairs, to tell his father what they had decided—"Dad will be so pleased. I told him I was going to ask you"—she sat for a long time thinking about what her future might look like, about the feelings she had for Marcus and what they might mean, about risk and opportunity and the unknown. Then she opened her laptop and shut down her Findom Twitter account. She had already told her clients she would not be servicing them anymore.

She closed the laptop and put it on her desk. A whole chapter of her life had closed, and a new one was beginning. It was scary, but it was right. And she would have Marcus. He had said so, and she believed him.

Forever. That was the best of all.

Meet Jane Anstey

Jane Anstey has been writing since she was a child, having her first story published in the school magazine aged 11. She was born in London, UK, and grew up in Surrey and Oxfordshire, including three years at the University of Oxford, before moving with her husband to Hampshire, where they lived for 25 years. The family then moved to Cornwall, where she was living during the start of the Covid 19 pandemic—hence the setting of *Priest-Hole*. She now lives in Shropshire. She loves reading, singing, gardening and taking the dog for walks, and is active in her local Anglican church.

Other Works from the Pen of Jane Anstey

Beauty for Ashes – When Hollywood actor Luke Caron falls for English college student Samantha, he finds himself on an emotional roller-coaster to disaster.

St Martin's Summer – Reverend Jeremy Swanson investigates an unpopular farmer's death and its connection with a village love affair and a small boy's disappearance.

You Owe Me Five Farthings – A parishioner's failing marriage and a mysterious ancient book keep Reverend Jeremy Swanson busy in this sequel to *St Martin's Summer*.

Thirteen Forty-Nine – When the Black Death ravages her village, neglected wife Alys finds comfort in caring for her neighbours, and discovering a new relationship of love.

Dear reader,

I hope you've enjoyed reading this tale of love and tragedy.

Your opinion is valuable to other
readers like you,
who may be looking for books like mine.

Please consider taking a few minutes to post a review,
however brief,
on the site where you purchased this book
or on the Wings ePress web page.

You may also want to visit my author page
at the Wings' website, where you can find
all the other books in my series.

Thank you!

Jane Anstey

Visit Our Website

For The Full Inventory
Of Quality Books:

Wings ePress, Inc

Quality trade paperbacks and downloads
in multiple formats,
in genres ranging from light romantic comedy to general
fiction and horror.
Wings has something for every reader's taste.
Visit the website, then bookmark it.
We add new titles each month!

Wings ePress, Inc.
3000 N. Rock Road
Newton, KS 67114